The Palm House

The Palm House

Tarek Eltayeb

Translated by
Kareem James Abu-Zeid

The American University in Cairo Press
Cairo New York

First published in 2012 by
The American University in Cairo Press
113 Sharia Kasr el Aini, Cairo, Egypt
420 Fifth Avenue, New York, NY 10018
www.aucpress.com

Dar el Kutub No. 24414/11
ISBN 978 977 416 482 8

Dar el Kutub Cataloging-in-Publication Data

Eltayeb, Tarek
The Palm House / Tarek Eltayeb; translated by Kareem James Abu-Zeid.—Cairo: The American University in Cairo Press, 2012
p. cm.
ISBN 978 977 416 482 8
1. English fiction I. Title
892.73

1 2 3 4 5 6 16 15 14 13 12

Designed by Adam el-Sehemy
Printed in Egypt

For Ursula, my Palm House in Vienna

1

Poor cities are more merciful to the poor and the destitute than wealthy ones. In poor cities, everyone is equally impoverished, and there are no contrasts to show the destitute just how far down life's ladder they actually are. Wealthy cities, however, are excessive in their cruelty, for they allow the rich to flaunt the luxuries that others cannot afford. In these cities, you often hear sentences that begin with the words "we've got" or "you've got." People like me, people who have so little warmth and so little joy in their lives, feel this cruelty, this great gap, even more intensely.

Vienna seems to be the cruelest city in the world, at least to me. The loneliness here is a cold death to the soul, and the bitter cold is a slow death to the body. I can feel a crack in my body and my mind: it runs through my days and nights, my memory, and no measure of oblivion can set it right.

I am here now in this lovely old city, this city that brutally kills the likes of me, the displaced, the marginalized. I never ask myself those naive questions any more, the ones so often repeated by the destitute: Why am I here? What am I doing in this city? Why don't I go back?

I've found myself asking the following instead: Is there a way out of this mess? Is there any way to cut my losses and leave the game? How can I survive this?

I am here now. I am here in Vienna.

It's Saturday night. I'm up late reading a book on German grammar. I cannot sleep, despite the many light blankets and tattered covers on my bed, which somehow resembles a pharaoh's sarcophagus. This long bare room of mine with its high walls and layers upon layers of wallpaper has always reminded me of an abandoned temple. I've added one last layer on top of all the others, something to lend a bit of warmth to the room and help ease my mind.

I live on the top floor of an old building that was saved from the destruction of the Second World War, but not from that of time. Its windows were never repaired, not a single pane. This city's residents do not like the upper floors of these old buildings for several reasons, the most obvious of which are the lack of elevators, the narrowness of their spiral staircases, their dark entryways, and the dank and bitter cold that prevails in them. This is where the unemployed and the impoverished make their homes, those who live off welfare or meager wages. Foreigners and poorer Austrians are the only ones living here—another reason most well-to-do Austrians prefer to keep away.

No one piece of furniture in my apartment resembles another. It's like I'm living in a flea market, or a junkyard. There's an old brown wardrobe with one door that refuses to open and another that refuses to close. There's a plastic chair that belongs in a cheap restaurant, and a metal chair that belongs in a hospital. There are two sofas: one with stripes like a zebra, and the other made of bright red leather, as if it were from a brothel. The uneven white plywood table from Ikea is riddled with cracks and cigarette burns, like a relic from a torture chamber, and the cheap linoleum floor covering has a deep burnt red color to it. I won't talk about the kitchen or the cramped bedroom with the creaky bed. The apartment could almost pass for a nineteenth-century museum, were it not for the wallpaper I added, which takes me to a more pleasant place, a place I love.

It's the end of December, and the weather is as cold as can be. Last night, the heating oil I bought with my last shillings ran out. The apartment retained some warmth for most of Saturday, but by evening the temperature had dropped to just seven degrees. I cannot fall asleep. It's as if I'm lying outside, my fingers and toes frozen to the sidewalk. There's a crack in the bedroom window that's wrecking me. Another crack, this one in the peephole of the apartment's front door, has created a draft. I've tried to cover up the first crack with cardboard, but the wind prevails, and the cardboard tears apart and flaps against the window like a trapped bird. The cold wind and the irritating flapping ruin my night. I curse Frau Olga, the owner of the apartment. I wish she'd suffer through just one night in this awful museum of hers, this museum of ghosts.

After her husband's death, Frau Olga began collecting shabby furniture—either for free or at very low prices—to fix up and then resell. She soon discovered that she could afford to buy some old apartments in run-down buildings and take advantage of bank loans that were being given out for repairs and renovations. She filled the apartments with old furniture and then rented them out to foreigners, immigrants, and other low-income people such as myself.

Frau Olga always comes by on the first day of every month to collect the rent without delay. It doesn't matter to her if it's a Saturday or a Sunday or even a national holiday: she still always comes running up the five flights of stairs so quickly that she can hardly breathe. She feigns politeness and good humor until she has the rent from me, then escapes as lightly as a bird. I know she's worried about me complaining, and afraid that I might explode one day. I also know she's making a lot of money from all the apartments she owns, and that it wouldn't cost her much to repair these ruins. But she banks on my patience and my lack of alternatives. Each time she comes by, she promises to make all the necessary repairs. She even gets on the phone—though I'm not sure who she actually calls—to try to reassure me. But nothing is ever repaired, nothing at all. Every time I see her, I repeat my requests; and every time, she repeats her promises; to the point that these have become stock phrases to us, our own ritual way of saying hello and saying goodbye.

For someone who has lived his whole life in the places where the sun is relentless, where you can still feel its presence even at night, this cold is the cruelest of tortures and the heaviest of burdens. My one comfort is Hakima, who is breathing calmly in my arms, and whose warmth makes up for this great lack. She always stretches herself out when she sleeps, resting her head beneath my chin and her body on my chest.

I wake up early. That is to say: I've been awake all night. Hakima stretches her body, and I follow her lead. She yawns and seems to smile, so I do the same. I search for my slippers with the soles of my feet, and as they touch the ground the cold linoleum devours what's left of my warmth. I get out of bed and head toward the communal bathroom outside in the hallway. Its upper glass window is broken, of course. As usual, the bathroom door is off-kilter, and I have to yank it upward to open it. It's stiff from the cold, and grates and scrapes reluctantly against the ground, like a goat being dragged to the slaughter. I wipe off the plastic seat with some toilet paper and sit down. It feels like I'm sitting on a block of ice. Even the water in the toilet bowl is half frozen. My muscles are twitching from the cold. I hurry up and finish as quickly as possible, then head back to my apartment to wash my hands and face with freezing water. As usual, the water heater isn't working: it splutters and sounds like it's working, but the water passes through it unchanged. I make a cup of tea with milk, not realizing that the milk's gone bad. I pour it out in the sink and make another one, drinking it plain this time. For a few moments, I can almost feel my body again. The tea courses through me, warming my lips, my mouth, my throat, and finally my stomach and even my hands. It's an incredible feeling.

Last night's battle with the wind has made me hungry. There's a last can of sardines in the refrigerator, and a solitary egg. I heat up some oil in a pan to fry the egg, but as I crack it I realize that it too has gone bad: its odor fills the air, throwing my stomach into turmoil. I rush out of the apartment with it, opening the door with my elbow and hoping to throw it into the toilet. But the bathroom door won't budge, and the egg begins to seep through my fingers and onto the ground in long sticky strands. I try to hurry, but the egg falls onto the ground with a smack, and the stench rises up, like that of a sick dog emptying its bowels. Before I can make it back to my apartment to find something to wipe up this disgusting mess with, I run into my neighbor, Herr Novak, who is over seventy years old, on his way to our communal toilet. Wrapped in a thick robe, socks, and wool slippers, he stops in front of me, leaning on the wall and breathing heavily. He points his trembling hand at my face—at the face of the culprit—before lowering it to the crime itself, the remains of the damned egg, while repeating, "Pfui! Um Gottes Willen!"

"What is that smell?" he asks.

"Eier kaputt!" I reply.

He's hard of hearing, so I'm forced to repeat these words several times in a loud voice, "Eier kaputt! Eier kaputt!"

He shakes his head in displeasure and slowly returns to his apartment. I hear him say "Scheisse," that oft-repeated word I know quite well, despite its not being in my German language book.

I run back to my apartment and grab one of the many *Krone* newspapers—the most famous Austrian daily—that are stacked in a corner. I wipe up the mess with it and throw it into the toilet bowl. Then I flush the toilet several times until the paper completely disappears, and return to my kitchen.

I've lost my appetite. The whole apartment smells like rotten eggs now, and I can't get the stench off my hands. I open the can of sardines for Hakima, who quickly gobbles them up.

I head for the closet and pull out one of the bottles of lotus perfume I bought from a souk in Omdurman. I daub a bit on my wrists and breathe it in deeply, which grants me a temporary reprieve from the stench. As I do this I stare at the wallpaper in front of me, and soon enough my mind is wandering through the souks of Omdurman, reliving the day I bought the perfume.

I know I can't spend my entire Sunday in this cold apartment, just as I can't even begin to fall asleep on that sarcophagus that passes for a bed. I think about heading out for a walk, but the downcast weather and the first hints of snow scuttle that plan. And going to a café would kill two hours at most. I do have a few friends, but no phone with which to call them. We usually run into each other by chance, and only rarely actually plan our get-togethers.

I feel sad today, but I'm not sure why. I feel as if I had a disturbing dream last night, one that's still somehow clouding my mind. I try to remember, but it's no use. However, a comforting thought raises my spirits a bit: I'll catch the N Tram by my apartment and ride it all the way to the Prater Gardens, the last station. I have a monthly public transportation pass, so the trip won't cost me anything. And I'm an expert on where the warmest tram seats are.

Trembling from the cold in my apartment, I strip off my pajamas, and see my own breath steaming in front of me. I quickly put on my clothes: two undershirts, long underwear, socks, a shirt, two light pullovers (they're all I have), my thick brown velvet trousers, my shoes, and finally the one overcoat that I own. Frau Martha gave me the coat after her husband, a fireman, died. She had offered me many of his clothes, but I only took this heavy overcoat and a pair of his thick gloves.

I place Hakima against my chest inside this big coat, and wrap a scarf around her. Hakima can hardly be called a normal cat. She's less stubborn than most cats, and is very calm and friendly. She often seems more like a small dog to me. And whenever I put her inside my coat, she sleeps there like a baby kangaroo. She comes with me everywhere: to cafés, outdoor markets, the supermarket, and so on. And she's always with me on long days like this, when I ride the tram for hours to escape the cold.

Before I head out, I grab the last bread roll—the kind they call *Semmel* here—and put it in my pocket, just in case my appetite comes back.

I named my cat Hakima after my two younger sisters, Karima and Halima, whom I last saw years ago. I didn't make it back in time to say goodbye to them before they died. They suffered so much, and I could do nothing to help them: neither delay their deaths nor ease their pain.

My habit of always bringing Hakima with me caused me some trouble once, though she was not to blame for it. I was shopping in the Billa supermarket near my apartment. I had paid and returned the cart, and was heading toward the exit when two young men attacked me. One of them twisted my arm while the other violently pressed his knee into my back and yelled, "We've finally caught one of the rats!"

Suddenly, I found myself kneeling on the ground in the middle of my scattered groceries, with no idea of what was happening. I simply tried to protect Hakima from the onslaught of these two men, who had found easy prey in me and were hoping to make heroes of themselves. I later learned that one of them was in charge of supermarket security, or something like that, and that the other one was in charge of stocking the shelves. The two idiots thought I was stealing a can of sardines or a chocolate bar or a piece of meat or some other precious Billa product, and that I was hiding it inside my coat. I tried to protect Hakima as best I could, skinning my knees and one of my elbows in the process. They twisted me onto my back, triumphantly revealing the bulge at my chest. Their search turned up nothing but a small cat, however. The two of them didn't seem embarrassed in the least, and none of the people who had gathered around us said anything to them. They were there to enjoy the show, to watch what was happening to the strange thief in front of them. I could tell they felt sorry for Hakima when they saw her, but they couldn't care less about me.

A woman with glasses and lovely hair almost the color of henna picked up my groceries for me and put them back in the torn bag, all the while cursing the two 'heroes' under her breath. She petted Hakima, who had become quite worked up by all of this, and reached into her own bag and held out a can for me. "Here's some food for your cat," she said.

I thanked her and stood up sorely while the two men tried to help me. I wouldn't let them touch me, and yelled, "I'll never come shopping here again! I'll never buy anything from this Billa! Scheisse!"

I berated myself later for not having thanked the kind woman properly. I felt so abused at the time that I completely forgot about it. Back at my apartment, I recalled the smile she gave me, and the enraged look she leveled at the two men on my behalf. My poise returned to me as I thought of this, and I reconciled myself a bit to the people of this city. I had to laugh at my own stupidity when I looked at the can of cat food the woman had given me for Hakima: I'd been buying these cans for months because they were so cheap and I liked the picture of the cat on them, but I hadn't realized they were cat food, . . . I had thought I was sharing my food with Hakima, but in truth she was sharing hers with me!

I walk outside to find the street covered in a white shroud of snow, which is still coming down like flour from the sky. The tram approaches, and I run to the Radetzkyplatz stop and jump in just before the door closes. The conductor sitting in the back ignores all the passengers that have just gotten on, except for me. He stares at me silently, and I can tell he wants to check my ticket. I make my way over to him and angrily wave my transit pass in front of his face. He thanks me with exaggerated courtesy.

I know exactly which seat the tram's heating unit is under, but it's occupied at the moment, so I take a different one not too far from it. It frees up after three stops, and I quickly switch seats. The Vienna public transportation system is the only refuge I have from my greatest enemy, the cold. It's the one warm place I know where I won't be forced to order another drink if I stay too long, which usually happens at the cafés. I've tried everything to escape the cold: cinemas and cafés and even train stations. And I've tried every type of transportation too: trams, buses, trains, and the subway. The trams are the best of all of these, and I quickly discovered that a monthly pass buys the most heat for the least money. Yet I've become tired of this routine, tired of all these oppressive faces that stare at me in obvious disapproval, as if I were from another planet. I don't know why these people always show me their worst features. Their morose faces instantly light up if there's a single dog in the tram, a sight that practically turns them into children: they start talking to the animal and smiling at it and petting it, and sometimes they even let it lick their hands. Yet as soon as these people—the very same people who have just shown the animal all of this kindness and affection—sit up in their seats again, the stern features return to their faces, faces that seem revolted by the world and so many of its people.

The heat almost puts me to sleep on the tram, that heat I had been denied the previous night. It feels as if thorns are pricking my hands and feet, and even flowing through my blood. It burns at first, but then it stops, and a delicious torpor follows the pain. Warmth has become something of a rarity to me, a great chance to feel alive again. It always intoxicates me, and Hakima too: she stretches out across my chest, feeling warm and safe.

A woman with a kind and smiling face gets on the tram and sits down near me. Her fragrance brings back memories. It's as if I've met her before. I try to examine her face, but she's sitting directly behind me. So I close my eyes instead and try to recall the features of that scent as I slowly fall asleep. Now I know where it's from, where I first encountered it: it's the scent of my mother's hair from my childhood. My eyes still closed, I draw nearer to the source. That warm fragrance always made me feel safe. Whenever I drank it in as a child, clinging fiercely to my mother, I'd fall asleep. I know where I am right now, but I push the thought aside. I don't want to wake up. Instead, I set off with that fragrance, off into a dream.

I'm an infant in my mother's arms. We're riding in a litter on a camel, heading toward the north, as if to emigrate. I become older the further north we go, and begin to feel cold. At sunset, the caravan stops to rest at a small oasis. My mother puts me down, and I immediately learn how to walk. A short while later, I'm a young boy sitting beside a palm tree, its ripe dates all around me on the ground. I put a few of them in my mouth, but they taste different: more bittersweet than normal dates, and lacking flavor. I eat a couple and examine the pits, then turn my gaze to the tall palm as I sing:

> *"Turn, palm tree, turn,*
> *Throw me your dates and your light,*
> *Hide me from the bat,*
> *From the soldiers' servant,*
> *The one who steals jars and steals people,*
> *The spineless Devil.*
> *Turn, palm tree, turn,*
> *Throw me your dates and your light."*

I circle the palm until I'm dizzy, then I lie down and fall sleep beside it. When I wake up, the others are gone, and I've become an adolescent. The caravan vanishes into the distance: my mother has forgotten me. This place suddenly seems so strange. When I call out to my mother, I hear myself uttering words I do not understand.

Now I'm in that muddled state between waking and sleeping, caught up in the smell of perfume and the tram's warmth. I'm beginning to understand: My melancholic mood this morning must have something to do with that dream. This is the same dream that unsettled me last night. Yet how does it end? Or how *will* it end?

I hear some commotion around me, but I don't want to open my eyes. I can also hear the names of stations being announced on the tram's speakers, and I wait for those last words, "End of the line! Everyone off please!"

The commotion increases. Some sort of bright lights are flashing. People are talking loudly in a language I don't understand, and I can hear Hakima meowing timidly. I open my eyes and see her head sticking out of my coat. Some children have gathered around me, but they're only interested in Hakima, not me. A group of tourists has also appeared, and are taking pictures of us without asking permission. Their faces stretch out in broad smiles—smiles for Hakima, not for me—and they ask a few asinine questions in weak English, feigning politeness. I'm annoyed at being woken up, and I feel violated by their cameras and their laughter. It's as if I were a statue or a painting. Frightened by the strange voices, the flashes, and the incessant clicks of the cameras, Hakima curls herself into a ball and digs her sharp claws into my chest, something she rarely does.

I stroke Hakima's back, and am finally forced to give up my warm seat. I head for the back of the tram and sit down, but these people are everywhere. Fortunately the end of the line comes quickly. A part of me wants to stay here in the warmth, but I get off anyway, and am happy to see that the group is staying on and heading back with the same tram. I stomp around in the cold, waiting for the next tram. Hakima meows to let me know she's hungry, and I realize I'm hungry too. I pull out the cold bread roll and split it with her. She calms down a bit, and so does my stomach. I try to figure out the time—without my watch, which has stopped working—but it's useless. It's impossible to tell the time in this dim neon glow. Morning, noon, and afternoon all look the same; the features of time have all disappeared. Here, neither the trees nor anything else have shadows. You yourself have no shadow, so you become hazy, unfixed, and featureless, just like time.

I walk in funereal silence, watching the snow coming down relentlessly to cover the trees: there's not a single trace of green any more. The peace is broken by a scream from the sky, the sound of a low-flying plane. I can hear it, but I can't see anything through this haze.

When I was young, I used to bolt from the house anytime I'd hear a plane. They only ever rarely passed over our village. It didn't matter if I was in bed or in the bathroom or at the table. I'd still come rushing out to watch the plane as it soared above us like a cloud. Sometimes I'd stumble over things in my haste, but I didn't care. I just wanted to see the strange loud bird leaving its traces in the sky. The cloudy line behind it reminded me of a wagging tail at first, but then it seemed to swell up like someone's intestines, before finally disappearing. I was always amazed at how the plane would be in one part of the sky while its sound would reach me from somewhere else. Someone—I can't remember who—once tried to explain to me that some planes travel faster than sound. But it didn't make sense to me at the time because it didn't look like sound was actually traveling. In fact, I couldn't *see* sound at all. Back then, I simply dreamed of riding that wondrous metal bird and seeing our village from above. But the bird never came down from the sky for me.

I got on a plane many years later, and have been on a couple more since then. But flying has never brought me any real joy. I feel disjointed every time I fly, as if I were split in two: one part of me forever in my homeland, and the other a phantom venturing out into the world. Now I look at planes with a cold and sorrowful eye. I know they can carry the body from place to place with ease, but the soul always stays behind. Souls do not fly planes. They can't be moved so easily.

I suddenly remember Khalifa Wad Nafisa. He was the one who told me that some planes are faster than sound. How could I have forgotten that tall young man? I only spoke with him twice. He mostly kept to himself and didn't talk much, but he was very knowledgeable and open-minded. He had studied at one of the universities in Egypt, but his real interests lay in music and painting. Every time he came back from one of his trips, I would hover around his house in the hope of seeing him and hearing his stories about the places he'd been to and the people he'd met. The man was always smiling. I remember the one time he came with me to the tombs. The whole way there, he sang beautiful songs I'd never heard before. And I remember his words to me, words that he repeated the other time I saw him, to the point that I practically had them memorized.

"You'll see wonders when you set out into the world, Hamza. You'll see people much more decent than the ones in our village, but also people who are much worse. You'll see all sorts: idiots constantly worrying about their possessions, and other people who want to destroy the world. You'll see pious people and atheists; women and men; old and young; rulers and the ruled. You'll see all sorts, Hamza. Some of them will laugh at you, and some of them will trick you with their lies, with their fake respect and piety. They'll try to take advantage of you and suck your blood like oil for their own survival. You'll see wonders, Hamza. By God, you'll see wonders!"

The new watch that Sheikh Rikabi gave me back in Egypt still isn't working. It's in revolt against the time of this country, and tells it however it pleases. I've set it over and over again against the clocks on Vienna's squares and train stations, and here I am setting it against the one at the Schwedenplatz. I get off the tram at Taborstrasse, thinking to kill some time at the Karmeliter Market.

I'm hungry, and I know there's nothing to eat back at the apartment other than some dry cat food, which I keep to give to Hakima in emergencies. I had planned to spend the little money I brought with me on food for Hakima today, for I can't bear to hear her meow in hunger. But maybe I'll buy something we can both eat instead.

I love all open markets. I often buy fruits and vegetables from them on Fridays or Saturdays. Whenever I hear about a market in Vienna,

I make sure to go visit it. I'm almost certain that I know all of them by now: the Karmeliter Market, the Nasch, the Hannover, the Viktor Adler, the Brunnen. I love their hustle and bustle, their vitality, the cries of the vendors. But they really bring me down when I pass through them in the evening. At that time, after the working day is done, tons of perfectly good fruits and vegetables fill the trash bins or are thrown carelessly onto the ground, where they are either sniffed at by dogs or trampled by the feet of passersby. I often want to pick up this food and take it with me, but I'm always too embarrassed, and too proud: it would only add to my humiliation.

When I was young, I never threw out a single morsel of bread, whether stale or fresh. My mother taught me to kiss anything that anyone dropped on the ground and to set it to the side of the path, so that a bird or some other animal might have it. For all things that fall to the ground are the apportioned lot of animals and birds—that's what my mother told me. But where was my share among all these scraps? No pain is worse than being hungry and walking through all these piles of food without being able to stretch out your hand to them. Wealthy cities are cruel to those with only a few shillings.

Mehmet, the roasted chestnut vendor from Turkey, is there in the market. Every time he sees me he greets me in Arabic, and always in the form of an invocation, "May God preserve you—prayers and greetings!" This is how he says it, believing it to be an actual greeting in Arabic, and so I reply in kind. I buy some of that sourdough bread the Turks call ekmek and some cheese from the adjacent Turkish stall, and return to sit down beside Mehmet: the stove he roasts the chestnuts on gives off some very friendly warmth. I speak with him for a long time, more to warm myself up than because I actually want to talk.

When I get up to try to walk around a bit, I feel as if my head has remained seated. Black spots dance in front of me, growing larger until I can no longer see. The vertigo sends me reeling, my mind weighed down with all these distant memories and unable to break its bonds. I sit down again, and am immediately gripped by that very same feeling that accosted me long ago on the day I visited the graves of my mother and my sisters, the day of great thirst. I sink into the vertigo, resuming the dream that was interrupted in the tram:

I circle the palm until I'm dizzy, then I lie down and fall asleep beside it. When I wake up, the others are gone, and I've become an adolescent. The caravan vanishes into the distance: my mother has forgotten me. This place suddenly seems so strange. When I call out to my mother, I hear myself uttering words I do not understand.

I stand there and try to cry out again, but this time no voice emerges. I see a greenhouse not too far off and head toward it, thinking they might be in there. As I draw near, the scene inside it piques my interest: I can see a garden filled with birds, a water fountain, and people too. They're wearing strange clothes and walking in a silent, mechanical manner. I enter to look for the caravan, and hear the door close behind me. The air inside is sweet and fresh. The people approach me, still walking in that mechanical way of theirs. They stop in a line and stare at me strangely, absently, and then carry on with their walking. I ask them if they've seen the caravan. My voice has returned, thankfully, but it's hoarse now, the voice of an old man—I've grown older without realizing it. The people reply with puzzling gestures and words I cannot understand. The whole thing upsets me, and I make to leave.

Two giants are standing at the door. They order me to take off my clothes and put on the same clothes as all the others. Through the glass, I can see the specter of the moving caravan, and I can just barely hear the echo of my mother's voice calling me. I try to leave, but the two giants lay hold of me. They strip me down and dress me in the uniform: a blood-red wrap. These clothes somehow make me compliant. I begin to understand their words, and my memory slowly fades. I imitate their manner of speech, taking on their tones and inflections. I start to walk as they do, mechanically, though I have no idea where we are heading. We're all the same now. Young and old, men and women—it's all the same now.

Hakima wakes me up from my nap with an irritated meow, so I pull out some bread and cheese for her. She keeps using her left paw to grab at the cheese, something I've never noticed before. I try putting the food down to the right of her, but she still uses her left paw. "You sweet little southpaw!" I say to her, smiling and petting her happily, for I too am left-handed.

I was born left-handed. My mother thought it was sweet, an auspicious sign. She didn't know of a single left-handed person in our entire family. She used to love to play with me when I was a child and watch how I used my left hand for every action. My father was of a very different opinion, however. To him it was a defect and an evil omen. My mother told me that she cried one day when my father said that "the boy has been touched by Satan." He said that the Devil is left-handed, and that if I kept using my left hand for everything, I would not be granted very much of God's bounty in this world. As for Sheikh al-Faki, who considered himself a religious authority and also quite erudite, he told my father many things about the left hand: that it was originally the hand of Satan; and that it was also the hand of impurity and filth, and whoever eats with their left hand takes no pleasure in their food or drink, and receives no strength from them.

My father once told me a ridiculous story that Sheikh al-Faki was circulating in the village: When God first created mankind, He gave each person only one eye, one ear, one nostril, one leg, and one hand. The people were content like this, until they saw Iblis, the Devil. He had two of everything, and mocked them for their lack. So they complained to God and asked Him to give them what the Devil had. God replied that the left side is an evil that Satan must bear until Judgment Day, and that they could take it from him if they wanted to. But God warned the people, saying that this would mean they would have both good and evil in them. The people, however, rejoiced at this chance, and since that day all of us have had two of everything, just like Satan.

Sheikh al-Faki forced me to use my right hand for everything, as did my father. It was so hard for me to write with my right hand, and using my left one would have made things much easier for me. But whenever Sheikh al-Faki noticed me writing on the board with my left hand, he swooped like a vulture and lashed the back of my hand with his cane, yelling, "This is the hand of filth, the hand of Satan! No verses from the Quran may be written with it!"

Nothing exasperated Sheik al-Faki more than my remaining silent while he beat me. He used to explode in rage while I gazed at him calmly. I protected my head from his blows and the lashings of the cane, but I would not run from him despite the pain, which made him even more infuriated. Seeing him like this helped me persevere against his malice. I will never forget that one day when he beat me with such fury—as I held my ground—that he very audibly broke wind in the process. All my classmates immediately burst out laughing, and Sheikh al-Faki started raining chaotic blows down on everyone as they laughed and yelled. I was the loudest and taunted him more than any of them, of course. From that day on, we started calling him "the Farting Sheikh," and mocked him by make farting sounds.

In Quran school, Sheikh al-Faki used to have us pupils wipe the board with stale water from an old bucket made of rusty tin. At the end of my first day in the school, I wanted to do something useful, so I took the bucket that we washed the board in—we used to write in either chalk or ink—and poured the water in it onto the ground outside the school. The sheikh was outraged, and started cursing me and raving, "God's letters! God's words! God's water! Goddamn you Hamza Wad al-Rikabi, you left-handed devil!" I had no idea what I had done wrong. I ran home in terror, while he charged after me like an enraged bull.

That was my first day in Quran school.

I stayed away the following day. I feigned illness to my father, but I told my mother the real story, and she took pity on me. Sheikh al-Faki came by in the evening to inspect his victim and tell my father about my atrocious deed. My father cursed me and cursed the Devil too, as if we were one and the same. My mother went outside to where they were sitting and leered at the sheikh until he changed the subject to stories of other heroic deeds of his, which always delighted my father. They started laughing in that strange way of theirs—something between a cough and a hiss—while they sat on the prayer rug sipping hot tea with lots of sugar.

I went to school the next day and after the lesson Sheikh al-Faki ordered us to drink the dirty water in the bucket: he considered it holy water in which God's Quranic verses had dissolved. I was the only pupil who refused, and he laid into my head and body with violent blows from his reed cane, scared that my refusal would cause a mutiny among my classmates. They all stood there for a moment dumbfounded by my refusal, but they started to drink when they saw how he went after me with his long cane. I protected my face but didn't run away. And despite the pain he inflicted, I didn't drink the water that day.

He stopped and spoke with my father once again as he was making the evening rounds to dole out extra punishment to some of the children before their bedtimes. As usual, my father sprang up and made a big show of his anger, "Idiot! You miserable ass! You won't drink God's water, you son of the Devil?"

My mother replied loudly to the two from inside the house, "God's words aren't in some bucket, Sheikh al-Faki! His words are in books and in people's minds, not in their stomachs!"

"Don't ever listen to women," my father answered in a low voice, in collusion with the sheikh. "They lack both reason and religion."

I was happy to have my mother's support. In the days that followed, the sheikh ordered everyone to drink only after he had sent me off to do something else. Or sometimes he turned his back to me, as if he were afraid of my rebellion.

One time, another pupil, Ilyas Wad Farah al-Nas, hurried toward him saying, "Hamza didn't drink God's water, sir!" So Sheikh al-Faki screamed out, "God's curses on Hamza, that ass, that left-handed devil! He'll enter Hell through the widest of its gates!" Then he furiously beat Ilyas as if he were beating me, and the poor boy stopped telling on me after that. I stopped my good friend Uthman Darab Sidru from giving Ilyas another beating during the break later that day. Uthman wanted to teach him a lesson, since he was always on the sheikh's side and was always telling on us, even though he was a very poor student in both memorization and writing.

Uthman Darab Sidru, who was known for his courage, was so called because his mother said that when he was small, he used to violently beat his own chest like a gorilla whenever he got angry. And as he grew up, he started doing the same thing whenever he wanted to fight someone. Everyone was terrified of him and the harm he could inflict. I was a good friend of his, and I knew how harshly his father used to beat him, often for no reason at all, as if they were archenemies. That man had a child every year with his poor wife. In her youth, she was the tallest and strongest woman in the village, but she later became gaunt and sickly from all the children she had borne. Her husband, however, strutted around like a rooster, bragging about the eight children he had and wearing that spotless turban of his, which belied the dirty crumbling house that he and his family lived in.

Uthman was a handsome boy who looked a lot like his father, yet had the large and powerful frame of his mother. But his father's senseless beatings gradually wrecked his beauty. His face took on a despondent hue as the wounds and the suppurations, the sores and the scars, increased, until all his beauty was gone. His radiance gradually gave way to a look of subjugation and despair.

I was very sad when Uthman was kept away from school and could no longer come play with us. His body was wrecked, emaciated. Something was wrong with his kidneys. He was in a lot of pain and had problems urinating, and his pee would come out all bloody. All the cauterizations they gave him and all the burning 'holy' oil they rubbed onto him only made it worse—there was no doctor there.

Uthman Darab Sidru died when he was eight or nine years old. He had drunk from God's buckets dozens of times.

I remember all this while watching Hakima use her left paw to tug at the Semmel bread, and to play, and to do everything else as well. I can't get these stories out of my mind. I keep thinking about all those beliefs and traditions, and all the humiliating tales they told me about the left hand of Satan.

2

On the last steps of the narrow spiral staircase leading to the fifth floor, my paper shopping bag finally breaks. I had been pressing it tightly against my chest, worried that this would happen. There was a very light drizzle the whole way home, so light that I did not think to open my umbrella, but I was quickly soaked to the bone. I shifted the heavy and overloaded bag from one arm to the other every hundred meters or so, but when I realized that it was almost as soaked as I was and was about to tear, I lifted it up and held it against my chest. Now it has split at the bottom, and I can hear its contents falling to the floor. The loaf of bread rolls down to the bottom of the staircase. The eggs land safely on the sugar and the tea. The fruits and vegetables are covered in yogurt, and the milk spills all over everything. I instinctively try to protect the bottle of cooking oil with my leg: it falls hard onto my left foot, but does not break. The bottle of vinegar shatters, however, and its penetrating smell fills the air. For a moment I stand motionless, holding the empty bag absurdly between my arms, cursing the rain and the stairs and the bag while glaring at the scattered groceries.

I start picking it all up and setting the items at the top of the staircase, slowly working my way down the stairs to retrieve the groceries that had rolled away from me. A beautiful woman with a radiant smile is making her way up the stairs, holding one of my cans—a can of cat food—in her hand. Without saying a word, she helps me pick up the scattered groceries, her silver bracelets clinking softly as she does so. I accidentally touch the warm palm of her hand: the touch is soothing, and immediately brings back memories of a distant place.

"Thanks! Thanks a lot!" I say to her.

"You're welcome! Do you have a cat?"

"Yes."

"What's its name?"

"Hakima."

"Hakima?" she says, mispronouncing the hard Arabic 'h' at the beginning of the word. "It's a lovely name. What does it mean?"

"It means die Weise."

"Die Weisse? Is it a white cat?"

"No, she's not white! She's wise."

"How old is she?"

"I think she's about two-and-a-half years old."

"Did you get her from the animal shelter?"

"No. . . . It's a long story."

I gather up everything I can carry and head toward my apartment, and she follows me with some of the groceries. I can tell she's curious and wants to see the cat. I open the door and Hakima, as always, greets me with that long drawn-out meow of hers. I've always considered it her way of welcoming me, but everyone else who's heard it thinks that she's complaining about something.

The woman—whose name I still don't know—squats down and strokes Hakima's back with the warm palm of her hand while Hakima purrs in pleasure. The scene is breathtaking, as is the woman. I wish I were a painter or a sculptor right now so that I could hold onto this magical creature forever, capture that enchanting face from every possible angle—especially her hair, which has been done up elegantly but without affectation. Hakima is good at welcoming guests. She circles around, her meowing loudly, a welcome that delights the woman. I leave her to play with Hakima while I grab a plastic bag and go back to the stairs to get the rest of my groceries before making a final trip with a dustpan and a small brush to gather up the shards of the vinegar bottle.

When I return, the woman is still squatting just inside the open door of my apartment. I watch her as she goes through a host of spontaneous motions: sitting, standing, half-sitting, leaning over, squatting, circling on one foot, then on two. She looks like a ballet dancer with those light feet and nimble movements. Hakima circles around her, once to the right and once to the left.

"Come in, please!" I say.

She enters bashfully, her eyes widening in surprise as she looks at the apartment. I address her in the plural, a form of politeness and respect in this country, "Do you live here?"

"No, my brother lives here with his wife. But I help them take care of their baby girl sometimes."

"I think this is the first time I've ever seen you here!"

"I've been coming here once a week for two years, every Friday. Have you been in this apartment long?"

"Four years, two months, and five days."

"You've got quite a precise memory! You must not be very happy here."

"No, that's not quite right. It's just that I'm afraid of time."

"Afraid of time?"

"Yes. Time can be treacherous. It turns on me every few months and changes my life without a word of warning. I've lived through many different times."

"I'm not sure I understand."

"I've slowly become like everyone else here. I'm afraid of time, and every second I expect my life to be turned upside down. It's as if I've started waiting for something. I don't know what it is, but I'm scared of it. These days, I live the time of the people here. Their time is a menace. Do you know what I mean? I come from a country where people tend time like sheep. You tell it to stop, and it stops.

You tell it to march, and it marches. You can swat it away while you lie down under a tree to rest. You can sleep on it without any sort of alarm clock, and if you wake up you can drive it off into other people's homes and go back to sleep. But here, in this country, time chases after people like a wild beast, mangling the slow and devouring the weak. It hovers like a bird of prey. The people here run from it. They keep running and running until they collapse. I lived the time of the people over there, and now I'm living the time of the people here. There's nothing for it, and I'm not sure which one is better. To be honest, I've become tired of both of them. That's why I philosophize like this."

"It's all very interesting."

"I'm just joking around. It's all in my head."

Her voice is as enchanting as her footsteps: light, clear, soothing. She's piqued my curiosity, so I stop my rambling and change the subject, "Would you like some tea?"

"Thanks, but I should get going."

"I've got a delicious hibiscus drink from Sudan called karkaday. I know you'll like it."

"I don't want to trouble you."

Her reply puts me at ease. It seems that she's no less curious than I am.

"It's quick and easy to make," I say.

"All right! I'll try it!"

I quickly make her a hot cup of karkaday. At the first sip, her features change ever so slightly. In the mirror across from her, I can see the surprise and curiosity written on her face as she stares at the drink. For a moment, I reproach myself for assuming that other people's tastes are the same as my own, and for always offering them only the food and drink that I myself like. But I quickly put my mind ease: this is a token of affection, after all, a way I have of welcoming people. She doesn't let go of the cup, and takes sip after sip of the drink. It seems that she's slowly coming round, but I can't be sure. Her silver bracelets keep clinking delightfully, filling me with a childlike joy whose source is a mystery to me.

Hakima is sitting submissively in her lap now, as if she were holding onto her. There's a short silence, but the woman breaks it, "I'm Sandra. What's your name?"

"Hamza."

"Chamza?" she asks, mispronouncing the hard Arabic 'h.'

"No, Hamza."

"Khamsa?"

"Hamza, with a hard 'h.' Ha. Hamza!"

She keeps trying to repeat it, laughing all the while. She's gorgeous when she laughs like that, revealing those two white lines of teeth behind her pink lips and ever-present smile.

Her skin has the hue of wheat at the beginning of autumn. The confident smile that never leaves her face reminds me of that ancient pharaoh, Queen Hatshepsut. I can't tell the color of her eyes, but they too have something of that forgotten ancient enchantment.

Hakima conspires with me to keep Sandra here a bit longer. Sandra looks around at the walls and smiles.

"Why are you smiling?" I ask inquisitively.

"Your walls are covered with palm trees, even the ceiling! But you forgot to wallpaper the floor!" Her graceful laughter serves as an apology for that quick joke of hers, and I laugh with her.

"Do you really like palm trees that much?"

"When I first came here, the apartment was run-down and there was horrible wallpaper everywhere. I thought I'd catch a cold just by looking at the walls: there were white mountains covered in snow, and the sky above them was practically white as well. As you've no doubt noticed, this apartment is already as cold as a freezer, and it really can't take any more of that. I found this wallpaper as I was walking through the flea market one Saturday. It was cheap, so I bought every last piece of it, and then covered over all the frost that had been hanging on the walls for years. From that day on, I've felt a bit of warmth here. I feel as if I've moved somewhere just a little closer to the sun. I'm deluding myself a bit, I know, but in time maybe I'll actually start believing it."

"Have you ever visited the Palm House?" she asks me while stroking Hakima's back, who is now lying with her head on Sandra's thigh.

"No. Where is it? Is it a museum?"

"No. It's a beautiful greenhouse on the grounds of the Schönbrunn Palace where they keep tropical plants. It's called das Palmenhaus. You might like it."

"It must be new."

"Not at all. It was built in the days of Kaiser Franz Joseph the First as a place to keep plants that cannot stand the snow and fierce cold here."

"Incredible."

"What's so incredible?"

"How is it that I haven't heard of this place? I should have visited my family there by now."

"Your family?"

I laugh out loud. "Yes. If there are palm trees and tropical plants there, then the ghosts of my ancestors must be there too."

She looks at me inquisitively, and a bit taken aback, so I make amends. "I'm only joking," I say, "but there's some truth in it all the same!"

She laughs at this. "I don't know what to believe any more!"

"Some people believe the first part of what I tell them, and others believe the last part!"

"And which part do you want me to believe?"

"All of it!"

She laughs again. Then I ask her about the Palm House and how to get there. She tells me the way, with a bit of hesitation, however, as if she thinks I won't be able to find it on my own. But then she quickly changes the subject, "Can I have another cup of that delicious drink, that karkatay?" she asks.

This polite request makes me happy, for my first impression was that she had not liked the taste of it. My eyes must have deceived me. "I was convinced you weren't enjoying it! Are you sure it's not too bitter for you?"

"Not at all, it's great! It does have a lot of sugar in it, but who doesn't like sugar? You said your name was 'Hamsa,' right?" she asked, once again mispronouncing the hard Arabic 'h.'

"Hamsa is a nice name too, but my name is Hamza. Hamza! The first letter is a bit more in the throat—you don't have it in German. The word you said, hamsa, means something else in my language."

She laughs enchantingly. "What does hamsa mean?"

"It means 'whisper'."

My residence registration form is in a clear plastic envelope on the table. She sees it and asks my permission before taking a look at it—she wants to see how my name is spelt. But suddenly she starts and says "My God!"

I'm caught off guard, unsure of what's taken hold of her. I can't tell if she's happy about something or afraid.

"My God!" she says again. "Is this true?"

"What?"

"Is tomorrow your birthday?"

"Yes!" I say, a bit frazzled, but also relieved, as if I had committed some great sin and was now confessing it.

"And how are you going to celebrate?"

"Celebrate? What do I have to celebrate? I never do anything for my birthday." The harshness of my words is not at all in line with Sandra's joy. Hakima comes over to me now and sits down in my lap just as she had done in hers, as if to show her support.

Sandra falls silent for a moment, but then continues, "Let's celebrate your birthday tomorrow. What do you say? I've got an idea."

I look at her apprehensively, making sure that the karkaday hasn't gone to her head.

"I'm inviting you to the Palm House for your birthday," she says. "What do you say?"

I agree at once. She gets up nimbly and says, "I'll come by tomorrow at ten, and we can head over there together."

I don't reply. I don't have to—it feels like we've known each other for a long time. I look at her face hidden behind her hair as she leans over Hakima. She strokes Hakima's back before excusing herself to leave, and Hakima lets out a strange, almost humorous meow, as if she wants to say goodbye or tell Sandra to stay. I pick up Hakima and walk Sandra to the door, uncertain of what her eyes are telling me now. I leave the door open to watch her disappear, standing at the threshold with Hakima in my arm. Sandra waves to us from the end of the long corridor. "See you tomorrow!" she says.

I hear the sound of her bracelets one last time as I slowly go back inside to think about this remarkable visit. Overjoyed, I kiss Hakima and spin her in the air like a child. I feel as if my body wants to leave me for a moment to go dance in complete freedom, without any inhibitions.

"Your food is to thank for all of this!" I say to Hakima. "You're the one who brought us this charming visitor, you sweet thing—the sweetest Hakima in all of Austria!"

This time, I pronounce the name like Sandra does.

My sleep is troubled that night, and not just because of the cold. Sandra has left a trace of her lightness in the apartment. Uncharacteristically, I get up in the middle of the night to drink a cup of karkaday. It's more delicious than it has ever been before. I gaze at the wallpaper, examining the palm trees as if they were part of some exhibit. They're not the same as the ones in my mind, the ones I've seen for much of my life: they don't quiver in the wind or cast off dates. But they still somehow comfort me at this late hour of the night. I pretend that the weather has become warmer now, and take this thought with me to bed.

I fall asleep at dawn, and wake up at nine to the ringing of my loud alarm clock, with its copper bell that sits atop it like a crown. It too is from the flea market. I liked it because it reminded me of the alarm clock of our neighbors, Abd al-Malik's family, back in my village of Wad al-Nar. That alarm was so loud that it always woke me up, even though it wasn't in our own home. I get up sluggishly now, my feet and fingertips frozen. But my energy returns when I remember yesterday's visit, and also today's, which is rapidly drawing near.

I take a quick shower, praying for the water heater to work for just five minutes. But as usual, it refuses. Exactly two minutes into the shower, it stops working, and the water turns cold. I tremble as I get out, and quickly put on my clothes. I feed Hakima, and have some Semmel bread with butter and jam for my own breakfast, along with a cup of tea with milk.

Time passes slowly, my ears glued to the door of the apartment. Any time someone passes by on his way to the bathroom, I think that it's Sandra. At exactly ten o'clock, I hear a couple of light knocks on the door. At first I think I must be imagining it, but then I hear them again. I open up and Sandra comes in, smiling beautifully and looking even more radiant than yesterday. The scent of jasmine enters the apartment with her, a perfect addition to this morning that has suddenly become so much warmer. She's elegantly dressed, but there's a certain spontaneity to the way she dresses and acts that really attracts me—a lightness that she has about her. A change comes over me, and I feel a bit embarrassed. It gets worse when she presses my hand to wish me a happy birthday. Her face is so close to mine that I have the impression she wants to kiss me, but maybe I'm just imagining it. She becomes embarrassed now as well, and we both draw back a bit, but her warm hand remains in mine just a little longer. Hakima joins her as if she has known her forever, and yesterday's rituals are repeated.

"Can I get you something to drink?"

"A karkatay, please."

"It's called karkaday, but I'll change its name to karkatay if you like!"

I'm ready to go. Sandra addresses Hakima sorrowfully while drinking the karkaday, "We're going to have to leave you here all on your own, you poor little thing."

"No we're not," I reply. "Saturday is Hakima's day out."

"What?"

"I always take her out with me, or rather, she takes me out with her."

"Out in the streets?"

"Yes! And on the trams, and to the supermarket, and everywhere else. She won't let me go without her. She knows Vienna better than I do now."

"Don't all the people and noise bother her? She's a cat, not a dog!"

"You'll see for yourself."

I put on my coat and call Hakima, who is lying in Sandra's arms. She jumps up and comes over to me. I put her inside the coat at chest level, and she settles in. Sandra approaches in surprise, peering at my chest to make sure there's no trickery and that this is really happening. She doesn't notice how I'm looking straight at her, how intoxicated I am by her smell.

Out on the street, Sandra smiles and keeps her eyes fixed on my chest. We make our way down to the Danube Canal by the Urania building and walk until we reach the Schwedenplatz. It's not a long walk, but it's very cold out, and we can see chunks of ice floating down the canal. Everyone outside is walking quickly in their heavy coats with steam coming from their mouths, as are we. As soon as we're on the subway—line four—Hakima sticks her head out like a small kangaroo and takes a look around. Sandra laughs in delight and pets Hakima's head, and I do the same. The people around us are, as usual, surprised by this. Some of them smile, and some shake their heads in displeasure, and some of them take no notice of us.

We get off at the Hietzing station, and the three of us cross the street and enter the grounds of the Schönbrunn Palace. We keep walking for a bit, and the large steel-framed greenhouse that she described to me yesterday comes into view.

"This looks too new to be from the nineteenth century," I tell her.

"They've renovated it," she replies, "but it's the same building."

As we approach the entrance, I try to get ahead of her to pay for the tickets, but she's firm in her resolve. "We agreed yesterday that I would take you out on your birthday," she says.

As we open the door to step inside, an incredible warmth floods through it. It's as if I've entered a womb, a refuge from the cold of the outside world. An old familiar feeling comes over me, the feeling that I'm wearing a robe made of sunlight. It puts me at ease, as do these familiar smells and this warmth that I know so well, this rare warmth that I had lost for many years. Here it all is again, with Sandra, in the middle of these flowers and plants and trees. I hear birds as well, but they turn out to be a recording, nothing more.

I slow down a bit to look around, my face beaming while Sandra gazes at me with the joy of a child. "This place is amazing," I tell her gratefully. "I've been in Vienna for five years and four days, and I've never once come here."

"Five years and three and a half days!" she corrects with a laugh.

I walk around in a daze, looking at all the plants. "Where are the palm trees?" I ask her.

"In the right wing of the building."

We head over there together, making sure to close the door behind us. A familiar smell welcomes us and brings me joy: the smell of humid tropical warmth. We sit down on a white bench in front of a solitary palm tree. A question is troubling me, but I don't want to give voice to it, "Where are the rest of the palms?" I'd rather sit and watch this one palm tree instead, with no questions asked. A single palm in all of Vienna is enough; I feel comforted here, despite the many confused and competing memories being stirred up by this place.

Sandra is sitting beside me, playing with Hakima in my coat. A few people look at us curiously from a distance, but they refrain from invading our privacy. A few others peer at us stealthily from behind the plants, trying to figure out why she's plunging her hand into my coat like this.

That Saturday, I spend one of the happiest days of my life with Sandra and Hakima in the Palm House. It's the first time I've ever been inside it, yet it feels as I've lived there for years. I walk around a bit, but then head back to my original spot by the tree. "Do you feel at home here?" Sandra asks. "Do you like it? Or are you disappointed?"

"I can't find the right words to express how grateful I am. This is an incredible gift. When's *your* birthday, then?"

"I had mine a while ago. I was born on May 2, 1979."

I take Hakima out of my coat and set her on Sandra's lap. Sandra is worried about Hakima, and keeps a firm hold on her with her hand. I reassure her that Hakima won't become frightened and won't wander off: that she'll stay close to either her or me; that she never goes far when we're outside the apartment; and that even in the apartment she stays nearby, like a small child.

I close my eyes and let my mind wander. The warmth, the smells, and the deceptive sounds of birds send me off into the depths of another life.

I'm walking in the dark, and cannot see anything around me. I don't know where I came from or where I'm going. I take off one of my leather sandals and gently touch the ground with the sole of my left foot: it's as hard and cold as concrete. It must be ice, for an electric chill shoots through my body. I put my sandal back on, but my foot remains as cold as before. I suddenly walk into what seems to be a soft, cold wall. I take a few steps back and bump into another wall that is even colder. I feel trapped here, and stop to try to figure out where I am. I can hear the wind and feel its chill on my skin, as if someone has just opened a door or a window.

I hear a cat. Its meowing gladdens me, and draws nearer until I can see two glowing eyes in the darkness. I can see the eyes and feel the warm soft body as it circles around my left foot. I squat down and pet its fur, grateful for the touch, and for the beginnings of warmth that I feel. The cat slowly moves away and starts meowing again. I follow it, walking carefully with my arms raised in front of me so as not to bump against another wall. The meowing cat is my compass. Every time it looks back and I see the gleam of its eyes, I speed up. I suddenly find myself walking on what seems to be warm sand. I take off my sandals, carrying them under my arm, and feel the sand's warmth as I follow the cat, joyfully walking behind this good omen.

The light of dawn appears on the horizon, and morning arrives in just a few seconds. I can see the cat running in front of me. It seems so small in comparison to the wide eyes that I saw in the darkness. Its ears are long—a cat of ancient pharaonic descent. A little way off, a young woman is standing at the door of a house. There's a lemon tree in front of it, and a large glistening water jug made of clay. I walk over to ask her if the cat is hers, but she disappears inside the house. The door is open, so I go in after her. I catch a glimpse of her disappearing into the inner garden of the house. I enter into it, and find myself standing in the middle of many different types of trees: pomegranate trees and orange and lemon and mango. I can smell guava trees somewhere as well, but cannot see them. A single tall palm tree towers in the middle of the garden. It seems to be close, but I cannot reach it, no matter how many steps I take—it's as if it were moving away from me. The smell of lemon and jasmine fills the air. I can see the palm tree towering in the distance now. I make for it, crossing a small stream as I do so, and feeling the humid warmth of this place. The birds are singing their songs of dawn while the sun slowly appears, an astounding disc of the deepest red. Now I know where I'm heading.

I feel something warm moving on my thigh, and open my eyes to see Hakima there. She circles around a bit and then settles into her favorite spot: on my lap. Sandra is looking at me. "You were smiling and speaking softly," she says. "But I couldn't understand what you were saying."

I consider telling her about this marvelous dream, but I ask her another question instead, "Are you hungry?"

"Yes, I am. But I'm taking you out to one of my favorite restaurants. Hopefully you'll like it! Don't forget that we're still celebrating your birthday!"

"Let me get the meal, please!"

"We agreed on this yesterday. Don't make me angry!"

I realize that I don't have enough money on me to take her out, so I quickly propose an alternative, "I'm an excellent cook," I say. "How about I make something for us at my place?"

She thinks about this for a moment, looking at her watch. "All right! Let's go!"

We head back to my apartment. I try to impress her, cooking quickly, like an expert chef, while she watches. She asks me where I learned to cook and whether that's my job, and has me tell her the names of the spices she doesn't know. Incredibly, until now neither of us has asked the other about their work, which is usually one of the first questions people ask in this country.

It takes me about a half hour to make the food and put it on the table. We eat and laugh, and Hakima eats with us, then falls asleep on Sandra's lap—her new habit. Sandra relates bits and pieces of her life to me, and when she falls silent I tell her a little about mine. I can see that she wants to know more, but she keeps her curiosity in check, which puts me at ease.

"The apartment's cold," she says.

"Yes, a little."

The apartment's not cold—it's freezing. Both of us are wrapped up in our thick coats, like two people sitting in a freezer. I ask a few questions about the Palm House to change the subject. I want to stay there in my mind, draw out this lovely afternoon as long as I can. At 5:15, she excuses herself, asking one last question before she leaves. "What year were you born, Hamza? And where?"

"I was born in 1974, in a village called Wad al-Nar in the middle of Sudan."

I say nothing more, and she too falls silent. The unspoken words lie between us like a sea.

Hakima and I are once again standing at the door to say goodbye to her. I can still smell the jasmine. "You've given me such a wonderful day, Sandra. I'll never forget it."

"Happy birthday, Hamza!" she replies, mispronouncing the 'h.'

She kisses Hakima's head, and as she does this I lay the lightest of kisses on her own head as well, a kiss I don't want her to notice just yet. She looks at us with her big eyes, and then walks nimbly ahead of me into the corridor. "Could I come by every Friday to visit Hakima?" she asks, still having trouble with the 'h.'

I smile and put my ear against Hakima's head, as if I were listening to her reply. "Hakima says she'll wait for you every day, not just Friday."

Saturday evening comes.

Then Saturday night.

Sunday morning.

Sunday afternoon.

Sunday evening.

Sunday night.

An entire week slowly goes by in this way, and the much-anticipated Friday becomes the most important day of the week. I do as much as I can to spruce up my humble apartment.

Friday finally comes, and I wake up much earlier usual. I cook moussaka with rice and vermicelli, and make a green Arab salad, some tahini sauce, and some baba ghanoush. I also go out and buy some Arab bread.

The morning passes slowly as I listen for the door, thinking that every noise outside is surely Sandra. At exactly seven minutes before ten, she knocks softly at the door. I open it, and Sandra enters, bringing her scent and her smile in with her, and chasing away my anticipation. The awkwardness of the previous week returns, until Hakima comes and dissolves some of the sweet tension. Sandra has a plant wrapped in green paper in her arms. I take it from her as she removes the wrapping: it's a small palm tree with three long straight branches. "I found it today all by itself at the flower shop," she says before I can utter a word. "I thought it might like living with all the palms you have here."

"Thank you. This is too much."

"All I did was save the poor tree. It's your job to protect it."

"Would you believe that I went to the Palm House three times this past week?"

She blushes and tries to control her emotion, but the clinking of her bracelets betrays her. "Do you like it there?" she asks.

"Yes, a lot!"

"Then why don't we go back there tomorrow?"

Her hand is on Hakima's back, and mine is on Hakima's head. She starts purring even more loudly than usual, and both of us laugh in one voice. Time passes lightly, warmly.

She really likes the food, and asks how I made the different dishes and what spices I used. This brings us to a topic where I can more than hold my own. I ask her if she's ever had cardamom, and she says no, so I jump up to get some for her. She smells it and takes a taste of it, which she likes, while I tell her about the dishes in which it's generally used, and those in which it should be used. Then we talk about cumin and mastic; and then about saffron and dill; and so on and so forth until we reach the end of my long list of spices. I keep to this topic, and she seems happy to ask me questions, and to smell and relish everything slowly. She mistakes some hot chili powder for turmeric, letting out a loud and trembling cough that captivates me. I seize the opportunity, "You've done it!" I say. "You've pronounced the first letter of my name! Keep at it!" We double over in laughter, the tears coming to our eyes.

Hakima intervenes anytime there's a moment of silence, meowing to lighten the tension, which brings us even more laughter. A new dream takes hold of me, the dream I'll live tomorrow.

We go there the next day, to the Palm House. I feel like a child rushing to my favorite playground. This time I'm quicker than Sandra, and she watches uncomfortably as I pay for the two tickets. Inside, I head straight for the spot where we sat on our first visit, and where I'd been three other times since. Sandra excuses herself for a minute and comes back with a gorgeous smile on her face, blushing ever so slightly in that enchanting way of hers. She asks Hakima a question, "My apartment is pretty close. Would you like to see where I live when we're done here?"

I translate the question out loud for Hakima, who meows as she always does whenever I speak to her in Arabic. Sandra is delighted by this. I tell her that it means "with pleasure," and then continue, "I forgot to say that you look like an Austrian actress I've seen in a lot of the old black-and-white movies I watch. I don't know her name, though." She mentions several names, and I apologize for not knowing any of them. She says several people have told her this before, but that she can't see the slightest likeness between herself and any Austrian actress.

At three o'clock, the three of us head to Sandra's apartment in the seventh district. We take the number four subway to the Karlsplatz, then make our way to the Ringstrasse—the road that encircles the city center—and take the number one tram past the Opera House, the National Library, and the Museum of Art History. We get off at Bellaria station, near the parliament building, and hop on the number 49 tram to the seventh district. The building looks like a museum, both inside and out. Sandra tells me it's an old building that was spared from the devastation of the First World War and the destruction of the Second. It used to be owned by a Jewish man, one of the most famous watchmakers in Europe at the time. His workshop had been on the ground floor, the offices of his workers and employees on the second and third floors, and he had used the fourth floor as his own office. The fifth and sixth stories had been his private residence. Semper, a famous architect who was a personal friend of his, had overseen the construction of the building. That same Semper also designed Vienna's Museum of Art History and its Museum of Natural History, two buildings that are virtual mirror images of one another, with a sculpture of Queen Maria Theresa and her entourage set in the middle of the courtyard that separates them.

Sandra's apartment is on the fourth floor. It's a small apartment with two rooms, a foyer, and a small kitchen. The faint perfume of the place is the first thing that grabs me. Plants have been placed around the apartment with care, and all the walls are painted white, yet there's still a warmth to them. An elegant tiled stove stands in one corner of the apartment. In the living room, a bookshelf that stretches to the ceiling is crammed with books and a few other things, and there's a record player in the other corner of the room. Posters of Paul Klee paintings hang on many of the walls—I always recognize the warmth of his work.

Sandra offers me her favorite drink, which is called Holundersaft, or elderberry juice, and comes from a plant I've never heard of before. It tastes great, and Sandra is pleased that I like it. She sets a plate of fruit on the table and puts on a record by Mozart. It feels as if I'm hearing classical music for the very first time—it must be the magic of this place, Sandra's magic. Hakima moves around as if it were her own apartment. She loves all the plants, and spends the whole time rubbing herself up against them. We pass the time engrossed in a long conversation, a sign of things to come, perhaps. At midnight I excuse myself to catch the last tram home—I'd lost track of the time. Now she's the one standing at the door of the apartment while I say goodbye. She stands on the broad landing, her hand raised, until I've made it down the stairs.

I'm in no hurry to get back to my place. I tuck Hakima inside my coat and take the long walk home, paying attention to nothing but the signals at the crosswalks. I program myself to stop on red, while my mind wanders off into a beautiful dream. I move slowly, despite the cold, and arrive at my apartment door at 1:15 in the morning.

We get into the habit of seeing each other three times a week: Friday afternoon at my apartment, Saturday afternoon at the Palm House, and Sunday at her apartment. She also takes me to many places around the city that I've never really seen before, even though I walk past them all the time. We stop using the polite plural form of address—which I've always considered absurd in any case—and address each other like normal people instead.

"Where do you go when you leave me, when you seem to be asleep?" she asks me one Sunday at the Palm House.

I tell her about the dream I had the first time we were here together, the dream about the cat in the darkness, and the house with the young woman, the garden, and the sun. "Your dreams are lovely," she says. "If all dreams were like that, I'd start dreaming too. But take me with you one time so I can see what you see. Or come back quickly to tell me about it."

I do indeed enter into a wonderful lucid dream, this time through Sandra's two large eyes, and I set off into a world of her colors, of her suns. Then, half waking, I see her holding my warm left hand with both of hers, while Hakima is pressed against my chest. My heartbeat quickens at the rare feelings inside me. "The dream has become even lovelier," I say to her. "Now I really am taking you with me. Can you see what I see?"

She flashes that captivating smile of hers and says nothing, clinging for a few moments to that silence I love so much. "In your dreams," she begins at last, "you look as calm and peaceful as an angel, and I can see what you must have looked like when you were a child. I wish I could always see you like that." She gives me a quick kiss at the edge of my lips. I smile, still feeling the trace of her soft lips by my mustache and at the beginning of my beard.

"Can I give you a present?" she asks.

"You've already given me so many," I reply. "I can't turn them down, but I can't give you anything in return either."

She puts her fingers to my lips. "Don't say that! It's just a simple gift."

She opens up her bag and tells me that she has bought me an annual ticket to the Palm House. She says it's much cheaper than I think, and that she'd be very grateful if I accepted it, because she loves to see me happy like this, together with Hakima. She also says that if I don't accept it, then she'll give it to Hakima, whom she liked from the very beginning. She looks at me for a long time, saying nothing more. She's holding the ticket toward me, her outstretched hand cutting off any reply or refusal. I almost give her a wild passionate kiss right then and there, but I control myself, afraid of ruining the moment and the wonderful gift. The way she's looking at me now drives all the world's languages out of me—I can't say a word. She blushes lightly, and warmth spreads through my entire body. I remember our second visit to the Palm House, and how she excused herself for a few minutes and then returned, flushed and happy—she must have bought the ticket then.

I stare into her eyes as if I were reading some book, or looking at a painting. I slowly shift my gaze from her face to the solitary palm tree across from her, and then to Hakima, who is now sitting on her lap. Sandra does the same, looking at Hakima, and then at the palm tree, and then at me.

It's been so long since I've felt this way. I had almost forgotten what it was like to tend time in front of me; to feel family and warmth; and to feel the soothing gaze of someone who loves me.

3

I draw my 'devil's' hand to my nose to smell that soothing fragrance with which I perfumed it before heading out. It makes me feel as if I'm walking in a veil of enchantment. It's like a drug that gently draws me into distant worlds, into the past. Hakima curls herself up at my chest and falls asleep on her side. I open my coat up a bit for her—it's warm here.

I'm here again, after just a few days' absence: here at the Palm House.

I seem to be addicted to this place. It's becoming the wellspring of my memories and my happiness. If I die in this far-off country and they bury me here, I have no doubt that the warmth would bring joy to my soul, and that it would be a gift of beauty I would cherish until the end of death.

What a gift you've given me, Sandra! What world did you come from? Which gods sent you here to my fifth-floor apartment in Vienna's third district? I wish you were beside me now. But that would also make me uneasy, for I'd still be going into that distant world of mine without you. I plunge into my own longing, damming up the cracks in my memories with it, in order to feel that I once had a life like that of other people: a life with a mother and a father and two sisters; a life with a house and neighbors and classmates; with my own language and voice; a life with a sun, and a shadow.

I wish I could cry now and release this sad tension, a tension whose source I do not know.

As a child, I never cried like the others. I was largely denied that natural comfort, that great gift that lets you let go of your feelings. When I was a still a young boy, my father—before he left us—taught me that real men do not cry, and that tears are a disgrace. He shackled me with that notion until my feelings had hardened within me and I could do nothing to change them. I lost the grace of tears when I was young, and have yet to find a substitute.

I don't know when exactly my mother Habiba bit Nur al-Din al-Shilani died, or when my sisters Karima and Halima died. I consider the day I returned from Europe to my village of Wad al-Nar to be the day of their passing from the world. I buried the bracelet I had brought back for my mother and the two dolls I had brought for my sisters. That was the funeral for the remnants of my family in Wad al-Nar. I marked the spot with one large stone and three smaller black ones. The three smaller stones I had chosen for the grave were covered in dust, and were it not for the sweat on my brow on that hot day—sweat that stung my eyes and streamed across my lips and chin before pouring onto the ground—I would never have noticed the lustrous black color of those three stones, nor the scratches and scrawls that covered them. I paid them no further heed that day, however—my eyes were burning, and I was in a hurry.

Tranquillity envelops the Palm House. Hakima is purring happily in her sleep, and she feels warm against my heart. I can see Sandra's face in my mind. I remember how she sat right here beside me and let me have my dreams and my memories, calmly waiting for me like a patient mother whose child is playing. I can see her relaxed and smiling. Her face is always like that, even in my dreams.

I shut my eyes against the exhausted rays of the sun. Half asleep, I set off into a distant day, a day of celebration.

It was Eid al-Adha, the Feast of the Sacrifice. I had been staying in the village of Wad al-Kababish, the one closest to where Wad al-Nar used to be, but separated from it by a vast desert. Exactly forty days had passed since the funeral I described. Quivering, I made my way through the crowds that stood in the shade like palm trees leaning over a riverbank in the morning. They were standing all in a row, as if they were waiting for God's mercy to bring a ram down from heaven for them. But that didn't happen. Walking through the village in my flowing white robe, I looked like the mast of a ship whose sails are caught in a gust of wind. Wad al-Kababish: of the twenty-seven villages in the area, this was the last that remained. The mere mention of its name aroused sorrow. The elders said that this village was once an oasis that stretched to the horizon, a vast green disc against the yellow of the desert, and that it supplied rams and goats and camels to the north, east, and west. They said that no other village raised such large numbers of animals, and none had broader pastures, for none of them had any lakes that were as big or had such sweet water as the one that had been here. Sometimes the treacherous currents in its deep basin would cause it to overflow in rage, wreaking havoc on the surroundings, but that lake provided every living creature grazing in that vast valley with ample water the whole year round.

The next valley over was called Wadi Malkamani. One afternoon, as I was on my way to the tombs, that handsome artist Khalifa Wad Nafisa joined me for a bit and asked me if I had ever visited the valley, which I hadn't. This was the same man who told all the splendid stories about people in distant countries, and who told me that planes can move faster than sound. He later left the village, vanishing into the wide world. That was the only afternoon he ever came with me to the tombs, and I remember him talking to me about the adjacent valley, whose edges we could make out in the distance. He said that its real name was not Wadi Malkamani, but rather Wadi al-Malika Amani Shekhtu, the Valley of Queen Amani Shekhtu. He told me that she was a glorious queen, exceedingly tall, and that 'Shekhtu' was a title reserved for men, for kings. She was the first and only woman to be given this honor in the history of those dynasties. Some people now mistakenly call her Sheikha Amani, but her actual name was Amani Shekhtu. Khalifa told me that her beauty was renowned: her enchanting eyes, her long thick hair, her lovely breasts. There's a statue of her that's been largely worn down by time, and around which many legends were woven. It still stands there on a great crop of stone that juts out from Jabal al-Rutab, the Mount of Ripe Dates. That mountain is a marvelous sight: there's a green meadow on its plateau that's covered with grass and bushes and roses, and entirely surrounded by sand and massive boulders. Everyone who sees it is always amazed at how there can be so much green in the midst of all that rock and sand. Her statue towers over the place, and is visible from all directions. Some say that the pharaohs built that enormous statue for her and her father, and others say it was for her husband. Still others claim it was for her son Sirandub, whose name means 'the one who walks among the people,' and who always wanted to converse with his subjects. Toward this end, he refused to ride on any mount so as not to elevate himself above his people, and so he could walk with them.

The queens of that kingdom were not your usual slender queens, but rather the custom was to have large powerful queens to show they were from powerful houses. They were to avoid slenderness at all costs, for they also needed to be strong enough to perform the divine rites and undergo the rigorous coronation ceremonies that were prerequisites for any ruler.

That day, I thought of my dear friend Uthman Darab Sidru's mother and how she used to call him in that powerful voice of hers. She was a strong, solidly built woman, and I remember the heavy loads she used to carry without a word of complaint. Perhaps she was of the same stock as these pharaohs, and my dear friend Uthman Darab Sidru—who died so young—was the last descendant of Queen Amani.

It was Eid al-Adha that day, the Feast of the Sacrifice, and the people were congratulating one another on the holiday in spite of their weakness and sorrow. The village imam, Sheikh Hamad Wad Atbar, was the owner of the only goat in Wad al-Kababish, and was unsure of what to do. Should he slaughter it in obedience to God and be rid of the animal at the festival, or should he let it keep trickling out the little milk it had? I could hear its sad bleating over the murmurs of the men and women and the cries of the children. The people were looking at it voraciously, with eyes that were practically eating it alive. It appeared that they would spend the Feast of the Sacrifice eating kisra, a dish made out of cornmeal, with nothing but a bit of salt and water on it—if they even had any kisra left, that is. They used to top it off with sharmut or weeka, but these were long gone.

It was about a third of a day's walk from Wad al-Kababish to Wad al-Nar. I had filled a waterskin with silty, turbid water from the deep spring of Ain Bilal, and flung it over my shoulder along with a few dusty dates from the remnants of last year's crop. I was neither hungry nor thirsty, and I did not feel like asking anyone to take me to Wad al-Nar on the back of an animal. I wanted to make the pilgrimage to my family alone and on foot. Perhaps I would even be following in the footsteps of Sirandub, the king who walked among the people. I set off in the direction of my mother Habiba bit Nur al-Din al-Shilani and my sisters Karima and Halima.

The people kept congratulating me on the Eid, and I absentmindedly did the same. "Happy Eid to you, Hamza!" they kept saying, and I replied in kind, "And to you too, Khal Jafar. And you as well, Amm Ayub. And Khala Thuraya." I didn't see any of my old friends there: it was mostly either children or elderly people, and a very small number of people closer to my age. They all looked like sticks, so gaunt and weak. I noticed that the phrase "Many happy returns!" had disappeared from people's tongues—it had once been a very common felicitation here.

At first, everyone thought I was heading to visit Anbar Bab al-Khayr's family, whose house was at the end of the village, but I passed it by at a distance. Abd al-Karim called out to me, "Hamza! Hamza! Where are you going?"

"I'll be back before sundown," I replied.

He looked at me in surprise, unable to fathom why I would want to head in that direction. Of late, the people of the village had come to consider the north a place of evil, and they believed that whoever went that way would bring back penury and misfortune, for Wad al-Nar was a land of death now. The elderly would ask God to have mercy on it with harrowing words. And people—especially the children—began to make up horror stories about the place. They told stories about demons and owls—the servants of the jinn—that came from the north and made their nests in the ruins of Wad al-Nar. Any owl that stopped on top of one of their own homes was regarded as an ill omen that would bring a curse upon them for forty days. Some disaster or other invariably befell the afflicted house, vindicating the belief. But in truth, these disasters were happening to everyone all the time, owls or not. They said the same of the white-necked ravens, the ones they call "corpse ravens" here: those birds had never been seen before in these parts, but now here they were in large numbers, taking over the place.

I walked onward, descending into lifeless valleys and climbing a few hills, the village of Wad al-Kababish vanishing and then reappearing as I did so. The morning heat was shimmering, and growing hotter by the minute: I felt as if I were walking into some invisible furnace. The world was swimming before my eyes, and sweat dripped from my face as it slowly roasted. I could hear the sound of my steps on the sand. My sandals kept sinking in like shovels and scattering the sand behind me as I walked.

After I'd been trekking for a long while, the sweat began to pour from me. My feet dug deeper into the sand, slowing me down, while my breathing quickened and the horizon swayed in front of me, above the soft bright sand. Yet I felt no weariness, and my resolve did not falter. Above me, I heard the crowing of a black raven—the kind they call "Noah ravens" here—and looked up at this familiar creature with joy. I used to love them back in the old days, and never saw any evil omens in them. My eyes followed the bird as it flew into the sun, and I was suddenly blinded by the light. For a moment, I could see only darkness—the same dark black color as that of the raven flying above me. When I regained my sight, I could no longer see it, as if it had been nothing but a phantom. The feeling comforted me. I was trembling inside, and a sudden fit of sweating came over me, cooling me down and reviving me.

Inside the Palm House, I can still feel the sun on my face, cleansing me with its rays. I keep my eyes closed to hold onto the vision of that place, of those sands. The sounds of artificial birds blend in with those of another bird, one that I used to be a master at imitating.

The sound of those other ravens comes to me now: the white-necked—or 'corpse'—ravens that I had seen all over the village after I returned from my first journey away from Wad al-Nar. But they were very different from the black Noah ravens that I so loved, and that would caw to me among those tombs where I always sought refuge by myself back in the old days. Those Noah ravens looked so funny when they cried out, doubling over as if they were about to vomit. Their strange cacophonous cawing always drowned out the sounds of all the other birds, overwhelming that wonderful choir of warbling doves and plovers, and also the bird we called abu harun, which was a kind of nightingale or finch. How I loved those ravens!

The ground was flat, devoid of any trace of man. I felt as if I were treading on virgin sands, a place no human had ever set foot on before. It was as if I were on a different world, or as if I had just come down from the sky. The sight of my sandals brought me back to reality: no one coming from the sky would wear sandals like these. In the silence, the noise of the waterskin swaying and gently beating against my back was soothing, and strangely melodious.

Hakima, wedged in between my sweater and my coat, happily turns over. I can feel her against my heart, and gently lay my hands on her.

As I listened to the rhythmic knocks of the waterskin, I started to hum, and soon I was softly chanting something that was half recitation and half song. I only realized what I was doing when I raised my voice a bit and heard it echo around me. At that moment, I caught a whiff of an old smell that immediately brought back memories of a different day of Eid, years earlier. I was very young then, five or six years old. A few weeks before Eid al-Adha, my father had brought a large billy goat into the house, and was carrying a big sack of millet and a bundle of clover over his shoulder. He was laughing because he had gotten a great deal on the goat from an Ethiopian shepherd who used to bring droves of ewes and goats around to sell them before the Eid. The goat gave me a menacing look that day, but I ignored it, happy to have found a new friend to play with, and I quickly forgot that it was going to be slaughtered at the festival. Sometimes I would draw it toward me with millet and then make it angry, so that it would come after me with its horns. And whenever it passed me by, I attacked it playfully from behind. One time it caught me off guard, however, and with a solid thrust of its horns it lifted me up into the air and then hurled me to the ground in a single motion. I landed on my stomach like a tormented frog, a sharp pain running through my belly and my backside. I was powerless, and didn't even try to resist the goat. It put its warm nose—much warmer than a dog's—on my forehead, opened its mouth and let out a peculiar raspy sound. A strange odor filled the air, neither pleasant nor unpleasant, but something I had never smelled before, though not unlike the smell of molasses. The goat scratched several clear lines into the ground with its front hooves, as if it were writing out a warning to me, and then went on its way.

That same smell came back to me as I was approaching Wad al-Nar. I quickened my pace, hurrying along the soft sand like a swift old camel and taking off the wrap around my head, which was starting to burn me. My robe was a sail caught in the wind, pulling me toward my destination, while my leather sandals continued to dip in and out of the sand.

I could almost see the village dancing in the distance, along with all its people. I could almost breathe in that smell that brought me back to those far-off days: the smell of molasses. Confused voices were carried on the wind, and I heard distant felicitations: the words "Many happy returns!" repeated over and over again. I could hear the shrill voice of Karima: she's three years old and trying to say my name. "Amza! Amza!" she says softly, before bursting into laughter. And I thought back to the weaning of Halima, that poor child who clung to my mother's breasts for two whole years without letting go. My mother felt sorry for her and kept putting off the weaning until Batool, Abd al-Malik's wife, reproached her, saying it was bad for both her and the child. A week later, my mother brought home a cactus. As Batool had advised her, she breast-fed Halima a little before breaking off a spine from the cactus and smearing its bitter oil all over her nipple in disgust. She was in tears as she let Halima, who was eager and smiling, finish suckling her breast. I looked on as Halima suddenly cried out in disgust and started to vomit. She writhed and quivered as if she had just been poisoned, while I grabbed a cloth to wipe up the last of my mother's milk, which Halima had just thrown up. She beat at my mother with her tiny fists and bit her while letting out loud sharp cries. She fell silent as she stopped to gasp for air, but immediately started up again with those excruciating screams, her face glistening with tears. Her pain hurt my mother much more than her blows. She let Halima finish venting her anger, then tried to kiss her while Halima pushed her away, still trembling from the shock.

I carried her outside that day and tried to distract her. I carried her on my shoulders, and even on my head. I threw her in the air. And I played the waterwheel game with her too, spinning her round and round in the air. Even her laughter was sorrowful that day, a kind of laugh I had never before heard from her, and that was punctuated by intermittent crying. I hugged her tight, hoping to squeeze this sadness out of her. I made up a story for her about a one-eyed genie with three legs. The genie wrote words on the ground with one of his three feet and spat on them, and whatever he wrote came into being for a moment before disappearing. If he wrote the word "camel," then a camel would appear, and if he wrote "tree," then a tree would appear. Every now and then he'd make a mistake in his writing, and some wondrous creature that had never been seen before would momentarily come into being. I gave that story my all, hoping to make Halima forget her pain: she loved it.

That afternoon, I made a doll for her from the fabric of one of my mother's old dresses, stuffing it with millet and drawing a face on it. Then I asked my mother if she would cut off some of her long hair for the doll. She did this, and braided the strands together with small brightly colored beads. I sang to Halima as I made the doll, telling her it was hers and that its name was Salwa. I chose this name in particular because I adored Halima's lisp. She called the doll "Thalwa."

She fell asleep much earlier than usual that evening, clutching at her doll with an exhausted look on her face. She was very restless, though, so my mother lit some cyclamen-scented incense to calm her. She whimpered so reproachfully while she slept that she almost brought even me—the one who cannot cry—to tears. I woke up the next morning to find Halima playing with my hair.

I could tell my mother was very grateful for what I had done. That morning, she brought me new locks of her hair, and said, "Make a sister for Salwa and give it to Karima! And God be with you!" I did this with pleasure, letting Karima pick the name this time. "I'll call her Tuti!" she said. I don't know where she found this incredible name, but we all approved of it, and the new doll Tuti became a sister to "Thalwa."

The silhouettes of the houses seemed to be lined up together in the distance. There were palm trees all around the village, a sight that made me tremble in wonder. My heart throbbed violently as I lifted my feet higher into the air so as not to sink even deeper into the sand. The back straps of my sandals had slipped off my heels, causing my sandals to smack rhythmically against my feet. I drew nearer while the vision swayed and quivered, becoming ever larger. The palms towered ahead of me, their fronds murmuring in the wind, and the houses seemed to draw closer together.

As I approached, the noise began to fade, and the village and all its palm trees slowly vanished, until all of Wad al-Nar was gone. It was only a mirage. And I, the great expert in mirages, hadn't recognized it. My friends used to always be amazed at how I'd visit the tombs, not the slightest bit afraid, and how even at the height of summer I'd be able to walk through the heat without any trouble at all. And now this fleeting mirage had managed to toy around with me, to play with my mind. Of all my friends, I was the only one who never once had sunstroke, even though I often spent long hours in the midday heat. Sheikh al-Faki always heaped scorn on me for this. "By God, you lefty! You've got something of the Devil in you!" he used to say.

My head was teeming with confused dreams and strange apprehensions. I could feel the end of my pilgrimage was near, could sense that I was returning home, drawing ever nearer to the place of my birth, to my mother Habiba, and to Halima and Karima. I could almost hear Halima speaking incomprehensibly in that sweet lisp of hers.

In the Palm House, I wake up to the sound of a girl's voice. She's holding her mother's hand and asking her the name of a tree—of the palm tree. She has the same childlike lisp that Halima had, but she's speaking in a different language.

The girl smiles at me and raises her hand to greet me in that way that children have about them, while I happily return the smile. Her mother scolds her in a sharp firm voice, and pulls her away. This saddens me for a moment, but I quickly forget it when a young man walks by. He's wearing headphones, and I can hear the loud techno music blasting into his ears. I don't know how he can stand it—he must be deaf. Actually, it sounds less like music and more like someone banging on a bunch of metal pots, but he still sings along in a loud and jarring voice, imitating the singer whom he's clearly such a big fan of.

This strange scene brings the smile back to my face, and I doze off, abandoning myself once more to the lucid dream. The place is calm now, and I can smell the warm earth. Hakima is asleep at my chest, measuring out my heartbeats for me.

I lifted the waterskin to my lips to slake my thirst a bit, taking in a single gulp and letting some water drip from the corners of my mouth onto my neck and my robe. The way was longer than I expected, so I started singing to cheer myself up a bit. The old songs I used to sing came back to me easily. I simply changed the tunes a little, turning them into sad hymns, uncertain where this sorrow had sprung from. My heart thumped violently, like that of an exhausted old man, or that of a boy out of his mind for some girl who does not love him back. Before setting out in the morning, I had promised myself that I would control my emotions, and that I would give my family a simple greeting and leave it at that.

The desert stretched to the horizon, devoid of any trace of man. A familiar feeling came over me, one I always have when I'm alone in the desert—the feeling of being at the end of the world, or at its beginning. I felt as if I had just been born, innocent; or as if I were about to leave this world.

My instincts showed me the way, and my shadow was enough of a compass: I did not get lost. The soft bright sand beneath my feet gradually began to disappear, giving way to darker dirt that seemed dead and cheerless. Features appeared in the distance. This was no mirage. This place knew me. My feet had met this dirt before. Now I had to figure out exactly where I was, and look for the graves I had marked with a large stone and three smaller black ones: I wanted to sprinkle a little water on them, wash a bit of dust off those tombstones.

When the village had appeared to me in the mirage, it was our old paradise that I saw, the paradise of my early childhood. But now, as I was drawing near to its borders, the skeleton of a dead animal greeted me. Half of its white skull and ribs and legs were jutting repulsively out of the earth. Not a trace of flesh was left. Its bones were white as snow, all desiccated and brittle. Nothing remained for the hyenas and jackals to gnaw on. It must have left this world—and Wad al-Nar—a long time ago.

The heat intensified, and everything started dancing before my eyes. The wind was gone, as if it too feared to approach this place, as if it were afraid of choking and dying here.

From a distance, the contours of Wad al-Nar looked the same as always. I thought back to the many times I had passed through the village on my way to the tombs, fleeing my father's punishment—those sights were etched in my memory. The sun was directly above my head now, swallowing my shadow whole and convulsing everything before my eyes. I could no longer tell east from west, or north from south. And the closer I came, the less I recognized of the village. I had been so certain before, yet confusion overcame me now, and I lost my mental image of the place, momentarily worrying that I had come the wrong way. But the dirt beneath my feet reassured me that I was in fact in Wad al-Nar, as did the smell that still wafted into my nose, the smell of that goat my father had bought for the Eid: the smell of molasses. And the dry white bones scattered all over the place, the bones of dead animals—they too reassured me that I was here in this wretched village. I could not believe how many there were. In the final days of Wad al-Nar, we had nowhere near this many birds and animals. Even dogs and cats were rare back then. I shuddered when I realized that some of them might be human bones, the skeletons of people who died without a proper burial, without any respect for the body.

I loved animals when I was young, especially the smaller ones! In the old days, I used to collect dates from the palm trees to give to that wonderful Bedouin woman with the enchanting eyes. She always walked elegantly and confidently, driving on her goats and sheep with the staff in her hand. Sometimes she sang sweet songs in a dialect that I did not recognize. She didn't seem to have a husband or any children—I never saw anyone at all with her. She used to pass by in the early morning and then again just before sunset with her animals, which left large clouds of dust in their wake. I loved the dust that took so long to settle, for it reminded me of the fog that descended on the village on very rare occasions.

I used to gather unripe dates that had fallen from the palms for her, and that she would later give to the animals that could not come with her, either due to sickness or because they were in the late stages of pregnancy. I loved looking at the baby goats and the pregnant ones up close and petting them. I remember how happy I was that day when I saw her carrying a newborn goat in her arms! She said the mother had given birth to it on the way. From that day on, I stopped harassing and chasing after the goats that sometimes strayed near the houses. We children believed that anyone who raced among the goats would grow up more quickly. "If you want to grow up, run with the goats," we used to say. And so we used to circle around them and dart into their midst, while the Bedouin woman yelled at us to stop our mischief.

Her name was Hilya. She had stunning black-on-white eyes and tawny skin, and was always smiling. She had the sweetest voice, and smelled incredible. She used to play around with my disheveled hair whenever she saw me, laughing happily. For every large jug of unripe dates I brought her—the 'jug' was actually a small lard container that I filled—Hilya gave me a jug of fresh milk in exchange. I enjoyed watching her milk the goats. I loved that strange bubbling sound the milk made as it gushed out in long white strands, before foaming up and giving off its distinctive smell. I always had one or two sips right away, then happily licked the white mustache off my upper lip.

One day, a wicked shepherd from one of the Jandul Arabs' distant villages raided our palms, and his goats ate up all the unripe dates that had fallen to the ground, leaving me nothing but the pits and a few tiny dried-up dates, not even enough to cover the bottom of the lard container. I angrily cursed the Arabs of al-Jandul and that shepherd in particular for keeping me from my share of milk. Hilya might not even let me milk any of the goats that day, something I had truly come to enjoy. But Hilya was very generous, and did not disappoint me. She still gave me my full share of fresh milk, content with the few dates I had brought her.

I remember the first time I ever touched a goat's udder: it was warm and smooth despite the hair, and my attempts at milking it only succeeded after some difficulty. Hilya taught me how to squeeze forcefully on the nipples and gently slide my hand downward, using my palm and one of my fingers to draw out the milk. She laughed at my small fingers, and taught me by placing her hand on mine. I was a bit embarrassed by this physical contact, despite my being so young, but my curiosity and desire to learn prevailed.

I'm still sitting in that remote nook of the Palm House with my lucid dreams. I can feel Hakima stretching out inside my coat and scratching at my chest, as if to remind me that she's still there. Or perhaps she too is dreaming of another life.

The rays of the sun vanish for a moment, and all is still in the Palm House. I lazily shift my position.

We had a cat we loved, and who lived with us for a long time. All of us used to feed it and take care of it—all except my father, that is. We called her Kadis, which simply means 'cat' in the Sudanese dialect, and sometimes we also called her Biss or Bissa. She loved to play, and always delighted us with her curious movements. We never let any boy or girl from the village throw stones at her or hurt her. The people even started calling me Ibn Kadisaas as if it were an insult. And they nick-named Karima and Halima Banat al-Kadayis after Kadis bore us five kittens, which brought us much joy in that arid place. I always wanted to have a dog, but my father said they were filthy animals, much filthier than cats, and that a dog would ruin the whole house. He heard this from Sheikh Ali al-Faki, and of course believed him. He also added that seven animals would not enter Paradise: dogs, pigs, hyenas, owls, rats, snakes, and anyone left-handed. Then he'd taunt me cruelly, "Did you hear that, lefty?"

All the same, I made friends with a stray puppy who had something of the nobility of wolves, and whom I had found on a hot day at the tombs. It warily stopped at a distance, and kept looking at me while I sang. It started wagging its tail, so I kept singing to it, and repeated the word 'samih,' which later became his name. Back in the good days, days long gone, I used to smuggle chunks of bread and the scraps of bones to him. He loved seeing me, and used to hang around the house and bark for me to come out and give him some food. The strange thing was that whenever he caught sight of Sheikh al-Faki—who always asked God to protect him from the Devil anytime he saw the dog—Samih would bark at him and run away. It was as if each of them saw a devil in the other.

My father startled me once while I was playing with Samih, who was happily letting me pet his head and back. "Get out of here!" my father yelled at the dog. "God's curse on you, and all the other filthy animals!" He grabbed a stone and threw it at him, gashing his forehead just above the left eye. Samih bolted, yelping painfully, and started running toward the tombs, blood dripping from his head. I ran after him, angrily disobeying my father who was ordering me to stay. Samih halted at the tombs, his tail between his legs, and finally stopped howling. He gave me a look of despair and submission. His left eye was covered in blood, and his right eye bore a mixture of shame and disgrace. He was trembling from the pain, as if we were in the depths of winter. I took a close look at him, and was a little comforted to see that only his forehead was wounded, and not his eye. I wiped the blood off him—he let me do this, giving himself over to his fate. I blew on the wound and gently applied pressure to his forehand, which was still seeping blood, before going to the place where I hid my matches. I brought over a dry branch from the sweet-smelling zaynab tree that had been planted at the tomb of our patron saint Bab al-Shafi'. I was imitating how Awf al-Attar used to treat the wounded in the village. I burned the branch, and then rubbed its ashes into the wound. Samih's tail began to wag happily again, and I sang to make him—or perhaps myself—feel better. He wagged his tail while he listened, looking into my eyes as if he were thanking me.

I had many exciting adventures with Samih, but he too disappeared one day. I looked for him for days on end but could not find him. I couldn't even find his body for some peace of mind. I was certain that it was a plot by my father and Sheikh al-Faki. I heard the two of them joking that the village was finally rid of the "filthy thing," but that there was still more filth that needed to be disposed of. The sheikh told my father that all dogs became rabid after a certain age because they ate bones and carrion. He even cited a fatwa that forbade any woman to be naked in front of male dogs or to let them see her genitals. If this happened, he said, she would either have deformed children or multiple miscarriages. He cited cases of this that had happened in the village, linking each one to certain dogs. He said that if a dog sniffs a man's pubic region, then that man must wash himself six times with water, and once with sand. If a dog does that to a woman, then she must clean herself with water soaked in alum while burning sandalwood, and not have sex with her husband for at least a week. He assured my father that Hooma, a mentally disturbed woman in the village, was responsible for her own condition because she had taken off her clothes in front of a male dog of hers, and that it had afflicted her. She started speaking to it as if it were a man, asking it questions and answering its barks with either words or barks of her own, as if she understood what it was saying. I hated Sheikh al-Faki for all this nonsense of his. And I was angry with my father because he listened to it, always calling on God for protection while loudly slurping his tea. He constantly put down others in the village, ridiculing them in that agitated way of his, while Sheikh al-Faki spat all over the place, especially if the words 'Iblis,' 'dog,' or 'Hooma' were mentioned.

I loved Hooma—she used to play with us when we were kids. She was much bigger than we were, but her famous shrill laugh sounded like that of a small child. I always considered her a child in a woman's body. She was the only one who could make fun of Sheikh al-Faki without him talking back. If he ever did talk back to her, then she would spend days or even weeks pestering him as he went about his business, making his life a living hell. He always got out of her way, muttering curses and supplications, which he then said out loud as soon as she was gone.

Wad al-Nar was indeed condemned to desolation, but the dogs had nothing to do with it. I used to follow every new dog around, and also all the female ones in heat, thinking that Samih might approach them. I looked in other villages and out in the wild, but I never found a trace of him. I tried to forget him, but as soon as I heard any barking outside the house I would jump up and run out, hoping that Samih had come back. But it was always one of the other stray dogs, never him.

I saw a protrusion in the sand ahead of me and made for it, very curious about what it might be. It took me some time to lay bare the smooth stone, for it was covered in sand. It was a strange sight: the bust of a lion with a man's head in its open mouth. The lion's features were clear, but the man's were more difficult to make out—it was hard to tell if the man was terrified or delighted. When I dug deeper, I found more pieces of the statue, and I remembered the day when Sheikh al-Faki had some of the fanatics from the village help him destroy that very same statue, which he called an idol, saying it was from early pre-Islamic times. They wore themselves out for an entire day trying to destroy it, striking it with hatchets and pickaxes. The tools kept breaking on them, even though the statue was not that large. At the time, it seemed as if they were wrecking a mountain of stone. They scattered the bits and pieces in the middle of the desert, angrily reciting spells and exhortations over them. They said that they were getting rid of an evil pagan idol that could curse the village and wipe it out of existence. We children had no idea what the words 'pagan' or 'idol' even meant. I was amazed at Sheikh al-Faki's energy that day, how he led these men to work, calling on them to help win God's reward and gain the high ground in Heaven—a first-class seat, as it were. I could not believe that these people who professed piety and firm belief could be so afraid of a simple stone. Perhaps the stone was stronger than their faith. Otherwise, why would they act this way? No one thought to actually determine the statue's age, but it seemed ancient. They simply smashed it up, cursed it, and buried its scattered remains in the sand outside the village.

And here the head is again, sticking out of the sand and challenging that madness. It lay near the bones of the dead, as if it were a testament to them, and a witness to time.

The ground beneath my mangy sandals began to be covered with bones. They were like shells that had washed up onto the shore. I again trembled at the thought that these bones belonged to the people of the village, to those I lived with, even to the people closest to my heart. The graves had been scattered outside the village, and were marked only by stones or sand heaps. There was no other protection for these naked open cemeteries against the jackals, the hyenas, and the carrion birds that toyed with the remnants of man, leaving nothing behind but scattered bones. My steps became slower and more difficult. I walked with my eyes on the ground, trying not to step on any part of that sea of buried bones. The houses were barely recognizable. Their doors were gone, their walls and windows were destroyed, and their roofs were falling into their floors.

I sat in the shade under what was left of a wall of a house I did not recognize. I couldn't even tell if I was sitting inside the house or outside it. Once again, I found myself sunk in thought, looking around me like some crazed vagabond. And I once again found myself holding a dry stick in my hand, my many competing thoughts flowing into one end of it, while its other end sketched strange lines and letters in the earth. If there was any meaning in these forms, it was unintended, for I was lost in my sad thoughts. I pressed the dry stick into the sandy ground in anger and disgust. All the violence and bitterness inside me rose to my throat, and I spat on the ground, cursing the times, and cursing the world.

I gazed at the wall opposite me as I was sitting there, for there were deep scrawls on it that looked familiar. I threw away the stick that I had broken several times by now, spat, stood up, and brushed off the dirt that was clinging to my hands. I approached the scrawls: they were letters. Yes, this was my handwriting. It was a sentence I wrote when I was about eight years old on the house of an unmarried in-law of our neighbor Abd al-Malik. In the evenings, he would sometimes take us in and tell us marvelous stories. Most of the sentence was still etched deeply in the mud brick of the wall, and I remember how it originally read: "al-samih yamsah al-samij al-zirrit," or "Samih foils the disgusting farter." "The farter"—al-zirrit—had been our secret name for Sheikh Ali al-Faki since the day he broke wind while beating me. Some of the letters of the original sentence were no longer visible, so now it read "al-samm masah al-zirt," or "poison foiled the disgusting one." I marveled at this new meaning, for in our dialect the word 'zirt' was what we called someone who was either incredibly overweight or who greatly exaggerated their 'heroic' deeds. I was delighted by this new sentence!

I stood there, trying to remember how these ruins looked back in the day. This one sentence allowed me to figure out the contours of the village and restore the image in my mind. I closed my eyes for a few moments, vanishing into that fantasy, then opened them and began walking southward toward our house. I stumbled upon what was left of it. It seemed smaller than it had been, or at least smaller than I had imagined it. The walls were wrecked, and were at most only half a meter tall now. The tips of palm fronds stuck out from the dirt like the spikes of a hedgehog. I was standing in the middle of the house. I sat down. I kneeled. I stood up. I bent over. I sat down again. I got up again. I took a step forward. Then two steps back. Then sat down again, stood up again, bent over. . . . It was as if I were leading some unconscious ritual, the details of which were buried deep inside me, leaving me with only vague knowledge of them. I realized I must be standing right on top of the remains of my father's sheepskin, above his place of prayer that was now entirely covered with dirt. I dug a little, but found only two things: our old white iron teapot with its green and red spots, which was now rusty and full of holes; and beside it a gourd that we used to use as a container. The gourd used to have brightly colored patterns on it, but most of these were faded now.

I picked up the teapot and the gourd, and took them with me as I headed toward the trunk of the palm tree where I had buried my mother's bracelet and my sisters' two dolls. My instincts, this old feeling in my blood, pointed the way and served as my compass.

It wasn't far. Or perhaps I had run the whole way without realizing it. In any case, I could roughly make out the features of the place, and realized that this long protrusion in the ground must be the buried trunk of the palm. I put down the dates and the waterskin, took off my robe, and got to it. I started digging, sometimes with my bare hands and sometimes with the gourd. Dust flew into my face, but I paid no heed. The sharp edges of the palm fronds kept slicing into my fingers, which I would then press into the dirt to stanch the bleeding, before continuing the dig. My hand bumped against something hard. I was elated—I thought I had reached the trunk. But it turned out to only be the stone that marked the place. I dug around it, and before long my hands finally struck against the trunk of the palm. I kept digging like a mole until part of the palm's dusty rind appeared, which looked like it was covered in old dirty hair. A large straw mat covered this part of the palm, and when I removed it, the trunk finally appeared.

I felt the sweat streaming off my forehead and into my eyes. I stopped for a moment to grab the waterskin, which was now completely covered in dust. I gulped down a mouthful of water, and then started digging around the rest of the long trunk. I brought an old image of the place back to my mind, trying to remember where exactly I had performed the burial: it had been at the head of the palm tree. I kept digging at that spot until my hands struck against a dust-covered stone, and then a second, and then a third. They were the three stones that I had buried. The symbolic graves must be directly underneath them, the ones I had dug for Habiba bit Nur al-Din al-Shilani and Karima and Halima.

The sweat was still pouring off my face and into my eyes, and some of it dripped onto one of the stones, causing its color to darken. I rubbed at it, but the dirt refused to give. I scratched at it with my nails until it hurt, then used an edge of the gourd to scrape off more of the hard dirt, before washing it with some water. I was astonished by the sight. I had placed these stones here forty days ago without paying much attention to them, but now I saw that there were clear lines on this stone's surface—these were signs, not random scrawls. It was some kind of ancient drawing, but it seemed incomplete. After I had cleaned off the other two stones, I realized that the three had originally formed a single stone. Some parts of it were worn away, but on the whole it was still in very good condition. I put the three stones together on the ground, and the picture became clear. I sat and rested, looking attentively at it.

The image was of a woman lying on her back. Her hands and feet were raised in the air. She looked like a ship in that strange position, and when I gently wiped the dust off the inside of the ship, I noticed groups of people in lines, standing on their heads. I turned the stones over, and now it seemed that the woman was protecting these people with the arc of her body. I trembled at the sight of these rare stones. I knew it would not be easy to reveal the meaning of the image and solve the stones' mystery. The etching had been done by a very fine and artistic hand, with painstaking precision and skill. The woman's face, her large round earrings, and her long hair all reminded me of my mother. There was a sun in her open mouth, but I couldn't tell whether it was leaving her body or entering it. Five similar suns were above her, in the midst of many stars. And on the right at the end of her womb was one more sun—again, I could not tell if it was entering her or leaving. That was all I could make out of the scene. I turned each of the stones over on its other side, and all of them were smooth except for their backs, where I found several orderly markings in the form of scarabs and birds, as well as the crocodile-headed god Sobek and the jackal-headed Anubis.

I considered digging some more for the bracelet and the two dolls so that I could bury them somewhere else, but the thought of going through the burial ritual all over again was too much for me. I stood up. I sat down. I kneeled. Then I filled up the hole I had just dug and picked up the three stones. Each one on its own was very heavy, but when I picked them up together it somehow seemed as if the three were much lighter like that than they were individually. I tried it several times, but my impression remained the same. I attributed this to my exhaustion, and to the heat that had started to scorch my body. I sat down again, and took out three dates and ate them. I buried the pits at the spot where I had removed the stones, then sprinkled a bit of water on them before getting up wearily, the thirst burning inside me.

I returned to the ruins of Wad al-Nar, picking up a buried straw mat and a few long branches on the way. I went back to our house—or what was left of it—and made a temporary shelter from the sun with the branches and the mat. I sat down and ate the rest of my dates, and also a piece of bread that was now damp with my sweat. I lay down on the remains of a low bed to look at the stones. The middle of the bed, made of woven leather and rope, had sunk almost to the ground, and one of its legs was broken, so I propped it up with a broken demijohn that my mother used to keep corn and millet seed in. I dozed a little, and when I woke I felt as if I had come out of dream that had shaken my mind and disturbed my breathing. I had been playing with a strange round luminous object—that much I remembered—but I did not know what it was. The dream must have really taken hold of me, for when I woke I found myself standing up stiffly, and silently gazing at an empty spot on the ground, as if I were trying to read the sand. I tried to recall the strands of that puzzling dream, but they were gone. For a moment, I was utterly overcome with fatigue: I had no recollection of anything at all, and could not even remember where I was or what I was doing there.

Late in the afternoon, I gathered up my things and headed back to Wad al-Kababish, returning the same way I had come: across that land strewn with bones, the bones of my family and the people of my village. The Noah raven joined me, hovering above me as if he was the head of the village. I struggled forward—it felt like I was wading through mud. Conflicting feelings took hold of me as I made my way back: I was comforted and glad that I had visited my family, but also sad that they were gone. I remained in this muddled state for some time, now quickening my pace, now slowing down; now smiling, now frowning. And all the while I tried to recall my mother's features, the shape of her body, the color of her skin, her voice, the way she smelled; and I tried to recall Karima and Halima too. It was as if an eternity had passed—their features were so hazy in my mind. I finally managed to form a fixed image of them, which comforted me. My sweat started pouring forth even more profusely, streaming onto my chest and dripping onto the sand. The heat had not let up since morning. It was as if the day had not changed at all, as if time had stopped at that brutal midday hour with its lethal heat. The only things that had changed were my feelings, my feelings from this rare pilgrimage that I might not make again for a long while.

I was racked by exhaustion—it convulsed me and coursed through me until I saw darkness for a few seconds in broad daylight, like a reverse flash. My heart beat tumultuously. The wind had died down, and all the smells were gone too. I was beginning to feel the weight of the stones I was carrying. I had no water left, and my throat was burning with thirst. I saw the features of a village in the distance. At first, I was afraid that it was another mirage. But I had been walking a long time, and had covered a lot of ground. That had to be the village of Wad al-Kababish quivering on the horizon.

The sun appears for a few moments in the Palm House, its rays piercing the glass roof to come down and visit me. At once I feel the warmth course through my body, feel the light penetrating me and shimmering through me. It's too bright for me to open both my eyes, so I look through one half-closed eye at the steel-framed glass above me. The sun is unusually strong for that hour of the day. Its veil is gone, if only for an instant, but this is enough to renew my strength, replenish my stores against the bitter cold of the coming days. Hakima is off on another dream inside my coat. The whole place is silent, so I pass into and out of sleep, before finally entering the long-forgotten dream. That dream comes back to me now, here in the Palm House, as if all the memories that had just passed through me had merely been paving the way for it.

I see myself as a young child playing with the sun. It lies between my hands like a light golden ball. I roll it in front of me and laugh. At the crossroads, I see a boy about my age with a featureless face. He's carrying a moon under his arm, and wants to trade it for my sun. I refuse, saying, "No, I don't want to swap! But you can play with me if you like." He agrees to this and starts playing with me, setting his moon on the ground. But then he catches me off guard and snatches away my sun, running off with it and vanishing. His silver moon is lying beside me, but all trace of him is gone. I see the sunset on the horizon and realize which way he's escaping: toward the north. He's already long gone. I'm disconsolate. Darkness starts to fall, and I'm forced to carry this heavy moon with me, which seems to be made of lead. The sounds of the many birds I had heard vanish, and the place falls utterly silent. A strange and unfamiliar fear takes hold of me. I look at the moon. I had thought it was luminous and silver, but it is actually a pallid and lifeless ash-grey color. I wipe it off with my elbow a few times, and part of it starts shining. This delights me, for perhaps its silver will turn to gold if I keep wiping at it like this, and I'll have my sun again. I sit down and give myself over to wiping it off, until I hear a strange sound whose source I do not know.

4

When I wake from my dream, the sun has disappeared entirely. Hakima is restlessly shifting about, and I can tell that she wants to move. I get up sluggishly. The dream weighs heavily on me here in the Palm House. As Hakima and I leave, I call Sandra from a phone booth at the outer gate. She's happy to hear from me, but I don't say much because I prefer listening to her voice. After she asks me how I'm doing and what I'm up to, her first questions—as usual—are about Hakima. She asks what Hakima has done today, and what she's doing right now, and whether we have been to the Palm House. She also asks me if I want to stop by. I tell her I'm a bit tired and that I'm going to go home, even though I really want to see her. I'm not sure why I say the opposite of what I actually want. Sandra does not insist too much, but she tries to entice me by telling me about the Tafelspitz she had made earlier that day, which she knows I love. I promise her that I'll come tomorrow.

At the subway station, I play with Hakima while waiting for the next train and thinking about Sandra's invitation. Had I disappointed her without realizing it? Or was my reply simply idiotic? Suddenly,

Abu Darsh appears before me. As usual, he doesn't ask me how I'm doing, but rather jumps straight into other questions, speaking quickly and changing the topic of conversation at will, as if we were continuing a conversation from the past. This habit leads some people to think he's not listening to them, but I've never met anyone in all of Vienna with such sharp hearing, or who remembers things in such detail. He's carrying a plastic bag from the Hofer supermarket, and is constantly shifting it from one hand to the other. When the train arrives, he starts talking very heatedly, putting a smile on my face.

His name is Khalifa al-Darwish. The people in Vienna call him 'Herr Caliph.' I'm not sure exactly how long he's been in this country. He's been here several years longer than me, in any case, and speaks the difficult Viennese dialect fluently. Most of the time, he appears unexpectedly at the door of my apartment. He always comes in quickly, and if he's hungry he'll open the refrigerator without any inhibitions and squat there to figure out what he wants. After this, he usually gets up to make tea, as if he were in his own house, always making two excellent cups for us with enviable skill.

I don't know his full name. Sometimes he says his name is Mustafa—Abu Darsh is a common Arabic nickname for anyone called Mustafa—and sometimes he says it's Jibril. Some days he says he's Muslim. And other days he claims to have Coptic roots, and tells me in great detail about church ceremonies and prayers. I don't know if he's actually Muslim *or* Coptic, and it's really not important to me.

He always says he was born in Sudan, in the region called Kosti on the White Nile. And he usually says that his father was Egyptian, but sometimes he tells me that his father was actually Sudanese and that he lived for a long time in the Gharb Suhayl area of Aswan after the great emigration caused by the flooding of the High Dam project. His family later moved to Cairo, he says, but he always insists that he's of African origin.

Everything he says seems plausible; all of these wondrous stories seem true. I never wanted to examine the truth of any of them, for the only thing that interested me was the fact that he was a truly noble person. Anytime he heard that I was sick, he would rush over without delay to be by my side, even going so far as to spend a night or two at my place. And when I got better, he would disappear without waiting for a word of thanks. I don't know where exactly he lives, or how he supports himself.

Those who speak Arabic here call him Khalifa al-Darib, by which they mean that his mind or intellect is afflicted or disturbed. But he pays no heed to all the nicknames he has, and they only ever bother him if he feels that someone truly wants to ridicule or mock him. Whenever this happens, he wipes the floor with his adversary, for he knows very private details about everyone. He has lived with many of them at different times, but some moved up in life and started putting on airs and showing disdain for the poverty of the newcomers. Abu Darsh always ridicules this nonsense and haughtiness, often making use of details about their lives they did not even realize he knew. They never cease to be surprised at the embarrassing stories he knows about them, at how many of their shameful deeds he can narrate. Anyone with merely superficial knowledge of that man might think he's a bit slow or stupid or even mentally ill, but in truth he has a very sharp mind. He's quick in his retorts, and has a whole dictionary of astounding insults that none of us have ever heard before. When he lets those barbs loose, everyone around him erupts into loud laughter—or sometimes muffled laughter, depending on the circumstances. They all fear that sharp tongue of his, and that he'll bestow some injurious nickname on them that they won't be able to get rid of. He's done this to many of them, and their annoying nicknames have stuck. There was Muhammad Wirk and Sami Abu Libas, and Sulayman Mama Mabsuta, and many others. But none of these poisonous names or stories were created out of thin air. They all had some truth behind them, or some situation that was embarrassing to the person under consideration. Abu Darsh always told these stories with great suspense and excitement, until the audience would practically fall to the ground in laughter. As for myself, he nicknamed me Abu Hurayra a long time ago.

Abu Darsh prays in the mosque and fasts on occasion, and he also sometimes goes to church on Sundays. He does all of this without talking about it or ever letting anyone make it a subject of conversation, like someone secretly and calmly going through some lengthy training. I have never seen anyone who knows so much about so many different types of wine, or who drinks it with such pleasure, without ever overdoing it. He tells the most enjoyable stories when he drinks.

This is the way of Mustafa Jibril Khalifa al-Darwish, 'Herr Caliph,' a dear friend to me, and one of the very few I have in this city.

He's seen the best and worst of times in this country. He's had important jobs that no one would ever believe he's had, and he's worked in the lowliest jobs as well. He fell in love and married, and then got divorced, and for all I know he might even have children.

When he sees me in the street, he sometimes greets me with great joy and proceeds to follow me everywhere without asking any questions, and other times he merely waves to me quickly, as if he were in a hurry or angry about something. And on very rare occasions, he does not greet me at all, but avoids me as if we had never met. These peculiarities have lost him many friendships, especially with those people who lead lives as orderly and precise as clockwork, and who hate his chaos and laxity, as well as the way he lashes out at the world and pokes fun at it.

I love most of these traits, and have gotten used to him. He feels the same for me. For this reason, whenever he's angry at life and the world, he comes to me in my apartment without any prior warning. He sits and tells me countless long stories, creating suspense in that theatrical way of his while constantly moving around and smoking and cursing certain names and personalities.

Today, without any warning, he says, "Believe me! All of these people are being dragged around by the watches on their wrists, just like they themselves drag their dogs around. They're like maniacs hurrying through the streets. They rush off to their endless meetings. And if they're just a couple minutes late for these trivial appointments, they get agitated and start to go mad. They stand like statues at the tram and bus and subway stations, all of them looking in the same direction while they wait for their ride. But once they're inside, they sit down as if they'd just had a fight, saying nothing at all and intentionally sitting as far away as possible from one another. Their faces are tense and sad, and their eyes flit to their watches every minute. They read anything and everything just to avoid making eye contact. And they're the quickest of God's creatures to apologize if they accidentally touch one another. Their entire lives are planned out and programmed, and nothing is left to chance. That's why their joy is so fleeting—because they've already mapped out all their happiness. They even plan their periods of sadness. As for their melancholy, well, that never ends."

"You're exaggerating, Abu Darsh," I reply. "Maybe a few of them are like that."

"I'm exaggerating?" he screams. "I'm exaggerating, Abu Hurayra? You're so naive, Hamza. Take a look around you!" He signals with a nod of his head to a well-dressed woman with a large hat on her head, sitting some distance away from us. Her husband, who is sitting beside her, is sweating profusely in a suit that seems quite tight on him. It was as if they had got on just to illustrate Abu Darsh's theory. He finishes what he was saying, "Can you tell me what the purpose of that hat is, that trough she's wearing on her head? It's bigger than the seat she's sitting on! And what's the purpose of her husband's tie? It's a noose around his neck! He's practically choking, and yet he's proud of it! The men here respect that sort of thing—they suffocate themselves and can't move their necks, but they still insist on wearing their ties, thinking that it lends them dignity and prestige. It's a uniform, Hamza! And woe to anyone who strays from it!"

I laugh at this description, and he smiles. With a single smile, Mustafa Abu Darsh can turn any sadness into joy. He has a contagious and enchanting smile, and a laugh that is even more beautiful and contagious—one that that always incites people's curiosity. As soon as he laughs, the severity of his features turns into a gentle grace that's pleasing to the eye. That smile of his attracts the women without his even realizing it, even as other men struggle to win a single smile from one of them, a single moment of gentle sustenance on a rough day.

Mustafa Abu Darsh has a beige-colored face, and is constantly changing his hairstyle. Sometimes he has African-style dreadlocks, and sometimes a more 'normal' hairstyle of medium length, and sometimes he shaves it bald. Every now and then he'll wear a white cotton skull-cap or a beret, but he hates wearing most kinds of hats and goes off on amazing tirades against them. When he laughs that pure and powerful laugh, which comes straight from the heart, he pays no heed to where he is or who's watching him. It resounds in the silence of this calm city. I've seen so many faces turn in displeasure because of that crazy vagabond laughter!

One day I saw him standing with a famous Austrian actress on the chic street called Graben. She was laughing very affectionately, and with no affectation. When I asked him how he knew her, he told me that she used to be his mother-in-law. I thought he was joking, and I forgot all about it until I saw him one day with a large photo album in his hand. There were several pictures of that actress and her husband and daughter in it, along with several other actors and actresses whose names I didn't know but whom I recognized from television. That day, he told me a long story that no one would ever have believed, but that he corroborated with pictures.

Mustafa was the first person with whom I was comfortable enough to talk to about my past life—his questions never bothered me. He helped me remember things I thought I had forgotten. Only two people in this entire city have ever succeeded in getting me to answer their questions: Sandra was the other one.

I'll never forget what Abu Darsh once told me, "I swear to you, Abu Hurayra! The only thing you have is your long story, and it's up to you to tell it to the horrific invisible Shahryar in this country before he robs you of your soul. Try to enchant him with your story so that he forgets his deep-seated evil for a while. Do what I say or you'll regret it! Your life is your only story, so tell it while you live, before someone else tells it for you after you die."

Mustafa comes with me to my apartment. He does not tell me this, but rather simply walks with me, laughing and talking, until I find myself opening the front entrance of the my building. I try to get him to lower his voice as we go up to the fifth floor, for the people in this city go to sleep very early, and are also some of the earliest risers in the world.

Mustafa has to stop and set his heavy bag down several times as we go up the stairs. He keeps talking and laughing, while I urge him to lower his voice and come up quickly. I open the door of my apartment. Inside, the first thing I do is free Hakima from the captivity of my coat. She walks over to her litter box to relieve herself, then returns to meow and circle around my feet while Abu Darsh comes in and puts his heavy bag down on the kitchen table.

"You starved the cat, Abu Hurayra!" he reproaches me. "And you must be hungry too!"

Before I can reply, he starts emptying the bag, which is filled with cans and fruits and vegetables and some other food as well. He gives Hakima a bit of cheese, telling her, "You should come live with me, you poor thing, and leave this simpleton. I'll turn you into a veiled Arab housewife who doesn't leave the house. I won't be like those damned Europeans, those tolerant men who dote over you all the time!"

He cooks quickly, and we eat and drink in laughter. He asks me that painful and oft-repeated question of his: he asks me about Sudan. He doesn't actually want an answer, but rather asks because it helps him recover somewhat from his suppressed anger. He asks me if the people and the conditions there have changed a lot, and how the people have been living since the National Salvation Revolution, and whether the revolution actually saved the people. He begins by cursing the fat generals and army officers, and ends by cursing the religious men with robes and long beards, whom he calls al-kizan. I have no idea where he has learned this name. We talk at length about things I thought I had forgotten. Then he suddenly dozes off on the red leather sofa. I lay a couple of blankets over him as he falls into a deep sleep. It's past one in the morning, so I hurry to bed, for I have oppressive work waiting for me at dawn.

I can't fall asleep. Abu Darsh's questions have stirred up sorrows and troubles in my mind. Hakima curls up on my chest and starts to purr. Instead of sleeping, I depart into distant memories.

I simply go back a few years, returning to what remains of my memories as they solidify and take hold, though I have no say in which events

I remember. I was in the same van I had left the neighboring village in the first time, many years earlier. Spots of rust covered its run-down body like pustules. From a distance, it looked like a total wreck, and no one would ever believe that it was still working. I had begun my trip to Khartoum in it that day, on a road that was even worse than it had been on my first journey. I had the same driver as before. He was older, weaker, and quieter now, and all of his front teeth were gone, but he still smoked with the same disgusting voracity as before. He didn't recognize me. He was still uttering the same repulsive words to ease his anxiety and let go of some of his tension, spitting out the window from time to time as he did so. Like him, the van had fallen on hard times. The feverish noise of its engine was louder now, and if you wanted to say anything to anyone—even if it was just "Praise be to God!" or "How are you?"—you now had to scream. Everyone preferred to keep quiet. I too sought refuge in silence, despite the questions in my mind that troubled me the whole way there. The exhausting journey was repeated, along with the same stops to figure out where exactly we were: it was as if I was caught in the same absurd game, or an oppressive nightmare that refused to go away.

Then I boarded the train heading to Khartoum. Its 'windows' were empty wooden frames without any glass in them. The car I was in was torn up and dark, and the people who were rushing into it looked apprehensive. Everyone was jostling one another with their arms and their bags and baskets, and cursing and insulting each other. This was not how I knew these people to be, even with all their hardship. It seemed that something had happened, something stronger than their forbearance. Some disaster was lurking, leaving its mark on their faces and spurring on this inconsiderate behavior. The gloomy journey to the north continued. I had some dates in my bag made of palm fronds, as well as a few pieces of bread and the waterskin. I had also put the three black stones in the bag—the burial stones I'd found in Wad al-Nar.

The city seemed different now. Most of the men were wearing olive green clothes—the color of the army. Every face I encountered seemed to be frowning. A stern military life had taken hold here: there were new faces with long beards that were wary of anyone who looked different.

The women, who used to let their hair flow out beneath their beautiful long wraps, had now bound their hair with headscarves beneath the wraps, so that they almost looked like they were wearing space helmets. And they had much more makeup on now too, although the colors did not match the color of their faces. The people's smiles were gone. The joy and laughter that had once distinguished this city had given way to shouts and suspicious glances. The people seemed to be ordering each other around now, rather than speaking to one another.

I had the address of a student dormitory where I planned to spend the night. Many of the students leave to visit their families during the holidays, and some of the rooms become available then. I went there and the man asked me if I was a student at one of the universities. When I said I wasn't, he told me that this place was only for students. After that, he refused to answer any of my questions, grumbling about my coming here as he returned to his seat inside the room to continue watching a soccer game on TV. He was one of those people who works at the lowest rungs of an institution and exaggerates the importance of his position to anyone who comes by looking for information. The type of man who seems to make matters even more difficult for others every time his rank at work is reduced.

"Go away," he said to me. "You can ask about a room once you have a student ID, though I may or may not answer you, depending on what's going on. We're busy with more important stuff right now." Then he let out a scream that I thought was directed at me, but it turned out that somebody had just scored a goal. On the television, I heard names like al-Hilal, al-Marrikh, and al-Murada, but I did not know what they were.

I decided to walk around a bit in the afternoon. I had a destination in mind, though I did not admit it to myself: I wanted to go to the souk. On my way there, I passed the place where the Odeon Cinema used to be, but could not find a trace of it at first. The posters had been taken down and a sign had been put up which read, "The Piety Company for Islamic Clothes." A few moments later, I noticed the old beat-up neon sign for the Odeon, with its frayed wires, laying at the corner of the wall.

I didn't recognize anyone at the souk, and no one recognized me. I passed through it like a stranger, surprised by all the changes that had taken place in such a short while. The people seemed so different now, in this time of misery—it was all quite perplexing to me. I had drawn near to al-Kayyal's old store, and was about to take a look inside when a slightly overweight man who was reclining on a low bed called out to me while leafing inattentively through a bunch of books at his side.

"Greetings, young man!" he said. The voice seemed familiar to me, and had I not quickly and nervously turned to see whom the voice belonged to, I probably would have known who it was. The sight of this large man confused me, for it did not match the voice I had heard.

"Come in! Sit down! Don't you recognize me?"

He was wearing an expensive brown wrap on top of a clean white robe, and had an elegant scarf around his neck. He had white shoes on, like the shoes that pilgrims making the Hajj usually wear, and he was chewing on a toothpick. I studied his face, and when he smiled I saw that he was missing a tooth. I also saw a deep scar on his left check, which ran down toward the bottom of his mouth. At that moment, his voice merged with the old image I had in my mind. It was him. I remembered now. And I was certain of it when he spoke.

"How are you, Abu al-Nar?" he asked.

It was al-Hut but he looked so different now: he had changed so much. He got up from where he was sitting and greeted me joyfully, taking my load off me and motioning for me to sit down beside him, while I stood there like an idiot, confused. His entire body was giving off an odor that I couldn't quite identify, but which reminded me of that penetrating oil sold at mosques and mausoleums. He was holding a long string of amber prayer beads in his hand. He said a quick prayer and then ordered a young man—an adolescent—from southern Sudan to bring us a cold drink and quickly prepare some food for Sheikh Hamza, a title he gave me very casually. I laughed out loud, thinking he must be joking around with me, but he scowled and thrice asked God for forgiveness in a loud voice, while the boy ran off to prepare his orders. I knew he was being serious now, and that it had been no joke.

"The Whale?" I asked him. "The king of gasoline?"

I could tell that this name bothered him. He took the toothpick out of his mouth, which had dropped open for a moment, and said, "May God protect me! We've humbled ourselves before God and repented of our deeds!" His words seemed quite dramatic to me.

He put his soft and heavy hand on my shoulder and smiled that old sly smile of his, a shiny gold tooth appearing in place of the old one he had lost, and the wide gap between his front teeth coming into sight as his eyes vanished entirely. "Don't you know my real name yet? I am your brother before God, Abd al-Qadir al-Qammash," he said, pronouncing the two qafs in his name like the letter ghayn. He said God had cleared a path for him, and that he was now rightly guided toward God and the path of truth, and that God had blessed him, for he now had a large shop in the spice market, another one where the old cinema used to be, and also owned a small gas station. Here, he asked God for forgiveness three more times, before telling me that the "The Piety Company for Islamic Clothes" was his company, by the grace and favor of God.

"You're my guest tonight! Where are you staying?" he asked.

"I was just looking for a place to spend the night," I stammered.

He laughed and said, "God the Munificent has shown you the way!"

The cold Coca-Cola came, followed by two plates of tripe cooked in chickpeas and tomato sauce, a ground peanut salad with onions and tomatoes, and a small basket of warm bread with a bundle of arugula. I ate with unusual voracity, for I was both hungry and worried, and also confused and shocked by the enormous changes the people here had undergone. I was afraid of the fates that always controlled things without my having any say or any power to change them. Although my questions were endless, I remained silent, for every word he spoke was already an answer to any of the thousand questions in my head. I preferred to let him talk about whatever he liked while I collected my thoughts, trying to form a picture of what might have happened here, and of what would happen in the future.

He excused himself to go do work of some sort, but before he left he told his helper—the adolescent—to look after me. I needed to use a toilet, and I also needed to wash my hands, feet, and face, at the very least. When I asked about a toilet, the young man from the south led me through an archway beside the store, and I found myself in a large clean courtyard whose sandy ground was firm, presumably from being watered frequently. There were some straw mats and two large clay water jugs in one corner, and several cactuses by the walls. An arcade at the other end of the courtyard had rooms beneath its arches. The young man pointed to a side room, saying there was a toilet inside. I found a faucet and a small chair beside the toilet. I washed one foot and then the other, before washing my hands and forearms. As I sat down to wash my neck, I lifted my head and discovered a shower above me. I stepped to the side to check if it worked—it did. So I took off my clothes, put them in a pile, and had an incredible shower. Once I had finished and was feeling relaxed and born again, I saw the man approaching with a towel in his hand.

"You've got to go perform the afternoon prayer now. It's already almost time for the evening prayers," he said at once.

I thanked him and went to one of the corners and pretended to begin the prayer rituals for him, and he went away. I sat down and tried to remember the events of my first trip to this place, several years ago now. I thought of the souk at Omdurman that I was so eager to see again. . . . Had it changed? Was it even still there? Everything in life was different now; everything had changed during my absence.

Things grew quiet, and a calm breeze blew across the water dripping down my skin. A soothing grace and childlike tranquillity flooded through me, and I fell into a deep sleep.

I rush down a long road until I come to a huge giant of a man sitting on a golden throne. There are smaller people behind him, who are wearing masks. "Why have you come to us?" he asks me. I cannot speak. As the face of the giant gradually disappears, the other people scream at me as they take their masks off, revealing invisible faces. They terrify me.

I woke to the piercing voice of a muezzin making the call to prayer. The courtyard was filled with a large group of young men now. Some of them were sitting down in rows, and others hurried to go perform the ritual ablutions while I stood up to watch them. The Whale entered a few minutes later—or rather, Sheikh Abd al-Qadir, as he now called himself. A young muezzin made the call to prayer one more time, and the Whale signaled me to approach so that I could be in the front row, directly behind him. There was no way for me to excuse myself or find some pretext to get out of the prayer, so I took my place up front.

The Whale was our imam. Years had gone by, and the leader of our gang was now an imam. I used to follow him back then, and here I was following him again. I knelt when he knelt, and bowed down when he bowed down. And when he asked God for protection, or praised God, or testified to God, I did the same. After the prayer was over, a group of men gathered around the Whale, asking him questions and seeking his counsel on religious matters.

The Whale had become a scholar and a religious authority!

I excused myself from the Whale to go out and walk around a bit. He told me not to be late this evening, saying it in such a way that I wasn't sure if he meant that I shouldn't be late for the evening meal or for the other evening prayer. He then rose from his place, leaving the people around him for a moment, and tried to put a few dinars in my hand. I refused unequivocally, but he insisted. I was forced to open my wallet and pretend that I had enough money, looking him straight in the eyes. He wasn't convinced, and he muttered angrily as he returned to the circle of young men. The Whale Sheikh's anger hurt me much less than taking his money would have.

I don't know how I made it to the souk so quickly. I walked through it absentmindedly, my steps quickening whenever I thought of the past—as though I were trying to escape from something—and slowing down whenever I thought of the present. And whenever I thought of the future, I almost came to a full stop. The smell of the souk was the same as always, and hadn't changed. It smelled like a mix of spices, the more pungent of them entering my nose first: chili and black pepper; and then cumin, which never failed to dominate most of the others; this was followed by the penetrating smell of incense. But after a while, I discovered a new smell, which hadn't been here before: the oppressive smell of plastic. Countless plastic products filled the market now: bags, dishes, plates, spoons, toys, combs, and many other household items. I had never seen so much plastic before. The handmade wooden and metal products were all gone. The stores that were still there from the old days seemed older than they actually were, perhaps due to the influx of all these newer shops. The souk was now full of new vendors, young teenage men from the south and the west, and old women selling useless trifles that no one would ever buy. And there were other people selling new products: paper tissues, combs, buttons, sewing needles, lighters, soap, and also brightly colored plastic dolls shaped so strangely that you couldn't tell if they were modeled after humans, animals, or monsters. There was a lot of contraband stuff too. There was a wealth of worthless junk.

Most of the stores had begun to shut their doors for the night. There were some newer stores that stayed open late and which dominated the souk with their bright neon lights. They generally sold things other than spices, fruits, and vegetables. One of them was selling tape recorders, radios, and cassettes—I could hear the sound of sermons, delivered in some distant country's dialect, coming from inside. Another small shop was selling cheap watches, along with toy pistols, tanks, and revolvers. I couldn't tell what exactly most of the remaining stores were selling. People were standing in groups around some of the shops, and other shops had no customers at all, their owners standing alone at their doors. As I neared the end of the souk, I approached a store that held many memories for me—al-Kayyal's store. I stopped in front of it. The sign was still up, but it was quite run-down and one of the dots beneath the letter ya was missing, so that the name al-Kayyal was now al-Kabbal.

I thought about going back through the gold and silver souk, but decided to return through the spice souk instead. As I walked through it again, I took in all those smells I love, the mix of spices I could distinguish effortlessly: ginger, cumin, and cinnamon, and peanuts, tamarind, and sesame, as well as the one called hilw-murr, from which a bittersweet drink is made. I could also smell incense and sandalwood, and the mahlab spice. With my nose, with my sense of smell, which has never erred no matter how much time passed, I remembered how the place was in the old days. I went to the spot where I had first started selling spices. A cart was there now, and a vendor was selling a soup that looked like it was made from the same type of chickpeas I had often seen in Cairo. I wanted to stay there for a bit, but the vendor stood up when I drew nearer; I ordered a cup of the soup. Its taste was indistinct; I couldn't tell if it was made from chickpeas, stewed wheat, or salep, or if it was perhaps madida. I simply did not know. I ate—or rather drank—it quite slowly, until I had finished half of the cup. It was tasteless, neither bitter nor sweet. I paid for it and left.

I felt as if I were wandering through a different city, or as if I were in some dream in which a place I had once known now had very different features. Yet dreams are more merciful than this, for we accept the changes we see in them. In a dream, all things seem normal, and we only compare them to the fixed images in our mind after we've woken up.

I went back to the Whale's courtyard. At the door, I greeted the young man, whom I thought was from the south, and sat down and talked with him a bit. He told me that he was actually from the west, from Darfur, and that he had come here after the people of his village had been driven away by an armed raid in which his entire family was killed. He had been gathering firewood some distance from his village when he saw a gazelle. He chased after the animal for a long time and lost his way—fortunately for him. When he returned in the evening, he watched the unimaginable horrors from a distance, heinous acts that no one could endure: livestock being stolen; houses set ablaze; men, women, and children murdered; and young women raped. Miraculously, he managed to escape to a relative here in Khartoum but the relative wanted to get rid of him, and so tried to send him to the army. As for how he arrived in this courtyard, he said that that was a long story. His name was Abil Karkamani. The name of Queen Amani came into my head once more. When I asked him about his name, he told me that it was the name of one of the ancient kings, who was said to have ruled the Napata Kingdom around the year 500 BC. We spoke for a long time. He was eager to answer my questions, and eager to know who I am. Yet, from time to time he looked fearfully into the courtyard, as if he were afraid that someone would hear us.

Abil Karkamani was seventeen years old.

I entered the noisy courtyard after I had finished talking with Abil. The light there was dim, and I saw a throng of men in full olive-colored military uniforms. The uniforms were flecked with yellow and green, like autumn leaves, and were far too large for those gaunt bodies. The men had gathered around the Whale, who was sitting down in his white robe. His right hand threaded the amber prayer beads with mechanical regularity, while his left hand stroked his thick beard, which stretched down to his chest.

I stood there, dumbstruck and rooted to the spot, my mind in a muddle. The Whale greeted me from a distance and motioned for me to come closer, so I was forced to approach and greet everyone. As I sat down, they fell silent, awaiting the words of their sheikh, who calmly closed the session by saying, "O Almighty One!"

They filed out like dazed ants until I was alone with him. He called Abil to prepare dinner, which had been delayed on my account. We ate dinner together, and then I went to sleep.

As yet, I had had no opportunity to figure out what exactly the Whale did, but my intuition warned me that catastrophes were lying in wait with him, and that I should rid myself of his hospitality at the earliest opportunity. This shelter of his seemed so peaceful from the outside, but inside it was a hive of strange and disquieting activity. I was ill at ease when I went to my bed to sleep that night. I felt that something was wrong with this place. I tossed and turned anxiously. The days of stealing gasoline came back to me, the days when I had first heard that laughing voice of the Whale, a voice whose devilish tone had not changed. Despite all this apparent piety, his ringing laugh was still dishonest, his voice still varnished with cunning deceit. The Whale had managed to change much of his old appearance and his manner of speech, but he hadn't been able to change the tone of his voice, nor the piercing brazen clang of his laughter, which was still clearly untouched by piety or devotion. That impetuous laugh was the same as always, in line with his old nature. I could hear it now from the courtyard, mixed in with the laughter of others, and punctuated by litanies evoking God's name, seeking God's protection, or asking for God's shelter. None of this fit. I dozed off, overcome by exhaustion, and slept anxiously in this strange place.

The next morning, on my way to the bathroom, I noticed a large room with only three walls opening out onto the courtyard. There were disorderly piles of books everywhere. On my way back from the bathroom, I stopped inside, and found books that were newly printed, and whose pages had not yet been cut. Most of them were of poor quality, printed on faded yellow paper, but a few were leather-bound. Their strange titles had been written on the covers in gold ink without any skill or artistry: *Precepts Relating to Marriage with the Jinn*; *The Torments of the Tomb*; *The Greater Hell*; *The Hell of the Misguided and their Evil Fate*; *The Virgins of Paradise*; *This World is Theirs, the Afterlife Ours*; *The Greater Fatwas*; and so on and so forth in this vein. There was also a big pile of cassette tapes with similar names on them. This must be the library that the Whale had proudly told me about yesterday.

This room led to another room in which some young men were engrossed in silent work. I entered, curious to see what they were doing. At first I thought they were binding books. But then I saw that they were blacking out, with mechanical regularity, parts of what looked like magazines or newspapers.

"What are you doing?" I asked the man closest to me.

"Our task is to get rid of any objectionable material," he said proudly.

"How?"

"By stopping this godlessness—this licentious material—from reaching the people."

He pointed to a picture of the famous singer Umm Kulthum in one of the magazines. It appeared he didn't know who she was.

"Can you really stop that?" I asked.

"Of course—easily. We simply cover up any naked women we find."

"Naked women?"

"A woman is only allowed to reveal her face and the palms of her hands. And the true sharia states that no part of her at all is to be seen.

Aren't you Muslim? Don't you see the truth of this? We do this work for the glory of God the Exalted."

I stood and looked at these new religious marvels. They were following specific instructions. Pages from newspapers and magazines had been hung on the wall, their page numbers enlarged, and parts of them had been blacked out to serve as models for their work. If a woman in one of the pictures wasn't wearing a headscarf, they veiled her with black ink. And if a woman was wearing a swimsuit, they blacked her out entirely, leaving only the text. The art pages were their greatest enemy, and they were very aggressive in blotting them out. I could see how excessively they made use of this wretched power they had been granted, sordidly signaling to each other and speaking in words from their secret dictionary. Not even the sports pages were spared: they blotted out the legs of the athletes, both male and female.

I left my bag with Abil the next day. I was a bit worried about the Whale seeing the three stones in it, the ones I had carried from my family's grave: I was afraid that he would open my bag and dispose of its contents, either in the manner of the old Whale or that of the new sheikh. I went to Omdurman to walk around the souk, hoping to visit al-Kayyal's old store and see what the place looked like during the day. I bought some limes from an old lady standing near the front of the store, even though I didn't want any. Inside, I could see a thin young man tirelessly moving about and selling stuff to people, as well as an old veiled woman who moved slowly and calmly in the back, loudly repeating people's orders, although she wasn't actually selling anything herself. I didn't know who this woman was. Everyone was in a big rush. I wanted to ask the young man a question—any question—but that seemed silly, so I moved on, slipping the limes into the pocket of my robe. I walked beneath the scorching morning sun, a sun that was melting my thoughts and memories.

I walked like a tourist for a while, and then started on a long and aimless route, hoping to escape for a little while from this place so laden with memories. I kept on going, despite the heat, crossing the street to walk in the mercy of the shade. I looked at the faces of all the passersby in case I recognized any of them. At last, I noticed an old face that I could never forget, the face of the first person to speak to me, years ago, on my very first day in this city: it was the man who had dragged me to work with that gang, the Whale's gang. Al-Khattaf still had that distinctively sardonic face of his, and the sarcasm had yet to disappear from it. I saw him busily working at a gas station that had a wide sign with the word 'hell' on it, for the letter 'S' had fallen off the beginning of the sign. He was wearing threadbare filthy overalls, which were covered with grease and oil stains and had the Shell Oil Company's logo printed on the back. His hair was disheveled, and he had a pen behind his ear. He was rolling a large tire into what appeared to be the station workshop, and both his hands were smeared with oil. I approached him.

"Good morning, young man!" I yelled.

He lifted his head. "Ah! Abu al-Nar? How are you? Welcome! By God, it's been a while!"

I wasn't sure how to greet him or whether to embrace him, and he made a playful quip, "Watch out that you don't bleach my clothes!" he said, warning me not to get my own clothes dirty. He followed this up with a series of questions and remarks: "What are you doing here, Abu al-Nar? Where have you been? You were gone a long time . . . . It's good to see you!" Then, after hearing someone yell in the distance, he quickly said, "Listen, I'll be done with work in exactly one hour. I still have to change the oil and one of the tires on an army trailer . . . . Where are you staying?"

"In the Whale's courtyard for the moment," I replied, and then added sarcastically, "With Sheikh Abd al-Qadir al-Qammash!"

He scowled for an instant. "We have to meet," he said. "I need to talk to you. It's important . . . . Do you remember our old coffee-house?"

"The Adhab Coffeehouse?"

"Yes."

"Is it still there?"

"Of course. But we changed its name to the Uzzab Coffeehouse. The owner wrote the one letter unclearly, something between a dhal and a zay, so the name can be read either way now . . . . It's good to see you, Abu al-Nar!"

I was happy to have found someone I knew, but the way he scowled at the mention of the Whale was cause for alarm. I said goodbye and left with my head hung low.

I saw another face that I recognized as I went on my way: that of the grocer Hagg Nur. I greeted him, and he recognized and welcomed me, insisting that I drink something with him at his store.

"Boy! Get some karkaday!" he said to someone, conjugating the verb in the feminine form. I always loved his distinctive stutter, and the way he used the feminine forms of address for men and the masculine forms for women. He swore that the old days—by which he meant back when I used to live here—had been good days, in spite of the hardships, "Life was good in the old days, Hamza. . . . People have changed. The way they treat one another has changed. Everything's changed. . . . But the good Lord is generous, Hamza! Your Lord is merciful!" I considered Hagg Nur's words while drinking my cold karkaday, for I hadn't been gone all that long. Was it possible that things had become this bad here?

We talked about this and that. He repeated his welcome, as well as his complaints about things having changed. I got up to go, and he insisted that I come by and see him again, saying he would always be happy to see me. I promised him I would, and said goodbye.

Unfortunately, I did not meet al-Khattaf again that day. I waited two hours for him at the Adhab Coffeehouse, and then went all the way back to the gas station to ask for him, but no one knew the name: al-Khattaf. It was my fault, for I hadn't thought to ask him what his real name was earlier. He had been so serious when he proposed that we meet, and I thought that he really meant it. Something must have come up. This made me even sadder, for I was very curious to hear his story about the Whale, and was sure that it would be an exceptional one.

All of these things pass through my mind on this night, holding sleep at bay. Abu Darsh's questions were not unfamiliar, but they somehow stirred up my memories. Perhaps my answers to him had been a bit short, as if I'd wanted to keep the details to myself. The tape of memories is easily rewound, just like a film. Hakima's fast asleep, and I can hear the clear sound of Abu Darsh's regular breathing coming from the other room. I begin to feel a mixture of sorrow and relief, which helps me finally sink into the sleep that I had longed for.

I'm not sure exactly when I fell asleep on that cold night. I dreamed that my cat Hakima was meowing strangely, as if she were sick. I start from my sleep to discover that the wailing is in fact coming from the old alarm clock whose batteries are dying, causing it to emit an awful rattling sound. I suddenly realize that my watch is forty minutes ahead of the clock.

In less than ten minutes, I manage to go to the bathroom, wash my face, and put on my clothes. Abu Darsh is still fast asleep. I leave him a note saying I've gone to work and that he should help himself to breakfast. I also write that he's welcome to stay until I return, but that if he decides to go he should leave the key in its usual place in the flowerpot outside the front door. I feed Hakima and leave the apartment, closing the door behind me.

It's now 4:58 a.m.

I hurry toward the Praterstern station—I have to catch the 5:10 subway. It usually takes me a quarter-hour to get there, if I move quickly.

The weather is extremely cold today. My breath steams in front of me: I look like a dragon spitting fire. The cold rises from my toes to my fingertips, and even to my ears, increasing my pain.

I stop at a red light. There are no people here, and no cars as far as the eye can see, so I cross. Suddenly, at the other end of the intersection, I notice a police car lurking like a crocodile, and now moving in my direction as if it had just hit upon a criminal. I enter the nearest alley, and hear the noise of the police car turning on its loud siren and its annoying blue lights. Fortunately, the alley connects with a narrow back passageway at its other end. Despite my quick pace, I can still hear the police car stopping at the narrow entrance to the alley. The doors slam and an officer yells out roughly, "Stop! Stay where you are, you animal!"

At the end of the passageway, I put on my *Krone* jacket and cap. I hurry up, panting, and head down into the subway station to platform one, in the direction of Kagran. As I reach the platform, I see the red taillights of the 5:10 train at the end of the tunnel, and I'm forced to wait for the next one. I enter wearily once it arrives, and collapse onto the nearest seat. The warmth takes hold of me.

I'm rushing on a long road toward a lofty house perched on top of a mountain. I enter the house and see a man with an indistinct face. His name has been handwritten on a broad leather-like cloth hung above his head. I've never seen such strange letters before, yet I can read his name clearly, "Bah." He's sitting on a large golden throne that has five legs shaped like those of a lion—three in the back and two in the front. I can make out three men behind him, each wearing a mask: one is that of a mountain goat, the second the head of a crocodile, and the last the dog-like face of Anubis. He's been expecting me, but it seems that I don't know the rites of welcome, for someone comes up behind me and whispers in my ear that I should kneel and bow my head. When I refuse, the person haughtily tries to shove me down. I resist, but his hand is so powerful that it seems to have electricity coursing through it. At that moment, Bah cries in a loud voice, "Leave him!" Then he looks at me, raising his head, and asks, "Why have you come to us?"

"I'm looking for my mother and my sisters," I reply.

"They're here. But you must answer my questions before you can see them."

I glance around me and say, "Go ahead."

"If a person dies, what's left of him?" he asks, as if this were some absurd test.

My voice falters for a moment, and I stutter, "Nothing, nothing, . . . nothing is left of him!"

I feel a silence unlike any I've ever felt in my life. The echo of my words reverberates, convulsing everything, until the masks fall from the three men. Their faces are featureless.

The letters hung behind Bah become muddled, and the three men threaten me with their fists. Bah looks anxious and sorrowful, and scratches his chin with his thumb and index finger. I can see him clearly now, and I repeat my words, "Nothing, nothing, . . . nothing is left of him!"

"Then let him go so that he may see for himself!" Bah says in a voice like thunder.

I don't know what he means. Will I see Habiba and Karima and Halima? And why does his face look like that? Why has my reply filled him with such sadness?

I hear several noises in my sleep: the meowing of Hakima, the splintered sound of the alarm clock, the sharp siren of a car, and the rough voice of a policeman. Then I hear a voice inside the subway listing off the names of stations, and I simultaneously feel something digging into my shoulder. I open my eyes. A man with stern features is standing in front of me. He's wearing a leather jacket with a large badge pinned over the left side of his chest. He says something I don't understand, and I answer in shaky German, "Okay . . . I crossed on red!"

He looks at me in surprise and irritation, then repeats himself, "Your ticket please!"

I see other passengers pulling out their tickets and putting them away again. I stand up to take mine out of my back pocket, but in my haste I accidentally give him my ID card from the *Krone* newspaper, where I work. The look of irritation is still on his face, but now mixed with some schadenfreude. "Your ticket!" he says once more, drawing out the vowels this time.

I dig through my pocket and pull out my monthly pass. He looks at my picture with a policeman's suspicion, tilting his head to the left and then to the right. Then he turns the pass over to read the name and address on the back before returning it to me in disgust.

He walks over to his colleague, who is standing with a terrified young woman near the door. He's writing down her information in his notepad so that he can fine her, and he tells her to get off at the Vienna International Center station.

I get off at Kagran and take my bundle of newspapers from Yousef. My place number is on the bundle, as well as the number fifty, which indicates how many newspapers I receive.

"The boss was here today," Yousef says to me sadly. "I flipped over your bundle so he couldn't see your number, but he flipped it back over and recognized it. He asked me why you were late, and if you were always this late."

"Damn the boss!" I reply. "And the *Krone* and its owners!"

An elegantly dressed woman in an expensive fur coat comes to buy a newspaper from Yousef. "The weather is very cold today," she says. "It's sixteen degrees below zero!"

"Ahlan wa-sahlan!" I say, bidding her welcome in Arabic.

The woman looks at me in surprise while Yousef laughs sadly.

I pick up the newspapers and leave, going to wait for the tram that will take me two stops away to my gloomy spot. The tram is running late, and I decide to walk to the next stop, for movement is a blessing here, and I'd turn to ice if I stood still in this freezing air. The tram arrives just as I make it to the next station. I get on quickly and warm myself up, for I'll have to stand out in the cold for several hours.

I arrive at my spot. With my frozen fingers, I try to cram the newspapers into the bag. Then I put on my cap on and rub my hands against each other. I put the bag of newspapers on a short pole and stand there. I notice someone in a car with tinted windows across the street, and for a moment I think that they want a newspaper. But it turns out to be the boss, Goldman, sitting in his black BMW and watching me. He must have stopped to note down my place number and how many minutes late I was in his dictaphone so that he could impose the customary penalty on me.

The street is glistening with snow. I almost slip when I try to move from the sidewalk down into the street, and I don't try it again. The cars go by in funereal silence, their headlamps approaching slowly like the eyes of animals in a forest.

It's still dark. My few regular customers prefer to keep their car windows closed today, shaking their heads and raising their palms apologetically behind the steamy glass that they've wiped off with their hands. The meaning of their signals is clear, "No."

In my haste to leave the apartment, I forgot to put on my thicker socks, and I also forgot my scarf. The cold is unbearable: I can no longer feel my feet. I walk up and down a bit, but am worried about slipping. So I move around in my spot instead, like a caged panther.

Someone stops in the fourth lane on the far end of the street and asks for the paper. I carefully walk—or rather, glide—over to him and give him the paper. The man hectically looks for his money, but the light turns green before he can find it. The car behind him honks, and he speeds off and mutters "Morgen!"

I recognize the man's face. He only buys the Friday newspaper, and he only ever utters a single word: "beide," by which he means both the *Krone* and the *Kurier* papers. "I will wait for you, Mister Beide, no matter how long it takes," I say to the disappearing car.

I slip on my way back. As I get up, I curse the boss, and the newspaper, and this situation of mine, and the damned cold weather. No sooner have I reached my spot on the other side than I see the boss in his car right beside me, as if he had just come out of the snow. He lowers his window about two centimeters, and a strong smell of cologne comes streaming out, along with a blast of warmth.

"You're not a good worker, Mister Muhammad," he says in a smoky voice, with a mixture of derision, conceit, and sadism. "Your cap's on crooked. You don't have your bag. Your jacket's undone. And you showed up late to top it all off. This means you're not getting paid this week."

He closes his window and darts off to find some other prey.

The extreme cold sinks into me. My fingers and toes are in even more pain now. My body is stiff and numb. This weather leaves me with no strength at all, not even to utter a fleeting insult. I rub my right hand and put it in my pocket while I try to zip this awful jacket all the way up with my left. I finger the few icy shillings in my pocket. I look at my watch: it's not even six o'clock yet. I've got to stand here in this huge freezer for four hours without a scarf or thick socks, and now I won't have any money left at the end of the week.

I think about Hakima: Did I leave the window open on this cold day?

5

My absurd work selling papers ends at ten o'clock, and I leave this place where I've almost frozen solid. I ride the tram two stops to Kagran. Inside the tram, I take off my cold *Krone* jacket and put it in a different bag, and then count the unsold papers that I'll be returning to the man we call "the paper boss" at the station. He too counts them, discovering that there are ten unsold newspapers too many, and says that he can only buy five from me. I wait for my colleagues to return, hoping to find someone whose sales were better than mine on this cold day to buy a few from me. But everyone comes back with long faces, and asks the same question I do, "Can you buy a few papers from me?"

As usual, I'm forced to pay for the five unsold newspapers out of my own pocket. For each vendor, the newspaper always sets a limit to what we call the retour, that is, the number that they'll buy back. Anything over the retour is not refunded. Thus, the vendor bears the brunt of a bad day, while the newspaper takes pride in its high sales, which are steady in both the summer and the winter.

I call Sandra. She says she wants to meet today, but that she has to go to a lecture at the university first, and also swing by the library to return some books. She asks if I'm planning to go to the Palm House, and I tell her I am. She says she'll come by there between two and three so that we can go back home together. I head home quickly. Hakima greets me with a lazy yawn and stretches out in front of me. I discover that the wonderful Abu Darsh has cleaned the apartment and cooked shakshuka and left me a portion. He also bought me some heating oil before he left. I eat with pleasure. Warmth takes hold of me, and I doze off on the sofa. I wake up at noon, fearing I've missed my meeting with Sandra. I put on my shoes, pack up Hakima, and head for the Palm House.

I go straight to my favorite spot. I still feel drowsy, for I did not sleep well last night. I check my watch, but it has stopped. The place is very calm. I gaze at the palm tree, and then fall asleep.

I wake to the sound of nearby whispering, and see an Austrian soldier sitting on the other end of my bench and giving a young woman a long kiss. His uniform is olive green. I've seen that color somewhere else, on other soldiers who lived in the most wretched and miserable conditions: they were squandering their youth and their short lives for the sake of mad and marauding leaders, who saw themselves as the country's keepers and caretakers and who believed that all others were traitors.

I remember wearing that khaki—or rather olive—color myself; that hated color that robbed me of all of life's colors, all its splendor. I was its prisoner for many long months, in the name of defending the holy fatherland and battling the rebels, aggressors, and enemies—and all the other clumsy designations they had for them. In those days, I had neither a place to stay, nor a family, nor a salary. I didn't have any days off either, no chances to go out like this young Austrian soldier—though if I had it would have been without a woman, of course. My greatest wish at the time was simply to leave the barracks. It would have been such a luxury to have even just two hours to sit on the banks of the Nile until sunset—to clear my head and cast some of life's burdens into the riverbed.

I've tried, over and over again, to suppress the memories of my conscription—I don't like it when they come back to me. But now I remember it all in detail again. I was at the Whale's courtyard, lying peacefully on my back and thinking about trying to find al-Khattaf again and then leaving this country to go somewhere—anywhere—else, when a group of army officers entered to examine the papers of everyone present. They found my passport and took me with them in a military truck, which was already full of other young people, to some sort of center. There, I saw a large number of young men squatting on the ground. They put me through a quick interrogation about where I lived and the countries I had visited. I had to undergo further questioning about all the distant places I had been to: Why had I gone there? And how could someone like me, who was from a remote village that no one had heard of, have managed to travel to such faraway places? Then we stood in a long line while they wrote down our information and took pictures of each of us. The place looked like some sort of army camp. I didn't know what they were going to do with us, but one of the young men said that they would almost certainly conscript us.

I spent the night in those barracks, crammed amid an enormous number of young men. I have no idea how they managed to round up so many people in such a short time. They brought us all into a large dark room, which resembled a pen for animals. Its walls were made of cement, and had small circular openings near the top. The room was packed with rusty iron bunk beds, which creaked at the slightest touch. The mattresses and blankets on them gave off a putrid smell—they looked like fertile ground for insects and disease.

The next day, they moved us like pack animals in the back of trucks to huge barracks on the outskirts of the city. There, they called out our names and divided us into groups, with a 'corporal' in spotted olive green military fatigues standing at the head of each group. We moved in a line to go stand in front of another room in which some military doctors were sitting and scowling. The atmosphere was tense, the orders harsh, and the punishments cruel. We entered in groups of four. It was a physical and mental check-up to find out whether we were fit for service. They examined some of us slowly and with boring repetition; we opened our mouths like idiots so that they could see our tongues, teeth, and throats. And they left others alone, paying no attention at all to them in an obvious display of laziness. Then all the questions of the previous day were repeated in a blunt interrogatory manner, just to make sure of our answers. They decided that all of us, without exception, were fit for military service. There was one person among us with a clear case of polio, and another who could see no more than a hand's length in front of him without his thick glasses. Both of them were included in our ranks without any further ado. Then a 'sergeant' with two ribbons on his chest came and gave each of us a kit with some necessary military equipment, including boots and a uniform. They only had two sizes for the boots, and the same was true for the uniforms. They told us that this was army property, and that we would be punished if we lost anything.

It seemed that a war was on. The officers came by to give us pompous and frivolous orders. They commanded us to take off our civilian clothes and put on our uniforms as quickly as possible. We did as we were told, and all of us looked absurd. I felt as if I were an extra in some comedy that was about to be filmed. I remembered how ridiculous I looked in Port Said, during those smuggling trips with my old colleagues in Egypt. Yet, at least we were able to laugh about it back then. Matters were more serious now, and laughing was forbidden. My trousers were too short and too wide on me, and my shoes too small. I fortunately managed to exchange my shoes at the last moment with someone who had received bigger ones. I tried to exchange my trousers with several of the others, but these were the longest ones around. After shaving all the hair off our heads, they ordered us to go wait in the large courtyard outside. We stood there lined up, completely still, until they brought us back inside to the pen.

As simply as that, they stole our lives and gave us new ones that were full of death. We didn't know what to do with them, nor when we would be done with them.

Forty days went by in that place, and I counted every single hour of it. We woke up every day at five in the morning to the awful sound of a trumpet, and did rough physical exercises for three hours. Then we ate a colorless breakfast, one with so little flavor that we couldn't even tell what we were eating and drinking. But we still devoured the food like animals. We lined up again outside in the intense midday heat, while the officers squatted in the shade to find creative ways of tormenting us. They doled out punishments to the whole group if a single one of us made a mistake, always repeating the same revolting principle, "Reward is individual, and punishment collective." Whenever people collapsed on the ground from malnourishment and ill health, the exercises always continued without interruption, with one of the officers usually yelling out, "Ha! Another actor!" Then, after a while, the officer in charge of the drills changed this to add another element of mockery, and started yelling "Another *actress*!" instead.

Then the officer began nicknaming anyone who collapsed or vomited, giving them the names of Egyptian and Lebanese actresses. We had a Layla, a Nabila, and also someone called Hind. Some of the meaner men among us seized the chance to relieve themselves of some of their anger by repeating these random nicknames, and thereby consolidating them. My nickname was Abu Kura'ayn because of my extremely long legs, which they said made me look like a heron or a flamingo when I walked. It was quite nice compared to the other nicknames—a trifle, really—and didn't anger me. But the awful names that others received, along with the sick scorn of the officers, caused clear psychological damage to several people there without them even realizing it.

For forty whole days we were forbidden to leave the camp or receive any visitors. Our families had been notified and informed about our conscription. But I had no family, neither in Wad al-Nar nor anywhere else. Wad al-Nar wasn't even there any more. After those forty days, those among us who had family or relatives were allowed to receive visitors here in this remote camp. All of us, without exception, came from poor and destitute homes, and only a few people came to visit, bringing foods that we hadn't seen for a long time, as well as some snuff and other tobacco that we divided among ourselves. The visits were short—a single hour once a week—just like visits to a prison. Since there was no one to visit me, I used that hour to go out by myself into the camp's courtyard and walk around. I walked in circles like a bull tied to a waterwheel, and thought about the three stones in that bag of mine that was lying somewhere inside the Whale's place, with Abil. Was it still there? Was Abil even still there?

After the end of our basic training, an officer, whose rank I had never heard of before, arrived. He showed up in a big car with two flags at the front, and seemed very important. The car stopped in the middle of the camp, and the driver jumped out to open the door for him and then salute him. All the camp officers had lined up to carry out the military greetings. This great officer emerged from the car like a peacock, adjusting his uniform over his big belly and holding a small cane with a leather grip in the shape of a crocodile in his right hand, while tapping it against his left. The military ceremonies and salutes began at once. The head officer of the camp stood and presented him to us with quivering words that contained more fear than respect or reverence. He recounted his many deeds and the battles that he had taken part in to liberate the country, and said that he was considered one of the leaders protecting the country from the oppression of the aggressors. The head of the camp said his esteemed visit today was a historic occasion, and that we—the new troops, his sons—were proud to receive him. This man of great rank stood there, decorated with badges on his shoulders and medals on his chest, and a huge military cap like the ones the Russians wear, as well as enormous dark glasses. I could not see his neck. After the introductory speech, he got up on a platform and droned long words into the microphone about the homeland and the jihad, and said that we were the heroes of the future and the keepers of the country's flame, and so on and so forth. When he was finished, we applauded him, then stood to attention and gave our salutes while our head officer passed pompously through our ranks to inspect us. We held our heads high to show how proud we were of our great accomplishments and the lofty calling for which they had chosen us. The national anthem could be heard in the background as they raised the country's flag. We were supposed to sing the anthem, which they had tried to teach us over the past forty days. We recited it discordantly, for many of us had no more than the first sentence memorized, a sentence we repeated clamorously but without any real passion. Then one of the officers suddenly yelled out "Allahu akbar."

The visitor raised his cane in the air several times, and cries of "God is great" resounded from all sides—I'm not sure if this was due to the rapture of the moment, fear of punishment, or our submission to their orders and oppression, or whether we let out these cries because of the hopeless situation we were in. The time passed slowly and heavily, until the exhausting ceremony finally came to an end.

They later divided us into smaller groups, and we did additional exercises for the officers in blind and mute obedience. Everything was done with order and severity: waking and sleeping; eating and drinking; walking and standing to attention; even speech and silence. We were turning into machines that they ordered around. We obeyed like pack animals, always doing as we were told, for there was no way out of this captivity. We received brutal punishments for the most trivial matters, and were often made to stand for hours in the murderous blaze of the sun. They forced additional grueling exercises on us. We were deprived of sleep, food, and drink. We were constantly subjected to ruthless derision and psychological torture. We suffered the cruelest and most organized forms of oppression in that army that was sending us to our ruin. We couldn't understand why they were doing all of this to people as young as us. We were like hired slaves, as if this land and country were not our own. We were defending something of theirs, not of ours—something that belonged to the powerful, to the ones who sat around with their bellies hanging out while they held their staffs or threaded their prayer beads, laughing scornfully.

After this, they trained us in bearing and using weapons, but the training was poor and inadequate. Then the hasty orders came, and I found myself entangled in a mission that was surely leading me to my death, or to some other unknown place. It was like being in a nightmare.

I was alone in a forest on a searing day, neither a leader nor any companions by my side. I had a pack on my back and a Russian-made rifle in my hands. Munitions belts were hanging across my shoulders and around my waist, along with an olive green flask for water. The ground was boggy, and my feet kept sinking into the mud. I could hear the strange intermittent cries of an animal or a bird, and was worried that those were actually enemy signals. I suddenly realized just how much of a stranger I was in that place, and how miserable I was carrying a military pack instead of my bag made of palm fronds, and a metal flask in place of my leather waterskin. My hands were no longer free, but were fettered to this rifle. Instead of my address book, I had the tattered remains of a poorly scribbled map. And in place of my mother's amulet, I was wearing a metal tag around my neck with my military ID number on it, as well as the number of my unit. I had been told that it could withstand thousand-degree heat, though I myself clearly could not.

I had lost my way. It was broad daylight, and I was in the middle of this marshy forest, uncertain of how I had gotten there. The branches of small trees—the likes of which I had never seen before—were all about me. I couldn't recognize the pesky insects that were stinging me either. The muddy ground I was standing on resembled henna paste that had been dipped in water. I was in the middle of nowhere and didn't know which way to go, nor why I was here. I called out at the top of my voice, but there was no reply. All I could hear was a rustling in the branches, informing me of the presence of animals or reptiles or birds of some sort. I saw a tall tree in the distance and hurried toward it, falling into several of those wretched boggy holes in my haste. I must have looked horrible, but I didn't care. The feeling of danger here in this isolated place was overwhelming. I felt as if I were waiting for sudden death in this unfamiliar land. I didn't even have a proper map on me—it was with one of my fellow soldiers. He had lost me, or I had lost him. I had no radio with me either, and no means of contacting my unit. I kept stopping and spinning around at the slightest noise, an absurdly heavy rifle in my hands. I scouted out the place as I advanced cautiously and silently, fearful of being taken by surprise.

This was such a ridiculous situation I was in. They had left me here to fight the rebels. Those mighty men split open the country for us. They lit the fuse of civil war, and we were its fuel. I was enraged at the leaders who mercilessly sent us here, into this war where we don't even know who exactly we're fighting, or why we're fighting them. They gathered us up and trained us to be obedient sticks in their hands, using us to strike anyone they hated, before stopping to gaze at this majestic sight and congratulate each other and pin ribbons and medals on one another, all the while striking at the peace of the republic. Then they would play the national anthem and soak in the applause and the "long live so-and-sos," and have their photos and slogans hung up on the walls, all of them precisely mapping out and protecting their careers, with no thought for the rest of us. We were the fuel of war, the bodies strewn about like dust, the cheap souls they called martyrs of the country. They said we were gaining paradise, a paradise they themselves did not want to enter just yet, preferring to sacrifice us for the sake of their own survival. They said that each of us would have forty virgins waiting for us in heaven, as if we actually wanted forty virgins. We were leaving our mothers and sisters and wives behind to go to a whorehouse in the sky.

I remember how confused and bitter I felt on that first day when we drove away from the barracks and passed by those throngs of women. I couldn't believe my eyes. I saw a huge number of girls and women wearing white uniforms and veils that covered their entire heads—everything but their faces. I couldn't tell whether they were there freely or by force. They were shouting out slogans in shrill voices and raising their weapons as part of their basic training, looking wretched and utterly absurd. Their shrieking gave me goosebumps. The big shots were sitting on their comfortable seats in that big open arena, raising their fists or wooden staffs, or pointing with their fingers. All the while, we young men and women were being led like lambs to the holy slaughterhouse. I didn't understand what was happening, nor did those around me. We looked into each other's faces, but no one dared ask any questions. Sirri, a fellow soldier, had closed his eyes and was shaking his head in pain, like someone suffering from a migraine. He was on the verge of tears. Or maybe he was actually weeping—I can't remember.

I reached the tall tree, which had broad flat branches, and began climbing up its trunk with some difficulty. I got about halfway up the giant tree, which offered a clear view of the surroundings. I saw a wide expanse of green land with narrow dirt paths running through it like red copper. Herds of cattle were grazing peacefully, and there were neither people nor houses nor villages anywhere to be seen. From my vantage point, I could make out some animals: spotted gazelles, some giraffes, a few zebras, and also a couple of monkeys jumping and swinging among the lofty trees. I envied them, their calm and peaceful grazing, and wished I too could be an animal like them. I was relieved that there were no lions or hyenas, however. Then I heard movement near the top of the tree, so I struck the branch above me with the butt of my rifle, and something withdrew into the branches. I climbed down a little ways to sit down on a broader branch. A few bustards landed near me, which reassured me that the tree was devoid of danger. I gazed out at the horizon, but I couldn't see any of my fellow soldiers. It was as if I had come down here from the sky, all by myself.

I was exhausted, but I thought there was no way I could fall asleep in a tree, like some panther or bear. Yet, I was so tired I dozed off then and there. Often, when I feel the pressure of the world on me, I depart into a trance-like sleep and have strange dreams that I share with no one, dreams that I myself am unable to interpret.

A movement in the Palm House wakes me up. I glance at my watch, which is still stopped. The young soldier is looking at me with a relaxed and smiling face. His girlfriend's face is flushed, but she seems to have quenched her thirst for his kisses.

"A lovely place, isn't it?" he asks.

"No." This odd answer upsets him, but I continue, "This place is more than just lovely. It's incredible."

They both smile and wave goodbye. Then the young woman sees Hakima, who is meowing and has come out to announce her presence, so the two come back. She picks Hakima up gently, and they ask me several questions—questions I've become quite accustomed to by now. Before they leave, I ask them the time and set my watch. Hakima is sitting beside me now, and I shift over to where the two of them had been sitting.

I'm surprised at how easily the sight of that olive green color brought those distant days back to my mind. I'm still drowsy, and I have some time before Sandra will arrive, so I fall asleep again.

I'm walking with a group of young men at the end of a wedding night. We're accompanying the groom to his new house, according to custom. We laugh with one another and joke around in loud voices, in a state of joy and harmony. More groups of smiling young men in white robes appear at the intersections and join us. The girls and the women keep a bashful distance, letting out their joyful ululations while they wave their hennaed hands and skillfully parade their beautiful hair and enchanting braids. We walk a long way, and I don't notice that the young men behind me have begun to disappear, one after the other. I'm at the front with the groom. I climb up a tall mountain, walking quickly as usual, and am the first to reach the summit. I stop to take a look at that strange place, but when I turn around I find that the groom and our companions are all gone. Against my will, I rush down to the foot of the high mountain. As I approach the bottom, I see a group of people whose faces I cannot make out due to my speed, and I tumble onto the ground before them. In the flash of an eye, and without a word of greeting, they take off my shoes, my robe, and my underwear, until I'm naked. I feel half-numb, almost paralyzed. I'm surprised to see that my pure white robe—a robe fit for weddings and nighttime celebrations—has suddenly, as if by the trick of some conjurer, taken on an olive green color in their hands. I hear a clamor behind me and stand up, thinking my friends are on the way. But instead, a young woman comes out of a tent, and screams when she sees me naked. As the woman screams, everyone around me disappears, except for her. I pull hard at her tent, hoping to use it to cover myself up, only to find a second young woman bathing naked in the middle of the tent. I start up at the sight and cast off the tent, which falls onto an infant. It doesn't seem to hurt the child, but it does upset him, and he too starts screaming. Suddenly, the group of young men appears again. They approach with malice in their eyes and weapons in their hands. They've cut my olive-colored robe into small pieces, which they've tied like tresses into their hair, though I cannot understand why. They say nothing as they draw nearer, while I scream out silently, unable to move. One of them grabs my arm. I'd expected his hand to be coarse, but find it soft and warm instead.

I wake from the dream, reminded once again of the day I fell asleep in that tree in the forest. I keep my eyes open, first looking at the palm tree and then piercing the ceiling of the Palm House with my gaze, and recall that distant day. I woke up, horror-stricken, to the movement of something soft and warm slithering across my bare forearm. I opened my eyes and saw an enormous boa making its way down the tree. I was terrified by how large it was—I'd only heard of this animal in stories and legends. I fell on my back onto the soft grassy earth, my rifle bouncing beside me. The broad branch shook as I dropped from it, and the snake's enormous tail fell onto me. I thought it was attacking me, and grabbed at my rifle to defend myself, but the snake vanished lightly into the thicket as I panicked. I tried to shoot a round off in the air, but it didn't work. I tried two times, and then a third, until a bullet finally went off. Its echo rang out louder than I had imagined, and I immediately regretted my rash action. Would I really have killed it if it had attacked me, or would I have run away? An old myth came back to me, a myth about not meddling with snakes or killing them—for it's said that whoever kills a snake will himself be killed by one.

I sat there, worried and confused, and stared at the ground. And so it was that I didn't notice, at first, the large ring of people who had surrounded me.

During my military training, I learned neither the names of the weapons and equipment nor any of the military ranks. I demonstrated the greatest ineptitude in using all kinds of weapons, and I didn't know the difference between a brigade and a battalion, or a platoon and a legion, or a regiment and a squadron. There were some who became drunk with joy at the mention of these groupings, and learned all the military terms by heart. Those were the lifelong soldiers. I myself was never interested in any part of this military life. I felt bored, and greatly resented being kidnapped like this. I rebelled, in my way, by being apathetic.

We had left as a full company three days earlier. They divided us into smaller squads or units or whatever they called it. One squad was light infantry; and another was heavy infantry with old army equipment that only had a very short range. Some moved in armored cars with the heavier equipment and ammunition. And I, with my ill luck, went with the air force. They said that our mission was to approach the enemy, that is, the opposing forces, and destroy them. They transported us first in an old single-propeller Russian warplane they called Antinov, and then in a helicopter, since there was no suitable landing strip at our destination.

There were officers at the head of every company in our squad. During those three days, we camped inside threadbare tents along the rough road amid mountains and forests, taking turns on watch. The weather was tropical, a combination of extreme heat and rain showers, and the nights were grueling. We didn't know how to set the tents up properly, so we spent our nights soaked to the bone, openly cursing the world and what it had come to, and secretly cursing the leaders and so-called heroes who had sent us to this miserable place.

The head officer's plan was to drop paratroopers into the front lines, and to transport some of the other squads to the closest landing strip. The soldiers they were sending had not been well-trained in the use of parachutes. We were with them at camp before we were sent off, and they were all nervous and afraid. They told us they'd only had three days of training, during which time two of them died when their parachutes failed to open. They had no practical knowledge of how to use the parachutes, and most of them had never even been in an airplane before.

They were supposed to arrive at the front lines before us, but we saw no paratroopers or infantry when we made it there, neither in the sky nor on the ground. I wound up with a company that consisted of one higher-ranking officer and four lower-ranking ones, along with one hundred and twenty-eight soldiers. Our head officer gave us a map, on which he had scribbled a few details. He said that the rebels over there didn't have any of the ammunition or supplies that we had, and that they hadn't been trained for warfare. Our comrades would be dropped behind the rebel lines so that we would come at them from the front and the rear. God willing, he said, we would hold that position within twenty-four hours, and bring it under the control of our forces. He gestured toward a large tree where his car and driver were, and told us we were to meet back there after four hours of reconnaissance. He walked a few steps with us, pointing out the features of the road, before getting in his car and making off like the wind.

I was sure I would meet my end in that place. I realized this when our squad's head officer, who was reading and stammering off orders received from on high, divided us arbitrarily into two groups of sixty-four soldiers, with two of the lower-ranking officers in each group. He said that we should keep splitting ourselves into smaller groups as we advanced. We proceeded aimlessly through the forest, with no guide and no means of communicating among ourselves. Most of us were utterly exhausted. There was no clear plan; everything was extremely chaotic. "Who's this enemy inside my own country?" I asked myself. "And what's this wretched rifle doing here? And where are those supporting troops? Where are the supplies and munitions, the planes and the transports? Is all of it a ruse, a conspiracy?" We kept dividing ourselves into smaller groups until there were only four of us left, and no officer. I saw the misery, fear, and nausea on the faces of my three remaining companions. We were all exhausted from this aimless journey.

Then there were two of us, and we would not divide ourselves up any more.

"You know what, Hamza? I made a big mistake!" Sirri, my only remaining companion, said without any warning.

"A mistake?"

"I was just a week away from proposing to my sweetheart Azza, and then the raid happened!"

"The raid?"

"Yes. They rounded us up in our homes like cattle and drafted us. I wish I'd proposed to her earlier. I spent three and a half years building a house for myself near my parents' home. And for four years I was busy with my sisters' marriages."

"Did they all get married?"

"Two of them did, and the third's engaged."

"Why didn't you propose to Azza?"

"Her mother—may God repay her!—kept delaying the engagement. She wanted a better husband for her daughter, someone better off. I'm just a poor farmer! All I own is a piece of land. Azza is incredible, Hamza! And loyal! She had dozens of proposals, but she stayed true to her word. But I'm afraid of those vultures."

"Vultures?"

"Yes, vultures!" The angry words kept pouring out of him. "Hovering vultures! I'm scared of those rich Sudanese men who live abroad and raid the country once a year, their wallets crammed with dinars and riyals and dollars. Their promises throw even the strongest of families into confusion. They take away the most beautiful women in lightning-quick marriages, and then imprison them in foreign countries, where the women lead dull and stifling lives—lives that are comfortable but devoid of any real pleasure. Those men leave the old lovers behind—young men like myself who've never been attracted to the flash of travel and life abroad. They leave us behind to swallow the bitter pill of our defeat and misery. Those vultures are the hopes of all the girls now, of all the young women who wait for these 'princes' to come from their faraway lands with their money and cars and flashy promises. Those of us who stayed behind and refused to go abroad can't match any of that. A lot of those vultures are panting after Azza, and her mother is hoping she'll pick one of them."

I try to keep talking about her, to distract both of us. "Do you love Azza that much?"

"Love her? I'd die for her! I'd give my life for her! I'd do anything for her! You haven't seen Azza's eyes. You haven't heard her voice. She haunts my days and nights. She's like a goddess of love. She's my palm tree and my flower, my heaven and my earth. Azza!" I noticed what looked like tears while he was talking. He was trembling from the excitement.

"Are you married or engaged, Hamza?" he asked me.

"Neither one nor the other!"

"How come you don't have a fiancée, Hamza? Engagement is the loveliest period in life, and marriage is the most beautiful catastrophe in the world! Especially if they've drafted you and dragged you into this damned life. At the very least, you'd have the memory of a brief life you lived before they robbed you of it, along with your dreams, and gave you this miserable life instead. You won't be good for anything if they ever release you—you'll die alone, in tatters, abandoned like a mangy dog."

"Sirri, if we can just get out of this mess, then you can engage me to anyone you like," I answered him sadly.

I don't know how I lost Sirri, or where he wound up, or what exactly happened. I was there in the middle of all those staring eyes, without a companion or an officer or anyone at all. This was crueler than any nightmare. A large circle of people had surrounded me at a distance of about five meters. They looked warily at me. Their bodies were strong and athletic. Their clothes were different, as were their faces. In those short moments, I couldn't distinguish between dream and reality. It seemed, from the loads they were carrying, that they had been busy farming and grazing animals. There was a woman with an infant suckling at her breast and a hoe in her hand, and another one with a large bundle of straw on her head and a sleeping child swaddled at her back. One of the men looked like a shepherd, judging by his clothes and the staff resting on his shoulder. They were speaking a language I couldn't understand. I knew that I was a prisoner, and that I had fallen into the hands of the 'enemies.'

I threw my weapon onto the ground at once, afraid that a stray bullet would shoot off accidentally and hit someone, and also as a sign of my peaceful intentions and surrender. The people before me looked like neither warriors nor rebels, contrary to what they had filled my head with over there, and my gesture seemed to move an old man standing at the front of the circle. He approached and spoke to me in his language. I didn't understand. I mentioned my name in Arabic and the name of my company. The man smiled reassuringly. I was relieved when he spoke in Arabic that was clear but a bit broken, for he couldn't pronounce the hard 'h' sound, "You're an Arab from the north, and belong to that mad government. You've come here to fight . . . . Had you not thrown down your weapon, we would have slaughtered you. They send you here in the hundreds every year like locusts . . . . What are we going to do with you now?"

I took this last sentence as a threat, and backed up against the tree that I had fallen from to protect myself. The man remained calm while several younger men with powerful athletic bodies advanced on me, the anger clearly showing in their eyes. The old man let out a strange clicking sound, and they stopped in their tracks, in deference to him. He signaled me to come with him. I was squatting there, defeated, so I stood up. I had to follow his orders. He signaled to two giants among the young men, who grabbed me under my arms with iron fists. One of them took my weapon and carried it in his right hand like a toy. I walked between the two of them, following the old man. I expected my fellow soldiers to arrive, whether attacking from the ground, or dropping out of the sky, or even as prisoners. But no one came. I felt as if I were prisoner to some long nightmare. My pack kept beating against my back while I headed toward that new and unknown world that awaited me. I could feel something warm on my face, and something touching my lips. I was incredibly thirsty.

I awake to Sandra kissing me with her soft lips. She apologizes for being late, and picks up Hakima, who is yawning lazily after having fallen asleep on my lap. She kisses her. I tell her about the long and distant journey that I had just taken, right here in this calm seat—and all because of that olive green color. As I tell her the details of the strange story, her face looks pained. She's holding her breath, and also my hand. And anytime she hears something that was painful to me, she gives me a kiss. A new feeling comes over me while she listens attentively to every word and lovingly presses my palm: a feeling of rare grace.

A loud clamor arises, and I hear a language that's not German. A bunch of tourists are looking at the plants and taking pictures of them. One of them is shouting like a goose. She looks like a teacher or a professor, and must be their guide. She's standing at the head of the group and calling out the names of the plants in a very loud voice, as if she were in a lecture hall, while the others listen to her silently and nod their heads in wonder and delight.

I hear her say a word that sounds a bit like "Tafelspitz," and I seize the opportunity to tell Sandra that I've been craving the Tafelspitz she cooked since yesterday. We go out, and Sandra holds onto my hand as if I were going to run away from her. Her eyes kiss me dozens of times as we head to her place. We make it to her neighborhood with unimaginable speed. I can't remember which trams or subways we took, nor how we got there so quickly. We walk the rest of the way with our arms around each other.

6

Hakima has everything she needs in Sandra's apartment. I ask her if I can take a quick bath, and she reproaches me for asking, saying that this is my home too. When I get out of the bath she surprises me: she's prepared the table with the delicate touch of an artist. There are two roses in a small vase at the middle of the table, beside a beautiful blue candle she has lit. She opens a bottle of red wine from the Krems region for us. The sight of her face partially covered by her hair in the quivering candlelight mesmerizes me. My heart slips out of my chest, and my breath quivers. She puts on a record by Mozart and, with that melody and that enchanting atmosphere, stanches the flow of my memories and pain. I savor the meal of Tafelspitz and sip the wine in my glass. And every time she smiles, I give my lips over to her, letting her flood me with that torrential love. The music flows through my body electrically, turning me into a new man. I feel light and enchanted, as in an exquisite dream.

Sandra surrenders to me in such a way that she actually controls me. I adore the fragrant smell of her mouth. Our clothes fall to the ground as easily as autumn leaves. Her body is soft and warm, supple yet strong. My lips glide gently from her mouth to her cheeks to her ears. I plunge my face in her hair. Her breathing speaks the loveliest of languages to me. I know every letter of those breaths. Our hands read each other's bodies in slow excitement. We begin to melt into one another. The space between her navel and her waist undulates slowly. The waves become faster. I sink into that sea, into her islands, while her voice rises coquettishly and she coos and moans into my ears. She kisses me again, her two lips stretched out in a rush of pleasure. They take on a pink hue, like the color of her two firm nipples. Her tongue glides from my ear to my temple to my chin, then makes its way back to my mouth and stays there, quivering with tension. Her palms are in mine now, and when I tug at her wrists she surrenders, and gains even greater mastery over me. I plunge my fingers into her fragrant hair. I see the color of her eyes for an instant, and her eyelashes quiver in exciting shyness. I go beyond her eyes into her inner world, and see what she sees. I gently run my palms across the full length of her arms until I'm just beneath her shoulders. The touch excites her, and she lets out an even deeper moan. She gets on top of me, and I run my palms down the soft skin of her back. We switch positions. My hands move from her calves to the graceful soles of her feet. I apply some light pressure there, at points that never fail to excite her. The fragrance of her wet body intoxicates me. Our moans grow louder and blend into each other, rising and falling. She pulls at my hair—not too roughly, but not too softly either. She gently bites my shoulder while lightly clawing at my back, which always excites me. I can feel my body dissolving into hers. Ecstasy. Desire. Submission. Domination. Attraction. Touch. Smell. Passion. Peace. Warmth. Oblivion. Absence. Presence. Moans. Sighs. Pleasure. Laughter. Screams. Touch. Sight. Ecstasy, ecstasy, ecstasy.

In spite of our exquisite exhaustion, Sandra still wants to know more about me. She's still holding onto me as if I were going to slip away from her. Her body is asking me those questions that have been locked up between us for so long. Although she says nothing, I find myself speaking, as if I were answering her questions. She brings over the bottle of wine, and I drink and tell my story, stopping from time to time to gather my thoughts. Then Sandra asks me a single question, "Where did they take you, those two young men and the older one?" The words flowed out of me.

Tense and quivering, and under the guard of the two giants, I followed the old man while the others looked on in surprise and anger. It was hot and humid, and the sweat was pouring from me. I was a prisoner that day, and did not know what fate awaited me.

I reached a group of circular mud-brick huts with thatched roofs of twined palm fronds. The huts were pressed together, and each one looked like a giant onion planted in the ground. I walked into a hut over whose entrance two ostrich eggs were hung. It was comfortable and clean—a place fit for guests, not the prison I had expected.

I opened the door from the inside and saw that the two giants were still on guard. Children had gathered near the hut and were screaming and pointing at me with their long slender fingers, and a few women were stealing glances at me from a distance. Some of the women were on the backs of bulls while others were walking and carrying clay jars and gourds and other large containers. In spite of their loads, the women there walked lightly and elegantly, with smiles on their faces. I closed the door and sat in my hut, with neither my weapon nor my pack. A few moments later, one of the two men knocked on the door and entered, then said something in his dialect that I couldn't understand. He put my pack on the ground in front of me and left. I was surprised at this, and amazed that they knocked before entering, as if I'd actually come here as a guest. I opened the pack cautiously: everything was still inside.

The giant knocked again a short while later, and two lovely young women with naked breasts entered, their waists wrapped in beautiful loincloths. They were smiling like children. The first one put down a large gourd full of water, and also a bundle, and the other one set down a large basket with some bread and fruit and other food in it. The first woman had beautiful braided hair filled with colored beads. And the other was no less attractive with her short hair and large black eyes, and her pure white teeth in perfect rows. Their skin looked soft and smooth, and they had a light but distinctive fragrance.

The water was heaven to me, for it had been three days since I'd had any to wash myself with. I'd been disgusted by my own smell, but my worries and dire straits had not allowed me to think like a human. I found an old clean robe and underclothes in the bundle. I wanted to wash myself quickly in the far corner of the hut first, but I was extremely hungry, so instead I attacked the food with great voracity, not even stopping to see what it was. I ate as if it were my last meal. It was delicious and had just the right amount of chili. I was still surprised, for this wasn't how prisoners of war were treated. After the meal, I felt extremely tired. I wanted to go to sleep, but I mastered myself and got up to bathe before this heavenly opportunity passed me by. Standing in a large basin, I washed myself quickly with the little water they had provided. It was an incredible bath, one that I'll never forget. I was worn out, and all the unanswered questions were making my head spin. But I felt that if I were to die now, after that wholesome bath and in this state of calm exhaustion, then it would be a lucky death, and a generous one. I put on the robe, and have no recollection of when I fell asleep. I slept on the low bed like a child in his mother's lap.

I woke to the sound of someone knocking at the door. The old man entered with three men of differing features: two of them were older, but the third was somewhat younger than the others. The third one looked like an experienced soldier. The old man introduced them to me, and I still remember their names, for the man translated them for me: the first one's name meant 'lion,' and he had a thick neck and strong arms; the second man's name meant 'oak tree'; as for the third, he was the old man's son, and his name was Tihraq, which was the name of an old king and meant 'the strong and courageous one.' As for the old man himself, his name meant the same as Sharif does in Arabic and so I called him Sharif from that day on. Their names were similar to ours in their meanings and descriptions. I asked Sharif if he was the leader of this village or the head of this tribe. He smiled, showing me all of his healthy white teeth. He said that for a long time he used to be the meeram, or the sheikh and leader of this small tribe, but that now he was just an ordinary man here. He was the oldest person in the village, however, and they still sought his counsel on important matters, but they were not bound to follow it. He said that his father had been meeram of this tribe as well, which had once comprised twenty-one villages and had seen a long period of peace and prosperity. The old man resigned when he got older and gave the title to one of his children—the one he thought was best for the job—and kept an advisory role for himself. He said that they had decided almost ten years ago to select a new meeram every autumn and have the previous one remain as an advisor. The meeram did not have to be one of the elders, but should be someone poised and wise, someone accepted by the community.

"The selection process is a very simple and traditional one," he said. "On the morning of the appointed day, the people go stand in line in front of the house of their preferred candidate, while others count the number of people at each house. Whoever has the most people is appointed meeram that evening, in a lovely celebration in which all the candidates take part."

He sees my astonishment and continues, "It might surprise you to learn that women also govern here. In the past ten years, two women have been meeram. But we're humans like everyone else, my boy, and aren't free from evil. This place of ours is no paradise. We too harbor hatred. There are disputes and killings over pastures and grazing land, but the council keeps them within limits."

After this, they spoke in their own language, looking at me from time to time. They seemed to be deliberating peacefully, without raising their voices. Then Sharif told me that I had to stay with them for a while until they figured out what to do with me. He stood up as lightly as a young man and put on his shoes. He told me that I was invited to his home for dinner that day, and that one of the two men outside my hut would take me there. Then he noticed the food in front of me, "Don't eat too much of that!" he said laughing, and went on his way. I too laughed—the first time I had done so in that place. The other men also stood up to leave, after having made way for Sharif, and went out respectfully behind him. I said goodbye to all of them as they gracefully walked out.

At that moment, I thought of my training in the army camp, and the drill-sergeants who were only good at barking out orders. Those officers wore uniforms that were far too tight on them, yet they considered them to be very dignified. Their bellies inevitably hung down in front of them, and whenever one of them stood up to demonstrate some exercise or drill to us, he would almost burst out of the uniform.

I threw myself onto the low bed and thought about the world, about the circumstances that had been hurling me about in both the north and the south, before finally leaving me here with no way out.

I was eager for that evening's meeting with Sharif. At sunset, one of the men knocked on the door and I knew that the time of the visit had come. I had no gift for Sharif, and was a bit confused about my status: Was I a prisoner or a guest?

I walked into his big house: there was a large central courtyard open to the sky, its ground covered with the skins of sheep and goats, as well as rugs made from other animals. The walls were made of clusters of palm trunks bunched together, and they too were decorated with furs and animal skins. The wooden doors of the house had a simple captivating beauty about them—they'd been made with an artist's skill. I hadn't expected to see such a place here. A large number of men and women, young and old, were gathered there. It looked like a wedding celebration, except that the men and women weren't separated: everyone was sitting together. Sharif had me sit down beside him and offered me a sweet drink similar to foamed milk, but which I was not familiar with. He told me it was made from a fruit that doesn't grow in the north. He called to one of the young men and asked him to bring one of the fruits, which they called guwannabana. He said that they mix an infusion of this fruit with fresh cow's milk to make the drink, and that it's especially good for women who are pregnant or breast-feeding, but that the men also drink it to give them strength. Then they brought out several delicious types of food, many of which were grilled. He told me what they were and taught me the names of everything.

As soon as night had fallen and the moon appeared, some of the people brought out instruments that resembled tunboorasas well as drums and tambourines. They played them, singing in pure and powerful voices, and lovely African dances ensued. Sharif encouraged me to participate, so I got up and began to imitate the dancers. I forgot myself with them, and entered into a state of ecstasy, like a dervish. A strange feeling came over me, as if I were no longer in this world, or as if I were in the sweet trance of death. Perhaps that boa had actually bitten me, and now I was living a wondrous feverish dream. I can't remember how I made it back to my bed that night, or when I fell asleep.

The next morning, Sharif took me and a small group on a long journey by foot. He walked lightly, like a camel-driver in the desert. We reached some ruins: the rubble of houses and the remnants of fallen trees. The further we advanced, the clearer the smell of carrion became. I saw a village that had been utterly destroyed. It looked like Wad al-Nar. Sharif told me that this peaceful village had stood between two warring sides, and that it fell victim to them. Fighters had come from both sides, and the village fell between the anvil of the one and the hammer of the other.

The place needed no further description from Sharif. We walked in silence among those ruined huts and houses, encountering lacerated and rotting animals on our way. The vultures were fighting over the carcasses, while jackals and hyenas circled at a distance.

"We buried most of the people with our own hands," Sharif said to me. "And we brought those who remained to live with us in Sumit, our village." Sumit was the word for 'bead' in their language.

We all suddenly stopped at one corner of the village, for an old bare-chested man was rushing toward us, screaming, and raising a spear. Sharif ordered me to remain calm and not make any sudden moves. He held my hand firmly. The man came bristling with anger and eager to kill. He looked us straight in the eyes, but after a few moments—very tense ones for me—he left us, still raving incoherently in a loud voice. We continued on our way.

Sharif told me that that poor man had lost his whole family and everything he had during that absurd war. He went mad after they tortured him, and now he thinks that every stranger in this place is an enemy.

We continued on our way toward what looked like the ruins of a destroyed fortress. It seemed ancient. We entered through its broken gate, and were greeted by one of the most amazing sights of my life. There was a vast lake and enormous trees on the southern side of that elevated place, and also many animals, the likes of which I'd never seen before. And at the edge of sight, I made out what appeared to be scattered villages.

"Take a look!" Sharif said to me. "The people here are all peaceful. They're brave, but not warlike. We've seen all kinds of people come. Those who want to live in peace have stayed with us, and we've banished those who don't. The coming of the slave traders was horrible here. They wanted to take our people as slaves, but we didn't let them take a single person. We fought fearlessly against their cruelty and barbarism. Many of us died, and those who fell into their hands defended themselves to the death. They chained up anyone they captured, starving them until they died. They couldn't understand that we're nobody's slaves. It's a long story, my son!"

That was what Sharif called me, "my son." He considered me his own, even though I had come to them as an armed invader.

I spent almost eight weeks in that village. Sharif's hospitality did not slacken, and neither did his efforts at familiarizing me with the place and the tribe. I went to his gatherings every night except Thursday. He always spoke to me gladly and answered all of my questions. He had learned Arabic from a man from the north, someone he had lived with for a long time during his youth. He told me a remarkable story about how he had been captured by a group of soldiers when he was young. He managed to escape and was taken in by that man from the north, who proceeded to teach him Arabic. The man knew his father, the meeram of the tribe at that time, and treated Sharif very well. He stayed with him for almost a year and a half, until he was able to go back to his family in the south.

As the days went by, Sharif told me about many events, most of them sorrowful. He told me about this lovely place that could have been so much more beautiful had all those madmen simply stayed away.

"In time, my son, the bonds between the north and south were broken. Slave dealers came from one direction, and missionaries from the other, and chaos spread across the country. I kept my religion while I was in the north, and the man who took me under his wing—his name was Hamad al-Nil—said that I shouldn't convert to any religion unless I was convinced by it. I believed in the religion I'd grown up with, which had been passed down to me from my forefathers, and most of the people didn't seem to mind. But I remember how Hamad al-Nil warned the extremists not to force me to convert to Islam. Who would stand up for me like that now, my boy?

"The missionaries came to the south with their Bibles and built churches here. They tried to get our people to wear strange clothes and pray to white prophets—prophets who weren't our own. And my father told me about Austrian missionaries from a group called 'Maria' who'd come with the help of Emperor Franz Joseph to convert us pagans to Christianity. They pretended they were there to abolish slavery, but then they set up the Holy Cross Organization, as it is now called in the Church. Some of those missionaries died from illnesses or from the harsh climate, and the few that remained began selling slaves to Hursid Pasha. Afterward, supposedly for the sake of converting us, a large number of lazy drunkards and smokers came looking for servants. They decided to take some of us back to their cities in Europe to convert and instruct us, and then send us back here as local missionaries. They founded an organization they called 'The Good Missionaries.' There were several branches of it.

"We tried to make those missionaries understand that we had older beliefs and religions, but they laughed at us. They said there was only one true religion—the eternal religion of Jesus Christ the Savior. They hung up their crosses everywhere and made our children memorize church songs in European languages. They dragged our people into another religion, and tempted us with gifts and clothes and medicine, as well as promises of Paradise, and turned us against everyone from other religions.

"All they cared about was teaching us the prayers and the rituals, and about the new clothes we wore. Now they bring us Bibles and t-shirts that advertise companies we've never even heard of, and jeans and caps as well. We've started walking around like cheap ads. As you can see, many of the men here still go bare-chested, but now they wear jeans at the same time! Others still wear our traditional garments, but with European shoes on their feet!

"They built twenty-four churches for us in the past thirty years, but not a single building for us to pray in as we would like. A few of them come every year with photographers and a television crew to give out some clothes and sweets, in addition to an extraordinary number of crosses. They gather the children around them and smile for the cameras, though we're not sure why exactly they do this.

"They think they know the world—and religion—better than we do. They think they understand our land and our history and our traditions. They're convinced that we're inferior and that we should imitate their lives. But we see only the worst of their people here, the ones who are always scowling in despair: they hate the world. They're overly conscious of the little they possess, and are in constant fear for their lives.

"Fanatics came from the people of the north as well, wanting to bring us their religion in turn. Once again, we tried to make them understand that we have older religions and older gods. They mocked our beliefs, considering them a form of ignorance and backwardness, and called us pagans for worshiping things in nature. They too said there was only one true faith—Islam, the religion of Muhammad. They dragged the people into yet another religion, tempting us with good jobs and more promises of Paradise, and they too turned us against everyone from other religions.

"Those people are still trying to Islamize the south, while the others are trying to Christianize it. Some of our people have indeed changed their beliefs, along with their clothes and skin. People have different faiths now, and they struggle with one another over the quickest way to Paradise. One woman here converted to Islam, and her sister converted to Christianity—they got into a bitter feud over their faiths, and all they accomplished was to rip their family apart. There are men here who want to see their wives fully veiled, with Qurans in their hands and its verses on their tongues. And there are others who want to see their wives with Bibles in their hands and crosses on their necks. And there are some who don't want any of this.

"As for me, my only wish is for oil never to be found here. That would certainly be the end of us, my boy!

"We're a people of peace, not war, my son. Your insane people in the north are waging war against the rebels without knowing exactly who or where they are. And the insane ones in the south are waging war against the so-called traitors in the north. We're caught in the middle here. The northerners invade to look for rebels hiding among us, and the southerners attack to look for hidden nests of northerners. One side takes home the spoils, the other the casualties and blood. Not everyone who comes from the south brings protection, and not everyone who comes from the north brings salvation!"

Sharif also told me horrific stories about the smugglers who were not only intent on gold and ivory and rare birds and animals, but were also involved in human trafficking. His words were hard for me to bear.

Then came the day that Sharif had decided upon. He had made arrangements for my safe passage, for there was no guarantee against raids, and he was concerned about rumors of my presence there spreading. He took counsel with his people on Thursday, and decided that I should leave on Sunday. His people would take me from here to the borders of the first northern military encampments—he said that those were a difficult three days' journey from here on horse, and that he hoped the roads weren't blocked.

I spent Friday and Saturday playing with the children, and using my hands to communicate with the young men and women and learn some words from them. I gave serious thought to staying in that place, for it was possible that I would simply be forced to go somewhere else after I returned to the north. It was even conceivable that they would send me back here. But then I remembered the three stones in my bag, which I had left with Abil at the Whale's place. Those were my only possessions in this world, and I had to go back for them, whatever the price.

I spent Saturday evening sitting with Sharif in his house, and had my last supper with him. After giving me some words of advice, he opened a wooden container beside him, took out a smooth deep red stone, and put it in my hand. It was flat and very warm, and covered my whole palm.

"This, my son, is a stone from this place," he said. "It comes from Sumit, where you've lived and whose land you've walked on for a little while. It's not a holy stone, but it is a rare one. It's been here for thousands of years, maybe for millions, but now it will go with you. My one wish is for you to come back on your own one day—on a day of peace—to return it. For this is its land, and its place is here. Consider it a gift from me. I hope my wish comes true one day."

I thought of the three stones once more, and at the same time felt that I myself was that fourth warm stone, the stone that still had life in it. I felt a strong desire to stay alive, to seek something I did not know, something that was waiting for me, somewhere.

Sharif entrusted the task of accompanying and protecting me to the two men who had guarded me on my first day at the hut, in addition to his son Tihraq. We all sat outside and waited for Sharif. When he arrived, he gave me a small and incredibly fragrant oak container and told me it was a gift for Hamad al-Nil. He had a paper with Hamad's address on it, and I promised to deliver the gift. He said it was best for me not to keep any papers on me during my journey, so I quickly memorized the address.

He told me they would have to burn my uniform, and that I could take neither my weapon nor my pack with me. He also said that I was to remain silent for the whole journey, pretending I was mute until I was free from harm, and that my three companions would speak for me if necessary.

He bade me a warm farewell. Then he got up as lightly as ever, to not draw out the goodbyes, and left the men to their task.

I went to my hut and smeared myself with oil that repels gnats. I couldn't sleep, for I knew the next day would be a crucial one for me. I would either be saved, or I would die and have some rest from the nightmare of this wretched life. The thought of burning my uniform eased my mind and calmed my nerves a bit. It was as if I were burning an awful period in my life, one that had nearly wrecked my soul.

I don't know how or when I finally surrendered to sleep that night.

I'm wearing a pure white robe and running in the middle of a bunch of barking dogs and amid people who are also running and shouting. I can't tell if I'm running with them or from them. After a long while, I find myself alone. The ground beneath my feet is changing colors—from sandy yellow to a dull grey. Then it turns to green, then to wheaten beige, and then to gold. The colors change quickly as I run and listen to the noise of my quivering breath. The dogs catch up with me, and I'm afraid. The color of my robe turns to khaki, and then to olive green, and stops changing color after that. I take it off to help me run faster, and I throw it to the dogs. They stop to voraciously tear apart the robe with hideous noises. I see the bank of a river in front of me, and throw myself into the water. I'm not a good swimmer, but I float as the water carries me along. Naked, I savor its warmth, and can feel my childhood coming back to me. When I approach the other bank, I find myself caught in the water's ebbs and flows, as if I were in a sea, and I start to lose my ability to float. I struggle until I've made it up the other bank. Darkness falls, and I can see many eyes gleaming in the shadows, but I don't hear anything that helps me figure out whose eyes these are. The eyes draw nearer, so I draw back. Without any thought or hesitation, I throw myself into the water, and I find myself swimming in the warmth once more. As the water's white foam touches my skin, a delicious numbness comes over me. At the same time, the foam tickles me and I laugh out loud—I'm relaxed, happy.

I tell the long story without stopping, narrating even the dream in full detail. I polish off the entire bottle of wine without realizing it. Sandra hasn't said a single word the whole time. Her large eyes seem even wider than usual. Hakima is asleep at her feet. Sandra gives me a long, deep kiss. Her hands are on my face, as if she were reshaping my body and soul, while her breath quivers.

"Hamza!" she says, pronouncing the 'h' properly for the first time. The sound is beautiful and exciting—I've never heard my name spoken with such grace before.

I'm in her power once more, and she starts moaning again. Hakima leaves for the other room. I feel my body waking. Her fingers are pulling at my hair, now more strongly, now more softly. Her teeth gently sink into my shoulder and her nails scratch softly at my back. My body melts into hers. We become a single person, all boundaries gone. I feel an indescribable joy. I want to stay in this warm world of Sandra's. I don't want to go back to the coldness of that other world, the one lying in wait for me.

7

I draw Sandra closer to me, pressing our bodies together. I seem to have tired her out with my story. There's a look of purity to her face as she sleeps, and I catch a final glimpse of it as the candle goes out, melted away, after having performed the most exquisite of its tasks. I sink into a wholesome sleep with Sandra's breath on my face. That night I sleep as never before, deliciously exhausted. I sleep naked for the first time in my life, and the amazing thing is that I'm doing it in the middle of winter. It must be Sandra's abundant warmth. This carefree sleep is all I desire now. I draw the splendor of these wonderful hours beneath my eyelids.

I'm walking in a public garden, peacefully examining the roses. I can turn myself into any shape I like. I pause in front of a red rose, which captivates me and I become that rose. Some bees hover by me—they like the look of me, and I can hear their lovely words. One of the bees alights on me. I like the look of it, so I become that bee. I fly in the garden, drinking all the nectar I want. Then I catch sight of a butterfly, and change my shape again. Then I turn into a sparrow; then a blackbird; and then a dove; and finally into a tree. I try to turn back into myself again, but I can't. My power is gone, and I know I have to pass through all the states through which I've just lived. I'm going to have to go back in reverse, from the soul of the tree to that of the dove; and then the soul of the blackbird; and so on and so forth until I've reached the soul of the rose again. But I can't tell which dove I was, nor which blackbird or butterfly, so I remain lost in the soul of the tree for the whole long day. A young woman passes by me, and I feel as if I know her. She stops to look at the tree. It's Sandra. I shake, although there's no wind. And I speak to her, and she hears me.

"Sandra! It's me! Hamza!"

She responds with a cry of joy. "I knew this would happen," she says. "Come with me my love!"

She embraces the tree, putting her arms around me, and I flow out of it and into her, and become a part of her. I've never been so happy.

"You'll stay with me like this until the end of time!" she says joyfully.

I laugh through her voice while she walks with a smile on her face. I can feel what she feels. My breath is her breath. The beatings of her heart are my own.

I wake up in the morning: Sandra is no longer beside me, but I can hear the shower running. Hakima's curled up in a ball at my feet. I remember my dream, and bring back the details. Sandra enters wrapped in a large bath towel. She comes over and kisses me.

"I've been up a long time," she says. "You were smiling in your sleep, and even laughed out loud. I was watching you, but didn't want to wake you."

"I had a wonderful dream."

She pounces lightly back onto the bed. The refreshing scent of the shower covers her soft skin.

"Tell me about the dream, please!" she implores.

I tell her about it in all its detail. She gives me a strong embrace once I'm done.

"Be careful!" I joke. "I'm a tree!"

I forget—intentionally—to go to work on this exceptional day. I don't want to leave this intimacy, this warmth. As if I truly had become a part of her, Sandra says, "I'm not going out of the house today. We'll stay here together—we've got enough food! But tell me the story, I beg you! What happened after Sharif burned your uniform? What happened the next day? How'd you make it back?"

I excuse myself to take a quick shower, not letting Sandra ask too many questions. I return a few minutes later, invigorated, like a groom the morning after his wedding night. I make two cups of tea with milk, and bring a plate with some light breakfast to the bed. Sandra's eyes—her entire body—are waiting for my reply.

I slept in my hut until daybreak that Sunday, when the two young men and Sharif's son Tihraq came for me. They had four stallions and one mare with them, and put some of the extra baggage on the mare. I had a basket made of palm fronds with me, in which I had placed a robe, the stone from Sharif, and the container that was a present for Hamad al-Nil. Tihraq pointed at the robe, and I understood that I was to put it on as we drew near to the border with the north. For now, I was to wear clothes like theirs.

My eyes bade a sad farewell to the village, and I set off with the men toward a new unknown. They were speaking in their language, of which I now understood a few words. The two young men explained the meaning of their names in gestures. The name of the first one was Koto, which meant 'thunder.' The other's name meant 'river,' but I don't remember the word exactly—I think it might have been 'Saraf.' After that I thought about everything that had happened the past few weeks. Then the same disturbed man, who had rushed at us with a spear a few weeks ago, began screaming at us again, startling me. We did the same thing this time, and then retreated.

The first village appeared in the distance. When we approached it three men on horseback came out to us. They dismounted and greeted Tihraq ibn Sharif with great respect. They joined us for more than two hours before saying goodbye and heading back.

By noon we had reached the branch of a river. We followed its course well into the afternoon, before resting from our riding in the shade of a giant tree. I fell asleep, exhausted, for I had never ridden a horse for so long before. Later, we ate a light meal and got up. We spurred on our steeds for a great distance, until evening fell, and then slept where we were until dawn of the following day.

We started off again. Whenever they felt it was safe, they would teach me the names of the things we were seeing. We laughed a lot, despite the tension that was visible on all of us. Tihraq was the strongest among us—I could see no weariness on his face. His eyes were ablaze the whole time, sharp and keen but not condescending. He was serious yet knew when to joke, even though he didn't do too much of it.

We arrived at a broad meadow where doum palms enchantingly lined the riverbank. Suddenly, several huge young men dropped out of a large tree like cats. They had arrows and spears in their hands, and quickly surrounded us. I looked at Tihraq, who stood calmly where he was and almost seemed to smile, while Koto and Saraf screamed and spun around their horses, lifting their spears at the others. I was surprised that Tihraq let them do this. I wanted to dismount and do something, anything, no matter how idiotic that might have been—I couldn't let the other two give their lives for me like that while I stood idly by. If death was to come, then we should all die together. I was surprised when Tihraq told me to not move, even as the men surrounded us. Suddenly, they let out a strange loud intonation, then screamed and planted their spears in the ground in a wide circle around us. At this, Tihraq dismounted and laughed, and everyone burst into laughter and greeted one another. Those devils all knew each other! That joke was the most dangerous thing that had happened to me since the day the boa had slithered across my arm.

Despite the difficulty of the last three days, they had passed well in the company of Tihraq and Koto and Saraf. The young men we'd met that morning had two small boats with them. The boats seemed ancient: they were made of papyrus reeds bound together with thick fibers, and their prows were arched sharply upward. For a moment, I felt that I was living in the time of the pharaohs.

Tihraq explained that this was as far as they could come with me, and that these new men would help me make it back to my land. He pointed to one of the men and told me his name was Deng, and that he understood a little Arabic. I picked up my basket and Tihraq moved some of our supplies to the boat. The three warmly said goodbye to me.

I couldn't believe that this boat could hold all that weight, but it did. After traveling down that smaller branch of the river for some distance, we turned into the river proper.

I had been wearing clothes like the others, clothes that had left the upper half of my body naked. And I had a small dagger tied to my forearm. Tihraq had reminded me not to talk and to pretend to be mute if there was any danger, so that no one would know I was from the north.

We covered a large distance on the river. Suddenly, I saw things rising out of the water not too far from us. A head appeared, and then several more. I cried in joy, pointing at them like a child. A large number of hippopotamuses were calmly lifting their heads out of their water to breathe and then submerging again. Deng lifted his hand to his mouth and fixed his eyes on me, and I understood that I was to keep silent. They began to row very delicately. I was surprised, for no one else was around, and I'd heard that these were peaceful animals. I thought that Deng and the others might consider them to be holy creatures.

After we were relatively far away from them, Deng told me that it was the mating season for hippopotamuses, and that human voices agitated them, and that they often capsized boats and attacked the people in them. Hippopotamusets don't eat humans, but a single bite from one of them was enough to sink a boat, and another bite was enough to maim the passengers. The crocodiles would finish off the job, he said. He also told me that crocodiles, on the other hand, never capsize boats, but tend to avoid them, and that human voices frighten them and drive them away.

Just before sunset I heard a voice yelling at our boats from the riverbank. The men rowed hard and quickly. Several people appeared, and the voices grew louder. They had long spears in their hands and quivers of arrows on their backs. More and more of them appeared, rushing along the shore to keep up with us and signaling for us to come out of the river. Deng told me to remain completely silent.

As we went ashore, I smiled, expecting the previous performance to be repeated. Two of the men dove into the water and dragged the boats to the bank. The men spoke for a long time in loud voices. Then they examined the boats and let us leave.

When we were back in the boat, Deng told me that that was a close call, for this was a fishing area that the tribes had divided among themselves a long time ago. Violating one of the tribes' territories could lead to trouble, and serious consequences. They had inspected the boats to look for nets or other fishing gear, and had let us go when they failed to find any. A tremor ran through me when I realized that the situation had been very real, and was no performance.

I opened my basket and found the stone and the container, but not the robe. I was annoyed at this, and explained to Deng that the robe had been stolen. He was silent for a bit, then said, "I'm sorry about that. We got rid of it when they came after us. We would have had no chance had they found out where you were from."

We reached an area with high banks that evening, and moored the boats there. One of them climbed up a tall tree to make sure everything was all right. At his signal, we came onto shore. I walked through a long woody marsh with them until we reached a dense forest. They continued on paths they seemed to know well, and soon I found myself not far from what looked like a military camp. My heart beat violently at the sight.

"This is where our task ends," Deng said, handing me the basket. "We've got to get back as quickly as possible now, before anyone discovers we're here. The way back is long, but we know it like our own faces."

He apologized for sinking the robe, and told me to be careful, as I was dressed in clothes like theirs.

Night was about to fall. I crept toward the camp intently, like a thief. I was worried that this was a different barracks, and not the one I knew. I heard a sudden movement behind me, and before I could turn around I felt a violent blow on my head, and lost consciousness.

I woke up in a dark place and felt hard ground beneath me, my head throbbing from the blow. I could see nothing, not even my own hands.

My feet were shackled. I felt thirsty and wanted to vomit. Had everything simply been a dream? Had I never left the camp at all? I did not know.

Two guards entered at dawn. They got me up and took me away. I felt exhausted. I was questioned by someone I didn't recognize. Voices spoke to me in Arabic, and I answered them. I told them my name and the name of my unit, and said that I had no idea what had happened the past few weeks. I told them I didn't know the name of the area the army had taken us to, but that I had lost my fellow soldiers there, and that I had stayed in a village called Sumit, where I had been treated well. I said that I had only suffered on my way back.

They asked about my weapon, and threatened me with a court-martial for losing it. They also asked about the strange clothes I'd been wearing, then threatened to court-martial me for being a deserter. I answered the same questions over and over again—dozens of times.

The interrogation continued for days, and became increasing rough. They ordered me to stand during all of it, without any pity for how exhausted I was or my need for sleep. They put me in an isolated cell that looked onto a square courtyard. Three sides of that courtyard were lined with more cells. I saw terrified swollen faces in tattered clothes: disgusting robes or threadbare uniforms, long unkempt beards, dirty nails, and lacerated hands that seemed to be begging me, as if I'd come to save them. I could hear tortured voices coming from somewhere—I'm not sure where. The heat and humidity were suffocating, and the air was filled with conceit and cruelty. People in army uniforms were rushing here and there with papers and files. I heard the same two words hundreds of times: "Attention!" and "Dismissed!" They often made me stand up like a statue in my cell.

The interrogation officer was polished and clean-shaven, and was decked out in full military pomp. He looked peaceful, but his outward appearance belied his cruelty. I didn't know his exact rank. His chest was covered with decorations and gleaming medals, almost certainly from a war he had not fought. When they brought me to him wearing my strange clothes, he ignored me entirely and continued barking out meaningless orders to his guard, making a big show of it. He wanted me to know that he was god here. He shouted and looked around, then repeated the same order to another guard, as if it were the most important thing in the world. Then he looked at me suddenly, and yelled as if he had just seen a rat.

"What's this?"

"This is the recruit Hamza, sir—the deserter," one of the soldiers answered in a trembling voice.

"And what's he doing here?"

"These were your excellency's orders," he said in an even more trembling voice.

He leered at me, the sweat pouring from him; anytime he said a word, spit sprayed from his mouth. He looked monstrous now, nothing like the peaceful man I had just seen. He started shouting again, "They're all queers and sons-of-bitches! We know how to deal with this type of swine!"

He pulled his jacket over his large belly and straightened the beret on his head. He shook the stick he was holding, then yelled roughly at the soldiers, "Dismissed!"

The four young recruits in the room all left. One of the soldiers was very fat; the poor guy was panting from the midday heat. He'd been running this way and that, trying to carry out the quick haphazard orders. His chest was drenched, and there were two large sweat stains beneath his armpits. He wheezed like someone suffering from asthma.

The officer feigned gentleness, and with a smile on his face asked me to take a seat. He was done demonstrating the awesome power of his position.

"I know that you got into trouble and deserted your company," he said. "I know you were only pretending to be tired. And you know the punishment for this: you'll be executed by the firing squad after a court-martial. We're in a state of emergency, after all, and can't be lenient toward deserters and traitors of the homeland."

He finished this threatening speech and leered at me to see the effect of his words. I was exhausted and slow to react. This nightmare seemed so boring to me, and I had no desire to think about anything. Sensing a preliminary victory in my despair, the officer continued his rant:

"It's time for you to confess. Confess that you conspired with them and came to us as a spy. By God, why else would those barbarians let you come back so easily? And then there's the fact that you spent quite a long time with them. You must have told them our plans, and perhaps they told you theirs, too. Confess, and I'll guarantee you a fair trial—you'll be dismissed from the army, nothing more."

The officer had enough experience to tell that I wouldn't confess, and that flashing his rank and fabricating charges like this was hopeless. He started shouting again, and this time the spit flew at my face. He cursed and swore at my mother and father with the vilest expressions. He cursed the dusty ill-fated day on which I and the likes of me were born. He looked completely different now. His eyeballs bulged out of their sockets, as if a mountain were pressing into his chest. Suddenly, with all his strength, he punched me in the stomach, and I doubled over in pain. He followed up the blow by kicking at my skull with his enormous military boots. I could see the neon light on the ceiling, and also the dizzying fan spinning there. My eyes spun with it until I lost consciousness.

At either dawn or dusk—I wasn't sure which—I found myself lying on hot concrete. I could hear voices crying out in pain, and the clanging of chains and shackles. For a moment, I didn't know where I was. Had the boa actually bitten me? Or had Sharif suddenly turned against me? He'd showed me such kindness—had it all been a trap, a cunning attempt on his part to lure me in? How had the comfortable hut become this concrete ground and these iron bars? Where did these dirty walls covered in scribbles come from? I tried to get up, but fell back down weakly, hitting my temple on the ground.

It took me a long time to gather my shaken thoughts, to realize that I was somewhere else, and that this was not Sharif's guest room, but that I was in fact in a cell under the command of that mad officer. The courtyard was in front of me, and it smelled damp and rotten here. The poor fat soldier was running around from place to place, following his strict orders.

What had happened was real, then.

I was in a two-meter by two-meter square cell. Three sides of it were concrete walls, and the fourth was a row of iron bars with a door that had two huge locks. A tattered sackcloth served as a bed in a corner of the cell, and there was also a bucket with some filthy water in it.

I felt pain in every centimeter of my body, and I had swellings and abrasions in several places. I remembered the angry blow that idiotic officer dealt me. Yet now I could see that he had vented his anger even more liberally while I was unconscious. It took me a long time to stand up, but when I finally made it I saw that my right foot was chained to a heavy iron ball. I dragged it along with difficulty until I was standing at the iron bars. Even if I did manage to escape from this cell, there was no way to walk more than a hundred meters in a whole day with such a weight on me.

One absurd day followed the next, until I was no longer able to count them or tell them apart. They kept repeating the same ridiculous interrogation, to no avail, each one ending with a beating before they returned me to my cell. A soldier brought each of us a piece of dried bread every morning. And the bucket of filthy water was replaced every other day—if the soldier remembered, that is. We all drank like animals, and every one of us prisoners was forced to turn a corner of his cell into a toilet.

Once, the bucket accidentally slipped out of my hands, and I spent an entire day without water. I felt as if I were dying of thirst. I called to a passing soldier, begging him for water, but he didn't even look at me, as if he were deaf. I repeated this scene with a second one, who acted in exactly the same way. It was as if I were trapped in a nightmare, and had no voice. I repeated my request to the wheezing overweight soldier. He turned to me without replying. How comforting that was! I felt that I existed. He stopped for a moment, and looked at me from a distance. He gave me a couple of short and nervous signals that I didn't understand. Perhaps he wanted me to quiet down. I did, and sat waiting, silently. After a while, I saw the fat soldier panting and bringing a rusty bucket with turbid water in it—it reminded me of Sheikh al-Faki's holy water. He put it down and gave me a strange look whose import I couldn't understand. There was no mug or cup, or any kind of receptacle I could drink with. My hands were swollen and I had no control over them, but I was dying of thirst. So I dipped my head into the bucket and drank straight from it like a cow. It was the foulest water I've ever had. Then I sat down and leaned my head on the wall, looking out at the courtyard with my one good eye. I had thought it was dawn, but I was wrong. Darkness fell a few moments later and dressed the place in desolation, while pained and tortured voices struggled here and there. I fell asleep right where I was sitting.

The next day, I woke to a disturbing din. One of the guards was walking by and dragging an iron rod against the bars of all the cells. I sat up feebly and with difficulty. All of the prisoners in the cells were standing behind the bars and staring out into the courtyard. The soldier who was making that racket came and told me to stand up. I could see the bruised and swollen faces of the prisoners, and I remember thinking that my face must look the same. I pulled myself together, stood up, and approached the bars. My neighbor in the cell to the right of mine said that it was just a show.

"What do you mean by 'show?'" I asked him.

He looked at me and let out a short laugh, half in derision and half in despair. "You'll see!" he said.

It wasn't long before the officer-god came out puffed up like a peacock in his uniform and dark glasses. The guards rushed to set up a chair for him in a shaded corner they had prepared with army blankets, and then stood behind him like statues. The officer sat down and tapped his thigh with his stick.

I watched the show: it was absurd, meaningless. They had tied the neck of one of the prisoners—an old white-haired man—to a long rope, and the soldier in charge of the torture dragged him out like an animal to the middle of the courtyard. I felt pity for the old man who was being dragged along like this. Half of his ribs were visible, as if he were from Wad al-Nar. The soldier stopped for a moment, then started running, and then stopped again. . . . He kept at this with the old man behind him, while the officer watched the game in joy and kept beating his thigh with that stick of his and yelling out obscenities. The rest of the soldiers laughed whenever he laughed, like an orderly military choir. And we stood there all the while—for we weren't allowed to sit down watching from behind our bars at the other end of the courtyard.

The story of that torture is a long one. I buried it in my memory, and don't want to bring back its details now.

I escaped with a very unlikely candidate: the fat soldier whose name I didn't even know. He had confided to me that they would be shipping me off very soon to some other place for my court-martial.

We escaped together at dawn one day. Two weeks earlier, he had given me a file to remove the chain of the iron ball. I'd spent several nights silently filing away at it. The traces of that chain are still visible around my ankle, like a white birthmark.

I'll never forget that guard. We escaped on the officer's day off, the one day of the week on which he didn't get up until noon. Most of the other guards also got up late that day. The guard had already made sure that I'd broken open the chain, but that I'd left it attached to trick the others. He came to me that morning, panting as always, and calmly opened the door to my cell. He pulled me out while I trailed the iron ball behind me, and treated me harshly so that none of the other guards would notice what was happening. When we made it behind the cells, I unfastened the ball and chain, and we ran together for over two hours. Then he described the way to the closest safe place for me, and said that we had to part ways now. He didn't explain himself, or say another word. But he embraced me warmly, still sweating and panting. Yet he didn't smell like sweat, even though he was drenched in it. His smell was not unfamiliar to me. It immediately reminded me of the goat that day back in Wad al-Nar—it was the smell of molasses. I stood there staring at him breathlessly. Before I could recover from my surprise, he pressed Sharif's stone into my hand, then handed me the container for Sheikh Hamad al-Nil. I couldn't believe it; I was so overwhelmed by it all. While I looked in wonder at what was in my hands, he started off. I watched him bound through the brush and into the distance with incredible lightness. For a moment, he even looked like a goat. Had it come back in this form to save me? It all seemed like magic to me, like some sort of enchantment.

I had to take that path; I had to follow the path of enchantment to its end and see how that end would be. It couldn't be any worse than what had already happened.

I break off my story for a moment here. Sandra hasn't eaten any breakfast, and neither have I, and the tea's become cold. I can see tears in her eyes. I kiss them away, saying, "I don't want to ever see your tears. I know my story's a bit tragic, but I'm still alive, and I'm still trying to live. I'm here now, with you, and that's enough for me. Do you know why I don't tell anyone my story? It's because I'm afraid people will feel sorry for me. I hate pity."

"But your life's been so sad."

"Then I won't tell you the rest of my story."

"No, please—I want to hear it."

"Do you promise not to cry?"

"I'll try. But what happened after you escaped? Where did you go? And what happened to the guard you were with?"

"That's a long story. I'll tell you the most important parts of it, which begin after I arrived back in Khartoum. But should we make some more tea first?"

I don't know how Sandra manages to make the tea so quickly. She comes back like lightning. Not wanting to keep her in suspense, I continue my story.

I returned to Khartoum via all the modes of transportation that God created for us, and all the man-made ones as well. I avoided the military police. I managed to get a robe. I drank from public fountains and ate anything I found along the way. It took me several days to make it to Khartoum. I had nothing in my pockets except the flat stone from Sharif—which was my only possession in all this vast country—and the small container that was in my charge.

I didn't know whom to turn to in this large city, this city that had shut its heart in my face. I no longer trusted anyone except al-Khattaf, so I went to the gas station, making a detour to keep well away from the Whale Sheikh's courtyard. I saw al-Khattaf doing the same work as before, with the same oil-spattered clothes and grease-covered hands. It was as if I'd never left the place, and as if he were doing some eternal job that had no end.

He was overjoyed to see me. He apologized for the last time: he'd been forced to rush home, for his wife had given birth to his first child—a girl—that day, and he didn't know what to do. I was happy to hear the news, and congratulated him.

"What did you name her?" I asked him.

"Sumayya!"

"A beautiful name!"

"Sumayya Izz al-Din al-Safi."

"You've got such a wonderful name, and we've been calling you al-Khattaf—'the snatcher'—all this time!"

"That's the way of the world, Hamza."

He listened to my whole story, cursing the Whale and the day that we met him, then told me a long story about the changes the Whale had undergone.

Al-Khattaf—or Izz al-Din al-Safi—found me a place to stay at the gas station where he worked. Since I needed money, he told me that I could work with him, for there were a lot of rush jobs at the workshop, and they didn't require much skill: I could change tires, wash cars, and do oil changes. He said he needed someone to help him, and that the owner trusted him and would let him take me on without asking any questions. The two other workers there didn't mind if a fourth person worked with them, for all of them had a fixed salary, and a fourth person might make their jobs easier, and even give them a certain feeling of seniority. I slept at the far end of the workshop, staying in a cramped room that was itself within a larger room. It was a clean space, and none of the others entered it if they were covered in grease or oil. Al-Khattaf told me that he used to sleep there when he was still a bachelor.

Although the smell of gasoline and oil filled the room, it was heaven to someone who had just escaped from a military prison, and was a paradise for someone who had just had a stay of execution. Al-Khattaf made sure I worked only in the interior workshop. I mended tires, and also cleaned and fixed up spare parts. I realized he didn't want to give me too many responsibilities, for he knew very well that this was only a temporary job for me.

Al-Khattaf gave me the most lovely gift imaginable during my first week there. He had gone to the Whale's courtyard and somehow gotten my bag from Abil. I found it in the middle of my room one morning after I woke up. He would never tell me how he managed to get it, and every time I asked him, he simply laughed and said, "Abu al-Nar, they don't call me al-Khattaf for nothing!"

One morning, I told him that I was going out on an errand, and that I'd be back in the evening. I hadn't forgotten the address I had memorized from Sharif. I went there, carrying the small container with me. Hamad al-Nil was a dignified man, and quite advanced in years. He gave me a kind welcome, and I told him my long story. He wanted me to stay as his guest, but I reminded him that I had work to get back to. He thanked me for the gift, and treated me with great affection, telling me to come back anytime I wanted, or if I ever needed anything. I thanked him and returned to the gas station, relieved to have delivered my charge, and to have met someone who made a kind impression on me in that brutal time of my life.

I worked there for nearly three months. The military police had set up a new checkpoint near the gas station, which made leaving late at night almost impossible for me. Al-Khattaf thought it best that I go somewhere else. I had saved up a little money by then, which I kept in an old tire that served as part of my bed in the corner of my room.

I had made up my mind to return to Wad al Nar. I was resolved to say goodbye to my mother and Halima and Karima one last time, and then to look for a way out of this country. My place was no longer here. No place that truly loves you can torture you at the same time. I had to leave. I had no family or relatives here. No one would cry if I left, and no one would miss me. I was nothing here, and it made no difference to anyone whether I stayed or not. Let me leave, then. Perhaps I needed to leave to gather up the scattered fragments of my soul.

I told al-Khattaf of my plans, and he insisted on giving me some money. That evening, he pulled out all the stops to give it to me, saying that the small sum was for the rest of the work I had done, and not charity. I didn't feel comfortable taking it, but he swore to divorce his wife if I didn't, so I finally agreed. I refused to take any more than half of it, however, for he was wearing himself out at work, and now had a family to provide for in these hard times.

I said goodbye to him on the morning of a hot day, carrying my bag made of palm fronds: the three stones were in it, along with Sharif's stone, a spare robe, and some underclothes. My money was in a pouch tied to my waist beneath my robe. I started off toward my destination.

The heat was cruel that day. The people of this country must surely have their fair share of heaven in the afterlife, after living all their lives patiently in this inferno. None of my attempts at warding off the sun succeeded—it had settled above my head and chosen me as its prey, the sun that sometimes seems to forget for days on end to go anywhere else in the whole wide world. It remained there, above our heads, for hours, watching our torture lazily and indifferently. There was no shade anywhere, not even on the streets. It was as if all things and all living creatures had swallowed their shadows. Who could imagine such an inferno? The sun that faraway people long for as a form of mercy was the cruelest of tortures in this place. I was so miserable that day. It was impossible to tell whether it was still morning or now afternoon. The people were grumbling as they walked about, cursing and becoming upset over the most trivial things. The storekeepers kept their doors half-shut, and were sleeping or dozing inside.

A penetrating smell was coming from somewhere, but there was no one near me. It was the same distinct smell—the smell of molasses—that had come out of the mouth of that goat the day it put its warm nose on my forehead and let out that strange raspy sound. The smell immediately reminded me of Wad al-Nar, and also of the soldier who had saved me from execution, and whose name I never discovered. Was he nearby now? I couldn't manage to escape into more tender memories. Nor could I manage to numb my mind with oblivion. The heat was mercilessly pouring its wrath onto my head, searing and convulsing the earth. The asphalt seemed to quiver, as did the people. Everything was swaying. The exhaust fumes of the slow cars rose into the air, adding to the convulsions. I felt as if I was standing in front of an oven—or rather, inside one. My body shed its copious tears, but my eyes remained dry.

Suddenly, a man walking quickly on the other side of the street caught my attention. There was a woman at his side carrying something. I recognized the way he walked.

"Father! Father! Abu Hamza! Yousef!" I yelled.

The man turned toward me. It was my father. Why didn't he answer? I hurried across the street toward him, and felt a painful blow. As I slowly lost consciousness, my eyes were fixed on Yousef—on my father.

The world was cloudy. I felt a shudder pass through me. I couldn't understand this dream, this nightmare. A young nurse was standing over me. In comparison to the rest of her body, her head looked like a large balloon. I thought she must be one of those angels who thrust the damned into Hell. She drew closer to look at me, and smiled, baring her teeth like a zebra.

"Doctor! Doctor!" she called. "The patient Wad Nilawi has opened his eyes!"

She was yelling as if she were at the souk. The doctor rushed over to me, and stood there looking at me with his enormous head and his huge glasses.

"What's your name?" he asked me.

I gave him another name, fearing that I might be at a military barracks, "Jibril Shal al-Bahr."

"Do you have any family or relatives we can contact?"

"No. I'm from the oasis of Salima in the north. I don't have any relatives in Khartoum . . . . What happened? Where am I?"

"God protected you! We'd lost hope that you'd come back to life. You were hit by an army car two days ago and went into a coma. We don't have an intensive care room here, so we brought you down to the basement by the morgue, where it's cooler, and treated you with cold water once every hour."

I tried to get up, but the room spun around me, as did the fan on the ceiling. Its languid rotations reminded me of the fan in the prison camp. They took me up to the higher floor. I had become something of a wonder to the doctors. They examined me, not to check on how

I was feeling, but rather to make sure that all of my organs were still functioning after the coma. They laughed, and marveled at my state. I was emaciated. In this gaunt body, I truly was one of Wad al-Nar's sons.

There was a lot of talk around me. They told me I'd been delirious in the first few hours when I arrived at the emergency room, and that I had kept repeating "Wad Nilawi." They gave me several injections after they told me this, and it seemed as if each one made me feel weaker. The light began to fade, and I fell asleep.

I was still exhausted when I woke up. I thought about my bag and the money that I'd had with me. They must have been lost on the street. I asked the nurse about them, and she said, "Your bag's in a safe place. They also found a leather pouch around your waist with some money in it, and that's being kept safe as well. You'll get it all back once you've recovered."

In the evening, between delirium and wakefulness, and amid the smell of medication and anesthesia, I had a strange dream.

Suddenly, a man walking quickly on the other side of the street catches my attention. There's a woman beside him with enchanting hair that flows out from beneath her shawl. She's carrying a baby boy in her arms, and a young girl with two long, thick pigtails is walking between her and the man. I recognize the way the man walks. It's him. It's my father. The street lies between us, and cars are rolling by loudly and spewing out an absurd amount of exhaust fumes. I stand there, astonished and drenched in sweat. In the loudest voice I have, I cry out, "Father! Father! Father! Abu Hamza, Abu Hamza! Abu Karima! Abu Halima!" And for the first time in my life, I call him by his real name as well, "Yousef! Yousef Wad Nilawi! Yousef!"

The man turns around. I can almost make out his features, but a large passing truck hides him from my sight. Then he appears again. It's him, my father. Why doesn't he answer? Why is he looking at me tensely like that? I gravitate toward him, rushing into the middle of the street. Then I feel pain, a pain more intense than the kick of that haughty officer's boot in the military prison. I slowly lose consciousness, my eyes glued to Yousef Wad Nilawi and the others with him. I can smell the awful stench of the asphalt. I can smell my own skin, as if it were burning. I see feet and boots, and hear voices around me. I must be in that Hell that Sheikh al-Faki had gone on about at such length. Yes. I'm in hell now.

I was a celebrity at that hospital. They started calling me 'Jibril of Seven Lives.' I got better as the days went by. I wanted to recover quickly so I could get out of this hellish city as soon as possible. And I got what I wanted.

I finally arrived at the village of Wad al-Kababish. I thought I would never see this place again, after all that I had been through.

I got out of the van, and trod on the sand that was so close to Wad al-Nar. I took off my sandals and closed my eyes for a bit, feeling the ground with the soles of my feet. The ground was flat here, and there were no traces of man on it. Once again, I had the feeling that I was the first person to pass by this place, and that these were virgin sands. I felt as if I'd emerged from hell out into this world, or as if I'd alighted here from the sky.

My sandals were what brought me back to reality; there was no way I'd come from the sky wearing sandals like these.

8

At the thought of my sandals descending from the sky, Sandra laughs until tears start streaming down her face, and I laugh with her. Hakima pounces onto the bed, as if to join us in our laughter. She meows in that loud familiar way of hers.

"Maybe she's hungry?" Sandra asks me.

"No, I don't think so. She always acts like this whenever I start laughing."

"What do you think she wants?"

"Maybe she wants me to keep laughing. Or maybe she wants me to stop!"

Sandra laughs again and strokes Hakima's soft fur. Hakima purrs and turns herself round and round to have as much of her body massaged as possible.

"I'll bring you some food," Sandra says, addressing her directly.

Hakima lets out several long meows in quick succession. We laugh again, as if to cover up the sadness of my story and get rid of this atmosphere of pain. Sandra jumps out of the bed and into the kitchen to get some food for Hakima. Feeling warm and secure, I fall into a gentle sleep.

I wake up to see Sandra sitting in a rocking chair and reading a book, with Hakima on her lap. I'm not sure how long I was asleep. I want to watch Sandra in peace, so I remain motionless, feigning sleep. My mind still isn't sure if I'm actually awake, and wants to be certain. But my heart wants something else, and I obey my heart. Sandra looks over at me several times, but it's dark where I'm lying, and she can't tell whether I'm awake or not. Hakima is more cunning, however, and can see that I'm up from my movements, so she jumps onto the bed and I start laughing. Sandra comes over to me as well.

"Aren't you hungry yet?" she asks.

"I could eat both of you right now!"

"I'll make some food quickly. I want to hear the rest of the story. I want—"

"And I want to eat you!" I say, cutting her off with a kiss and embracing her.

"I'll be right back—I'm just going to make some spaghetti. Please don't fall asleep again!"

I nod in agreement, then drop my head onto the pillow theatrically and pretend to snore loudly, and we start laughing again. I get up to go help her in the kitchen, apologizing for my laziness. We make the meal together and then eat. Sandra suggests that we go out to have a coffee somewhere peaceful, so we head to a place called the Amerlinghaus, a small garden with a restaurant and a café. Sandra tells me that they have literary and artistic events here, and that it used to be the home of a painter of the same name: Amerling.

We pick a quiet spot in the corner. Our drinks arrive: two large mugs of drip coffee with milk. I don't wait for her next question—before she can even get one out, I retell the part of the story about the sandals to lighten the mood a bit. This would later become a running joke for us, to the point that I'd even wear my sandals if I were running late to meet her. When she'd ask me where I was, I'd point to the sandals and tell her that I'd come straight from the sky.

I start telling my story again.

I arrived at the village of Wad al-Kababish after an exhausting trip. I greeted the people who knew me and told them many stories about my absence. But none of those stories were true, and no two stories were alike.

I left my bag with Khala Thuraya, who considered me almost a son to her. I packed a small bundle of bread and dates, and slung a waterskin over my shoulder: the same necessities as always. That day, I walked once more in my wide white robe through the village of Wad al-Kababish, like the mast of a ship without a single gust of wind, heading into the distance.

I came back again to say goodbye to my mother Habiba bit Nur al-Din al-Shilani, and to Karima and Halima. The way there was the same as before. Everything was the same as before. It was as if time were simply repeating itself.

I spent the whole day at Wad al-Nar, sitting by myself and singing. I fell asleep there, and had the same old dreams. But I was clinging so firmly to my mother and sisters that they came to me in one of my dreams. I greeted them lovingly, and said my goodbyes. When I woke up, I felt relieved, but also a little anxious. There was dust in my eyes, and I wiped them clean.

I went back to Wad al-Kababish, trying not to step on all the bones. The ravens joined me.

I slept in Khala Thuraya's courtyard for a couple days, waiting for the only van that took people to the north to come. I wanted everything to happen quickly, for I can't stand goodbyes, and I couldn't bear to look at all those things dying; nor could I hold up under memory's failure to bring back the faces of those I had loved.

The day came. I said goodbye to Khala Thuraya and told her I hoped things got better for her. I picked up the bag with all my worldly possessions: the three burial stones and Sharif's stone. And I also dragged the burden of many long years with me.

I took the same van as before, with the same driver, and left Wad al-Kababish with a fair number of people, most of them women and children. The passengers looked downcast and bereaved. They had crammed their bags and large bundles in with them for a journey of misery to the north. We were pressed together like sardines in a can. This time, I was in the back with the passengers, in the middle of the luggage and all the tattered worthless things the others had with them—the travel necessities for these destitute refugees who would never come back to the land where they were born and where they had lived. They would die in a new land, bereft of any real will to live. Yet they'd carry on, vainly hoping for the return of that which would not return.

I was afraid of us being stopped by the military police on this trip. I was worried they'd pounce on us like hyenas, and send me off to some pit that no one knows about—no one would even know I was gone.

The van's feverish old motor was screeching rhythmically, now getting louder and now falling silent, and then starting up again with its strenuous groans. There was a baby girl in the van who wouldn't stop crying. Her mother tried to breast-feed her, but she refused. She had a fever, and the road was rough and uneven. Her father sat beside her with three other children: young girls who were all older than her, and whose faces bore a permanent expression of fear. From my corner of the van, I watched the sweat on the face of that poor infant, and listened to her painful groans. The father was trying to feed the three young girls, who were chewing their food slowly, their eyes glued to their baby sister. The mother was trying to hide her tears from the girls. I started singing to myself—I don't why. Perhaps it was my own subconscious way of weeping. I sang louder, trying to drown out the noise of the crazed engine and allay the children's fears. The baby quieted down, and the tension gradually diminished. I sang and sang, not stopping for breath, as if I were now the one with the fever.

Every few minutes, the father went over to the mother and whispered in her ears. He put his palm on the baby's forehead, and then went back and embraced the three girls, who were calmer now. The other passengers began to dispense advice to the mother and father. They felt their own pain in the baby's crying. Some of them stared nervously into space, and others looked downcast and lethargic as they gazed out into the unknown, waiting. I kept on singing, and suddenly noticed that the baby was asleep. The passengers lowered their voices, but the feverish noise of the engine flared up. The mother was caressing her baby's head, which yielded completely to her touch, and lifted her onto her right side, and then her left. She barked at her husband to leave her and the baby in peace, instead of restlessly getting up every minute to check on her. The man stayed where he was, but his worry was still there. The three girls were looking at me. I wanted them to know that I was singing for them. At that moment, I saw their mother's face covered in sweat in a way I'd never seen before. But it wasn't sweat. Those were tears streaming down her face. The tone of my voice changed and started rattling—seizing up and quivering—but I didn't stop singing. I wanted one of the passengers to yell at me to stop, or to pick a fight with me or anyone else in the van. But they were all defeated and covered in dust, despondently traveling together toward an unknown fate.

The mother was weeping over her baby. The man rushed to her and picked up the child, shaking her like a toy. He kept on shaking her out of shock, then finally stopped, put his hand on her head, and muttered some unclear words and embraced her. The mother began to wail and sob, her whole body convulsing. I went over to the three girls to try to distract them. I asked them what their names were: Inas, Basma, and Halima. They seemed close enough in age to be triplets, so I asked them how old they were: they were four, five, and seven years old, respectively. Then I asked them the same questions all over again, as if I hadn't understood, or hadn't paid attention.

The mother cried out in a piercing voice, "Zahra is gone! . . . O Nur, you poor mother! God had mercy on her! God had mercy on her! Have mercy on us all, God! Have mercy on us as you had mercy on Zahra!"

The father was sobbing uncontrollably, utterly powerless. I never saw a man cry so submissively before. The other men went over to try to calm him down and remind him of God, "There's no power or might save in God the great, the exalted," they said. "To God we belong and to God we return." "Ask God for forgiveness!" "The Fatiha on the living and the dead!" "God, we ask for your mercy and forgiveness, and that you be pleased with us!" "God, lighten our hardships and bestow your vast mercy on us!" "There is no god but God!" "There is no god but God!"

The women were lamenting the deceased as well. And all of this was happening while the van kept on going, shaking and jolting. One of the passengers knocked violently on the glass to alert the driver, who didn't want to stop. But after more banging on the glass, he finally brought the car to a shaky halt almost a full kilometer further on. He thought that someone wanted to relieve themselves, and got out cursing and swearing. But when he saw the speechless indignation and anger on the faces, as well as the stricken mother sobbing, he fell into an uneasy silence. Everyone got out of the van saying "In the name of God" and asking God's protection from the Devil. The driver muttered a few incomprehensible words, and stepped out of the way to have a smoke by himself.

The mother wanted to take the dead child with her. The madness of that idea worried the father: they couldn't bring the child with them in that heat. They didn't even know where their journey would end. He wasn't sure how to deal with his wife, who was still clinging to her baby. The men tried to calm the woman down and convince her that the child should be buried as quickly as possible. They said that burial was a way of honoring the dead, and that mercy demands it be done quickly. But she was delirious, and all her anger at the world came out in insults and curses as she clung even more ferociously to her daughter. After more than a half-hour of this, she finally calmed down a bit. No one knew what to do. The driver had stopped smoking, but had started chewing some tobacco instead, for this was the only way he could keep spitting without arousing everyone's anger. The mother was obstinate, and vowed to take her child with her until she reached "the land of God"—that's what she called the city. They tried to break her resolve, but she paid them no heed. Things got more heated, with the women taking the mother's side, while the men were all for a quick burial.

I left the place. My steps grew longer, and I kept walking until their arguments were only a distant muddled tumult. Then the noise stopped completely for a moment, and suddenly I could hear them yelling "Allahu akbar!" The words came to me on the wind, a chanting in the distance. They had begun the funeral prayer. Dirt kicked up into my eyes, and hot dusty water streamed from them. My breath was a choking rattle. Yet I didn't feel the oppressive heat in that world of loss. I'm not sure how much time passed while I wandered aimlessly in that desert. I felt as if my own soul were being taken from me as I walked, or as if were somehow leaving the soul of this world.

Once again, I found myself in the middle of the desert, in that place where there's no trace of animal or man, and where the flat windswept ground only takes on a single color. In the middle of that desert, you look for your shadow but cannot find it. You feel as if you're outside the world there: in the afterlife, or in some kind of eternity. Your feet leave no trace on the ground to remind you of even the nearest past. Everything seems wiped clean in that place, but it's no virgin earth—it simply swallows up the marks of those who came before. We were in the emptiest of voids: that's what life was for us.

As I emerged from the half-conscious state I'd entered in that heat, I heard their voices. They'd been calling me. I stopped and looked back, and saw a group of people moving and shaking as in a mirage, the color there slightly darker than the color of the desert. I headed back. My feet had left no marks on the sand. And there wasn't a single trace of the sweat that had been pouring from me during the walk, nor of that hot and salty water that the wind had been causing to stream from my eyes. I headed back as if I were simply continuing on my way. It was all the same. I was walking in the void: there was void before me, and void behind me; a void beneath me and above me.

Everyone was standing in silence near the van. I was about two hundred meters away, but some of them kept waving to me as I approached, as if a whole kilometer still lay between us. The women were propping up the stricken and exhausted mother. The children looked like gaunt specters, and everyone was covered in dust. All of them, and the van with them, were the same color. But a little bit away from the van, I could see a small mound of dirt that had just been sprinkled with water, and whose color was not that of the void. It was the only other thing I could make out in that vast desert.

The silence drowned out everything in that miserable van, where anxious eyes opened onto worlds of sorrow and frustration. It was as if our road had begun anew from that dead landmark left in the desert, shrouded in dust and water, and protected by a prayer spoken hastily in the midday heat. The way was long and grueling, but we reached the end at last.

We arrived at the city station, and everyone got out. I said goodbye to Halima and her two sisters. And I said goodbye to her mother and father as well, and wished them the strength to endure. It seemed that the father wanted to tell me something, but the words only rattled in his throat.

My bag had become heavier since leaving Wad al-Nar, though I'd put nothing new in it.

I went to the station to find al-Khattaf, but he wasn't in the workshop at that late hour of the night. No one opened when I tried knocking on the window of the back room, so I looked for the spare key we kept hidden beneath a bunch of old tires just outside the workshop. I went in, closing the door behind me. I tried to pretend that I hadn't left this place since the last time I was here, that what had happened was merely a delusion or some confused dream, but it didn't work. I was exhausted, and slept like a dead man until I felt someone shaking me in the morning. I woke up, terrified. I wasn't used to waking up like that. Yet it seemed that this too was becoming a part of my horrible situation—waking up terrified of some new disaster that my nerves could not bear.

Al-Khattaf was laughing as he shook me gently. I got up and happily embraced him while he poured his loud greetings straight into my chest. I asked him about his daughter Sumayya. He told me about her with great joy, and showed me a picture of a beautiful girl. I wished her good fortune in these evil times. He slapped me gratefully on the back, and asked, "When will you do it? When will you get married, Abu al-Nar?"

I laughed and said, "People like me don't have that luxury. I'm scattered all across the world."

"In that case, we'll have to wait for Isis to come and pick up your pieces," he said, startling me with his quick and witty reply. I wondered how al-Khattaf knew about that legend. I'd read about it in an Arabic book when I lived in an old house in France, where a bunch of us had worked at a vineyard. The book was translated from French and filled with references and footnotes in some European language—presumably French. I devoured that fascinating book back then, for it was the only Arabic one we had. *Queens that Ruled and Kings that Dreamed* was its strange and fascinating title. I read it twice, and wish I could have taken it with me when I left.

I asked al-Khattaf about his work, and how things were in general. He sighed and said, "Nothing has changed, Abu al-Nar, though everything has changed."

He had prepared breakfast: fuul with cheese, tahini, watercress, and tomatoes, along with a couple of limes and some bread. I was hungry. I got up quickly to brush my teeth and wash my face, then sat down and ate with him, telling him about the past few days. I tried to hide the sad and painful events as much as possible, so my story seemed quite abbreviated.

I told al-Khattaf that I wanted to leave the country, and he promised to help me. I spent the next two days at the workshop, hardly leaving the place. But on the third day I made the visit I had promised to Hamad al-Nil, that kind and dignified man who had given me such a friendly welcome, and who had listened to my story when I brought him the gift from Sharif. This time, he asked me if I wanted to work with him at his sesame mill. It didn't take me long to convince him that it was impossible for me to stay. I'd already made up my mind, and had promised myself that I would leave. He disappeared for a few moments, then came back and put a bunch of money in my hand. I stubbornly refused, and a strange trace of sadness appeared on his face: a look of admonition and embarrassment, coupled with the gaze of a kindhearted grandfather. I didn't want to be harsh, so I reluctantly accepted the money. I could tell that it was a very large sum. I hesitated to put it in my pocket, wanting to give him part of it back. "A third of this would be enough to get me to the moon!" I said.

"Then go to Mars, Hamza, and don't come back too quickly!" We both laughed, and he continued, "If you leave this country, leave it from the west, passing by the Salima Oasis. And if you make it there safely, ask for Burhan Wad Qandil al-Jammal. Give him my greetings, and tell him I sent you."

It was a short visit, but a warm and comforting one.

In the evening, I told al-Khattaf that I wanted to leave this hellhole as soon as possible. I was surprised when he got up and picked up an old dusty case. He opened it and, like a magician, pulled out a passport for me. It looked real, and had an old photo of me in it, which he had cut out of a picture our old group had taken together. This was the second time he had surprised me. It was as if he had read my mind. "This is more than just a passport, Hamza," he said. "It's your ticket out of here."

The next morning, I packed the three stones in my bag, as well as the stone Sharif had given me—the stone I had promised to some day return to its rightful place. I also packed two robes, some underclothes, a pair of sandals, and a pair of shoes. Al-Khattaf gave me a picture of his daughter Sumayya, saying, "Take it with you so you don't forget her!"

This parting was like all the others in my life. I set out on that hot and hazy morning, looking at the world as if for the last time. I left like someone fleeing one execution only to head to another.

Al-Khattaf had generously planned out my route to the Salima Oasis, for I couldn't legally leave the country without a certificate exempting me from military service. He had arranged for a small car to take me northward from the capital through Shendi and Atbara, and then westward, following the curve of the Nile, through al-Dabbah until we reached Dongola. From there, I was to cross the Nile into the region called Koosha, and proceed on to the Salima Oasis. Back when I'd been in the hospital, I had told the staff there that I was from Salima, without really knowing where it was at the time.

I reached the Salima Oasis after a journey that was just like all the others. I asked after Burhan Wad Qandil al-Jammal, and was taken to him. He was an old man, but had the vigorous body of someone much younger. Short, cheerful, and respected by all, he was a camel trader with great influence. He was happy to learn that Hamad al-Nil had sent me, and asked how he was doing, saying that he hadn't seen him for six years.

I gave him the abridged version of my long story, ending with my desire to leave the country. "A caravan will be leaving here seven days from now," he said. "I'll have you go with them, and I'll make sure everything is taken care of."

The people there asked me the same questions over and over again, "Where are you from?" and "Where are you going?" I didn't lie. I made many friends in those seven days. They trusted me, and welcomed me even more after they saw the warm welcome that Burhan Wad Qandil al-Jammal had given me. I was able to relax in that remote place that had not yet been invaded by the olive green color. And I was touched by the rich simplicity of people's lives there.

Once the caravan of camel traders had finished their preparations for the trip to Egypt, Burhan al-Jammal placed me in their care. Their camels would be sold in Egypt, and they had gotten them ready, checking to see that were healthy and strong enough for the long journey. They had me ride a very robust camel, and asked me to feed and water him in days leading up to the trip so that he would get used to me. They told me his name was Sabir. I loved the name, and he accepted me as a companion from the very beginning.

I said goodbye to the oasis.

This was the first time I had ever traveled with a caravan. The camel driver led on the animals by singing in that lovely voice of his. His name was Asil. I adored the way he sang and followed his lead, and we became friends. He said that I had a beautiful voice, a voice fit for driving camels long distances across the desert. I learned his songs on the first long day of our journey. It took us three days to reach the Kharga Oasis. Asil told me that we were now in Egyptian territory, and that we had traveled almost one hundred and fifty kilometers from the Salima Oasis.

I felt relieved, as if the fear and anxiety of the past few months had fallen away with this announcement. I was saved. We got off the camels to give both them and ourselves a short rest, we started up again after we had watered the animals. We entered Bir Abu al-Hussein, and then passed through Bir al-Nakhila, and also the Baris Oasis.

When we arrived at the al-Bagawat graveyard, Asil explained to me that the name actually came from the word al-qabawat, but that the inhabitants of the oases pronounce the letter *qaf* as if it were a 'g' sound, so that they say al-gabawat. The word means 'vaults,' and the name refers to the vaulted roofs of the tombs there.

Asil pointed to elevations in the north and the east, and told me that its name was Jabal al-Tayr because migratory birds would rest on those summits during their journeys.

As we proceeded, I saw chiseled stones at the entrances of structures and tombs. They were covered in words and symbols and ancient pharaonic designs, and most were adorned with either proverbs or verses of poetry. "This road is an ancient caravan route," Asil told me. "It's called 'the Path of Forty,' because caravans used to spend forty days on it."

"Will it take us forty days to reach an inhabited area?" I asked, a bit frightened.

He laughed and said, "No. We've already reached the village of Qarbil. Can you see that fort?" He pointed at a simple and ancient-looking fort in the distance. "That's Fort Dosh. And those towers that you see were for keeping tabs on the caravans and looking out for intruders."

"Why do the entrances to all the tombs open toward the south?" I asked.

"No one's figured that out yet."

Asil answered all of my questions judiciously. He knew a lot about the place. We stopped to rest there by a spring, and watered the camels.

After two days and a night, Asil and three others split off from the main group, and I made my way with them from al-Mahariq to Asyut. I said goodbye to them there, and they wished me luck. I spent one day in Asyut, and found a ride in a small truck that was heading to the outskirts of Fayoum. Its driver agreed to take me for free, as long as I helped him load the earthenware jars that he was taking there, and also help him unload them once he arrived. He told me that he took jars to Fayoum, and came back with oranges and tangerines for some merchants here in Asyut.

As I loaded the jars onto the back of the truck with him, I noticed a very familiar smell, but I didn't ask him what was in the jars. Then we got going. He was the silent type. He offered me a cigarette, but I said I didn't smoke and thanked him. I felt drained, and quickly fell asleep.

I don't know where I'm going. I'm wearing a white robe and carrying a bag made of palm fronds that's filled with everything I hold dear. A camel is kneeling in the sand and waiting for me, so I get on. I say goodbye to many familiar faces. The camel doesn't stand up. Instead, she starts moving slowly through the sand, like a ship in the sea, her legs completely out of sight. After a bit, she quickens her pace, and her legs gradually appear, emerging from out of the sand, lifting me higher. The camel starts running, and then her legs turn into tires, and suddenly we're on asphalt. Then she gets rid of the tires and starts flying. I marvel at each of these changes.

We ascend into the sky, the land beneath us becoming smaller and smaller. I start to feel cold. The camel hovers for a moment and turns her neck toward the saddlebag. I know what she wants, and reach into the saddlebag to pull out a small earthenware jar. The camel nods at me to drink. A familiar smell comes to me from the inside of the jar, and I drink something sticky and delicious, something that tastes like molasses. A wonderful warmth overcomes me, while the strong smell clings to my nose. And now I see that the camel is calmly descending, and that the color of the earth beneath us has changed to a vivid green.

I wake up, the smell of molasses still in my nose, and eagerly ask the driver: "What's in those jars you've got?"

"I thought you knew. It's molasses. Ours is excellent, and they like it in the north."

I thought about the short dream I'd just had. I felt as if something had been with me for a long time, as if that goat from Wad al-Nar were still here somehow, protecting me on this voyage into the unknown—as if it had been the fat soldier who smuggled me out of prison, and had now become this silent driver beside me. He had muttered his name to me at the beginning, but I hadn't caught it, and I was too embarrassed to ask him about it now.

We arrived after several long hours of silence. I helped him unload the jars and said goodbye. He gave me a strange yet kind look—a look of long familiarity. I wanted to ask him his name this time, but he disappeared behind the truck with a bunch of shopkeepers and drivers and delivery people. I walked around the truck twice, but found no trace of him. I wanted to ask about him, but I didn't know his name. In any case, everyone was busy and there was a lot of noise.

We had arrived at the village of Umm Said, on the outskirts of Fayoum.

In Asyut, Asil had changed part of the money that I kept in a bundle around my waist—part of which was southern money that lost value the further I traveled north.

I rode in the back of a flatbed truck that was taking some workers to a tourist area called Wadi al-Rayyan. The workers told me that it was a nature preserve, though I didn't know what that meant at the time—I thought it was a fort of some kind, but I couldn't see any walls there.

I got off with my bag, my clothes all dusty. I could smell water, and I walked quickly in that direction, my feet kicking up dust like two thirsty mules. My steps lengthened and my heart opened up, for I knew the water was close.

I drank like a camel. No one was there, so I bathed myself under a small cascade. I wanted to take a nap in the shade of a tree, but no sooner had I lain down than I heard a rumbling coming from the southeast, the noise of engines churning feverishly. I could see a lot of dust flying into the air. The crazy idea came over me that they had sent tanks from the military camp to look for me. I started to cut across a hill toward the noise, but I immediately turned back: the workers in the truck had told me about people being injured, or even dying, due to German mines that had been buried there during the battles of El Alamein in the Second World War. A lot of those mines were still out there, like genies waiting for some unlucky person to free them from their bottles. In a few moments, dusty cars were passing by—cars that looked just like the ones I had seen in advertisements and in the sports pages of newspapers. They were followed by even dustier motorcycles, which flew by madly, their drivers wearing strangely shaped helmets. A bunch of curious people had gathered near the road, and I made my way over to them. A motorcycle driver was there, warning people through a megaphone to clear the road and keep back.

"It's rally time again!" one of the people standing near me said.

I looked at him stupidly and asked, "Who's Rally?"

"The rally's a race. Foreigners race across the Western Desert. They come from Morocco through Algeria and the deserts of Tunisia and Libya until Egypt, where they pass by Fayoum."

"Why?"

"It's a speed race. Whoever gets there first wins a big prize."

"Gets where first?"

"To the finish!"

"And where are they heading?"

"To Cairo."

I asked sincerely but naively, "Would one of them take me in his car to Cairo? I could cheer him on until the end!"

The man I was talking to looked at me in surprise, as if I had said something incredibly stupid, so I stopped talking.

I was now covered in more dust than I had been before I bathed. I wondered whether I should go bathe again, or continue on my way like this, covered in the grime and dust of the rally? While I was considering the matter, the flatbed truck that had brought me here that afternoon turned up again. I rode with them, and got off in the city of Fayoum.

I bought one fuul sandwich and one falafel sandwich, and sat down in a coffeehouse. I ordered a tea, and then asked the waiter whether he knew of any Sudanese people who lived here in this city.

"Of course!" he said. "Who doesn't know Amm Idris Abu al-Saba? He's lived here for a long time. He used to work as a taxi driver, taking people between the different districts, but he's retired now. He married a woman from Fayoum, and they have four sons and three daughters." He spoke very highly of the man, which gave me hope. I called to a boy who was sitting on the sidewalk in front of the coffeehouse selling tissues, and asked him to take me to Amm Idris.

Amm Idris was a generous, hospitable man. He welcomed me into his home even though he didn't know me. He lived in a large house that had modest but clean furnishings. There was an interior courtyard in the Sudanese style, with some citrus trees and ivy and loofah plants. He had me stay in the guest room. For dinner that night, we had duck, a dish that Fayoum is famous for. I told him parts of my story, but left out others, not wanting him to pity me, and not wanting to add to my own sorrows. I also told him that I wanted to travel to Cairo as soon as possible. So the next day, after an excellent breakfast, he took me to the bus station, and placed me in the care of Khalil, one of the taxi drivers there. Khalil was a playful Nubian man with a smiling face and a cheerful disposition. Amm Idris told him to take good care of me, and asked him to take me past Giza, all the way to the Midan Ramsis, because that was closer to the district of Ain Shams, where I knew people. He gave me a large package filled with many of the delicious things we had eaten together—honey and butter and citrus fruits—to take to a relative of his in Ain Shams. And he told the driver Khalil not to take any money from me.

"Ask for Sheikh Rikabi in Ain Shams," he said to me, "and give him this package, and also my greetings!"

I sat down beside Khalil, who was full of jokes, and who kept asking me the same question, "Have you heard this one?"

"No."

"Okay then! Once a Sudanese guy. . . . Once this other guy. . . . Once someone from the south. . . . Once a man from Aswan. . . . Once an Italian. . . . Once an American. . . . A Muslim. . . . A Christian. . . . A Jew. . . . " And so on and so forth, not sparing a single province or country from his sharp jokes. He would let out a guffaw before telling the joke, and then swallow it up, only to burst out laughing again as soon as it was over. He had a way of telling them that made you laugh even before you'd heard the punch line. He even made me laugh when he wasn't trying to be funny. Khalil managed to lift away my worries and my web of sorrows during that trip.

We reached Bab al-Hadid—or Ramsis Station—and Khalil said goodbye to me. I gathered my things, and stepped out onto the square by myself.

I once again set foot in Cairo, that ancient city of stories. It was early, and I thought I'd go visit my old haunts. I walked down the same long street opposite the station. I passed by the hotel where I had stayed back in the old days. It looked the same. Lukanda al-Firdaws was its name. The old sign was dustier now, and three of the letters had fallen off, so that it now read 'Lukan al-Firus,' which had no meaning. The shops were still the same, but there seemed to be more street vendors and noise than in the past. Most of them were selling imported things I'd never seen before, and people were gathering around them in large groups. I looked for our old favorite restaurant to bring back more pleasant memories with some fuul and falafel sandwiches. The owner of the restaurant, Mister Salama, was a man with six fingers on each hand.

"Greetings, my dear!" he said. "Welcome back! It's good to see you my man—my prince!"

"How are you, Mister Salama?"

"I'm well, praise be to God!"

He seemed to have forgotten my name, so I reminded him, "Hamza!"

"Of course I remember you!" he said in that pure Alexandrian dialect of his. "Abu Hamza the dark-skinned, the famous! What is your order, my prince?"

I laughed at these lovely words, for I knew how kindhearted this man was. He used to tell us stories in the evenings. He had been involved in leftist revolutionary activities, and had spent several years in prison. He used to work at the state electricity agency, but they let him go after his internment. Life had been hard on him, but things became easier when he opened up this famous restaurant that everyone knew as "Salama the Alexandrian's."

I ordered a fuul sandwich and a falafel sandwich with pickles, tahini, and some pickled eggplant. The boy who worked there put a cup of water on my table and I attacked the food. Mister Salama excused himself for a few minutes to finish preparing some falafel dough, then came and sat down with me after I'd finished eating the delicious sandwiches. I hadn't actually been that hungry, given the excellent breakfast I'd had that morning in Fayoum. I seemed to be eating for the sake of conjuring up my memories of the city and the good times I'd spent here with my friend al-Khidr.

Mister Salama came and ordered two cups of tea for us, and started happily telling me of the old days, and of his revolutionary deeds and his incarcerations. When he realized that he'd gone on for too long and had forgotten to ask after me, he cut his story short and asked how I was doing and where I'd been during my absence. I told him a little bit of my story, but didn't want to go into details. I quickly changed the subject and asked him about his son Muhsin. He was happy that I remembered him, but I could see that he was on the verge of tears. This reaction caught me off guard. He was silent for a moment, and then took a loud gulp from his cup.

"That's the way of the world," he said sadly. "The poor boy finished his studies and started his military service. After it ended, he spent two years looking for work . . . . He finally had enough, and left for America."

The man talked at length about his son before falling silent. I asked him about some of the people from the old days, and he remembered them. "You're a good man, Abu Hamza," he replied. "You're decent and friendly. . . . They're all well, praise be to God!"

I took my leave of Mister Salama, and asked him to hold onto my bag and the gifts I was carrying from Fayoum for an hour. I went for a walk on the long street. I stopped at a vendor, and ordered a hot drink made of chickpeas with spicy vinegar sauce, just to bring back my memories of the place. After I got tired of walking around, I went back to the restaurant, picked up my things, and said goodbye to Salama, telling him I'd see him again soon. I went to Ramsis Station and took the next train heading to the Ain Shams district of Cairo. The train was empty at that hour. I set my stuff down and peered out the window, looking for any changes in the city's appearance. After arriving at the

Ain Shams station, I went straight to the Sudanese Club. I knocked on the door but no one answered. I checked that the sign was still the same, then sat on the doorstep and rested for a few minutes before knocking again. After a while, Amm Fadlallah opened the door. He recognized me and gave me a hug, then apologized for the delay—he'd been leading the evening prayers. I went in and sat down in the club's clean and watered courtyard. I felt as if I were in Sudan again. He asked me how I was doing, and how things were back in Sudan. He said he'd heard that a lot of oil had been found there recently, and that Sudan would soon become one of the largest oil exporters in the world, rivaling the Gulf countries. He talked at length about the old government and the new one. I immersed myself in the smell of the courtyard and nodded my head occasionally: his words were sorrowful to him, and truly painful to me. When he noticed I wasn't speaking, he skillfully changed the subject, then got up and made two cups of real Sudanese tea for us. I withdrew into my shell a bit as I sat beside him, while other people entered one after the other. I stood up each time someone came in, and they all greeted me affectionately. Each newcomer asked me the same questions, and I gave the same replies, as did Amm Fadlallah, so that both of us were saying the exact same things over and over again. But all the people there still kept listening to us, as if they hadn't heard our words the first or second time around. My replies were short, for I didn't want to make them uneasy—these people who lived so far away, yet who were so near and dear to me.

I stayed at the club and slept in a small room on the upper floor. During the day I helped clean the courtyard and do whatever needed to be done in the club, and in the evening I sat with the younger men for a little while, but spent more time with the older ones. I was waiting for the arrival of Sheikh Rikabi, who, I was told, was away paying his condolences for someone who had passed away in Alexandria.

I tell this whole story without stopping, and without Sandra asking any questions. Her hand is in mine, and her face is pressed against my face. We drink one cup of coffee after another, paying no attention to the people around us.

"Will you come back to my place with me?" she asks.

We head out together, leaving behind the warmth and the smoke, and also those heavy stories of the past. I feel as if a load has been taken from me. Hakima pokes her head out of my coat and Sandra kisses her. I kiss Sandra quickly on her head, wanting her to feel it this time.

9

It's almost eleven o'clock. I head with Sandra toward Burggasse—the name means 'castle alley,' despite the fact that it's a long, broad street. I put my arm around her waist and feel her sun-like warmth flow into my fingers. As she too puts her arm around my waist, she repeats her question, "Will you come back to the apartment with me? It's close."

"I've got to get up early tomorrow for my damned work."

"Why don't you go straight there in the morning from my place?"

"My jacket's at my apartment, and the rest of my stuff too."

"That's not a problem. We can go get it now."

She kisses me, and I know there's no way not to accept her offer. Bus number 48A—the one heading to my part of town—stops in front of us, only a few passengers on board. But we'd rather walk, so we don't get on.

"How long have you been working at that newspaper?" she asks me. "You've never said much about your work."

I fall silent for a moment, so she makes amends, "I'm sorry if I'm troubling you with my curiosity."

"No, not at all. I'm just thinking about where to begin."

He eyes are gleaming with that delicate curiosity of hers. I don't hesitate for very long.

I arrived in Vienna in January 1992, thinking that there was plenty of work to be had. The story of how I got here is a long one, and I'll tell it to you another time. I was told that the only available work was at the newspaper company that publishes the *Krone* and the *Kurier*. I went to the address I'd been given in the nineteenth district. I had to pay a deposit of five thousand shillings for the coat, the bag, and the cap—all of which serve to advertise and promote the paper. I left the place and spent a week trying to figure out how to come up with the money. I was finally able to borrow it from someone, who himself had to go borrow it from someone else—which he was able to do because he'd been here longer and knew more people.

I went back to the newspaper office. There were large numbers of Egyptians, Indians, and Pakistanis there, and also a couple of Turks, and a few people of other nationalities as well. I paid them the money, and didn't receive a receipt for it. The translator told me that the three pieces—the jacket, the bag, and the cap—were my responsibility, and that I'd get the deposit back when I returned them. They gave us these things as if they were made of gold, and as if we'd try to make off with them at the first opportunity.

I later discovered that I'd be selling papers from a miserably empty spot, in an area of the city called Kagran. The boss, whose name was Goldman, told me, "If you do well, you'll get a better spot as soon as one opens up!"

There was a large crowd of us there, and also translators for our languages. They brought us into a room to watch a preparatory video. It was like walking into some sort of war room. We sat down to wait for the arrival of 'the boss,' who strutted in like a peacock. He spoke in very fast German, and I couldn't understand a single word. Behind him, four people were translating into four different languages for us. They kept starting and stopping the video, repeatedly explaining things as if we were cattle. I realized that he was to be my general, just like the ones in Sudan had been, even though he wore a civilian uniform.

The video was a training film that showed long-serving vendors selling newspapers in the streets and squares of Vienna. The places we saw were crammed with passersby on that pleasant sunny morning, and they seemed to have filmed this on a day when some big event had aroused everyone's interest, for the papers were flying out of the vendors' hands. As I mentioned, I later discovered that I'd been given an isolated spot where no one ever felt like buying a paper or even saying "good morning." I also discovered the weather in the video was not typical for Vienna.

We also saw a skillful vendor who darted among the cars with the lightness of a cheetah and the grace of a gazelle, before pouncing back onto the sidewalk like a frog to call out in his loudest voice, "Kroooone! Kroooone Zeitung!" The video was stopped at certain images so that the boss could speak to us in his quick, shrill dialect. The translators informed us that we were supposed to lift up the paper clearly, as if we were at a demonstration, so that the drivers and passersby could read the headlines, and that we were to call out in loud voices to catch people's attention. Then they played some more of the video, and we saw the vendor nimbly rush into the street as a traffic signal turned red: he weaved his way among the cars, and sold seven papers in less than a minute. They stopped the video, and the translators told us that speed was essential if we wanted to make a lot of money. I still remember the person sitting beside me that day: he was overweight and sweating profusely, even in that cold room. I felt sorry for him.

Then they showed us an Indian man who was inside either a train or subway station. He was standing there with a dignified look on his face, his mustache arched upward toward his hair. He had an Indian turban on his head, and had put the newspaper cap on over it, so that he actually looked quite comical. He was cheerfully and liberally selling newspapers as if he were giving presents to children on some holiday. All the people were talking to him and laughing, as if they were telling jokes. I remember thinking that he must have lived here for at least a century to be able to understand the language that the boss spoke so perfectly. Then the boss barked something out again, and the translators said that if we wanted bigger tips, we needed to smile at the customers, just like that vendor. They stopped the video at a close-up of the face of that Indian man whose smile knew no bounds, and a large green check mark appeared in the middle of the screen.

After this, they showed us secretly filmed scenes of lethargic vendors, with big red X's appearing on them. There was a vendor who had fallen asleep against a pole. And another vendor received a red X because he didn't run out into the street to sell papers to the drivers. And there was an X for a vendor who looked sullen and weary: he was supposed to be smiling at the customers, even though the customers themselves never smile back. There was another X for someone who didn't seem to be doing anything wrong, and, as if this were a quiz, they asked us why that man was going to lose his Fixum.

"What's a Fixum?" we asked in reply.

The translators told us that it was our fixed or stable pay for each day of work, and that it would be forty-five shillings—equal to nine shillings per hour.

None of us could see anything wrong with that man on the screen who had caused them to stop the video, but then a skinny guy sitting in the back cried out in English, "No cap, boss!"

"Well done!" the boss congratulated him, before taking down his name to give him one of the better locations.

Another red X appeared on a vendor whose jacket was open, and there was one for a vendor who was talking to a woman and who had left his sacred *Krone* bag on the ground, and another for a vendor who had his hands in his pockets and was walking around whistling and singing—the list of violations and red marks was much longer than the earlier list of good deeds. The video ended in an illustrative and statistical fashion. There was an image of a pile of shillings, and as the face of the smiling Indian man was shown, the pile grew larger and you could hear the sound of coins clinking together. His face was then replaced with that of the miserable vendor who had fallen asleep, and the sound of clinking shillings grew fainter as the pile diminished. Then there was a vendor who ran about like a horse while the pile of shillings increased in size again, and then yet another vendor who slept like a bear as the pile grew smaller.

We left the 'war room' and stood in line, each of us holding a piece of paper with our name on it. The man in charge of handing out the clothes was shouting out our names as if we were soldiers heading off to battle, "Mohammed Abdel Azeem! . . . Rasul Mamoud Mamoud! . . . Mehmet Tusun Oglial! . . . Sink Raja Muhareem!" And so on and so forth. He would then take the person's piece of paper, looking them up and down before giving them the bright yellow jacket, the plastic yellow bag, and the yellow cap.

The jacket I received was very big, and the cap very small. I traded the cap with one of my coworkers, but it was still too small on me, even though it was the biggest one they had—I hadn't cut my long hair yet because I was worried about the cold in this country.

I felt ill at ease when I returned to my apartment that day, as if new drudgery and servitude were in store for me. I fell into a restless sleep.

I see a man with cruel features wearing dirty overalls on top of sports clothes. The smell of his sweat is penetrating and repulsive. German words come out of his mouth like the barking of a dog. I don't know where I am or where he came from. Because of the way he's speaking and his pronunciation, it's difficult for me to make out what he's saying. Suddenly, the man brings out a sharp, glistening cleaver from behind his back. A bull is tied to a nearby tree with a rope made of thick fibers, and he clearly wants to slaughter it. One of the bull's legs is injured, and a strangely colored liquid—different from the color of blood—is streaming from the wound. The bull implores him in clear, calm, and high-pitched German: it asks for his mercy; it asks for him to let it go free, saying that it's the last bull on earth, and that if it dies the whole species will be extinct. But the man simply clamps his teeth in victory and satisfaction, and with a sudden movement he expertly draws the blade across the bull's neck. The animal starts braying loudly as a stream of light liquid—whose color is unfamiliar to me—pours from the wound. The liquid gets thicker and thicker, and then starts glistening, and finally turns into a golden color that's nothing like the color of blood. The liquid keeps pouring from the bull, and when I make to leave, I find that my feet are stuck in this molten gold, which is pleasantly tickling my soles. But the slaughtering of the bull has made me uneasy, and the man is now trying to reassure me that he is in fact doing good and warding off evil. I've been carrying a small meowing cat in my hands the whole time. At first, I'm afraid to set it in the molten gold, and I lift it to my chest. Yet once I realize how good the gold feels, I try to set down the cat so it too can have its share of the pleasure. But it digs its claws into my chest and clings to me, not wanting to go down. After a short while, my attention is drawn to my motionless feet. The gold has solidified now, and I can't see my feet any more. The gleaming color begins to fade, turning to that of lead, and then of rust.

Sandra listens in silence as I tell my long story, trying to get her to laugh at the strange things that have happened to me. She seems almost incredulous. "Are you still working at that newspaper?" she asks me.

"Yes."

"Haven't you found anything else?"

"I've worked seven different jobs here, and didn't make it in a single one of them. I handed out flyers, and I washed dishes in a restaurant, and I tried selling roses. I worked as a street cleaner too, removing the snow in the winter and cleaning the glass off the streets after New Year's Eve. But the best place I worked was at the market—the Naschmarkt—where I sold spices. I almost made it there, but the owner of the place fell in love with me, even though she was married. It was a difficult situation, and I left the job."

We're walking along the main city park now. I give Sandra a hug, and then call out to her in a loud and laughing voice, imitating the Viennese dialect, "Krone Zeitung, gnä Frau!"

Sandra laughs, but then says, "This work is killing you."

"Yes, but there's no way out of it, Sandra."

"What do you mean, Hamza?"

"There are those in life who would do any work at all to keep from dying, and there are those who would die any death to keep from working. I seem to belong to the former!"

"Your whole life is strange, Hamza. You've really piqued my interest. I don't know if I should ask you what you did in Egypt and how you left there, or if I should ask you what your life has been like here all these years."

Hakima turns over in my coat and pokes her head out a bit, so Sandra takes her from me. Hakima meows as usual, and we laugh. I try to change the subject, "Why don't you ask me about your delicious lips instead, the way their balsam wards off sadness? Or ask me about this hand of yours that holds all the warmth of the world. Or about your voice, if you like. Ask me about Sandra. Ask me about the woman I can't live without. I've found my home and my family now—I've gotten back the life I lost."

We stop outside the Urania building, a cold wind coming to us from the Danube canal. The few cars on the street pass by quickly. With Hakima between us, I embrace Sandra and kiss her passionately, then hurry to my apartment holding her hand.

I let Hakima loose in the cold apartment for a bit, and then put the newspaper jacket, bag, and cap in a large plastic bag, and we leave for Sandra's apartment. We take public transportation this time, and Sandra clings to my hand until we reach her place. Neither of us are tired, so I ask her, "Do you want to hear the story about Cairo, or the one about Vienna?"

"Cairo first. What did you do there, and how'd you manage to leave? And why did you come to Vienna in particular?"

I stayed at the Sudanese Club in Ain Shams, waiting for Amm Rikabi to come back from Alexandria. The morning after my arrival, I went out to look for my friend Adam, who had helped me get a visa for Italy over three years earlier. I ran into many mutual acquaintances that day, and they all told me that he had gotten married and was doing well. Late in the evening of the same day, Adam rushed into the club and greeted me affectionately. I was sitting in the middle of a group of young men and telling them about my memories of Cairo. Their questions were generally different from those of the older men—they were more interested in hearing about life in Europe, and they never got bored of hearing my story.

Adam told me that he had gotten married, and now had a girl and a boy. He said that he had traveled to one of the Gulf countries and worked for an oil company there for a year. He made a lot of money in that time, but the work on the rigs was hard and dangerous, and it had a clear impact on his health in the short while he had spent there. He realized that many of his fellow low-level workers were coming down with skin and lung diseases from working with those chemicals all day, so he decided to speed up his return, especially since he had fallen in love with a young woman back in Egypt, and wanted to get married to her—before he left, he had been too poor to even get engaged to her and have the traditional Fatiha-reading ceremony.

He told me that I would stay with him that night, and that he wouldn't take no for an answer. I felt embarrassed because I hadn't brought him a gift, not even a few citrus fruits from Fayoum. I told myself that I would buy a suitable gift for his son and daughter as soon as possible. On the way to his place, we passed by a kofta vendor and Adam bought a half-kilo of kofta and a half-kilo of kebab, as well as some salad. When we arrived he gave a special knock at the door, and then said in a voice loud enough for his wife to hear, "Hamza, please come in!"

I entered, clearing my throat, and said the traditional "ya Satir" to warn his wife of my arrival. I heard a noise inside, as if someone had fled further into the house. It smelled wonderful—the smell of Sudanese incense that reminded me of far-off days. The television was on, and a movie with the Egyptian actor Ahmed Zaki was just beginning. Its title was *I'm not Lying, I'm Adorning the Truth*. I knew the movie and liked it a lot, so I sat down on the couch while Adam went into the kitchen. Suddenly, a little girl appeared and greeted me in beautiful Egyptian dialect, "How are you, uncle? What's your name?"

"My name's Hamza."

"Uncle Hamza! My name's Yusra, and my brother's name is Basim."

Before either of us could ask any other questions, her mother appeared in a Sudanese wrap, carrying Basim. Adam introduced her, using the traditional form of naming parents after their oldest son, "The mother of the children, Umm Basim!"

She welcomed me bashfully, and asked me how things were in Sudan. I told them both that all was well back there, then fell silent for a moment, so Adam said we were hungry and wanted to eat. She excused herself for a moment to make the last preparations for dinner, and then we all sat down to eat together. I've only sat down and eaten together with a family like that a few times in my life, and the setting made me hungrier than usual. We had tea after the meal, and a long and intimate conversation began. I asked Adam what he was doing for work now, and he told me that he was renting a small shop near the house to weld car frames, taking advantage of the welding experience he had gained while working for the foreign oil company at the rig. He said the work was good, and that he was making reasonable money: cars never stopped getting into wrecks, and they always needed someone to weld them together again.

I watched TV with them while we continued our long conversation, and then slept on the sofa in the living room.

I woke up the next morning and ate breakfast with Adam and Yusra and Basim. Basim was a little troublemaker: he ran around and spun plates and flipped them over, then came over to me and sat on my lap and looked deep into my eyes, as if we'd always known each other. I went with Adam to his shop after breakfast. It was extremely small, and I was surprised that he could work in a place that was no larger than a narrow prison cell: roughly two meters by one-and-a-half meters, and crammed with tools, cylinders, cables, and sheets of metal. He took all of these things out onto the sidewalk and arranged them. The neighbors and owners of nearby stores said good morning, and they all wished each other a successful day. He brought out his chair and borrowed another one from the porcelain vendor next door, and we sat down in front of his workshop. He went in to make some tea for us and kept talking to me and laughing, while people passed by to speak with him, after which he'd continue his conversation with me. The people greeted me as well, and joked around as if they'd known me for a long time. Adam was asked several times if I was a relative, and each time he said that I was his cousin. That designation put me at ease, and I too began to call him my cousin.

I didn't want to spend too much time lazily enjoying his hospitality, so I jumped straight into the topic that had been preoccupying me since the previous night: I wanted to know if there was any chance of my working here. Adam wanted to have that conversation later, even though I insisted that I needed work as soon as possible. His work began to pick up, and I was only getting in the way, so I excused myself, saying, "I'm going to the Sudanese Club. Let's meet there in the evening."

The days went by, and every day I walked around Ain Shams to see the changes that had come over the place since the last time I was there. It had changed a lot in such a short time. Many of the villas that the area was famous for were gone, and tall buildings had sprung up instead. There were noticeably more cars as well. And what used to be the train station was now a subway station. I had noticed some of these changes on my arrival a few days earlier, but I'd been too preoccupied with going to the club to pay them much attention.

I was sitting in the club's courtyard one afternoon and thinking about what I could get Yusra and Basim, when a man wearing a clean white robe and a Sudanese turban and shoes came in. He was walking purposefully, and greeted me from a distance as he approached, "Welcome, Hamza. Welcome back!"

"Greetings! How are you?"

"I'm well, God bless you! I'm Rikabi, Rikabi Idris! They told me about you yesterday, but you weren't around."

"Hello, Amm Rikabi! How are you? I hope you're well!"

We sat down for a long conversation. This man asked different questions than the others. He was silent on occasion, and never asked the same question twice. I got up and brought over the gifts I had carried with me from Fayoum, and gave them to him. He thanked me and opened the package in front of me, then insisted on dividing it up three ways: a third for him, a third for Amm Fadlallah, and a third for me.

Amm Rikabi Idris was over seventy years old, but his big eyes flashed in a way that made him look much younger. He was an attractive man with a friendly face and a kind voice, especially when he laughed. His pure white teeth were particularly eye-catching, and he had a strong memory, sharp hearing, and even sharper sight. He told me he had come to this city as a young child in the twenties, after his grandfather had been exiled. His grandfather had been a powerful and influential man in the Sultanate of Darfur at the time, that is, until the Austrian Rudolf Slatin Pasha was appointed governor of Darfur by Gordon Pasha—the same Slatin Pasha who would later profess to embrace Islam when the Mahdi's armies captured him. He told me a part of the story then, and said he would tell me the rest another time.

Amm Rikabi noticed that I always said "Medinat Ain Shams," referring to it as a city rather than a district or area, so he asked, "Where do you have this word from? You're the only person I know who calls it a city."

"It looks like a big city to me. Maybe it's because I grew up in a small village and got used to calling everything bigger than our village a city."

He laughed and said, "You're not wrong, my son. It may surprise you to know that the real name of this place is actually Medinat al-Shams. It's located where Heliopolis used to be, which the ancient Egyptians called Awn, and which the Arabs called Ain Shams, by which they meant 'spring of the sun' or 'source of the sun.' The nearest place to the north of it, about two kilometers away, is the village of al-Matariya, where you can still find that famous ancient sycomore fig tree the people call the Tree of Mary. They say that Our Lady Mary rested with her child beneath that blessed tree, which some believe to be over two thousand years old. I don't think it's possible for the tree to be that old, since sycomores don't live more than five hundred years. I think the people, wanting to continue to receive the tree's blessings, must have taken a shoot from it and planted it, and then done so again with the new tree, and so on. The present tree probably represents the third or fourth generation after the original one. These trees took in water from the Well of Moses, which disappeared in time—it's said that Moses stopped there before leaving Egypt. That whole area is famous for its fertility: any seed that falls there sprouts, despite the fact that the soil looks more like the sand of the desert than it does any kind of fertile ground. Elder trees also used to grow there—they only grow in climates similar to that of Ain Shams. It's believed that they were irrigated with water from that well. In the old days, they used to grow them in the Hejaz, for example. In Egypt, these trees can only now be found around the mountain called Jabal Elba. When the people here saw the name 'Elba' written on the maps of the English, they believed that its real name must have been 'Ilba'—with the Arabic letter ayn at the beginning of the word. It's located in the south of Egypt on the border with Sudan, not far from the Red Sea. The only structure remaining in that area from the ancient days is the lovely tall Sun Obelisk, which the Arabs also call the Pharaoh Obelisk."

"Tell me about Ain Shams," I said. "I love knowing the histories of places where I've lived."

"This City of the Sun was the first green sight that could be seen by those coming from the yellow desert of Sinai in the east, and it was the first inhabited settlement for those coming from the green fields and farms of the Nile Delta in the north—though there were only a few people living here back then. Some of those people were ascetics who preferred to keep away from urban life. Bedouins also grazed their animals at the borders of this place. It was famous for its wells, and it was said that anywhere you dug you'd find delicious water. Some Copts also lived in a nearby monastery called the Monastery of al-Malak the Martyr—the French later turned it into an ostrich farm to export ostrich meat and feathers. But that monastery isn't the same as the other one that bears the same name."

"Is that the area they call al-Na'am now?" I asked.

He replied, "Yes, but the area used to be much bigger, and stretched all the way to the borders of Ain Shams. They raised so many ostriches in it that they started to call the men there al-Na'am and since then that entire place has been known by that name. In addition to the feathers and eggs of ostriches, fine surgical threads can be produced from their intestines and stomachs, and the corneas of ostrich eyes are very similar to human ones."

"But you can't see any traces of that history there now."

"It's incredible how much has disappeared, Hamza. Would you believe me if I told you that the horses of Ain Shams used to be exported all across the world? They were famously known as khayl al-zahra. One breeding farm is still there, at the end of this street. But it makes me sad to think about how they used to train those beautiful animals for the wars, and how the horses were used as shields against spears and swords and fire. They used them as pack animals too, and, even worse, had horse fight against horse. They had no pity on those noble animals. Horses were their tanks in ancient times.

"I'll tell you something else that people have forgotten. A long time ago Ain Shams was a place reputed for its therapeutic qualities. It's said that the mother of al-Murtada, the third caliph of his day, had a rare skin disease called ruqt, as well as a severe type of asthma from which she often suffered nighttime attacks. The doctors advised her to go somewhere dry, and they suggested three places that were near to the capital Fustat: the first was Medinat al-Shams; the second was Helwan or al-'Uyun; and the third was Fayoum. The story is that in ancient days they took fresh meat from all kinds of animals and birds and hung the meet outside for days in several different areas. The flesh took much longer to decompose in those three places, so they made them sanitariums for the caliph's family, and later on for the followers and aids of the sultan.

"Medinat al-Shams was like an oasis. It had grazing land for cattle and camels, and was a good place for horses as well. The ancient Egyptians used to rest their steeds there on their way to and from their wars."

I listened attentively to the man and lost myself in his stories. He continued.

"I've spent the best days of my life in this place. People gradually began to move here with their families, particularly some of the Sudanese who had settled in Egypt: a lot of them worked in the 'haggana,' a branch of the Egyptian security forces that keeps the peace and whose members ride on camels, and then later as part of the Egyptian border patrol. Many of them turned out to be very generous and sociable people, and they got married and raised their children here. Afterward, a lot of Gazans and Palestinians came and settled here too. Ain Shams wasn't like what you see today, my boy. Cars only very rarely ever came here. Only four people in Ain Shams that we knew of had cars: the agricultural inspector Boutros al-Asnawi, who also had a palm farm; Tahir Bek al-Manufi, an officer at the Khanka prison; the medical doctor Abu Shadi al-Dandarawi; and the imam Zayn al-Din al-Tahtawi, who lived to a ripe old age, and who lost his judgeship because of his legal ruling in support of women going unveiled outside the home. He was a contemporary of Qasim Amin, and was one of the few people truly convinced of his views. He wrote under a pseudonym in the newspaper *al-Waqa'i' al-misriya*, which Muhammad Abduh edited. The khedive was angered by an article of his, so he was exiled to Beirut with Muhammad Abduh, until Khedive Tawfiq pardoned him and allowed him to return to Egypt. He lived many fretful years here in Ain Shams, and he and my family used to visit one another from time to time. He was a great scholar, but the past had left its mark on him, and he went into seclusion, engrossing himself in reading. We didn't know he was a prolific writer until a long while later.

"Yes, my boy, Ain Shams has seen its share of the action. It looked quite different in the old days. The people built their homes right beside each other, and according to Sudanese custom all of these houses were only one story high, so as not to invade the neighbors' privacy, and the place kept expanding in this way. People watered the ground in the summer to strengthen the soil and lessen the dust, and they planted lemon trees there, and other citrus trees as well, and grew grapes, mangoes, pomegranates, guavas, and also palm trees. Everyone knew each other, all the way from the Sun Obelisk to the Ismailiya canal, which they called the Gulf of the Commander of the Faithful and which used to flow by here. Imagine this place, Hamza. Bedouins and fishermen and farmers used to gather here, and those camel- and goatskin carpet-makers as well. Women from Palestine and Gaza, who had made their living as weavers, settled here and taught the local women their craft. Nothing's left of that old place any more. The buildings are different now, and Medinat al-Shams has become crowded. The old spacious houses have vanished, and the lush greenness has turned into the arid yellow of the desert. There's dust and asphalt everywhere, and the wells have dried up for good. There used to be hoopoes and nightingales here, and doves and yellow and red canaries, and many other birds that made their nests in the trees—but they've all disappeared.

"This was a place of wonders, Hamza. The dervish or Sufi saint Wad Shirwani—or Wad Sharwani—appeared here. I saw that wondrous man with my own two eyes, though I could hardly believe them. The skin on one side of his body was white, and on the other side black, as if there were a split straight down his body. Even the hair on his head was lighter on the one side than the other. That man used to shake people to their core. They came to watch him and be blessed by him. He would appear and disappear suddenly, and no one knew where he lived. Anyone who tried to follow him always came back thirsty and suffering from sunstroke, as if they had come from a war zone, for the man mostly came in the summer, and only rarely showed up in winter. He would arrive before dawn and leave us at the hottest part of the day, plunging into the desert in the east in the direction of the Bedouin path—that's what we used to call it. The adults and the children used to follow him, but he just kept on walking, and eventually the people, exhausted from the long march and the extreme heat, would give up their pursuit, and he'd disappear from view. This usually happened in the summer. When he appeared in winter, he'd stay till sunset, and then head off at dinnertime. No one ever found out where he came from or where he disappeared to. The people said that he had an unmistakable smell. Whenever they smelled him coming, they would pray to be blessed by that holy sheikh. As for the children, they were afraid to hurt him or throw stones at him like they often did to other people, fearing that their families would reproach and curse them for it, or that the sheikh would become angry with them—for they believed he could turn them into animals or snakes.

"Only one person ever threw a stone at him, and that was Khayri, who they called 'the idiot' because he couldn't speak properly. He threw the stone while he was standing with a bunch of children, all of whom fled like birds, fearing the dervish's anger. But he simply turned to Khayri and said, 'Go, my boy, and may God guide you!' And for the first time in his life, Khayri said something comprehensible, 'Go, my boy, and may God guide you!' He repeated this with the same clear pronunciation and tone of voice of the dervish, and everyone was amazed. The next day, he started saying that same sentence to everyone who crossed his path, whether they were men or women. And from then on, anytime anyone greeted Khayri, he would utter those words. But he never said anything else that was comprehensible. In time, the people changed his name from 'Khayri the idiot' to 'Khayri the guided.'"

Adam came to the club late that evening and apologized, saying that he'd been forced to finish some work. He sat down with the younger men, while they listened attentively as I continued telling them stories of distant countries. They got me to play cards with them, especially the game they called 'al-kunkan,' but it soon became clear that I was no good at any of those games. Earlier, they had tried to play football with me, but I was horrible at that too. The one skill I had—and which they had apparently discovered without my realizing it—was singing. This discovery of theirs would later cause me some trouble. From time to time, I sang by myself, but the men forced me to sing at one of the weddings once, even though I wasn't ready to stand in front of so many people. But they insisted, so I walked timidly through the throng and got up on the stage. They put a microphone in my hand and asked me what I was going to sing. I told them I'd do a song by Salah ibn al-Badiya, and they all fell into a terrifying silence as I began to sing the song. When I finished, everyone clapped and cheered, and from that day on they started trying to get me to go to their weddings and celebrations, sometimes even asking for my singing services in particular. But I wasn't used to that kind of singing, and I didn't like singing to an audience. That's not how I am. I've always sung only for myself, sometimes to try to protect myself from something I wasn't fully aware of. I avoided going to weddings after that, fearful of being dragged into a similar situation again.

I went to the embassy one day, hoping to take up my old work of selling kisra bread there. But when I got there, I found an old Sudanese woman selling that bread in the very same place I used to, and I realized that my place there was gone, and that I had to start seriously looking for work.

After about six weeks in Cairo, I was down to my last few Egyptian pounds. It was a moonlit night, and I had just watched a soccer game with the men at the club, though I still didn't understand any of the rules. Amm Rikabi stayed for a while after the courtyard had emptied out, and he asked me, "Have you found any work yet, Hamza?"

"Unfortunately not."

"I saw an old acquaintance of mine yesterday who still works at the Zahra Horse Stables, near the Shams Club. He told me he was looking for an assistant stableman, so I said I knew someone who'd be perfect for the job. I gave you a good recommendation, and said you'd come by and see him."

"That's great news, Amm Rikabi! How can I ever thank you?"

"Don't thank me, my boy! It's the least I can do. Go there and ask for Sharaf, and tell him I sent you. Do you know where the Zahra Stables are?" He described the way for me.

I didn't sleep well that night because I was nervous about this new job possibility. I headed over there the next morning. Sharaf was a bit reserved and even a bit cold when he met me, and I could sense that there might be no work for me here. He asked if I had any experience with horses, and I said no, yet immediately added, as a last line of defense, "But I'm a quick learner. And I'm in desperate need of work."

I entered the stables with him. It was a large enclosure with several smaller enclosures inside it. The smell of horses was everywhere. Outside, there was a sort of paddock with men and women riding on horses in larger and smaller circles. Inside, the horses were looking at me with eyes that, for some reason, seemed sad to me. I fell in love with the horses the moment I set eyes on them. Sharaf quickly explained the work to me. He said that I was responsible for several of the horses on this side of the stable, and that I had to groom them, and clean and polish their saddles with various scented oils. He also showed me how to clean the ground of the stables, bringing in cleaning supplies and working quickly with his hands—this practical demonstration surprised me a bit, for he was wearing spotless clothes. He showed me where the water and the fodder was, and taught me how to comb the horses and clean their hooves and horseshoes, using a hooked metal rod that he said I had to be very careful with. He explained everything quickly and eagerly, and I learned it all. Then he invited me to come watch the show, and brought me a bottle of Coca-Cola and stood next to me. I found him to be kind and good-hearted despite the chilly reception he had given me at first. I watched the show and fell even more in love with the horses. He told me to come early the next day, and said that I could start off by working three days a week with Amm Diyab, one of the stablemen there. Amm Diyab was a very short man with a tiny body. He was very quick and alert, and loved to joke around.

I worked there happily for several months, but I didn't make much money. Sharaf was very pleased with me and liked how I treated the horses. Amm Diyab told me I should approach the high-society women there and be nice to them, for they tipped very well, but I was too shy to do this. He kept trying to teach me how, and even showed me all the money he had made, but I was still too timid to go after those alms, and was very cautious and reserved around the women. As for Amm Diyab, he was still crazy about women, even though he was almost fifty years old at the time, and despite the fact that he had two wives and had married four times in all. He used to tell me about his amorous adventures, which would make me keel over with laughter, for he often greatly exaggerated them. He loved it when I asked him questions in that Sudanese dialect of mine. "Is that really true, Amm Diyab?" I'd often ask. "By God, you're some devil!" He'd always burst into laughter and continue unloading all his exciting stories, none of which ever bored me. The best part were those incredible mythic exaggerations that even the wildest rakes and liars couldn't compete with. I listened to them with the same pleasure that I had from drinking that delicious sweet tea that he boiled over firewood. Amm Diyab enjoyed my company too, and he found in me an avid listener who never tired of his endless stories.

Sharaf came by regularly. I always did my work quickly so I could go out and watch the elegant horses strutting about in the shows. Amm Rikabi was happy that I had found work, as was Adam. The latter occasionally said, "Haven't you thought about getting married, Hamza? We'll look for a good girl for you. You're a kind and decent man, and there are a thousand girls who would love to have you."

I avoided the topic, not wanting to go into any details, but Adam kept alluding to it, and told me that I had some female admirers who had heard me sing and fallen for me, and that several of the young men were jealous of me. He said that the men were surprised at my indifference toward women and at the way I avoided the subject, and that were it not for a few references I had made to events in my life in Europe, they would have had some doubts about me.

I loved the horses, and I loved working with "Diyab the boaster," as I secretly called him. Sharaf supervised us from a distance, and told us what to do stiffly but not harshly. I liked the work and thought that it would last, but my dream of staying there finally vanished.

It was the beginning of October, and I'd been working there for ten months, during which time I had learned a lot. As for the rich women there, I only approached them very rarely, and gave only short answers to their questions before slowly leading the horses away to the stable and singing to them.

It was a beautiful sunny day, and I was in a great mood and singing to the horses. Diyab was off that day, celebrating the birth of his seventh child, and apparently my voice was louder than usual. I saw a young lady in a riding outfit at the entrance. Bright sunlight was streaming in from behind her, so that I couldn't make out her face.

"Do you know the singer Mohamed Mounir?" she asked me.

"Of course. He's an amazing musician with a lovely voice."

"Are you from Nubia?"

"More or less. I'm from Sudan."

She asked what my name is and where exactly I am from, and told me I have a beautiful voice. Whenever she took a step toward me, I took a step back. She started coming by the stables frequently, and would ask Amm Diyab about me if I showed up late. He was delighted at this turn of events, and urged me to "act like a man." I resisted the idea.

"What do you mean by 'act like a man,' Amm Diyab?" I asked him.

"I mean that you should catch the young dove and let the pigeon fly!"

"What dove? What pigeon?"

"You know, bridle the mare, you stallion! Ride that mare!"

Amm Diyab was speaking in that funny symbolic language of his. The woman was very attractive, and I was exaggerating my naiveté so as to enjoy Diyab's interesting figures of speech. Her name was Safinaz. Day after day, Amm Diyab told me that she had asked about me. When she came by, he would leave me alone with her and say something that seemed to be about work when in fact he was always alluding to her: "Water the mare, Hamza!" or "Tie up the mare!" or "Tighten the reins!" or "It's feeding time, Hamza!" and so on and so forth.

Safinaz was always very nice to me, but I didn't think that this ordinary relationship would ever develop into something more, and her composure reassured me in this regard. Yet there was a joyful and captivating gleam in her eyes, and whenever she brushed against me—whether intentionally or not—she always trembled in a way that made me nervous.

Trouble started creeping into my life once more. Rumors began to spread about me. Behind my back, I was being accused of having relationships with girls from the neighborhood, which wasn't true. There were two girls who went to a school in the area of Heliopolis, and I saw them once and greeted them very respectfully. Yet they seemed to be intentionally going the same way that I was, and when I realized this, I took a different way, turning at the end of the street toward the cemetery. But the grudges the young men bore against me were too far gone by then, and their ill will was even worse than I had imagined: there was no stopping it.

Adam defended me staunchly, but the situation worsened without any apparent cause. A few of the young men were always keeping a close eye on me, and I became annoyed by their idiotic behavior. My sad voice had brought all this trouble and misfortune upon me, so I stopped singing. If my voice was going to attract all this ill will, then I would silence it. I no longer greeted any girl in the street, even if she called out to greet me. That was the part I hated the most: that I was being forced to repay courtesy with rudeness and conceit. This place was becoming too much for me, especially since Adam was once again trying to win me over to the idea of marriage. Amm Rikabi defended me all the while, and raised his voice against anyone who slandered me. He was always on my side, and I often heard him berating the young men for the uncivil and arrogant way they were treating me. He warned them against meddling in my affairs, and said that any insult against me was also a personal insult against him—I was in dire need of that protection. I could hardly believe that my sad voice, which had always accompanied me and eased my mind of its hardships, was now bringing harm on me and arousing the envy of others.

At dawn, I wake up to the sound of the alarm clock. I can tell that I haven't slept enough. Sandra gets up with me and makes breakfast. "I don't remember falling asleep!" I tell her. "I must have talked a lot!"

"Yes, you did. Your story almost makes me want to go to work with you today to hear the rest."

I eat quickly, kiss her, and then head out onto the cold street. I ride the tram and the subway, and arrive at the spot where I work, half-asleep. But I can feel Sandra giving me strength and resilience. I feel more capable of bearing the world's burdens now—I'm beginning to laugh about it all again.

10

The days and weeks go by pleasantly. Sandra and I meet occasionally at my place, and more often at the Palm House, and most of the time at Sandra's. One Friday I leave Hakima at Sandra's. We'll be meeting at the Palm House in the afternoon. Once again, I'm filling in for a coworker of mine who distributes flyers at people's homes. As my luck would have it, it's a rainy day. I drag along the heavy trolley filled with flyers, which I've covered with plastic because of all the rain, and distribute them around a large residential neighborhood that the boss had pointed out on a map. It will take me over seven hours to go up and down the stairs of all these tall buildings, waiting each time for the residents to open up the building doors.

At the beginning, I choose one buzzer at random from each building's intercom system and wait for someone to answer, and then tell them that I'm distributing flyers. But this leads to long discussions about who I am, and what company I work for, and who ordered these flyers, and why I'd picked that buzzer in particular—which means I'm spending a lot of time waiting outside the building doors. The questions aren't offensive in and of themselves, but the insults and slurs I hear on account of my disturbing people's peace and quiet in their homes at that hour certainly are. Most people in this city hate anyone distributing flyers. They detest that type of trivial yet intrusive work, and also the disturbing creatures who carry it out. But as soon as the person distributing the flyers has left, they take the ads into their apartments and examine them with great care. Later on, I start pressing several buzzers at the same time, so that a bunch of voices talk to me all at once—there's always someone who's not interested in asking questions, and who buzzes the door open immediately.

I find myself standing in front of an old building that seems deserted. Wires are spilling out of the intercom system. I press all the buzzers, but no one opens, so I seek refuge from the rain in the archway of the building entrance. Suddenly I hear the door being buzzed open. I leave the trolley outside and push open the heavy door with one hand, holding onto a stack of flyers with my other hand. I head up the building's ramshackle stairs. The walls of the building are all cracked and run-down, and the place smells damp and rotten. Most of the apartments seem to be deserted, for flyers are scattered haphazardly in the corridors, covered in dust. In places like these, I take pleasure in dumping most of the flyers I've got on me to lighten my load. I know that my energetic boss usually picks a few buildings to pass by and check up on our work. He sometimes even asks the occupants of a couple apartments whether they've received flyers from us or not, to prove how shrewd he is to the company president, and to show us poor workers how far-seeing his police eyes are, for we know that he's capable of imposing harmful fines on us. But I'm fairly certain he won't pick a building like this one to check.

On the top floor of this dilapidated building, I hear music coming out of one of the apartments—familiar and alluring music. At first I think my ears must be deceiving me, for I'm starving and I can feel a headache coming on. Perhaps this is merely an echo in my memory from the courtyard of the Sudanese Club. I draw near to the door and listen. The music is clear, and I recognize it. I've heard this gentle Arabic voice many times before.

"Nights of joy in Vienna,
a breeze from Paradise,
a rich melody in the air:
when the birds heard it, they wept and sang.
There's bliss for the soul and the eye,
and your heart rejoices.
Lovers are all around:
what more is needed for Paradise?
Enjoy your youth in Vienna,
this garden of Paradise.
Why do you let the days
go by without delight?
Rejoice, enjoy the music!
Take joy, enjoy the music!
Let your heart swim and fly in this world,
and grant it a companion.
Enjoy him, enjoy his love,
and let your young heart be happy.
Vienna, garden of Paradise,
may your nights be full of joy.
A rich melody in the air:
when the birds heard it, they wept and sang."

I'm not proud of snooping at the door like this, but my attraction to the music is stronger than any rational thought. I robotically distribute the flyers no less than five times to each of the apartments on this floor; and every time I pass the apartment with the music, I stop to listen. I want to knock and find some pretense to ask a question, but I'm too shy. The apartment seems to be the only inhabited one on the entire top floor. The rain beats down violently on the old building, and I'm caught between joy and extreme confusion. I pull a small cheese sandwich that Sandra had prepared for me out of my bag. Just beside the apartment, there's an iron spiral staircase that climbs to the roof of the building, so I place what's left of my newspapers on the third step and sit down there. My eyes gradually wander off into a distant time, accompanied by a song that's close to my heart. I calmly close my eyes.

It was a warm moonlit night, and I was sitting in the courtyard of the club in Ain Shams, which had been deserted since sunset. Everyone had gone off together to take part in one of those weddings that I had come to avoid. It was late, and a song on the radio was coming and going with the wind. The voice was clear and moving, as if it had come from another time. It had a distinctive richness that seemed not quite human. I fell asleep that night to the enchanting sound.

It's my wedding day. I'm jubilant in my robe, and my skin has been adorned with henna. My mother is dancing in the middle and calling to me in a clear voice, blessing me and protecting me with magical incantations, while scattering salt on the people's faces to ward off the evil eye. My sisters Karima and Halima are dancing around me—they appear as two beautiful young women. Everyone is singing to me and my bride in clear and moving melodies, while my friends wave and congratulate me. I skillfully dance 'the hoopoe.' Everyone is surprised by this, and they ask me where I learned the moves of that wondrous dance. I myself don't know how I managed to do the dance, or where I got the idea to do it. I'm in a state of ecstasy, and they all want to learn the dance from me. I return to the center and repeat the dance while they imitate my moves. My mother sprinkles even more salt on everyone's heads and lets out joyful cries. When I go to my bride to dance with her, I hear her singing in an enchanting voice that almost seems not to be her own. I'm intoxicated by the rattling of her bracelets and her incredible smell. She takes my hand and draws me out of all this noise. In the bright moonlight, she lets me touch her long hair, then her neck and cheek. She smiles as I kiss her fragrant mouth until my lips touch her teeth and we tremble together. When we return, everyone is gone. The echo of my bride's song keeps coming to me as we sit down. The voice is clear and moving, as if it were from another time. It has a distinctive richness to it that seems not quite human. Yet when I look at her, I find that she's not singing, but changing her clothes instead. We fall asleep in each other's arms, wrapped up in that angelic voice.

The next night in Ain Shams, everyone had gone to an aqeeqa. I was in my room on the second floor of the club, feeling tired and sleepy, when the distant sound of singing came to me. It was the same melody as before. I slowly walked out to the courtyard, to the source of that peaceful voice. I saw Amm Rikabi there. He usually listened to Quranic recitations on the radio—especially to the voices of Sheikh Muhammad Rifaat and Sheikh Abd al-Basit Abd al-Samad—and also to the Umm Kulthum program. But that night I found him listening to that song instead, and singing along with it—he had it memorized, just like he had memorized the verses of the Quran. His eyes were closed, and he seemed to be in a state of rapture, almost entirely absent from the world. I too was captivated by that enchanting voice and clear melody. I closed my eyes, hoping to perhaps see what he was seeing.

Amm Rikabi sighed as the song ended, and looked a bit embarrassed when he realized I was there. He pressed at the cassette player to take out the tape, and then turned it over to play the other side. He greeted me kindly, a happy and relaxed look back on his face. He gazed at me, as if we had seen some distant apparition together. Since he wasn't saying anything, I asked him, "Whose enchanting voice is that?"

"Asmahan."

I heard 'ismaha Ann' so I asked him in surprise, "Ann? I haven't heard of her before."

"Her name is Asmahan, not Ann. Do you know the singer Farid al-Atrash?"

"Yes, from the movies."

"This is his sister. She was an amazing singer with a devilish voice."

"Don't you mean an angelic voice?"

"No, her voice was truly devilish. There are many angels, Hamza, but there's only one devil."

"Is she still alive?"

"The poor woman died young, but she left us her immortal voice."

"I thought you loved Umm Kulthum."

"Of course I love Umm Kulthum, but Asmahan enchants me too. Umm Kulthum's voice wraps you up; it hunts you down, and there's no escape from it; it shackles you, but with your consent. Asmahan's voice penetrates you, and soars with you into clear skies; then it leaves you there, free to fly as you please."

Amm Rikabi pressed the button on the tape recorder, and the voice gently streamed out, while he nodded off. I looked at him in surprise. I was certain that there was some secret in this ritual, and I waited patiently to hear it. I started on the surface of the melody, but was drawn deliberately and tamely into the depths, without knowing where exactly this secret attraction came from.

A few evenings passed, and one calm night I found Amm Rikabi alone in the courtyard and listening to the BBC news broadcast, as he often did. The group who normally sat outside in the courtyard had started to dwindle, for autumn had begun and the evenings were getting colder. But Amm Rikabi was one of those old romantics who loved sitting in the peaceful moonlight or in the darkness to listen to the distant sounds of the radio. He entered those faraway worlds with his ears, and made his home in them for a while. I brought him a cup of tea with fresh mint, and he was delighted at the gesture, and called me the hero of the age. I sat down and listened to the BBC Arabic broadcast with him. He mostly commented on the news with short bursts of mocking laughter. And whenever the signal of that distant broadcast weakened, he was forced to lift the radio in the air and move it around in different directions—sometimes even grabbing at the antenna—until the signal returned and the broadcaster's voice was clear again.

"Do you have that cassette of Asmahan on you?" I asked.

He was happy that I asked, and I could see the flash of his eyes and the gleam of his white teeth as he smiled in the half-light. "I do," he said. "Are you addicted, Hamza? I can see you've fallen for her."

I laughed, but made no reply. He sat up, pulled the cassette out his robe, and put it in the recorder: the devilish voice flowed out of it. I left for distant lands. I don't know what it was at that instant that made me think about Europe, but my thoughts traveled to Italy, France, and Holland. I thought of the many enchanting things that I hadn't been able to enjoy in those cruel countries that had changed me and then rejected me. Asmahan fell silent, yet the echo of her voice kept ringing inside me, opening windows onto unknown worlds, until the player clicked, announcing the end of the tape.

"I'll go make us another tea quickly," I said to Amm Rikabi, opening my eyes.

He thanked me but told me he needed to go to sleep early, for he had to go to the embassy the next day to help a friend of his get around paying the exorbitant fees for renewing his passport. As he got up with his usual lightness, he said, "I'll leave the tape and the recorder with you tonight, so you can listen to Asmahan whenever you want. But you should probably plug in the recorder—if you want to avoid angering Asmahan by letting the battery die out and distorting her beautiful voice."

"I wouldn't want to anger that devilish voice," I replied.

Amm Rikabi laughed. I thanked him for his lovely gesture, this unexpected gift whose secrets I wouldn't unlock until much later.

Over the course of the following evenings, Amm Rikabi began to notice that I was in love with one song in particular, "Nights of Joy in Vienna." We usually listened to the BBC broadcasts first, and then to Asmahan. I truly enjoyed sitting with that man who would tell me about the calm and beautiful days of his past, as well as many exciting stories about his life and other people's lives as well. He told me about things I never knew had happened. He talked to me about everything, the whole spectrum of life around us. He loved my endless curiosity and how eager I always was to ask questions. We listened to "Nights of Joy in Vienna" together, as well as to other wonderful songs by Asmahan. And every night he followed this up by telling me a new story about his past life. The songs seemed to be coaxing these stories out of him, bit by bit. He didn't divulge much, but it seemed that he had led a rich and exciting life—it was a well full of secrets that no one here knew about. I asked him plenty of questions, but never insisted.

"Would you believe that I was at Asmahan's funeral, Hamza?" he asked me one night.

"How's that?"

"She died a sad death that shook the country. Her real name was Amal, and some said that her father had actually named her Emily When she sung in front of Sheikh Dawood Hosni—the famous artist, composer, and singer—he was so overwhelmed that he gave her the name of Asmahan. Her strange death remains a mystery to this day."

He kept talking about her, until I could almost see her before me.

Asmahan's voice stops from inside the apartment. I tremble a little as I listen to the sound of the downpour outside. It seems that the rain won't be letting up today. Disoriented, I walk slowly down the stairs, a bit intoxicated, but also sad. I look at my watch, which has stopped, as usual. I try to get through my work quickly so that I can go meet Sandra at the Palm House as I promised, but the trolley is still crammed full of flyers—it's as if I haven't distributed any of them. I drag them along to the next building, and stand for a long while at the entrance as I try to convince one of the residents to let me into the building. When the door finally opens, I take the trolley straight to the back of the building. One after the other, I throw the bundles of flyers into the paper recycling bin. Then I pull the light trolley behind me, and walk outside with a broad smile on my face, heedless of the rain now, for my eyes are filled with visions of Sandra. I quickly head home, and chain the trolley up to the staircase at the entrance of my building, and lock it. I run up to my apartment and hastily change my clothes while gulping down a cup of tea. Then I grab a packet of cookies and eat them as I bound down the stairs and rush to the Palm House.

Sandra and Hakima are waiting for me inside the Palm House, and I'm delighted by the warmth and the kiss that greet me there. As I pet Hakima, Sandra asks me how my day was in all this rain. I tell her about the strange day I've had and about Asmahan, and also about Amm Rikabi, that wonderful artist who gave me back much of what I had lost in life.

"You said Amm Rikabi is an artist. Does he sing?" Sandra asked me.

"His story is a long one. Do you want to hear it?"

"Of course!"

Hakima moves to my lap, and I feel her warmth. Sandra draws closer and holds onto me, and I can feel the warmth of her thigh and her shoulder at my side as well. Her eyes are wide in anticipation, and looking straight at me. A very different thought crosses my mind at that moment. Sandra realizes what it is I'm thinking about from the deep look in my eyes and the sly smile on my lips, and lightly hits me on the chest, "Come on! Tell me the story!"

I look at the solitary palm, trying to recollect Amm Rikabi's words from that distant evening.

It was a clear moonlit night, and we were up late. It felt like the summer was bidding us farewell, sending us the last of its warm nights. Everyone else had left early. I longed to know more about Amm Rikabi's life. It was as if he were my father, a man whose story I wanted to know in order to help me live my own life. That night, he began telling me his story.

Many years ago, at the beginning of the sixties, I read an article in *al-Ahram* newspaper about an exhibit of works by a European artist at the gallery near the Egyptian Museum. At the time, I was much older than you are now, Hamza. These kinds of exhibits were frequent and by no means unusual, and this one might have escaped my attention had I not read its title, "The Palm House, the Sun House." I decided to go check out the exhibit the second I read that title. None of my friends knew I was passionate about painting. I was a painter myself, though I'd never shown anyone my pictures. There was a certain ostentation to the way people in the art circles used to live back then, and I couldn't take it, even though I admired many of their works. I used to work as a bookbinder at a press in the Faggala district: I could read most of those books for free, which allowed me to follow developments in literature and the arts. I sometimes visited the exhibits downtown, while living in lovely isolation here in Ain Shams, where I could live out my identity as a painter in all tranquillity. The reason I went to that exhibit in particular was that I had painted a collection of twenty-one large works that I had entitled "Houses of the Sun, Houses of Palms."

I went to the gallery. Valerie's paintings—that was her name—were splendid. I felt a tremor in me that I'll never forget. There were a great number of artists and patrons of the arts present, both Egyptians and foreigners, who were looking at the paintings. Some photographers were also there taking pictures. I really wanted to see her, to see the creator of those splendid paintings, and the person who had come up with the title we had in common. There was a group of well-dressed women standing in the middle of the gallery, but I didn't know which one the artist was, and didn't want to stare at them. I preferred to stare at the paintings, which were the reason I was here. I went to the other end of the gallery, far from the noise of the people, to look at some of her paintings in peace. I counted her paintings as I walked through the gallery: there were twenty-two of them.

A woman came up behind me and spoke to me in English, "I see you're interested in these paintings—I can tell by the way you look at them from different angles and distances. Are you an art critic?"

"No, I'm just a normal person who loves art. Are you the artist?"

"Yes."

Rather than ask me what I thought about the paintings, as many artists often do, Valerie quickly changed the subject, "No one else here is looking at my work with such attention. Where are you from? Are you from Nubia?"

"More or less. A bit further south. I'm from Sudan."

"Oh! It's a lovely country! I visited last spring. I loved the people's hospitality, and how friendly everyone was. I hope to . . . ."

Someone approached us and interrupted her, apologizing. He greeted me with exaggerated respect, and spoke to her in a language that I didn't understand. She gave me the catalogue of her paintings, and politely excused herself, saying, "If you have time tomorrow, come by the gallery between noon and two. I'll definitely be here then."

"With pleasure. I'll do that."

The young woman was wonderfully self-confident, and clearly knew how beautiful she was. I was amazed, both by her and her paintings. I had lost my objectivity at that point, and could no longer look at her work as I'd done before, for now she herself appeared to me in every painting as soon as I approached. I left the gallery, holding onto the exhibit catalogue that she had forcefully given me as if it were her own hand. I walked a long way that day, until my scattered mind finally made its way back to my body.

I went back to the gallery the next day, and stayed there from noon to three. She didn't show up. I wasn't angry, but I was quite sad that I couldn't see her again. And at the same time I was happy, because I got to experience her paintings again with less noise than before. I wrote down the names of the individual paintings, took a few notes, and left.

That same afternoon in Ain Shams, I took out my dusty paintings and sat down by myself to look at them. They gave me a mixture of joy and frustration. I had yet to choose names for the individual paintings. I read the titles of Valerie's twenty-two paintings, picked a suitable mix of titles, and finally gave some of my paintings names from among them, in memory of the lovely coincidence. Then I put them back, with the exception of a painting I had done of a woman with thick blue hair. I named that one "Valerie John," after that Austrian painter I thought I'd never see again.

Two days later, still spellbound, I went back to the gallery, wanting to see the paintings again. There was beautiful music playing that reminded me of the opening night of the exhibit—the music of Mozart.

"Are you an art critic?"

The same gentle voice repeated that same question from behind me, this time followed by a clear beautiful laugh. I turned around, laughing. She apologized for not showing up the other day, and said that appointments were hard to keep here in this country. She said she had been afraid that she'd never see me again, since she hadn't even caught my name.

"Even though you weren't here," I replied, "I still enjoyed seeing these unique and horrifying paintings again."

"Horrifying?"

"Yes. But that's a long story."

"What do you say we go somewhere else? I'd love to talk with you."

"Sure. Where would you like to go?"

"You choose the place, and I'll treat you."

"No, you choose the place, and it will be my treat."

"All right."

"Mine name is Ilyas Rikabi, by the way."

We made our way to a calm place on the Nile, a small open-air café with only a few customers. The unspoken questions increased while our eyes met, and then poured out what they couldn't divulge into the nearby Nile. We smiled timidly, like two adolescents. I talked to her about her paintings, and told her my opinion of them, which was different than what she had expected. I compared the paintings to places in nature—not to other paintings—and also told her the more spontaneous impressions I'd had of them. Valerie was amazed that I remembered not only the details and colors of every painting, but also their places in the gallery. We sat there until the sun was gone, the time passing like a summer breeze.

We continued to see each other, and for the first time I revealed the secret of my own shelved paintings. She wanted to look at them, and to visit Ain Shams. I invited her, and told my sister about the visit so that we wouldn't be alone in the house. Valerie came in a car with a driver. The cultural division of her embassy treated her as if she were the artistic ambassador of her country, and had provided her with a car and a driver for the duration of her stay in Egypt. In those days, it was a marvel for a foreign woman to go to Ain Shams. At first, everyone thought she that was either a movie star scouting out her next role or that she had the wrong address, or something along those lines—that's what people told me in the subsequent days. Some people said she resembled the Austrian actress Romy Schneider, which was true. My sister gave her a heartfelt welcome. She had lunch with us that day, and sat down with both of us for a long time while my sister took a good look at her. After that, Valerie said she wanted to see my paintings.

We climbed up to my secret workshop on the top floor. I took my paintings out from their dust and slumber—those paintings that no one else had seen except my sister. I remember that day well, the day Valerie entered my workshop, while I tried to clean the cobwebs off the paintings. I apologized to her about all the dust, but she simply waited without saying a word. It was as if she were somewhere else entirely, at some other place in the world. Her eyes were filled with tears as she looked on in silence. I wiped off the paintings quickly but gently, as if I were recreating each one of them with the act.

"You're an artist, Ilyas, a great artist!" she finally said. "Why are you hiding these treasures? It's a shame to dump such art in the middle of all this dust and darkness! These works should be in front of the people!"

Her words brought me joy, and a degree of self-respect. I told her about my artistic anxieties, and about my past, which was both bitter and sweet. That day, Valerie also talked to me about the modern European schools, and certain movements in painting, and told me that my work resembled that of several artists, none of whose names I knew. We discussed her vision of art, and it turned out that we shared many of the same views. I told her that I was familiar with the European arts and that I read whatever I could about them, but that I was more influenced by my environment here, by the clarity and richness of the colors here, the colors hidden beneath the dust, and by the light of the south as well—those were my greatest inspiration.

Valerie was originally supposed to spend two months in Egypt. She extended her stay to four months, and then to six, and in the end spent ten months and six days in Egypt. I also traveled with her to Vienna twice. Can you believe that, Hamza? She loved me and I loved her, and she became closer to me than my own breath and soul. She lost many of her supposed friends because of our relationship, which they couldn't understand, and because she preferred to spend most of her time with me, no matter where we were. She painted in my humble workshop, and I painted in her splendid atelier in the Neubau district of Vienna.

Hamza, perhaps it is destiny, fate, or chance—or some other unknown thing—that arranges the houses of life and death for us. All of us go down into the world twice, Hamza: once into life on this earth of ours, and once into death beneath it.

That beautiful flower visited me again, but the pressure from my family and friends pursued us. Painful questions were raised publicly on numerous occasions: Had Valerie converted to Islam? Would she become a Muslim? Would she change her name? The absurd yet oppressive talk increased, and vicious rumors started to spread, especially after my two trips to Vienna. They started to tease me by calling me a khawaga but I liked the name, and they were enraged when I started referring to myself as 'Khawaga Rikabi' in front of them.

I saw another world in Vienna. I saw great museums and exhibits with endless paintings and sculptures. I was enchanted by the live music there. Valerie took me mercilessly from one paradise to the next, from one city to another: Krems; Gratz; Salzburg with all its amazing lakes; and the beautiful eastern part of Austria, which I loved. I held exhibits of my paintings—all twenty-one of them—in Vienna, and in other enchanting cities as well. And I started painting again in Valerie's workshop, encouraged by her and some of her friends. I produced a lot of paintings in Vienna.

I tried to paint again in Ain Shams, but I couldn't. I was overcome by artistic impotence here. Something was preventing me from painting, but I didn't know what.

They suggested putting my paintings up for sale in one of the exhibits that Valerie organized for me, with the same title for the collection: "Houses of the Sun, Houses of Palms." Valerie exhibited her paintings with mine. We were very successful, and without batting an eye they said in that Western way of theirs that I had been influenced by the Swiss artist Paul Klee, and that many of my paintings were similar to his. I read about him later on, and was amazed at his work. I liked that he had been interested in poetry and music, because those were my interests too. And I appreciated his original style, which was free yet not overly complex. I felt honored that they were comparing me to him. Every time I saw a painting of his that I hadn't seen before, I had the feeling that I'd painted it before in my mind. I loved the captivating spontaneity of his works. But I swore to everyone that I didn't know his work, even after I began my long study of it. I was saddened by the fact that they always attributed the origins of all our art to Europe, no matter where it actually came from.

I sold all of my paintings, with the exception of two, which I gave to Valerie: the painting I'd named "Valerie John" after our first meeting at her exhibit in Cairo, and another painting that I called "Nights of Joy."

I got a lot of money for the paintings I sold. And when I returned to Egypt, the rumors increased. They said the usual crude things about that respectable woman, and then they claimed that I was part of a ring of spies and was conspiring with foreign elements against the interests of the country, and things even more absurd and degenerate than that. I left them for a while. I was saddened by my family and the people closest to me, who loved her not for who she was, but rather in the hope that she would become a Muslim. They wanted her to convert, but I refused outright, and avoided the topic at all costs with her. We lived in near isolation. And we suffered the painful bitterness of my tenuous position here.

I bought the house that I now live in with the money from the paintings. I planted a garden with some trees and palms in it. And I traveled to many beautiful places, enjoying my life. I live a secluded and peaceful life now—I have the means for that.

I had freed myself of the beautiful paintings that I'd left in the dust, and at the same time revived them. They were put in many great galleries, and I still have newspaper clippings and pictures from exhibits and conversations in Europe that I took part in. Back here, some of the people were proud of me for a while, and others criticized me for a while, but things returned to normal once I stopped traveling and became a regular person who lived a life like theirs again—after they had drunk their fill of the stories of my strange adventures abroad, that is. I tried to tell them only what I knew they wanted to hear. None of them ever asked me questions like yours, Hamza!

Valerie returned to Vienna and waited for me, while I stayed here alone in Ain Shams. We spoke on the phone and wrote each other letters. And I listened to Asmahan a lot, whom Valerie had also begun to love after I told her that the richness of her own voice was similar to that of Asmahan's. I became addicted to Asmahan as a substitute for Valerie, and I watched the films of Romy Schneider out of love for Valerie. She wrote me once to tell me she had adopted a girl whose name was Klara—Klara later started running a famous art gallery in Vienna. Valerie wrote me often and sent me pictures, but I didn't go see her. And she never came back to Egypt. Perhaps we both wanted to keep the other's home in our memory. The distance only increased our love for each other, and had one of us moved permanently to the home of the other, something precious might have been ruined. That's what we both felt, and what we both feared.

My heart was slowly breaking, and my soul burned up when I heard that Valerie had committed suicide. I couldn't believe it. I went and attended her awful funeral, and met her daughter Klara. Afterward, I received a translated letter from a lawyer in Austria, saying that Valerie had left a few paintings in my name in her will, and that she had wanted me to have them. Our relationship had been torn apart because of the ugly thoughts of our suspicious societies, and this caused me no end of sorrow. I regretted not having gone back to Vienna—the city of my last love—to see her, even if just for just one last time. I began to isolate myself after her death, keeping away from my family. In the old days, I used to feel the lack when I was far away from them in Vienna. But I also felt the lack—and so much sorrow—while I was here with them, so far from Valerie. I was split in two, and there's no cure for that. Now the lack, the loss, was here again, with Valerie even further from me, never to return.

That evening, as Amm Rikabi and I were listening to Asmahan, whose voice had added a deep dimension to my life, which I had not expected and which would remain with me forever, I asked him, "Do you regret not having gone to visit her again?"

"More than you can imagine."

"If you could go back in time, would you go see her?"

Amm Rikabi fell silent, and gave me no answer that evening. The next day, he invited me over to his beautiful home. The house had a strange but pleasant smell, one that I could never identify, in spite of my well-trained nose. He made me a hot cup of karkaday with lots of sugar, and put on a tape by Asmahan. He took a few paintings out from underneath the bed. They seemed to have been done fairly recently, and they were all of a woman of extraordinary beauty. I saw the same face in different scenes: once against a desert backdrop; once in the midst of snow; once at nighttime; and once in daylight. It wasn't hard to see how he felt about her. The works were truly breathtaking. Even though I didn't know much about painting, I felt the same enchantment that I did when I heard Asmahan's voice. He gave me a long look and said, "I painted these after Valerie died. It was a long time before I could take up the brush and colors again after her death. As you can see, the paintings aren't finished yet. I'll need the rest of my life to finish them."

Amm Rikabi let out a sigh that seemed as long as life itself. I stood there looking at the paintings while Asmahan sang that song of hers that was pulsing through me sadly. Amm Rikabi's story had become bound up with Asmahan's voice in a way I had not expected, and every note—even now, here in Vienna—seems to reveal more of his secrets to me.

I can almost see him before me now. I think of Amm Rikabi, and how he might have passed through this district, or walked down this road, or sat down in one of these cafés. He might have been in one of the newspapers I sell, or on one of the television shows I watch. He may even have been here, in the Palm House. I can almost smell him here inside this building: it's as if he were standing near me and looking at me with love. I can almost smell the karkaday and the oil paint, and his own distinctive scent, which always reminded me of the sweetest fragrances.

Sandra was still holding onto me. Her scent brought me back to myself. Hakima is on her lap now. I stop talking, and sigh deeply. Sandra sighs as well, and says, "It's as if you're narrating a movie, Hamza."

"There are no movies that can convey the feelings I saw in his eyes, Sandra. I don't think there's anyone like Rikabi in all the movies of the world."

Sandra's wide eyes reveal tears that I don't want to see. I surprise her with a mischievous look to get her out of this sad mood, and then claim to be hungry, and we silently leave the Palm House. As she presses my hand, I whisper in her ear, "Do you know how much I love you? I love you more than the number of beats in your heart."

"Really?"

"Hasn't your heart told you that yet? I'm telling it to you now, just in case it hasn't."

I kiss her, then move my lips to her ear and her cheek, until her skin starts trembling and she says I should stop. We walk among the people: some of them seem glad to see two people in love like this; and others seem bothered by it and shake their heads in irritation; and still others seem completely oblivious to everything going on around them.

11

The weather's improving, and that beautiful summer that I love begins. I can take off some of these heavy clothes now; and by telling my story to Sandra, I can also peel off many of the burdens of my past life. The Palm House becomes my favorite place to tell her most of it, this soothing place that has returned the balance to my life after many long years where I had no faith in anything at all in the world. Life is good with Sandra and Hakima beside me.

I call Amm Rikabi about once a month to ask him how he's doing, and to reassure him that I'm doing well. The past few times, Sandra has spoken with him a bit too. She learned some Arabic greetings from me, and he was delighted at how she pronounced the few Arabic words she knew, just as she was delighted at his own German expressions.

"I want to go to Egypt with you, Hamza!" She catches me off guard with these words, after having spoken with Amm Rikabi one day. This one sentence thrills me, but also troubles me. I've thought about going back to Egypt throughout the six-plus years that I've been here, but

I guess I never really took the idea seriously. There was always the difficulty of paying for the ticket, to say nothing of the presents I'd have to buy, so nothing ever came of the thought.

"When would we go?" I ask her.

"What about at the end of the year, after Christmas?"

"At the end of the year, in the middle of winter? No, it would be better in March. The weather's nicer at the beginning of spring."

For the first time, I feel that I'd be able to go back there if I really wanted to. And for the first time, I seriously consider working extra hours on Saturday evenings again—dragging around flyers—to save up some money. As if Sandra were reading my mind, she asks, "Would you let me buy the tickets to Cairo for us?"

"Slow down! You're in such a hurry!"

I say this while thinking about how I can manage to get the money for both our tickets.

One day, as we're on our way to the Palm House, I surprise Sandra with a remark, "You haven't told me much about your life."

"What would you like to know?"

"I don't know. Anything!"

She keeps quiet, and at first I think she doesn't want to talk about herself. But once we enter the Palm House and Hakima binds us together with her movements, looking for the warmest and most comfortable lap—and settling on Sandra's in the end—Sandra begins speaking, without any further prompting from me.

"I was born in the area around Krems, which you know, to a well-off family. My father played first violin in the Vienna Philharmonic, and my mother was a flute player. They got to know each other in Paris, during my mother's first trip there with the orchestra. She had always dreamed of seeing the Notre Dame cathedral, so my father took her there one morning. They had such a good time there they missed the plane that was taking the orchestra back to Vienna, and were forced to spend an extra night in Paris—which quickly turned into two extra nights—with a friend of my father's. It was one of the best trips of their lives.

"They got married in Vienna. The story of their love was full of passion, but also short-lived. They'd only been together five years when my mother left us—me, my brother, and my father. I was two years old at the time. She'd fallen in love with an actor, and went to America with him. My father wouldn't let her take us with her, so my brother and I stayed with him and his mother. He was wonderful, both a father and a mother to us, and we were everything to him. He was indulgent with my mother, and didn't harbor any resentment toward her. Nor did he ever say a single bad word about her when we were around, despite what had happened. And if she visited Vienna on one of her few trips to Europe, he let her come to our place and had us spend plenty of time with her. I slowly became estranged from her, and I could never undo this. I couldn't forgive her for going away and abandoning me when I was so young. And I couldn't forgive her for leaving my father like that. The shock of it never left him. He never remarried, and has been living alone ever since.

"You've met my father, Hamza. You've seen how much he loves and respects you, and how he only wants the best for me. And you've seen how my grandmother loves you, just like she loves me."

"I've never met anyone kinder than your father and your grandmother in this whole country," I reply. "And I like your brother too. But how's your relationship with your mother now?"

"We write from time to time. I visited her once in New Jersey, where she lives; she didn't seem happy. She chose a fast-paced life, but a practical and routine one, devoid of any real spirit. Her American husband is a vain man who's constantly going jogging to keep his figure. I can't stand him: he's the reason for my father's misfortune. I can't forgive either of them for what they did to him."

Here, I try to steer the conversation toward an important question that every lover wants to ask. It's a strange question, but also an entirely normal one that can set the tone for a whole relationship, "Wasn't there someone else in your life before me, Sandra?"

"Do you mean a man?"

I smiled, silently shrugging my shoulders as if to say: anyone.

"One single man, Hamza?" Sandra replied with a laugh. "No, there were lots and lots of men!"

"Really?"

"I'm just joking! There was only one other person before you, Hamza. I was eighteen, and I thought he was going to be there my whole life. I was studying painting and photography at the time. When we met, he was a sensitive man in love with music. He finished his law studies quicker than expected, and it seemed as if his life—and the way he looked at it—changed completely from one day to the next. He became paranoid, and thought he had enemies everywhere in society, and began to bicker with them by writing columns in a few of the newspapers that were opening up their arms to that kind of harsh language—newspapers that were widely distributed across the country. The people on his hate list grew with each passing day, and he found like-minded people who supported him, so he turned his energy toward politics and "ridding society of its filth," as he put it. He joined the ranks of those political garbagemen who think their task is to clean up the country and burn its human trash. Even his views on women were a concern to me. He became completely convinced that women were inferior to men, despite the fact that his mother dedicated her entire life to him. He quickly came to identify with the views of a political party I couldn't accept, and he clung to that ideology, working his way to the core of the party. This was the political career he'd been dreaming of. The gap between us kept growing, until he found someone else who shared his ideas and accepted his beliefs. There are many people like him here, Hamza, despite our supposedly civilized way of life, and its flashy exterior. He left me for someone who believed in his views and who helped him achieve his ambitions. I was extremely disappointed, and fell into a depression. But my father and grandmother were there for me when I needed them. They didn't interfere too much though, and let me go through it on my own. I needed several long months to recover from that painful experience. And now, now I have a partner who's only fanatical in his love for me."

I press her tight against me, and at that moment imagine how people in my own society would react to a scene like this. If a woman I loved spoke words like these to me, and if I kissed her with this kind of passion, everyone would call me insane. Most of my friends would abandon me, and I'd become an object for slander in their mouths.

Sandra tells me a lot about her childhood and her interests in the following days. These intimate stories are extraordinary, but she considers most of them to be perfectly normal. I'm truly amazed at how calm she remains, and the way she accepts life and whatever it offers her. Nothing upsets her. Nothing makes her lose her composure. I love her intelligence and her openness—she has so many qualities that make me fall even more in love with her.

"Doesn't anything ever bother you, Sandra?" I ask her on one occasion. "You're always so calm and composed."

"Many things bother me. But letting anger get the better of me doesn't help anything. I'd rather look for a solution to whatever it is that's bothering me."

"Have you never been angry at anyone?"

"Of course I have. I've gotten angry at a lot of people. I'm no angel. I was angry at my mother for a long time. But I've changed a little. I'm trying to forgive her now, but I need time, and I don't want to lie to myself. There's only one person I'll never be able to forgive."

"Who's that?"

"Do you remember how I told you that ballet used to be my whole life?"

"Yes, I do."

"My father brought me to the ballet academy, and they accepted me. I was preparing for a career in it. I was young and everyone considered me very talented. I devoted myself to it, and spent many long years training. Then, one unlucky day, we had our first original performance of *Swan Lake* at the Vienna Opera House. I'd dreamed of that day for so long. I put my outfit on an hour before the show for the warm-up drills. But on the first jump, I let out a scream that almost tore my chest. My toes were bleeding, soaking through my ballet shoes. I was in so much pain that I couldn't even take off the shoes by myself. There were shards of glass in them. A nerve in my foot had been cut, and I went through several operations. It took me six months just to learn to walk normally again. Can you believe that?"

"Who did that to you?"

"Several people were under suspicion, and they carried out an investigation. They finally discovered the culprit, and she was expelled from the troupe, but that didn't change the fact that I could never do ballet again."

Sandra tells me story after story, and I keep on asking her questions. She says she prefers my stories to hers, but I love the simple and unaffected way she tells me about her truly remarkable life.

Christmas comes, and I spend it with her family in Krems. Sandra finds my present for her underneath the Christmas tree: two tickets for Cairo, just as we wanted.

We set the date of the trip for the end of March. I tell Amm Rikabi, who is delighted and says he'll be waiting for us. Sandra can't believe she'll be in Egypt in just a few weeks.

One morning, while I'm at my apartment, I feel a sharp pain in my right side. I pull myself together and make a cup of herbal tea, thinking it must be something I ate, but the pain keeps getting worse until I can hardly move. I can almost feel death drawing closer, while Hakima meows beside me, not knowing what she should do. I drag myself into the kitchen to vomit. Fortunately, my neighbor in the adjacent apartment—who always gets up quite early—hears me. She hurries over and knocks on the door. I open and tell her I'm dying, and that I want her to call Sandra. At that moment, I think about how often Sandra has tried to get me my own phone line, and how I kept putting it off. Before I can finish telling my neighbor Sandra's number, I lose consciousness.

They remove my burst appendix at the hospital at the last possible moment. Sandra comes to visit me in the afternoon, worried, and stays by my side. I come down with an infection, and wind up spending three whole weeks at the hospital. Many confusing dreams visit me in my fever and delirium, and for a while I think that I'm back in Sudan again, until one dream brings me back to reality.

The hunchbacked man in front of us is wearing a new coat and an old hat. He descends into a long underground passageway, and we follow him. He's carrying a dim flashlight in his left hand, but I can't see his right hand. I can barely see anything in this darkness. The air smells dank. I bring up the rear, using both arms to hold a heavy bag with a broken handle against my chest. I set it down from time to time to dry my sweat off with my sleeve, before hurrying on after them again as they proceed in funereal silence. I can hear the panting and wheezing of the older men among them, and also the sounds of the heels of women's shoes—a large number of them—striking the ground. The hunchbacked man is still at the front: I can see his silhouette in the distance. We slowly make our way down steep concrete steps that are so narrow we're forced to turn our feet sideways, which is even more difficult for me because of the bag I'm carrying. I had hastily packed some books and dictionaries earlier, among them: the Duden, *a huge German dictionary; the* Kindler Encyclopedia of Literature*; and a book called* Learn German in Seven Hours. *I drop the bag, scattering the books on the ground, as well as some of the wool sweaters, scarves, and gloves that were practically bursting out of the bag. As I gather all this up, I find a large cookbook as well. I'm not sure why I packed it with all the other books—perhaps I thought it was some important dictionary because of its size and binding.*

I almost cry about having to abandon the upcoming trip. Sandra reassures me, saying that we can travel to Cairo a hundred times over once I'm better. Hakima is staying at her place now. My old neighbor comes to visit me as well—I always carried her bags for her whenever I saw her out on the street. Now I thank her for saving my life on that difficult morning.

Abu Darsh also visits me, and the whole time he's there he makes me laugh, until my stitches almost rip. He tells me he's printed pamphlets in Arabic and German calling for the closure of all the Arab embassies in Austria, and says:

"Hamza, all the embassies are worthless! All they do is spend the country's money—the poor people's money—on useless ambassadors and consuls and trade advisors; and on cultural attachés who know nothing at all about culture, but are simply there to pay the dues of student delegations. And they spend the money on military advisers, too! Military advisors, in Austria! Do you think Sudan will ever go to war in Austria? There are tons of huge offices with lots of employees. They're supposed to be serving those of us who live abroad, but they think they're here to lord it over us. The taxes of the poor pay for their ridiculous salaries. Most of them don't even live in houses—they stay in palaces they've rented, or that the country owns, and wash their hands of their fellow countrymen, as if we had rabies. Most of their 'work' consists of eating and drinking at banquets and parties they throw for each other until their bellies burst, while their wives hang around at their sides like decorations. They don't do anything to help the poor Sudanese people living here in Europe. Only on the holidays do they ever invite people for some meal or celebration or Iftar banquet, to show how pious and devoted they are. And some of the fools are actually happy about being invited to those events! They clean up their wives and themselves to rush over there and show their allegiance and loyalty. Then they're overcome with joy because the Honorable Consul shakes their hands. Or because His Excellency the Ambassador smiles at them! Can you picture it, Hamza? Those people are cogs in our disastrous machine as well!"

"But the embassies do useful work sometimes."

"You're so naive! You're practically a cog yourself! You must still have a fever. They call their get-togethers at the UN cafeteria 'important meetings!' They make private phone calls for hours to all the countries of the world while their secretaries wait on them and tell insignificant servants like yourself that his Excellency will deign to speak with you for a full thirty seconds! They deprive you of the few rights that the Austrians actually grant Sudanese people in this country. They're supposedly here because of people like you, Hamza, but in truth they only work for themselves. They only solve other people's problems when they themselves are affected. And as for their poor fellow citizens who work beneath them at the embassy: they get paid slave wages, and have no health insurance or social security. And if you ever complain about it or are unable to work because you're sick, then they throw you out into the street. And if you've suddenly become too old to work for them, they get rid of you like some old horse!"

He keeps on telling me about scandals involving ambassadors and consuls in Vienna, but I don't know to what extent the stories are true. He jokingly assures me that he'll be writing a book about all this, and makes me laugh until I forget all about my troubles.

Sandra continues to visit me regularly, and Abu Darsh irregularly. Sometimes he stays until the nurses kick him out. He always jokes around and laughs with all of them, and every time he leaves with some new story that he tells me about on the next visit. I want to see Hakima too, but she's not allowed in the hospital, so Sandra sneaks her in inside her coat for me—I'm delighted to see her after such a long absence.

I gradually recover, and leave the hospital. Since my job at the newspaper doesn't provide me with any health insurance—or any kind of insurance at all, for that matter—I'm forced to pay the hospital fees, and I lose all the money I had worked so hard to save for the trip to Egypt, even though Sandra helps me out by paying for part of the hospital bill.

I call Amm Rikabi. I never told him the truth about my financial situation here, even though he always said I shouldn't hesitate to ask if I ever needed any money here in this expensive country. When I tell him about my appendix, he asks if I'd like him to come visit me in Vienna. I feel so grateful for this paternal thought of his: the mere presence of this distant person who cares for me and is willing to be there when things go wrong comforts me greatly. He really does make me feel like he's family.

The days go by, and Sandra's presence beside me speeds up my convalescence. The newspaper fires me for being absent for so long, and I fall even further behind on paying the rent for my apartment, which is getting colder. Sandra decides that I should move in with her and say goodbye to my apartment forever.

A few days later, once I'm able to walk around a bit again, the three of us head over to the Palm House on a cold yet sunny day. Once we're inside, I tell Sandra, "I hope you can forgive me for ruining our trip to Egypt."

"Don't say that. Your health is more important to me than any trip."

"I'm sorry for disappointing Amm Rikabi as well."

"We'll go there Hamza. We will. But don't worry about it right now."

"I'm afraid I'll never see him again, Sandra!"

Sandra can tell how sad I am about this, and says, "You have no idea how much I love the man who sent you here, to me. And your stories make me want to see him even more, Hamza!"

"He's an incredible man. But there's someone else I haven't told you about. He and Amm Rikabi were the reasons I was able to come to Vienna."

"How's that? Who?"

"Amm Rikabi was the soul behind my trip. As for the person who paid for it, so that I could leave right away: that was someone who came close to being my father."

"What do you mean?"

I begin the story.

One night, toward the end of that autumn roughly six years ago now, a man entered the Sudanese Club's courtyard, wearing a clean white robe and an elegant turban. I was sitting with the older men, listening to their stories and drinking tea. The new guest was in his fifties, and had a dignified look about him. He was tall and had an athletic build. He showed respect to everyone seated there, and they all stood up to greet him—which they usually didn't do—as if he were someone important, or had been away for a long time. His name was Hashim. From their conversation, I learned that he had been living abroad in one of the oil countries for several years. They asked him if he'd finally bid the bachelor's life farewell, but he said that he hadn't, and so they joked around and teased him about it. He deftly changed the subject, then greeted me, saying that he hadn't seen me here before.

"Welcome," he said. "Are you from Ain Shams?"

"No."

"But you're Sudanese?"

"Yes."

"Where in Sudan are you from?"

"I'm from a village nobody's heard of. It's called Wad al-Nar."

The man quivered in surprise. "Wad al-Nar? *Wad al-Nuwwar*? How could I not have heard of it?!" he asked in a voice that seemed louder than usual in that silence.

He was the first person here who I'd heard mention the name 'Wad al-Nuwwar.' I thought that he must be joking, or that he had confused it with somewhere else, or that I had misheard him, but he continued, "I'm originally from Wad al-Ghazal, of the Basatin tribes, and Wad al-Nar is exactly sixty kilometers northwest of our village. But it had a different name a long time ago."

Hashim was for real. I had heard about that village several times from my mother. She'd told us that we had family there, but I don't remember any of the visits that we apparently made while I was still a baby, before my grandfather died and my aunt Warda married and moved to the north.

"What's your name?" Hashim asked me.

"Hamza Yousef Wad Nilawi."

"Hamza Yousef Wad Nilawi?! The son of Yousef Wad Nilawi? Is your mother from the Shilani family?"

I shook so hard that I was sure some of the men must have noticed it. Hashim was silent while some of the others laughed, and one person said, "Hamza! Finally someone's showed up who knows your village!"

Hashim said nothing, and seemed pensive. I was staring at him, and he was staring right back at me. I finally broke the silence with a question, "When did you last visit Wad al-Nar, Hashim?"

"In the mid-sixties. I was a colleague of your uncle Sharahbil. You probably never met that great young man, did you? Sharahbil al-Shilani."

I felt my chest freeze, and the trembling came over me again, for I could still remember some of my mother's stories about that uncle of mine. At that moment, I recall thinking that my history was buried in the mind of that man Hashim. I couldn't let him get away from me. I had to find out what he knew about the village and its people, and how much he knew about my family.

"How's your family, and how's Wad al-Nar?" Hashim asked me.

"Wad al-Nar is gone. It's not there any more. I don't know where my father is. As for my mother and two sisters, they're all dead."

Hashim flinched in his seat, then clearly spoke the name of my mother, "Habiba bit Nur al-Din al-Shilani is dead? There's no power or might save in God the great, the exalted."

All of us were in a state of shock. How did this man know my mother's name? He repeated the expression, "There's no power or might save in God the great, the exalted. To God we belong, and to Him we return."

The others repeated this last phrase after him, "To God we belong, and to Him we return."

He was silent for a long moment, then said, "I know your family very well, Hamza."

Hashim raised his hands and recited the first chapter of the Quran with me. He had a sad and shocked look on his face now—it was nothing like the face he'd entered here with a few minutes ago. For the first time, I felt a bit of comfort. This was the first time that all these people had ever mourned and asked God's mercy for those who had died in my family. It was the first time in years that a clear picture of Wad al-Nar came to my mind: it was as if I could see the village before my eyes. There was a sad comfort in the support of that silent group of men. That rare feeling of intimacy was soothing at that moment—the feeling that I was not unknown, and that I'd had a family and a home, even if they were no longer there. My history, which had almost been forgotten, was real. There was someone else who knew my village. There was someone else who knew my family and my parents, and who could confirm that I didn't simply come from nothingness. The merciless thoughts that had so often accosted me at night—that I was from another planet, or stuck in some nightmare—were not true. Wad al-Nar existed. My family existed. I had almost gone mad in my moments of weakness; I had almost thought the stories I told people about my childhood were nothing but delusions. Very few people believed them anyway, and in time I stopped telling any of those stories—whether good or bad—to anyone.

Silence hung over the place. Everyone was expecting Hashim to talk about me, and about my family and Wad al-Nar. But he skillfully changed the subject, asking the group the usual questions one asks when one has been away for a long time. Dozens of questions were spinning through my head the whole while. Hashim glanced at me from time to time, and I glanced at him. It was as if each of us were afraid of the other one slipping away. The group also asked him the usual questions about work, and about many people whose names I didn't know, and he in turn reassured them about so-and-so, and mentioned that he had seen so-and-so in such-and-such a city a while back, and that some other person they all knew was doing well, and that someone else was still alive and kicking. They continued talking about people, and mourning those who had died, bringing back memories of the old days. Then they decided to hold a karama celebration the next day in the club on the occasion of Hashim's return. They divided up the tasks for the ceremony with incredible speed, while Hashim kept glancing at me, and I at him.

"Where are you staying, Hamza?" he asked.

"Here in the club."

That night, neither of us would let the other out of sight, as if we were both on a hunt. Hashim was in no hurry to leave, and no one wanted to leave before him, as a token of honor and respect. But when everyone finally began to file out slowly and a bit embarrassedly, he said to me, "Why don't you come have a tea at my place now? I want to talk to you about Wad al-Nar."

I was ready to leave within a couple minutes. We headed out, and walked to his home in silence, despite all the unasked questions. Hashim put off the conversation. He bought some fruits along the way, but I couldn't tell exactly what kind he was buying. He also passed a few people he knew, and they greeted him affectionately and invited him to come visit them and have a meal with them the next day, or any other day he liked, but he politely declined, inviting them instead to the karama at the club the next day. I greeted them too, though I didn't know them, and he introduced me proudly, "This is Hamza Yousef Wad al-Nilawi, from Wad al-Nar and the Basatin people!"

The people were surprised to hear both my whole name and the name of my home in Sudan. For the first time, I seemed to have their respect and honor. Hashim looked at me proudly while I stood tall beside him, calmly smiling in my robe.

We entered his house. He lived in an area called al-Hilmiya, which was close to Ain Shams. I sat on the sofa and Hashim turned on the television. The program called "Twenty-Four Hour News" began, with talk of presidents and delegations and meetings and broken ties, and then some news about the renewal of relations between Sudan and Egypt, which was followed by sports. I watched all of this in boredom. Then an old performance by the Egyptian singer Umm Kulthum came on in black and white. It was a famous song of hers, and she was singing the words "This is my night and the dream of my life. . . . Caught between time that has passed and time that is coming." Hashim was singing along with her slowly, and I tried to make out all the words, but I was nervous, and kept glancing back and forth between him and Umm Kulthum, who was wearing a long dress and holding a large handkerchief in her hand. He made some tea for us after the song, but didn't drink any of it with me. He went to a nearby closet instead, opened it, and took out a bottle of cognac; he went and got some ice for it. He asked me if I would like some, and I almost said yes on account of how nervous I was, but I didn't want to numb any of my senses on that particular night, not for a single moment. For I knew the story he would tell me was part of my own, something I'd thought was dead and gone. He had held it prisoner inside him for many long years.

Hashim seemed even more nervous than I was. He wanted to shield himself from the nerves that were so evident on my face and body, but he wanted to talk as well. I wanted to listen. I wanted to gather up all the scattered words and record—fully and consciously—the lost and forgotten history of my family. There were so many times when I wanted to sit down with my mother and have her tell me about the family, but I always felt pity for her and put off my burning questions. The ghost of my father was always there, and I didn't want to upset her. Her eyes swelled up with tears every time she even touched on the subject, and I could almost feel the lump in her throat. So I always wandered off toward the tombs, dragging my feet, and sometimes humming or singing.

I knew that whatever Hashim was going to tell me that day would be new to me. I had so often dreamed of meeting some relative of mine—any relative, anywhere in the world—who could tell me even just a morsel of my family's history. I'd heard bits and pieces about my grandparents on my mother's side, and a little about my father, but these were scattered stories that contradicted each other, and I'd never seen my grandparents or any of the other relatives I'd heard of. We were on our own in Wad al-Nar, and far away from everyone. Our neighbors were our relatives; they were our whole family, and also our friends.

Like most Sudanese, Hashim began by talking about politics—and specifically about how confused relations between Egypt and Sudan had become after a long and stable history. He was looking for some way to get to the heart of the matter, but he broke off his introduction and didn't take it up again. Then he began.

"Wad al-Nar was practically an oasis in the old days. Its name was not Wad al-*Nar*, but rather Wad al-*Nuwwar*, because of all the gardens and flowers there. No seed would fall in that place without sprouting into a tree or a bush. Hamza, at the end of every autumn, a small lake of rainwater would collect there—would you believe that? We used to call it 'the sea.' Wad al-Nuwwar used to grow the best dates of the gondayl variety, and was one of the very few places where the argoun palm—which you may have heard of—grew. But you had to see it before the drought to believe it. No one who'd been there back then would ever have believed that it would turn into such a barren desert.

"Your grandfather on your mother's side, Nur al-Din, was a wonderful man from the Basatin tribes. He was supposed to come into a large inheritance from his father al-Shilani, who was a merchant and village leader. But your grandfather Nur al-Din committed an unforgivable sin against the customs of that time. He returned from one of his far-flung trading trips with a lovely wife whose name was Ansam. Ansam was extremely beautiful, and came from a family of good stock and standing. Her one fault was that she was from the north. And your great-grandfather al-Shilani had had bitter experiences with a few people from the north, who had collaborated with the slave dealers. He came to consider the northerners traitors, and refused to do business with them. So you can imagine what he thought of his son getting married to one of them! He was furious with him and denied him his inheritance, and banished both him and his wife Ansam. So your grandfather left Wad al-Basatin and moved to Wad al-Nuwwar, hoping that his father would go back on his harsh decision one day. Your grandfather Nur al-Din later traveled all over, and was very successful. Ansam bore him four children: al-Tayyib, Asiya, Habiba, and Sharahbil. But your great grandfather took his grief to the grave with him, and never forgave his son Nur al-Din for marrying your northern grandmother Ansam. Nor did his heart ever take pity on his grandchildren.

"Your grandfather Nur al-Din was al-Shilani's only son from his first wife, after she had borne him three girls. But Nur al-Din had a half-brother from a different mother, and when your great grandfather al-Shilani died, that half-brother received most of the inheritance, and the rest was divided among the daughters. Nur al-Din didn't get anything. The whole situation caused all of us a lot of pain.

"After Nur al-Din died, his half-brother considered himself to be in charge of the girls, and quickly married off Asiya and Habiba. He was the one who married the youngest of the girls, Habiba al-Shilani, to your father Yousef Wad al-Nilawi, and she lived with him in Wad al-Nuwwar."

"I remember my mother telling me once about the country of Shinqit, which is now called Mauritania," I said to Hashim. "It seems like a distant dream now. She mentioned years of hardship, and also how her own mother and father were married. She told me many things that are all a jumble to me now. Most of what she said about that subject seemed painful to her, so I never pressed her about it, even though I was dying to know more."

Hashim continued, "Your grandfather Nur al-Din used to trade in salt stones and dates and oils, taking them between the area around Shinqit, Mali, and Sudan. He also traded in spices from Yemen, and precious stones from Ethiopia. Nur al-Din saw that beautiful woman on one of his trips to the north. Ansam was part of a northern family from an area called Dumyat. He fell in love with her and set about to marry her. Her father loved your grandfather, and considered him one of the wisest and best traders around. For her dowry, Nur al-Din gave him many camels, and containers full of oil, and sacks of dates. He took her with him on a beautiful howdah, and they say that he sang to her the whole way back to ease the sadness and strangeness she felt at leaving her home. He stopped many times along the way and set up a tent for her so that she could look at all the natural beauty and grazing animals. She was eighteen years old at the time. After relations broke down between Nur al-Din and his father, he built Ansam a big house with a large garden in the middle of Wad al-Nuwwar.

"I was in love with your mother, Hamza. We were very distantly related. And I had arranged to marry her, but her father—your maternal grandfather—died, and the agreement we had was no longer valid, and your mother was married off to your father Yousef instead. He was from a good family, but he could be a bit quarrelsome at times. I couldn't bear to stay there any more, so I went away. I left the country and my own family behind, and never came back."

When he spoke about my father, Hashim was careful not to hurt my feelings, despite how bitter he felt about it all. He didn't want to add to my burdens. And in spite of the obvious anger and resentment that I myself bore toward my father, Hashim didn't let himself get agitated or say anything bad about him.

He kept on talking and drinking. His calm face was covered with light sweat and evident sadness, and his bloodshot eyes were gleaming. He got up to get some ice for his drink, and made me another tea. My whole body was listening to him, even while I pretended to follow what was on the television a bit. He had intentionally left it on to lighten the tension, and we both kept glancing over at the screen, but only to avoid each other's eyes—not because either of us were really paying any attention to it. I can't actually remember a single scene from the television after that song by Umm Kulthum. Our voices echoed in the room, as if they were coming from the inside of some glass bottle. We sat there talking from just before midnight until five in the morning. Hashim laid down exhaustedly on one of the sofas after having finished half the bottle, but all the tea I'd drunk was keeping me awake. I turned off the television once the silence began to lengthen, and laid down on the other sofa. I took a large gulp of cognac before lying down, thinking it might help me sleep, for my mind couldn't take any more consciousness that night. I looked at the ceiling as the drink's first effects took hold of me: it began to spin, reminding me of the ceiling fan during my interrogation by that mad officer at the detention camp. But that night at Hashim's, I was looking at a fan that wasn't there. I could hear the birds chirping, and the distant sounds of roosters announcing a new dawn, and also a muezzin calling to prayer in the distance, "Prayer is better than sleep! Prayer is better than sleep!" But I went off to a different prayer in the temple of the past—in the temple of memory. I'm not sure what time I fell asleep, but when I woke up to the loud bells of a nearby church, it was just past ten o'clock, and Hashim was no longer in the apartment. My head was bulging with the stories of the previous night, yet at the same time it was so empty that I kept hearing the church bells ringing in my ears long after they had stopped. My mind was a muddle, for I had just emerged from a strange dream.

An enormous man is standing in front of a long line of people, all of whom have their hands tied behind their backs. The man has a mask on his face, which makes him even more terrifying. He issues crude orders in a disturbing and incomprehensible voice, and colors each person's face red, blue, green, or black. They split up into four corresponding lines behind him. Some dwarves push each of these groups toward different pits. The strange thing is that everyone is walking into the pits in complete silence, as if they had no tongues. I don't know where these people came from. I feel foreign here, and my clothes seem strange on me. I'm scared that the same awful thing that's happening to them will happen to me. I run for a long time, getting further and further away until I'm sprawled on the ground and gasping for air. But the giant man with the mask and the rough voice is standing there above me. He starts coloring my face white—the color of limestone—and suddenly my voice is gone. I hear a familiar voice coming like an echo from the distance. I look up and see a man in a white robe and a big turban calling out to me: Hamza, Hamza!

I wake up late to the clanging of nearby church bells in the seventh district. I can't remember when my long conversation with Sandra ended and I fell asleep. I try to gather up the remnants of the last few hours, but to no avail. From the bed, I can see a slip of paper from Sandra on the distant table. I try to stand up, but my head is heavy, and I collapse at the edge of the bed as if I'd just been knocked out.

12

As I lie on the bed, all these events from the past run through my mind. I can't stop the memories from coming and going as they please. Hakima is looking for a comfortable nook beside me to finish her nap. People and places flow through my mind in quick succession. The loud siren of a passing ambulance fills the room, and its flashing blue lights flicker for a moment on the roof. At that instant, I try to focus on the difference between the sound of an ambulance and that of a police car. Suddenly, I remember I have an appointment with a Turk in the sixteenth district, at the Brunnen Market. I left a lantern with him to be repaired. I'd brought it back with me from Cairo, but never tried to light it on the long journey. It was still one of my most prized possessions, along with the three stones I collected and the stone Sheikh Sharif had given me. I planned to give the lantern to Sandra, but had to postpone doing so because it needed to be repaired first.

I don't know how long I've been in bed. Sandra normally goes to her job at the translation bureau in the morning, and then works on her thesis at the university after she leaves the office. I can see the slip of paper she's left on the distant table, but I stagger and fall back down on the bed when I try to reach it.

The door opens and Sandra enters with her usual bright smile. Hakima always hurries to the door as soon as she hears the key in the lock. I half sit up, happy, but also afraid of the vertigo I've had since leaving the hospital. Sandra asks how I am and kisses me, then picks up Hakima and kisses her, who in turn lets out that meow of hers, which is either a complaint or a greeting—I still don't know which. They disappear together into the kitchen for a little bit, then Sandra comes back to tell me about her day.

I take a warm bath, which revives me, and my vertigo gradually disappears. We eat together and have some tea with mint. Then I show Sandra a portrait of Valerie that Amm Rikabi had painted and given me as a gift. It's the first time I've shown it to her. I ask her if we could put it up in the room, and she's all for the idea. I also take the three stones and the stone of Sheikh Sharif out of my old bag and place them carefully on a table at the far corner of the room. It's as if I'm worried about dying before finding a suitable spot for these spirits I've carried with me all this time. I tell Sandra that she'll have the rest of my story when the time is right.

She looks at the picture of Valerie joyfully and says, "Valerie's so beautiful! I can't wait to meet the man who painted this!"

From my silence and frozen features, she can tell that her words have saddened me, so she surprises me with a question about two famous Sudanese singers, "Do you know Abd al-Qadir Salim and Abd al-Aziz al-Mubarak?"

I laugh at the sweet way she mispronounces their names, and ask, "How do you know them?"

"I bought you two CDs today from the Südwind store, but there's one condition!"

"Name it!"

"You have to tell me the rest of the story—the story of your journey."

She puts on the CD by al-Mubarak, and the songs soon have me in rapture. I keep my eyes on Sandra's face as I listen and sing along, and I can tell she's surprised at the way the harmony has taken hold of me.

She asks what the lyrics mean, but my translation is slow and clumsy, and only conveys part of the meaning, so she prefers to simply listen to the music without it. I can see happiness in her eyes—the happiness of a mother who has brought her child a toy that he adores.

After we've listened to the CD twice, I continue my story.

I was worried about my job at the stables in Cairo, for winter was just around the corner, and work was slowing down a lot. I got up early one morning with a desire to bring back memories of the old days. I decided to go to the Khan al-Khalili market and see Hagg Abu Faysal, a trader in gold and silver I used to know. Back in the day, I used to take the train and get off at Midan Ramsis—which is now called Hosni Mubarak Station—and walk all the way down Faggala Street. I loved just how crowded that street was, and was always amazed by the throngs of people I'd pass in that one kilometer.

I left the club at dawn. The transparent dew beneath my feet somehow calmed my agitated mind, and the fresh smell of the damp morning made me feel like I was somewhere else in this world. I walked in a state of near enchantment: perhaps it was the lingering effects of Asmahan's voice; or perhaps meeting Hashim or listening to Amm Rikabi's exciting stories had breathed new life into me.

The roosters were busy with their incessant crowing at that hour, and dogs were barking somewhere out of sight of human eyes. The echoing sounds of the call to prayer came from scattered minarets, and the birds answered them in song. Some cats were warring over scraps of food in plastic bags that had been thrown into the street. A solitary man was calling out in a calm and distinctive voice for people to buy fuul and balila from him. A solitary woman with a Bedouin accent was crying out and selling milk and that soft white cheese that they call arish. The sun came out as I turned from a long narrow alleyway onto a broad paved street. A small number of street vendors and other people began to appear, and the sounds of men gradually mixed in with those of the animals and birds, until the latter were all but drowned out by greetings and invocations, by coughing, spitting, and panting, and by the drone of car engines. Then all the sounds began to blend together, and the details were lost in a single indistinct mass of noise—the noise of everyday life. I walked on, my feet wiping up the dew and tracing my fate behind me on the ground.

It was the beginning of November. The marks of animals and birds and reptiles could still be seen through the cold morning dew. Those animals had swept the ground clear of our scraps in the hours before dawn: they erased our writings on the ground at night, just as we were erasing theirs during the day.

I could feel my skin trembling that morning, for I was wearing light clothes: I hadn't expected it to be so cold when I left my warm lair at the club. I picked up the pace, my mind clear of all thought, and walked until al-Zaytoun. There, I caught the first bus heading to al-Ataba, and got off at al-Muski market. I slowly passed through the long souk, which was alive and kicking even at that hour. I bought a newspaper and sat down in one of the coffeehouses to read it. I drank a hot ginger tea, and ordered a bowl of kushari from a vendor in front of the coffeehouse and ate it. After this, I made my way to al-Hussein Square. I wanted to see some faces from the old days, especially that of Abu Faysal at the goldsmiths' market in Khan al-Khalili.

I entered a narrow alley from the wide-open square in front of al-Hussein Mosque. The calligraphy on the walls of an ancient domed house drew me in, and I sat down to look at it from an elevated sidewalk not far from the fence of the mosque. The letters were Arabic, but I couldn't make out the words—they were like magic characters to me. There was a pretty woman there selling incense, prayer beads, and toothpicks. She had lit a few of the incense sticks, and was calling strangely and incomprehensibly to the passersby, gesturing to them with her hands. The captivating smell drew me to her, and I sat down near her on the sidewalk without attracting her attention. The smell reminded me of something in the past, but I wasn't able to gather up the fragments of the past and remember exactly what it was. The smell took hold of me, and I closed my eyes like an addict in ecstasy, transported from the world.

Some people were bargaining with her and buying prayer beads, while she gestured and haggled with them in return. Suddenly, she noticed me, and held out some incense. She didn't let out that strange coarse sound of hers this time, but smiled affectionately at me instead. I was both embarrassed and moved by the gesture, and I gave in, ready to pay her all I had on me. I had exactly 75 piasters, which was the price of a return ticket to Ain Shams, and a packet of incense cost 50 piasters. She could see how embarrassed I was as I put all 75 piasters in her hand, and she gave me two packets of incense, signaling to me that everything was fine. I smiled bashfully at this, and told myself that there were a thousand ways for me to get back to Ain Shams.

I sat down once more on the elevated sidewalk by the fence of the mosque, and looked at the lively world around me, at the people of this country whose features hadn't changed for thousands of years, and at the transparent smiles on their faces. I looked at the tourists who were all over the place. Some of them were moving as quickly as arrows and scowling angrily at the world and everything in it, as if they were seeing things that the rest of us could not. And other tourists were dawdling aimlessly about and smiling happily, as if the whole world were laughing playfully with them. I kept gazing at that wondrous mix of people, and from time to time I looked back stealthily at the lovely woman. I'm not sure why, but I thought that she somehow resembled my mother. Was it her smile? Or that scent? Or the color of her skin? Or was it the way her bracelets clinked as she moved her hands? What was it? She could not speak, yet there was something very deep about her, deeper than any description of her can capture. I sat there for a long time, looking at her. As the Friday prayers approached, the woman began to re-arrange the incense and other things she had hung on the fence of the mosque. A well-dressed girl who was about nine or ten years old and who looked just like the woman came and helped her. The girl communicated with her with the same types of hand gestures, and I assumed that she too could not speak.

The woman noticed me again, and signaled for me to wait. Then she promptly vanished into thin air. I stayed there watching the girl, who I thought must be the woman's daughter. Her beautiful braids reminded me of Karima's. The whole situation seemed strange to me: it was as if the woman had suddenly turned into the girl.

I took a closer look at the elegant calligraphy on the house, and finally guessed that it was in Persian. I read a little bit with difficulty, while the girl carefully hung more prayer beads on the iron fence near the gate that led to the mosque, and skillfully sold them to passersby and people on their way to the prayers, attracting them with her beautiful voice. She could talk after all.

The earth opened up to again reveal the woman, who waved to me from a distance. She approached and looked in my eyes, then said something that I could not understand. She opened a sackcloth and took out a lantern, which was dusty but still in good shape. The lantern had an ancient look about it, which was eye-catching, as if there were some enchanting story behind it. It could have belonged to Aladdin. I tried to explain that I didn't have any money on me, but she signaled that it was a gift. She wrapped it up in a newspaper and put it in a plastic bag for me. I thanked her and took it out of the bag. While I was rubbing the dust off it to have a look at its fascinating colors, she disappeared again, as if she were one of the jinn. I wanted to ask her why she had given this to me, but she was gone.

I stood up, with the lantern in one of my sweaty hands and incense in the other, and not a single piaster in my pocket.

As I walked past Fishawi's coffeehouse, I smelled a mixture of mint tea and spiced coffee and hookah smoke, and could hear the clinking of teacups and people ordering drinks and beggars imploring the customers. Further inside the Khan al-Khalili market, vendors were loudly calling out in every language, and other people were laughing. Once more, I remembered the old days. The market seemed more packed and crowded now. A few people recognized me and asked me how I was and how my old friends were, and offered me tea or coffee. This ritual was repeated several times, and I had drink after drink over the next two hours: black tea, ginger tea, mint tea, coffee, cola, Fanta, sahlab, and also hilba. I was very happy about this welcome—it brought back memories of the days when I used to smuggle goods from Port Said.

I went to Abu Faysal's store, but he wasn't there, so I headed back to Ramsis Station. I laughed at the situation the incense and lantern had landed me in, and was now determined to make the pilgrimage to Ain Shams on foot, no matter how much time and effort it cost me. I walked along Faggala Street from Khan al-Khalili through al-Ataba until I reached Midan Ramsis. I looked at the clock: it was two in the afternoon. A few clouds here and there were creeping in front of the mild sun. I decided to follow the train tracks to Ain Shams: I walked from Ramsis through Ghamra, al-Dimirdash, Manshiyat al-Sadr, Kubri al-Qubba, Hammamat al-Qubba, al-Zaytoun, and al-Hilmiya, and then on to al-Matariya, before finally making it back to Ain Shams.

I arrived at the club at ten-thirty in the evening, exhausted and dying of hunger. Amm Rikabi asked me where I had been all day. When I told him the story, he said, "By God you're crazy!" I laughed at this, and went to the bathroom to quickly wash up and put on a comfortable robe. Then I got out some bread and a plate of halawa tahiniya and went outside. I invited him to eat with me, but he politely refused, saying he had eaten earlier. The radio signal was weak, and he was looking for his favorite station so that he could listen to the BBC news. The dry bread was delicious. The halawa tahiniya was even more delicious: I gobbled it up voraciously. Then I made some tea with mint, as usual, which brought the smells of Fishawi's coffeehouse back to me. My legs were heavy and lifeless, but there was a light tickling sensation in my entire body that quickly sent me into a deep sleep that night.

There was no more work for me at the stables until the beginning of spring, which was a long time from then, and I could find no other jobs in Ain Shams. The young men's animosity toward me kept on growing, because of their suspicions about me regarding some of the women. So I sat with the older men instead, but their conversations were very repetitive. They even repeated their jokes, and some of them told the same stories day after day. I was bored out of my mind. Didn't these people have anything new to say? How is it that they don't realize that Amm Rikabi has the most—and the deepest—stories of any of them? I was certain that he still had dozens of untold stories to tell. He was a man of experience, someone wise and calm, and who was able to laugh at the world without overdoing it. I loved him, but it was difficult for me to define our relationship. Did I consider him a father or a friend? The carefree way he interacted with me made him a dear friend, but his concern for me was that of a loving father.

One evening, everyone had left except Amm Rikabi, as usual. "Do you like to read, Hamza?" he asked me without warning, once the news broadcast was over.

"I do, but I've only found a few books here at the club, and I've read most of them by now. It's mostly useless political stuff in that awful library: books praising the living and denouncing the dead, or unreliable works about politics or military history or those huge make-believe projects in Sudan. I haven't read anything that's actually taught me something about Sudan's history or about the daily lives of ordinary people there. These books talk about the exalted pious leader as if there were no one else around, until a new leader comes and the past repeats itself: the new one is always praised, and the old one condemned. And every single book in the library is about Sudan. Why aren't there any books about the country we're living in? Why isn't there a single book about Egypt? I bought seven books recently, but it's a luxury I can't afford any more."

Amm Rikabi took out four large and similarly bound volumes from a plastic bag beside him, and put them in front of me. "Do you know this one?" he asked me.

I looked at the title: *A Thousand and One Nights. Volumes One, Two, Three, and Four.*

"Of course I know it! But I've only read a few scattered stories here and there, and I thought it was all in one volume, not four. I asked about it once in the bookstore at al-Hussein, but the vendor got angry at me and said that they don't sell such immoral works there."

Amm Rikabi laughed. "No one here knows that it's one of the most important narrative works ever. They value it more in the west than we do. People here make fun of the west's interest and infatuation with our culture and literature. So much of our written heritage is prohibited here because it supposedly strays too far from religion and 'true morality.' They keep banning or destroying so many great works of literature on the pretext that they're indecent—they'd get rid of them all if they could. And the remnants of the more ancient civilizations are simply considered pagan idols. What's left for us, then? Religion is all around us now: above us, and in front of us, and behind us. The only place left to go is down—down into the earth to die."

"Do you really mean that?"

"Of course I do! A thousand times over! Those idiots who don't even read found some stories in this book that they say violate common decency. They read a few scattered excerpts and then decided to purify the whole book. They recently came out with an 'improved and civilized' version that's no bigger than one of these four volumes, some three hundred years after the book was first printed. And this isn't the only one: they've banned hundreds of other books, and there are dozens that they've altered to 'cleanse them of decay.'"

"That means that this collection here is a rare one."

"It's not only rare—it's banned. Take it and read it at your leisure."

"Thank you, Amm Rikabi. This is quite a surprise."

"By the way, this tape by Asmahan is for you as well. You'll need it on your long journey through life."

He smiled, as if he had some secret knowledge that I did not, or as if he were reading something in me that I myself did not yet know. I pressed the hard cassette in my breast pocket against my heart, and felt a new joy come over me. Then I took out the books in the dim light. I turned one of them toward the half-light, but could only make out the words *A Thousand and One Nights: Volume Four.* The books smelled like ambergris—everything that came from that man smelled like ambergris. I put the books back in the bag while Amm Rikabi prepared to leave. I, on the other hand, was getting ready to go inside and start reading this exciting text, this great work that was supposedly so lacking in decency. We parted ways until the next day.

"Why was it banned, Hamza?" Sandra asks me in surprise. "It's a fun book—I read it in high school."

"I don't know, Sandra. It seems that reading is hard work, and only those with strong wills are up for it. The people in our countries pass on what they hear. And those who call themselves the protectors of morals and religion make the decisions for everyone else regarding what should be published and what should be forbidden. They label one book indecent, and another anarchistic; they call one book immoral, and say that another one strays from religion. Not only that: they've gone so far as to kill some writers and artists. They'll go after anyone they think is straying from the path."

"I don't understand."

"Does anyone understand this, Sandra?"

"Tell me, what happened next?"

The cold set in, and one bitter night that month I suddenly said to Amm Rikabi, "I've decided to leave!"

"Where to?"

"To Vienna."

"Because of Asmahan?"

"She's not the only reason."

He smiled. And perhaps to test my resolve and see whether I really meant it, he said, "You've tried leaving to Europe before, and you weren't happy there."

"I'll try it again. I can't stay here like this, excluded and unemployed, and with neither a present nor a future."

"Do you know anyone in Vienna?"

"Didn't Asmahan say that Vienna is a garden of Paradise? That voice can't lie!"

I laughed as I said this, and Amm Rikabi laughed with me, "You're right, that voice doesn't lie!"

So I continued, "I think I had my portion of Hell in Wad al-Nar, Amm Rikabi, and I've had my portion of suffering all across the world. So perhaps it's time I go to Paradise. I don't think the angels of Vienna would oppose granting me a visa to enter their gardens."

Amm Rikabi laughed that long distinctive laugh of his, revealing two rows of perfect white teeth. Then he said, "Have you thought about what you'd do there?"

"When the angels question me, I'll tell them I came on a mission straight from Hell, and that the Devil sent me as a spy to figure out once and for all whether there really is a difference between Heaven and Hell. Maybe they'll believe me, and then I can write a report for the Devil; perhaps he'll come and see for himself what things are like there."

Amm Rikabi seemed to be lost in thought, and I thought he must be getting tired. He turned off the news commentary on the radio and said, "Vienna is beautiful, Hamza, but it's both Heaven and Hell. You'll have one portion of Heaven but two portions of Hell waiting for you there. It's Heaven because it's a refuge from this tedium and disgrace. But it's Hell because you'll be there without a language to preserve your history. And it's also Hell because you'll be starting all over again in that place, but with an older head on your shoulders this time—and that may be the cruelest of life's blows. But I know you're patient and persistent. And to the extent that you'll be a stranger among strangers there, you'll also be a friend among friends. I hope you survive the flames of that city, Hamza. It truly is an inferno, from the stinging cold to the hatred on people's tongues. Sometimes it will seem that even its love is fire, and that the people themselves are made of flames. You know that the angels were made of light, Hamza. But Iblis—Satan—was made from fire, and he refused to bow down to Adam because Adam was made from clay."

The first Hell I encountered was at the Austrian embassy. The consulate found creative ways to torture me, devising all sorts of problems and difficulties: they demanded that I buy a return ticket as well; they said that I had to have enough traveler's checks—in dollars, and in my name—for the duration of my stay in Vienna, in addition to money in an Egyptian bank account, and also health insurance; they asked for me to document the total assets I had in Sudan and Egypt; and they created other hurdles related to the job I had in Cairo and my work visa there. For three weeks I made a pilgrimage to the embassy at least every other day, and each time a new problem arose. Amm Rikabi came with me most of the last few times. He was disappointed that no one knew him there any more, and that they treated him rudely in spite of his age and how polite he was.

Hashim helped out with the traveler's checks and the bank account, and Amm Rikabi finally succeeded in getting me a four-week tourist visa.

I finished all my preparations to leave in just two days, for the visa had gone into effect a week before I actually received it. I said goodbye to Adam and his family: he was the only one of the younger men who still visited me from time to time, and I often visited him as well and played with his children. I said goodbye to Sharaf at the club, and to Amm Diyab 'the boaster,' who gave me some advice and warned me to represent him well in those distant lands and not be a coward with the fairer sex. I didn't have the chance to pay a final visit to downtown Cairo before leaving, for I had so worn myself out with the constant trips to and from the embassy that I simply couldn't handle any more trips into the city.

I said goodbye to Hashim and thanked him a lot for his help. He told me that I shouldn't even think about returning any of the traveler's checks that had helped me get the visa. We both insisted, but he was determined, and finally said that he considered himself indebted to *me*, and that it was the least he could do for me.

I prepared the suitcase that Hashim had given me. Amm Rikabi gave me a separate handbag, as well as a thousand dollars, and he too entreated me not to utter a word of protest, saying, "I've begun to paint again since you've been here, Hamza. I'm happy now, and I don't need a lot of money, as you can see."

Then he surprised me by giving me all four volumes of *A Thousand and One Nights* as a gift, and said, "Keep them safe, for if anyone here ever finds them, they'll either be neglected or burned. Take the books for own your nights of joy. Take them with you to Paradise."

Amm Rikabi made me promise to visit Valerie's grave for him. He said it was on the outskirts of Vienna, in the Zentralfriedhof, the city's largest cemetery. He gave me the exact location of her grave and said, "Tell her that Ilyas sends her his greetings and his eternal love from these miserable lands."

He gave me a small but beautiful painting of Valerie as well. "Every time you go to the cemetery, take this painting with you so that her soul can see it," he said. "Keep it in your home, so that she always has a place in Vienna."

Amm Rikabi gave me the addresses of three people in Vienna, saying that he trusted them completely and that they could help me. The first was of an Austrian painter and sculptor he had met a long time ago. The second was of an Austrian photographer who had been a friend of Valerie's. As for the third person, it was Valerie's adopted daughter Klara.

Amm Rikabi also wrote down the names of some places that I was to visit for him, and also the names of a few paintings that he said I had to see. Among others, he mentioned Gustav Klimt's *Adam and Eve* and *The Kiss*, as well as the paintings of Egon Schiele, who he had a great appreciation for, and also Rembrandt's sad work, and Breughel's paintings as well. They were all names I'd never heard of. He said some of their work could also be found at the Belvedere Palace complex and at the Museum of Art History. Not only did he talk to me about their paintings, he also told me about their lives and the periods in which they lived, which schools of art they belonged to, and many other interesting things. I promised him I'd go see their work.

As we said goodbye, Amm Rikabi said, "By God, Hamza, don't forget to write! And don't forget the lovely nights we spent listening to Asmahan and the BBC. I'll miss you and your dear company a lot. I hope you find your peace of mind."

Then he took off his watch and gave it to me, saying, "This is just a simple gift; don't turn it down. You'll need to know the time in that time-driven country: you'll come to know the meaning of it there. Time is so abundant here that we could export it! A watch is mere ornamentation here, Hamza. Take the watch with you so that it realizes its true value."

After all the difficulties, the time for leaving had finally come. In my first handbag, I carried the three stones that smelled of dust and sand, which were all that remained of Wad al-Nar; Sheikh Sharif's stone, which I had promised to return one day; the painting of Valerie; the collection of *A Thousand and One Nights*, which smelled like ambergris;

the cassette of Asmahan, which smelled like Ain Shams; and the seven books I had bought. I crammed some old clothes that I had hastily washed and dried into the suitcase, but I didn't have the time to iron them. And in the other small suitcase that I was using as a handbag, I packed a few small things that were of great sentimental value to me. I put the lantern from al-Hussein in there as well, after wrapping it in cardboard to protect it. I packed all of this as if I were never going to return, and as if these things were somehow substitutes for the people I was leaving behind.

Amm Rikabi brought me a thick winter coat, and said that it was from Vienna and that he had another one he could use. He told me that this coat in particular had a long history, and that it would certainly be happy to return home after being away for so long. Hashim gave me two new shirts, and also an elegant suit jacket that he said was too tight on him. And Adam had prepared some glass jars of food filled with Sudanese and Egyptian specialties, and he also gave me a bottle of perfume. I accepted all of these gifts gratefully.

The three of them—Amm Rikabi, Hashim, and Adam—took me to the Cairo airport in a Peugeot station wagon. I said goodbye to them there, embracing them. We joked around a bit and made light of things, but our eyes gave expression to different feelings altogether. Once again, I was giving up a family, perhaps the last one I would ever have in this country, to go off into God's vast country, into God's Paradise.

I went through the airport procedures. After all the trivial difficulties, the time to leave had come. It was time to drag on the burdens I was carrying from all the places I'd left in my life, time to say goodbye and look back a few times to calculate the extent of my sorrow, but also time to look ahead hopefully to the horizon. Soon, I would be further away from here than even the heavens above me. I remember how I used to sometimes see one of the divine and sacred planes above our village, and how I longed for it to land one day and take me away. Well here it was, waiting for me in Cairo. My secret dream was coming true. But how heartbreaking it was to have that naive dream of mine come true so simply and cruelly.

I took my seat on the plane. My winter coat and bag with the lantern couldn't both fit into the overhead bin, so I put the bag on my lap. I mostly looked out the window, into that dreadful emptiness, while the plane engines droned. Whenever my gaze returned to the inside of the plane, I saw people either absorbed in conversation or staring into the void. The crew moved about and answered the passengers' questions. A few people opened up Qurans to calm themselves and their fear of flying.

The pilot announced there would be a one-hour delay, during which time we sat in the plane without any air conditioning. But the lack of air conditioning was not what tormented me. It was excruciating for me to be on the verge of departure like that: I felt as if I were standing on the edge of a sword.

Finally, the plane edged onto the runway, and began moving faster and faster until the black pavement disappeared beneath us. The plane banked sharply as it ascended, and I thought that my poor soul could not possibly keep up with all that speed. I could feel my heart being wrenched downward. I was terrified, even though I wasn't at all afraid of flying. But my soul was a slow one, and couldn't handle flying, despite the previous flights I'd taken. It was as if that first trip to Europe had never happened. I wasn't sure if my soul was up in the sky or still on the ground, but either way it was still in Egypt. I left my soul behind there, almost calmly, in the care of benevolent spirits, not knowing how long it would be until we were reunited.

When the food came, I didn't have any. I was too nervous to be hungry, to say nothing of the fact that there was nowhere to put the bag that was on my lap. I took the *al-Ahram* and *Wafd* newspapers from the smiling flight attendant and tried to read them in my cramped position, but all I could manage was a look at the headlines on the front and back pages. I gazed out at the clouds from my seat by the window, imagining the distance that now separated me from Amm Rikabi and Adam and Hashim. Then I imagined how far I was from Wad al-Nar, and all the years that lay between me and Wad al-Nuwwar.

The sadness of those memories wore me out, as did the hum of the plane. I felt dizzy and empty, and fell asleep.

I'm a young boy. I head down a slope of ground behind Sheikh Ali al-Faki's Quran school. It leads into a dark underground vault. There's an old door made of palm fronds and rope. The door's ajar, and my curiosity gets the better of me. I enter into the vault, following rays of light that come from a high oval-shaped window of dusty broken glass. The place seems strange to me, and I keep my guard up since I'm alone. I bump into a closed chest in the middle of a room that's filled with junk. The chest tempts me to open it. I try to pry it with all my strength, but to no avail. I've been carrying a heavy bag with some strangely shaped stones in it, so I put it down and try to open the chest again, beating it with some of the stones this time. But it still doesn't open. I keep up my desperate attempts for a long while. And just when I'm about to leave in despair, the chest opens willingly, a cloud of dust rising from it. I cry out for my mother in fright, and rush out the door back onto the slope of ground outside. Once I feel that the dust must have settled, I head back to the door of the vault, but it's closed now, and I can no longer open it.

It's getting very late. Afterward, my mother would tell me that she'd been worried sick because I'd never stayed out so long before. The poor woman had been wandering around the village looking for me, and asking everyone if they'd seen me. I slowly head to my house late in the afternoon, still thinking about going back to the chest to try to discover its secret. My mother's waiting for me in the distance, and comes toward me quickly, and before I realize it she's standing in front of me, her anxious face devoid of color. In a single motion, she slaps and hugs me, erasing her anxiety with the slap, and then erasing the slap with the hug. Then she drags me into the house to scold me.

The plane shook violently, and I woke up in fright. I could hear a small child crying, and thought it was Halima. I stood up in my seat, my bag in my hand, not knowing where I was. The people sitting behind me looked at me in surprise, while the pilot's voice announced that we were passing through some turbulence. Then I heard the voice of a flight attendant asking us to sit down and fasten our seat belts, and I finally realized where I was. I sat down and sighed, knowing that for as long as I lived the crying of any child would remind me of Halima.

The fear I felt made me forget my dream for a moment. I looked out the window and saw nothing but clouds. The man sitting beside me had opened his Quran and was reading it out loud while bobbing his head like a pendulum.

I felt turmoil inside me: it came from this flight into the unknown; from the lantern at my chest; from those memories that flowed and multiplied; and from my mind's inability to distinguish between dream and reality. That unfinished dream came back to me, but I could see more of it this time. I began to doubt that these dreams had any meaning at all. I saw myself as a child again, separated from my mother; I saw Halima and Karima; I watched myself as I entered an empty palace; and then I lost my voice. Did any of this have anything to do with my real life? Who were these people who resembled me? They looked weak and emaciated, and were silently sweeping the ground with brooms made of palm stalks. And what about the color of this strange night, and the frost that I could see with my own two eyes? I had never felt such cold before, or seen such darkness. Or was this flight the dream, and my dreams reality?

The captain's voice rescued me, announcing that we were approaching Vienna, and that it was seven degrees below zero there.

A few people got up to get out their thick coats and prepare to face the cold that was lying in wait for them. I peered out the window to look at all the white squares and rectangles on the ground. The sun had vanished in the past half-hour, even though it was barely four o'clock. And as the plane descended through the clouds, the world became more overcast. The weather was dreary, matching my mood.

The plane landed, and the travelers enthusiastically applauded the captain, relieved to still be alive. My soul didn't land with me, as I had hoped. It had not even taken off from Egypt. It stayed in Africa. I stood up and got out Amm Rikabi's coat, which still smelled like him. I was glad I had it with me: it helped calm me down a bit as I got ready to face the unknown.

No one met me at the airport—except the bitter cold, that is. My knowledge of German was sparse. I only knew a few words, and even those I pronounced incorrectly. It seemed so much colder than the seven degrees below zero that the pilot had announced. I could feel it in the few meters that I walked from the ramp of the plane to the bus on the tarmac. It reminded me of the cold I'd experienced in France and Italy and Holland. The words came so quickly over the intercom of the bus that I couldn't understand any of them. There were signs as well, written in Latin script: very long words with dots on top of some of the letters. Before I left, Adam had given me a copy of an old book whose title was *Learn German in Seven Days*. The book had been quite funny, and I hoped that this country and its people would also bring me joy and laughter.

Once inside the airport, I headed for the passport window and stood in line. The officer looked me in the face, and then simply stamped my passport and let me through. After that, I went to get my luggage from the conveyor belt. I took my bag and walked toward the exit. Everyone seemed to be leaving—I couldn't see any customs officers. I turned around apprehensively, afraid that I was breaking some rule by simply walking out like that. Perhaps this was the exit for pilots or diplomats or VIPs. I stood there and kept turning around uncertainly, until a well-dressed officer came over and asked me some questions.

"Woher kommen Sie?" At first, even though it sounded like a question, I thought he was saying "Willkommen," which I knew, so I replied, "Danke! Dank you! Good!"

I was so flustered that I started mixing up the languages, thinking he would surely understand. *Learn German in Seven Days* hadn't even helped me decipher the first sentence I heard, and it didn't help me get out of my first jam either.

The officer pointed at my suitcase, and we started to communicate in earnest through our gestures. I spoke in Arabic mixed with English, French, and Italian—a mixture even the greatest linguist could not have understood. And he spoke to me in German and in English.

I understood the word 'Cairo,' but when he said the word 'Pass,' I thought he was saying 'bus.' He indicated for me to put my bag up onto a small moving belt. I thought he was going to weigh it, and was afraid that he would discover it was a full six kilograms over the permitted twenty. I was embarrassed, and was worried about how much the fine would be. But instead of weighing it, he turned a screen toward me, and I could see an image of the jumbled things inside my bag, and I realized that he was a customs inspector.

He pointed at the screen and asked me a question in English this time, which I understood, "What is that?"

Since the crisis over the bag's weight had been averted, English came easier to me now. "Cassette," I replied.

I was overjoyed, for I'd only heard the word before, and had never read it in either English or German. I said it again, and he nodded his head in comprehension and replied, "A cassette. Okay! What is this here?"

"Book. Buch."

He nodded his head in agreement. "And what's this?"

"Sandal."

"And this?"

"Khulal, misht ifriqi."

I said these last words quickly in Arabic while pointing to my hair to show him that I was talking about a type of African comb. We both laughed, but he quickly became serious again. "And this here?"

I didn't say anything because I didn't know what it was. I saw something that looked just like a hand grenade on the screen, stuffed between two shoes. It was hard to make out what it was on that x-ray image, which was like looking inside a sick person's stomach. He pressed a button and the image became bigger, but this only confused me. He looked into my eyes and turned the screen even further toward me, which flustered me even more. I shook my head and contorted my mouth to indicate that I didn't know what it was.

"Open, please!" he said.

Embarrassed and afraid, I opened it as if it were someone else's bag. Two other people came over and spoke with him in that quick nerve-wracking language of theirs. I didn't know where exactly in the bag that disaster I was carrying was located. I fumbled through the contents nervously while the officer looked at me sternly, which made me more nervous still. Then he pointed at a small clear container in the bag—I knew it was something Adam had given me, but I had forgotten what it was exactly. I opened it up, and as I was reading the label out loud, I remembered what it was. "Pino Silvestre," I said,

"Perfume." It was an oval perfume bottle that did indeed have exactly the same shape as a hand grenade.

The officer laughed again, but this time I didn't laugh with him. "Goodbye!" he said suddenly.

I walked a few steps, and an automatic door opened in front of me, and then closed behind me. Then a second door opened, and I found myself outside the airport. It was as if I had walked into a freezer. I'd left the heat of Wad al-Nar and of Egypt; and the warmth of the plane and the airport now gave way to the bitter cold of the street. I had only my memories to accompany me, and a heavy bag that would stay with me for years.

That kind of solitary departure has always caused me the worst pain. With communal departures, no matter how cruel they are, you have someone to share the pain with, and there's someone there to put their hand on your shoulder or look you in the eyes, as if to tell you that you're not alone, that you should hold firm and take heart. Or at the very least, they can do something to temporarily ease your mind. But when you're alone, you have to do all these things by yourself, silently. You have to comfort and console yourself. And you have to pinch yourself to make sure you're not dreaming. You have to curse the world on your own; and suffer; and weep, if you're able. When you're alone, you've got to remember everything, and cling to whatever fond memories are left, for those are your only comfort in solitude, and without fond memories there can be no nourishment for the soul; and at the same time, you have to forget the bad memories, for without forgetfulness the soul can have no rest.

The buses waiting at the airport looked like tourist buses to me—I didn't realize at the time that they were there for the general public. They seemed so luxurious, and there were words instead of numbers on them. There was a bus with the word 'Wien' on it, which I read as 'wayn,' and so I had no idea where it was going. I stood there, confused, in my poor Egyptian shoes that were failing me, for I could feel the cold coming through them. They weren't protecting me in the least, but seemed rather to contract about my feet as if they were made of thin nylon. So I trotted in place a bit, like someone who desperately has to use the toilet.

A man wearing a company jacket and a tie came up to me and asked, "Taxi? Vienna?" I nodded my head, thinking that he wanted to give me some information to help me get there, but instead he took my bag and started walking off with it. I was suspicious of him for a moment, but then I realized that he was the driver. His taxi was much more luxurious than the taxis I'd seen in Khartoum and Cairo. He put the suitcase in the trunk. I opened the passenger side door to sit beside him up front, thinking that he might want to stop and pick up some more passengers on the way. There were several newspapers and magazines on the seat, which he moved to the back so I could sit beside him. He asked me to fasten my seat belt, but I didn't understand him, so he demonstrated. No one used seat belts in Cairo or Khartoum—I felt as if I was riding in an airplane again. I gave him the address of Klara, Valerie's daughter. He read it and said, "Oyes klor!" in pure Viennese dialect. That sounded like the Arabic word for 'chlorine,' and I couldn't understand what that could possibly have to do with the address.

The taxi got moving, and the driver politely asked me in English about my country and the weather there, which, I later learned, was the first topic of any conversation in this country. I could barely understand him on account of my poor English. I didn't look at him very often while we were talking, which was unusual for me, but I was too busy looking at this strange country in which cars actually stopped at red lights. I had trouble saying much more than "yes" and "no," so I fell silent, and relaxed for a little bit, not knowing where I would be getting out. While I was looking at the cloudy sky and the snow piled on the side of the road, I heard a voice over the driver's awful intercom. I knew that noise, and was afraid of it: it was a noise of disasters and wars, one that I had often heard while in the army in Sudan. But I reassured myself that I had arrived at the country of joy, and that there were no wars here, and that I would soon be in Paradise—a somewhat cold Paradise, to be sure, but perhaps that's what Paradise is like, and I simply had not gotten used to it yet. Where I'm from, we use words like 'fire' and 'inferno' and 'flames' and other similar terms to denote hell, the home of Satan and the infidels. So the opposite must also be true: 'cold' and 'snow' and 'frost' and 'ice' must be the names for the home of angels and the benevolent.

I felt drowsy, but the lights of Vienna woke me up again. The driver was still carefully obeying every traffic signal, along with all the other drivers on the road. The other thing that amazed me was that I never once heard him or any of the other drivers use their horn the whole way into the city.

We arrived at the address I had for Klara, the owner of a famous art gallery in Vienna. The gallery was closed. The owner of the café on the building's ground floor told me in English that he knew Klara well, and that she had left a few months ago for America.

The driver offered to take me to the next address, that of the photographer. Fortunately, she lived nearby, in the eighth district. He took me there, but that too was to no avail. When the driver saw the third address, that of the sculptor, he explained to me in hand gestures that it was all the way at the other end of the city, in an area call Esslingen on the outskirts of Vienna, and that it would cost a lot to go there. I immediately gave up the idea of going there with him. But I still didn't know where to go that day.

A young man was standing at the intersection. He was wearing a yellow jacket and a yellow hat, and he was carrying a yellow bag filled with newspapers and calling out to people to sell them. When he heard us speaking in English, he drew nearer and asked me if I spoke Arabic. "Yes, I'm from Sudan!" I said, and quickly explained my situation to him. He said he was from the city of Esna in the south of Egypt, and that he loved the Sudanese. He told me that he knew a place where I could stay, and that I could wait with him for a while: in a half-hour, he would be handing the rest of the papers over to a co-worker of his, and he could take me there after that. I thanked him, and paid the friendly taxi driver the fare, which was much more than I had expected. I took my suitcase out of the cab and set it down on the sidewalk, and gazed at that cold world from the intersection.

I hadn't realized how cold it would be in this city. The people paid no attention to the other pedestrians as they walked around—or at least that's how it seemed to me. Their eyes were fixed straight ahead of them, and they never turned their heads. The only things they seemed to notice were the signals at the crosswalks. They stopped at intersections and raised their eyes toward the traffic signals. When the signals were green, they crossed; and when they were red, they stayed put. This system amazed me. I kept waiting for a single person to cross on red, but that never happened. Even the dogs that were out at that hour waited with their owners: they might run around a bit on the sidewalk, but they didn't set foot on the street until their owners permitted it.

From time to time, that kind young man from Esna came back to talk to me. He said his name was Abbas, and that he had been here for seven years, but wanted to go back because life here was much harder than he had expected. I felt cold, so I took another sweater out of my suitcase, but it offered no protection against that cold. And then it took me a long time to get the overflowing suitcase closed again. I couldn't tell what time it was by looking at the sky, for there was no sky to be seen. I looked at the watch that Amm Rikabi had given me, but instead of paying attention to the time, I thought about the watch's owner and the distance that now lay between us.

Abbas finished his work, or rather, he passed on all the things he had with him to someone else, who took them indifferently while greeting me with a bored look on his face—the man seemed to know nothing but boredom and apathy. I went with Abbas to a large train station called the Westbahnhof. There we met Jimmy, who told us that there was a free bed in the second district on a street called Nordwestbahnstrasse, and that it cost 1000 shillings per month. I had no choice but to take it. People in this country seemed to speak quickly, do their work quickly, and settle their affairs quickly. Jimmy called the owner of the apartment, who agreed to take me in. The owner was Egyptian, and he said I could pay the rent at the end of the month, which put me at ease.

I began to feel even colder, despite being inside the station. I went with Abbas and Jimmy to the apartment. On the way, Abbas told me about his two wives, and the story of how he came to Austria when he was quite young—he still seemed very young for someone with two wives and two children. It turned out his first wife could not have children. She was distantly related to him, so divorcing her was problematic. He married someone else on top of her instead, under pressure from his family—even though he had no desire to. Back in Egypt, he had worked as a driver for one of the hotels, but he lost his job when the hotel came under new ownership. He changed jobs several times, working as a taxi driver for a while, and then as a horse-cart driver, and then as a truck driver, but none of these paid well. A relative of his had traveled to Austria and written to him that life here was heavenly, and that he should leave everything behind and come immediately. When he arrived, he found that it was all a lie, and that he had fallen into a trap: his relative was lonely here, and had urged him to come so that he wouldn't have to be alone.

Just as he was asking me why I had come to Vienna in particular, we arrived. The three of us got off the tram together, and as we were walking, I almost crossed on red at several crosswalks. The two of them stopped me each time, and Jimmy said, "Be careful! The police will give you a fine, and if you get hit by a car, you'll find yourself with a bill from the driver's insurance company before you've even made it to the hospital."

We reached an old run-down building. I couldn't believe that buildings like this existed in such a paradise. Jimmy had a key to the apartment with him, and opened the door. No one was there. The place smelled rotten, and it was clear that it had never seen any sunlight.

The first thing I asked about was the bathroom. Jimmy took out a large key and told me the bathroom was outside. He went with me and opened the door. It too was run-down. I sat down on the cold seat. There was no bidet or any kind of running water, which annoyed me and reminded me of the toilets in Italy and France. But I had some tissues in my pocket, and I used them all.

I went back to the apartment to wash my hands with cold water. Abbas prepared a cup of flavorless tea for me, and then showed me which bed was mine. After he had pulled off the clothes that were on it, I put my suitcase on the bed and sat down. They said goodbye and left.

I sat alone in the apartment, which was moderately warm, but also a mess. I made my bed. Then, as I was trying to open the door of the armoire, it came off the hinges and fell to the ground. I spent a long time putting it back in place, but as soon as I had managed this, the other door fell off.

I took a look at the kitchen. I was hungry, but I wasn't sure what I would be able to find to eat at that hour. Abbas had given me the key to the apartment, and I thought about going out to try to find something. Suddenly, I heard the door open. A man who looked a bit like me came in and greeted me. He said his name was Mahjoub, and that he too was Sudanese: his father was from Sudan, and his mother was from Alexandria.

He took me to a Turkish store in an area called the Prater. He bought a few things for himself, and said, "Don't buy a lot here. Just buy enough for a day, or at most two." But I bought enough groceries for an entire week, fearing to have to go out into that cold again. He looked at me with concern, but didn't say anything.

We talked for a long time, and he promised to take me to the newspaper to ask about a job for me in a couple of days. We went back to the apartment and ate. Three other men came back late in the evening. All they did was curse the country and their miserable lives there. I was nervous about being in this new place, and there was an orchestra of snoring in the apartment, so I didn't fall asleep until quite late. I woke up at noon the next day. Since I was the only one staying there who didn't have a job, I cleaned the kitchen, which was a huge mess.

I couldn't find the rest of the food I bought, and I understood why Mahjoub had told me to buy only a little at a time. An hour after they returned that evening, the kitchen looked just as messy as before. And all of them denied taking any of my food.

This is the first time that Sandra has ever fallen asleep while I'm telling her a story. Her hand feels warm in mine. I know that she wanted to visit her brother today, so I try to wake her, but she seems sunk in a very deep sleep. I'm a bit worried about her, but also happy that she's staying here with me instead of going over to her brother's. I want to listen to the new CDs, but I'm afraid of waking her up. She seems exhausted today. Hakima is more tired than usual today as well, and has fallen asleep beside her.

I have a bit of a guilty conscience toward Sandra, for she always listens very patiently to my stories while I prattle on. I pull out the book by Ibn Hazm that I bought in Egypt. It's called *The Ring of the Dove: On Love and Lovers*. In the introduction, I read that it has been translated into German. I'm excited to share this information with Sandra once she wakes up.

My missed appointment to go pick up the lantern crosses my mind again. I originally wanted to give it to Sandra on some sort of happy occasion, but I decide to simply give it to her as soon as I have it—I don't want to wait for the occasion I have in mind. I try to read a bit of the book by Ibn Hazm, but my mind gradually drifts back to that absurd event that damaged the lantern and postponed my giving it to Sandra.

One miserable day a while back, a policeman stopped me in the street to check my papers. This had become a new custom among the police here—they'll stop and check anyone with dark skin. I had a leather bag around my shoulder, in which I was carrying the lantern the woman had given me at the al-Hussein Mosque in Cairo, as well as the three stones I collected, and Sheikh al-Sharif's stone. I never spent a single night out of my apartment without those precious belongings. I can't sleep well without them by my side. Sandra understood this, and always reminded me to bring the bag with me before I came over to her place. Sometimes she'd even take the bag herself without saying a word, which let me know that she wanted me to spend the night.

Late that muddy rainy evening, I was heading to Abbas' place in Favoriten, Vienna's tenth district, to spend the night there. I'd just heard that his parents had died in a train accident. He sounded horrible on the phone, and he had no one there to be with him, so I said I'd join him on that cruel night to try to comfort him a little. I got off the subway at the Reumannplatz station and headed through a narrow alleyway behind a church. I had only gone a few steps, carefully trying not to slip on the muddy ground, when a police car suddenly appeared and two officers got out. They ordered me to stop with my face to the wall and not to move. One of them grabbed my bag, and they gave me a full body search. They seemed quite worked up, and so was I. One of them asked me who I was, and for my papers. As he looked at them, he asked, "You live in the third district. What brought you here to the tenth?"

He asked me several other questions in quick succession, without waiting for a reply. The other officer opened my bag and scattered its contents on the ground in a single motion, and I heard the glass of the lantern shatter. Then he threw my Sudanese incense container onto the ground, and all the incense and sandalwood sticks fell out of it. He kicked the lantern to the side and pulled out a pair of white nylon gloves while his colleague trampled my scattered belongings with his dirty shoes. The strange contents of the incense container had led them to believe that they had caught a criminal.

"What's this?" one of them asked me.

I couldn't remember the word for incense, so I said, "Something like perfume."

He laughed and stared at me with mockery in his eyes, then spoke a few quick and incomprehensible words into his walkie-talkie. I thought he was either asking for reinforcements or telling them he'd caught a wanted criminal. "You're coming with us, monkey," he told me.

He picked up the muddy incense and put it back in the container, along with some cigarette butts and bits of tissue, and other trash from the street. He tossed the three stones and Sheikh Sharif's stone to the side, but his colleague told him that they had been in the bag as well, so he put them back there, and threw the frame of the broken lantern in with them. They put me in handcuffs and dragged me to the car. I sat in the back as we set off. They were making fun of me and telling jokes in their Viennese dialect. I could only make out two words: 'black' and 'nigger.'

I could smell the incense now, so I let go of my anger and followed the scent into a lucid dream while the car cut through the alleys and streets of Vienna. The blue lights were flashing and the annoying sirens screeching, clearing the streets and announcing the arrest of a dangerous criminal.

13

The Christmas holidays are just a few days away, and the city looks completely different now, and is much more lively than usual. Many Christmas markets have opened up, and the smell of steaming mulled wine is all over the place. The people seem different now too: they're more liberal in their greetings, but also more stressed. Everyone's walking around with enormous shopping bags, and there are crowds everywhere, and lots of traffic jams. The stores are all decked out in bright colors and lights, and people are hoping for snow during the holidays.

Sandra is busy getting gifts ready for her whole family, and especially for her niece Susanne—and even Hakima will be getting a share of the love. We'll be spending the holiday in Krems, as usual, where her family always gets together. Sandra has been quite tired the past few days, and even the smallest exertion has worn her out. She's sleeping more than usual too. But I figure it must just be the pressure of the holidays. I tell her about the new job I found by chance that morning. I was standing in front of a pet store, and saw a puppy for sale in the window that looked a lot like my old dog Samih. I walked in, as if to save the puppy from its captivity, but in truth I had no idea what I was going to do. "Can I help you?" the owner asked me.

"Do you have any jobs open?" I asked unexpectedly.

The man looked at me in surprise and said, "Have you worked in a pet store before?"

"No, but I worked for an entire summer at the Schönbrunn Zoo, and several years ago I worked for a long time at some horse stables. Plus, I love dogs and cats, and I know how to handle them."

"Do you have a work permit?"

"Yes."

"We don't pay very much."

"That doesn't matter!"

"Okay, then come back tomorrow, and we'll try you out for a bit."

Sandra laughs at this happy chance and asks me where exactly the store is. She knows which one it is, and wants to come visit me there tomorrow.

That evening, I sit down to learn some German. "Your pronunciation is a lot better now," Sandra says, "and you pick things up quickly. But your sentence structure is still all over the place."

"Maybe it's because I tried to learn German on my own," I said. "I didn't use the *Learn German in Seven Days* book, but a different one called *German for Foreigners*. At the time, I mainly needed to be able to interact with people in the stores and markets. I had a lot of trouble asking about fruits and vegetables at first, because I was using the language I'd learned from the textbook instead of the local dialect. For example, I said 'Blumenkohl' for cauliflower, instead of the local word, 'Karfiol.' And I said 'Tomaten' instead of 'Paradeiser.' I could see how annoyed the vendors were, and they gave me very sarcastic looks. They kept saying that I spoke like a 'Piefke'—a word I didn't know back then. I figured it was an insulting term for someone who can't speak German properly. I didn't realize that they were actually calling me a Kraut, and laughing at me because I spoke like a German instead of an Austrian.

"I had another problem with the language here: I couldn't simply imitate the way people spoke to me. Some of them would say things like, 'Ich arbeiten, du arbeiten. Woher kommen du? Du kommen Afrika?' I hated that stupid vulgar language that people here often use with us foreigners. But when they did speak normally, it was nothing at all like what I'd learned from the book. The dialect here is very difficult, and I couldn't understand it, so I became a Piefke in their eyes. But I made friends with the TV."

"The TV?"

"Yes. At the beginning of my time here, I kept up Amm Rikabi's habits: I listened to stations from the Arab world or Arabic-language stations based in Europe through a shortwave radio, but the signal was always quite poor. After a while, I thought about getting a TV, both for entertainment and to improve my German.

"An acquaintance who was leaving the country offered to sell me his TV for four hundred shillings. It was a lot of money for me, but I bought it anyway. Before that, Erika would sometimes let me watch TV in her room, but she usually fell asleep quite early in her chair, which embarrassed me, so I'd head back to my room."

"Erika? Who's this Erika? You never told me about her."

"Really? She was my first love in Austria. I lived with her for several months."

Sandra's eyes widened, and her lips tightened. She punched me jealously on the shoulder, feigning anger, "You never said a word about your girlfriend Erika!"

"You're right, I didn't. I used to call her 'Frau Erika.' She spent her childhood in the province of Steiermark. She was a strong and active woman, and had the severity that was characteristic of her generation. When she was feeling affectionate, which was rare, she would overdo it, and was almost too affectionate. But when she was being strict, which was the norm, she seemed sterner than a Nazi. She worked a simple job with the tax authorities. Her deceased husband had loved hunting and used to work for the forestry services. The floors of her apartment were covered with animal skins, and animal horns hung on the walls, and there were stuffed birds in glass cages as well. She used to clean the skins and polish the horns and the cases every single day, and mourn the loss of happier times. She was eighty-two years old.

The rising costs of living were what drove her to rent out a room in her apartment."

Sandra laughed when I mentioned how old she was. "How'd you find out about that place?" she asked.

"Through Abu Darsh. I moved from the communal apartment to a room in that woman's home. The rent was a bit more expensive, but the place was clean and peaceful. My new problem was that I felt as if I were living in military barracks again, due to Erika's sternness and extreme discipline. But she helped me get to know life in Vienna a bit better, as did the TV and my absurd job selling newspapers. Frau Erika practically taught me the history of both Austria and Europe. And the TV helped me understand the strange rituals of life here. As for my work, it was a source of frustration, and never failed to bring me back down to earth. Things went on like this for several months. I was happy spending time with Erika. She began to get used to me, and praised me for how quickly I was learning German. She corrected my pronunciation for me, and even helped me whenever I struggled to pronounce words with umlauts. She tried to make me feel that she was a grandmother to me, and she succeeded, but there were three things she was still extremely strict about: order, cleanliness, and quiet. I bent over backwards not to upset her. But she still complained that I hadn't arranged my clothes properly inside the armoire, pointing out that the shirts should be on the top shelf and the socks on the bottom, with underclothes in the middle. Her intrusiveness embarrassed me, but I forgave her, for she truly had become a grandmother to me. I knew she wasn't going through my things to pry; it was just the way she'd been raised. Anytime she entered my room, she ran her index finger across every single surface—from the desk to the chair to the closet—to check how much dust had accumulated and calculate when I'd last wiped everything down.

"I wanted to keep things clean as well—not because I was afraid of her criticism, but because I felt more relaxed in a room that smelled nice. I couldn't stand the dank and rotten smells of the poorer apartments in this rich country, apartments like the first one I'd lived in here. I could even smell those apartments on a lot of people, and could always tell if someone lived in that kind of wretched place, even if their clothes were clean. My nose got to know the smell of places that never saw sunlight, places with poor ventilation and cold, damp air."

The topic of Erika and the mood I'm in seems to have emboldened Sandra to broach a new topic: "Tell me about your first love, Hamza."

Sandra was bringing back things that had not crossed my mind in a very long time. We bury feelings like this in my country. We lock them up and throw away the key, sharing them with no one. And they disappear into oblivion until something reminds us—perhaps a telephone call or a whiff of perfume—and brings all the old longing back again.

"Her name was Layla," I said. "She was like a sister to me at the beginning. We were brought up together. She was the only one of Abd al-Malik's daughters whom I used to tease and joke around with whenever I saw her. She had a calm way about her, but she always stood up to me and defended herself with fierce words, and I loved that about her. We were sixteen when her older sister Asiya was engaged. That day, Layla came into the courtyard with my mother to put henna on Halima and Karima. I was lying down in a shaded corner, and she didn't notice that I was there. She sat there with the two girls, laughing in a motherly way that belied her age, and told them a story about a tree that grew money while my mother sat patching up some clothes. I quietly watched Layla: the wrap had slipped off her head to reveal her long braids. Her face seemed different than usual, and her voice was different too. The way she spoke, her smile, the story she was telling—all of this made her seem much older to me. I watched her and listened as eagerly as a child to the wonderful story of the money tree. I got up and greeted her once the story was over, then sat down across from her. She bashfully adjusted her wrap to cover her hair. I drew nearer to look at the intricate henna figures she was drawing for Halima and Karima, while she told them about how they too would get married one day, and how she would do the henna then as well. My mother blessed her. I'd drawn quite near to her, like a person with bad eyesight, eager to get a closer look at the lovely art on Halima and Karima's palms. I could smell Layla's perfume. I looked up: her eyes were a mere hand's length from my own. But there was no challenge or teasing in our eyes at that time. Her long lashes trembled bashfully, and she made a mistake with the rose she was drawing on Karima's palm. Karima informed her that the rose was far too close to the other one, and in fact almost touching it. She apologized and said she'd fix it. Layla shuddered, and I shuddered in turn, though I tried to hide it from her. I walked out of the house in a daze, and from that day on I no longer joked around with her, but instead greeted her with the affection of adults. And she began to bashfully lower her eyes in return, which made her look even more beautiful. I suddenly realized how lovely her voice was, and her mouth, and the way she walked as well. I felt feelings back then that I didn't understand until after her family left us."

"Where did they go?"

"The whole family left Wad al-Nar during the drought and the famine, but I don't know where they went. I asked everyone who I thought might know about them, but I never saw them again."

The Christmas holidays arrive. As she's driving us to Krems in her car, where we'll be spending three festive days with her family, Sandra tells me that it's time for me to learn how to drive as well.

Her niece Susanne is there; she's a little devil, and Hakima quickly makes friends with her. That evening, one of Sandra's presents under the Christmas tree is an envelope with a card in it: she's signed me up for driving lessons in Vienna.

The next morning, Sandra suddenly falls ill. We call the family doctor, who tells her to rest, and says she should have some tests done as soon as possible. Sandra lets me know that she's had two similar bouts of nausea and fainting in the past two weeks, which she hadn't told me about. She'd gone to the general hospital in Vienna and had several tests done, but they said that more were needed, and she had put these off until after Christmas.

I cannot sleep that night at the family's house, but I don't want to get up and move around for fear of making the other family members anxious. Sandra falls asleep early, while I remain entombed in my bed until dawn, my head a meadow for my thoughts and misgivings to run free in. Just before dawn, I fall into a troubled sleep.

The hunchbacked man with the new coat and old cap is still walking in front of us in the underground vault. We cross through a strange rectangular room that's different from all the others we've passed by: it's empty and clean, and its walls are completely covered in mirrors. A large piece of red canvas has been fixed to one end of the ceiling, and the other end has been painted the same shade of red. It's difficult to tell the two sides apart, and the whole ceiling reminds me of a big 'No Entry' sign. Here, we see ourselves in the mirror for the first time, in the dim reflected rays of the flashlight. Our hair and faces are dusty, and exhaustion and fear are written all over them. Seeing the fear in everyone's eyes terrifies me even more, and shakes me to the core. We leave the room quickly, for it seems as if the ceiling is slowly lowering and bearing down on us.

We keep descending, down spiral stairs, until we reach the deepest part of the subterranean vault. It's easier to see here. There's a high oval window in the distance with old and dusty cracked glass that lets in pale rays of light. I can hear what sounds like the rippling of water coming from that direction. We're standing in front of piles of old junk. Our leader says nothing. Everyone files in and begins hastily rummaging through the stuff like thieves, some of them coughing from all the dust. As for me, my bag is already breaking my back, and I have no desire to put anything else in it. I hear things falling, and the same questions being asked over and over again, "What's this?" and "What's that?"

From where I'm standing, I can see a man dragging along an old three-legged chair, and a woman hiding a dusty curtain under her dress, and someone else stuffing a flag into their briefcase. Another woman is holding what looks like the tusk of an elephant or a narwhal, and is stroking it with her hands in a state of ecstasy. In the distance, the others have stumbled upon a bunch of caps that look just like the one our hunchbacked leader is wearing. They're snatching at them and taking as many as they can, and piling them one on top of the other on their heads.

I hear a man cursing, and a woman sobbing. The sounds of people crying begin to resound amid the junk. I can still see the hunchback pointing the flashlight at every movement and every noise. I'm the only one who's remained near the steps that we entered the room from. I sit down on my bag to relax a bit, and feel the sweat running down my skin and making my clothes cling to my body. I feel cold, and an entirely unfamiliar scent enters my nostrils: the scent of something ancient and indescribable.

Sandra starts to feel better in Vienna, so she postpones the tests a bit. New Year's Eve arrives, and we've invited some of our friends over for the occasion. The apartment is filled with joy, and we all spend a lovely time together laughing, drinking, and eating. I make sure to call Amm Rikabi that night as well. He's happy to hear my voice, and also the sounds of the party in the background. I tell him that we might have to delay our trip to Egypt once again, and apologize. Then I call Sandra over, and she talks with him for a long time, and wishes him a happy New Year. After they're done, he asks me if I need anything. I thank him and say that the only things I need are his letters, and he assures me that another one is already on the way. I call Hashim after this—he always seems surprised to hear from me. He says he's glad to hear my voice, and assures me that he'll come visit me in Vienna as soon as possible. He wishes me happy days, and then he too asks me if I need anything. I thank him and give him the same answer I gave Amm Rikabi.

Abu Darsh arrives, accompanied by one of his girlfriends. She keeps laughing out loud at his side, and someone finally asks him what he's saying that makes her laugh like that. So he tells us one of his brilliant anecdotes filled with fictions and extraordinary exaggerations, and we all double over in laughter. Abu Darsh is one of my kindest friends, and also one of the finest liars I've ever known. He once said to me, "A lie has many advantages, Hamza! But not any lie. If you want to lie, then it should be a transparent lie, a lie that has no color at all and does no harm to anyone. The lie should vanish immediately in a puff of smoke. And you should only lie to someone who knows that you're lying, and who joins you in the game. Lying is an art. But don't tell colored lies, and don't tell black and white ones either—those are the lies of politicians."

I've missed this kind of intimate atmosphere. It's been so long since we got together in a group like this. Hakima is sleeping in the other room, for she hates it when there's too much noise. The sounds of the firecrackers outside have been bothering her all evening. Sandra seems very happy to have most of her friends here. I refill the food and drinks on the table, and keep telling everyone to keep eating and drinking. Sandra laughs at the way I insist on this.

"Why do you worry about that?" she asks. "They'll help themselves to whatever they want." But this way of hosting is quite ingrained in me, and I'd need a long time to change it.

A bottle falls to the ground and shatters. "Don't worry," Sandra says, and immediately cites a German proverb, "Shards bring good luck!"

The sound of that bottle breaking takes me back to the first New Year I spent in Vienna, back in 1992. Some friends had promised me that we would celebrate downtown, and that it would be a lot of fun. I was really looking forward to the night, but my miserable luck let me down. I had signed a contract with a company to shovel snow off the city streets. Whenever there was a heavy snowstorm, they contacted us to come shovel the snow into trucks, which would then dump the snow into the Danube.

A big snowstorm hit the afternoon of New Year's Eve. I was taking a nap in preparation for the long night of celebrations ahead when I heard loud knocks at the door. It was my Albanian neighbor, who kindly let me use his phone for emergency calls. I went to answer it, but I wish I'd kept sleeping instead. The call was from the company, telling me that we were to gather in the Stephansplatz in the middle of the city. We started work at four that afternoon, and the snow kept on coming. At around nine o'clock, people began to fill the square, and our work slowed considerably as the fireworks went off around us. Everyone seemed ecstatic as they took in huge quantities of alcohol. They kept on drinking without the slightest worry in the world, some of them no older than fourteen. Everyone was wearing thick coats, and many of the older women there had expensive fur coats on. They reeked of perfume and alcohol, while those warring with the snow reeked of sweat.

The excitement reached its peak just before midnight. The people counted down the last seconds of the year, then they all yelled and congratulated and kissed one another, and let off more fireworks in front of the cathedral. The merrymakers started shattering hundreds of bottles on the ground in the square to bring them good luck for the coming year. Some of them were so excited that they not only broke empty bottles but also ones that were still full of alcohol. The exhilaration was contagious, and soon everyone was smashing bottles on the ground. I wish I could have broken the shovel in my hands to join in the celebration! Despite the madness of that fleeting state, it took me out of my depression for a moment, for everyone was laughing together euphorically—a state of joy whose reasons I could not fully fathom.

Our boss came and told us that the company would pay us double that night if we stayed to clean up all the glass and garbage from the square. So we kept on working, for all of us needed every extra shilling. The city was covered in snow that now smelled of gunpowder and alcohol, and the people had reached a rare state of bliss that would certainly not be repeated until the following year.

I pick up the shards of the broken bottle, and go into the bedroom to check on Hakima.

The three of us—Sandra, Hakima, and I—go back to the Palm House after a long absence. Mustafa Abu Darsh appears out of thin air at the gate. He knows where we're heading, and says that he's never seen the Palm House before, and that he would love to join us if it's no trouble.

Abu Darsh starts laughing as soon as we're inside. "What's so funny?" Sandra asks.

"I just remembered a job I had many years ago. I used to work in a greenhouse a bit like this, but much less impressive. It was in an area near Vienna whose name I can't remember now. We helped grow the vegetables and flowers, and monitored the heating system to make sure the temperature stayed constant. We lived there as well. The owner of the place asked us to keep a low profile and avoid the police so that he wouldn't run into any trouble. He never let us leave the place, but he brought us as many cigarettes and as much alcohol as we wanted, deducting them from our pay. He used to charge us for the vegetables we ate as well, even though we only ate the ones that weren't fit for sale.

"One day, we noticed that he had brought in a bunch of brown wrapping paper and earthy colored cartons that reminded me of the thick paper that they used to wrap meat back home. The word 'bio' was written on them in big letters, and beneath it was a long description of how these products had come from soil on which no pesticides or chemical fertilizers had been used.

"One day shortly before the elections, he was standing in the greenhouse with his sons and his only daughter and telling them that they should vote for the party that was promising to kick out all the 'damned foreigners' who were ruining the country. He said this around us as if we were nothing more than statues! He seemed to think of us as only half-damned, as if there were still a chance for us. He used to repeat an absurd story about his neighbor: He said she was a fool because she'd married an Egyptian and borne him 'nigger' children—those were his words—who played with the other kids in the town and did even better than them in school. He said it was part of a conspiracy to take over the town, for foreigners like them got citizenship, and they were eating our food and taking our women.

"The air smelled awful in that greenhouse. Everyone knows that certain ventilation systems are required by law for places like that. But the man said that they were too expensive, and instead he had a cheap system from the Slovak Republic, which he said had been used in a kolkhoz. There were five us working there, and after a while he added a sixth person as well. He never told us where he was from, and he spoke a language none of us could understand. His name was Sunbat, and he did us nothing but harm. We discovered two months later that he was telling the owner of the farm about everything we ate and everything we said. We used to sometimes eat the better vegetables, and Sunbat told the owner, even though he ate all those vegetables with us. We started calling him 'Zunbat' instead.

"We also had a left-wing Iranian man with us: Daryush. He hated the Iranian regime, and led a vagabond life all over the world. And there was an Iraqi man, Badr, as well, who had fled conscription under Saddam. And there were two men called Samir as well. One of them was a Copt, and the other a Muslim. Samir the Muslim called Samir the Copt a 'khawaga.' And the latter always laughed and told him that both of them were wearing Austrian clothes, and so he started calling Samir the Muslim 'Hagg Khawaga.' All of us laughed at these exchanges, and we started calling them by these names as well.

"The owner of the farm was an alcoholic. He used to hide bottles of wine and liquor in the cellar under the vegetables. He often fled to the greenhouse to drink by himself and curse his wife. When he was very drunk, a spell of generosity sometimes came over him, and he'd give us a bottle to drink with him. He always drank to the dregs, and the first words out of his mouth were inevitably insults for his wife. He called her ugly and stupid, and said she thought she was the holy Mother Teresa because she went to church so much. 'Let's see how much the Pope helps her,' he said, 'in this world and the next!' He told us that she only ever slept with him when she wanted a child, and he swore that they had not had sex together more than forty times in the whole forty years he'd been married to her—and ten of those were in the first year of their marriage. He could still remember each and every one of those forty times. He said that had it not been for her stupid rich family and this farm that she owned, he would have divorced her years ago. And once he told us that he had always dreamed of becoming a musician. We were extremely surprised at this comment, but he did indeed entertain us on New Year's Eve with an incredible performance on the accordion."

Abu Darsh laughs all the while he's speaking. And he tells us more stories as well—the three of us can't stop laughing.

"This country is full of angels and devils!" he says suddenly.

"Especially devils who work at banks!" I reply.

Abu Darsh lets out that mad laugh of his again, which causes me to laugh even more. Sandra smiles in surprise, not knowing what's so funny. Abu Darsh quickly makes amends, "Haven't you told Sandra that you met the Devil in person at a bank?" he asks me.

I turn toward her and smile. "I'm so sorry, Sandra! I haven't told you the bank story yet. I just thought of it now.

"Back when I sold newspapers, the customers usually paid me in coins. And I got in the habit of taking all that change to the bank once a week to get cash for it, which made it easier for me to settle my accounts with the paper company. I went to the bank one Tuesday. I had rolled all the coins in a plastic bag, which I had then put inside a larger bag. When I was just inside the bank, I started to get out the plastic bag for the teller. But as soon as I looked up, I found myself standing face to face with the Devil himself. He had blazing blue eyes and his eyelids were covered in black. His face was pale, like the inside of a turnip, and he had two black lips with yellow teeth that stuck out like the fangs of Dracula. He was wearing a long black silk coat, and big fur boots that made his legs look like those of a goat. He had long black nails, and two red horns on his head. I was horrified, and asked God for protection from the Devil, while the Devil simply smiled at me. It was an absurd situation, and I really thought that Judgment Day had come and that I would have to pay for my sins in shillings. My fear was very real, partly because everything had happened so quickly, and also because I hadn't slept well the previous night due to the extreme cold and the broken window in my room. In a woman's clear voice, the Devil asked me in perfect German, 'Can I help you?'

"The two fangs seemed even longer and more evil now. I hesitated for a moment, and took a step backward. The Devil took two steps forward, towering in front of me. My eyes widened in fear. I turned around and saw a young woman who looked just like an angel approach me and smile. But a man's voice came out of the angel, 'Can I help you?'

"It was the last day of the Fasching celebrations in Vienna, and everyone was dressed up in costumes, as if we were all in some big movie together. I'd never seen anything like it before. I had noticed some children dressed as animals and birds and strange creatures that morning, but I thought it must be some children's holiday. I hadn't expected the adults to dress up as well! I had seen the bank director before, but I didn't recognize him dressed like a woman in that angel costume. He had plucked his eyebrows and colored his lips and cheeks. He was wearing a wig and a short skirt, and had clearly shaven his legs. As I left the bank that day, I couldn't tell if I felt more amused or disturbed by the whole thing. In any case, I was so tired that it all seemed like a strange nightmare to me."

We spend several lovely hours in the Palm House together. Hakima begins to get restless, which usually means that she wants to go home.

As we get up to leave together, Abu Darsh takes a look at the place, lifting his eyes to the ceiling, and says, "Incredible. I wonder why the Austrians haven't thought about putting a few of us in greenhouses before we all go extinct."

It's extremely cold outside, and Sandra clings onto me. I invite Abu Darsh to have a quick coffee at a nearby café to finish our delightful conversation, but he excuses himself, saying that he wants to go visit a friend who's having a hard time right now.

"What happened?" I ask him.

Abu Darsh takes a long drag from his cigarette and says, "My friend's been working in a nursing home for the elderly, and that's a hard job, as you know. His mother sent him a letter several months ago telling him that she was sick, but for some reason he didn't receive it. He was her only son, but he only rarely called the family. When he did finally call them yesterday, he found out that she'd passed away. The news hit him very hard. He's been caring for the elderly here in this country for several years and leading a hard life so that he can send a bit of money back to his family to help them get by; and now he can't forgive himself for not having been able to care for his elderly mother. He's always been torn in two, for the few measly shillings he earns here barely sustain him, and were never enough for him to go back and see his mother."

Sandra appears to be very moved by the story. I can see the tears in her eyes, and I too am speechless. We part ways with Abu Darsh and get on the subway. Hakima relaxes inside my coat, but Sandra seems strangely absent. I assume that Abu Darsh's sad story is the reason for her grief.

The next day, Sandra visits me in the pet store, looking at all the animals like a happy child. I jokingly try to get her to buy a cat or a dog. Then I excuse myself from the owner and go spend my break with Sandra in a nearby café. Her hand is in mine, and a question is gleaming in her eyes. I keep quiet and wait. Finally she speaks, making an effort to pronounce my name properly in that alluring way that she has, "Hamza!"

"Yes?"

"What do you think about us getting married?"

"Married? Us?"

"Is there anyone else here?"

"This is wonderful news! But . . . how? . . . And when? . . . "

My words are disjointed, and my questions aren't really questions. I kiss her, something I rarely do in public. I've always felt half-naked whenever I kissed her like that. It always made me feel embarrassed somehow, even though I have seen kisses like that all the time in this country, and find them a thousand times better than a fight or people swearing at each other in public—something I haven't seen once since setting foot in this country.

An overwhelming joy comes over me, for Sandra *is* my eternal wife. From the very beginning, I've felt that she's my wife, my lover, my friend and companion, my whole family. I gently kiss her fingers while my whole face beams with happiness. And it's as if she too is shining, as if these fingers I'm kissing are made of light. But I feel myself tremble in secret as well, for I had never imagined that I would marry, because of all the people I've lost in this life. I've longed so much for a family, but I was always afraid of losing it.

I look at the clock—I can't believe how quickly the time with her has passed. I kiss Sandra again, excuse myself, and hurry toward the store. Then I rush back to leave money for the coffee on the table, and kiss her one more time.

I return to the warmth of the apartment in the evening. I get back before Sandra, who's visiting her brother. Hakima sniffs at me like a police dog: the scent of all the animals from the pet store is new to her. I play around with her a bit, and she stays by my side. Then I turn on the tape player and listen to Asmahan, singing along with her as I head into the kitchen to make that special yogurt soup of mine that Sandra always loves. A feeling of bliss pervades my entire body, so I open a bottle of red wine from the Krems region to let it breathe for a while. As I recall our afternoon conversation about getting married, I feel embarrassed by my reaction: I wish I hadn't stuttered in reply, and I wish I had found better words for the moment. I wait for her to come home so I can give her the wonderful evening she deserves.

A flood of emotions comes over me as she enters the apartment. She smells the food and hurries to the kitchen, and within a few moments we've set the small corner table together. She brings in a beautiful blue candle, and also puts two roses in a small vase—I'm not sure where she has the roses from—while I pour two glasses of wine and serve the soup. She tells me how her brother and his wife and Susanne are doing. Then, at just the right moment, a moment that perfectly matches this warm and intimate atmosphere, she starts talking about the very first day we met on that staircase in the third district, the day Sandra came up carrying a can of Hakima's food. I fondly think back to that first period of our lives together, a time lovers often don't talk about.

"What did you think of me that day?" Sandra asks me suddenly.

I laugh and pause for a moment to bring back the memories, while Hakima jumps onto Sandra's lap, inadvertently helping me find the words I'm looking for: "I didn't actually see the can that you were holding that day. But I did see your outstretched hand and delicate fingers, as well as your eyes. The clinking of your silver bracelets drew me in. Your hand held me prisoner at first sight. I was too shy to look you in the eyes for more than a few seconds—I was afraid I wouldn't be able to pry my eyes off your face. But when you were playing with Hakima in my apartment, I couldn't help but stare at you. I was spellbound. All I could think about was how to keep you there with Hakima while I watched you."

"Really?"

"Well, that's not all I thought about. But before I tell you everything: what did you think of me? What was going through your head?"

Sandra strokes Hakima's back, who purrs appreciatively. "I wasn't thinking about much of anything at that moment," Sandra says. "I saw a kind man. Your voice had a sincere ring to it, and there was something calming and attractive about you. But I *was* really interested in the cat. Then, with each new meeting, I found something else in you that attracted me. And now your love has given my life new meaning. And when you tell me your stories, I feel that I'm a part of them – because you've become a part of me."

We spend one of our most beautiful nights together. I finally come to understand the meaning of Asmahan's song. It feels like our wedding night, but without the din and the guests; without the gifts and all the fancy clothes; and without any witnesses or forms to fill. It *is* our wedding, truly.

We have more nights like that one, and our feelings grow ever deeper. Now there really are nights of joy in Vienna. Sandra is my garden, my Paradise. I look at her pure face in the flickering candlelight. I can see her hair and her eyes; her cheeks, nose, lips, and teeth; her neck, her breasts, her arms, her hands. I gaze at her, enamored. I can hear her breathing, and the clinking of her jewelry. I can smell her delicate fragrance. I feel her in my veins and my lungs. My heart seems to be leaping out of my chest in joy, and I feel as flustered as a young lover again. I put on the tape by Asmahan—the first time I've ever done so on an occasion like this. Her sweet voice fills the night air, enchanting and clear. With that voice, Asmahan opens up all the doors of my memories with Sandra. I never imagined that I would ever have a place for such splendid memories, after all the pain I've been through. The warm music flows into my body, melting the frost and making a new man of me. I feel light, as if I were flying, or in some enchanted dream. I hold her hand as we enter the deepest parts of that paradise. Sandra gives herself over to me, yet also dominates me. With our breath and our whispers, we leave this world. We leave it for one of sighs and delight, laughter and moaning, oblivion and remembrance. We leave it for a world of pleasure.

Despite how sublimely exhausted we are, Sandra still wants to hear more about me. She's still holding onto me after the fall, as if I were going to escape from her. Her body now seems to be asking the questions, questions that have laid captive between us for a long time. She looks at my body stretched out beside her, and I too slake my eyes with her body. We've gotten used to lying together like this after returning from that sublime world of ours, and we always try to stretch the time out as long as we can. And whenever we fall asleep in that state, it's the loveliest sleep in the world.

I look at her and ask myself: How could that delicate body of hers make me feel such incomparable pleasure? How is she able to send me to such distant worlds, worlds I'd never dreamed of reaching? And how . . .

She interrupts the flow of my thoughts with a question, "When were you circumcised, Hamza?"

The question surprises me, and I let out a laugh: "I don't remember anything about my circumcision, because it happened when I was four days old. That's what my mother told me years later. She said I cried in agony until I lost my voice, and told me how bad she felt afterward. She refused to have Karima circumcised, convinced that this tradition was in fact harmful to girls, but the community came out against her, especially my father. She wanted an explanation from him about why girls should be circumcised and which holy book actually mentions it, in particular the horrific type of circumcision practiced in Sudan. She reminded him how much pain she had felt on their wedding day, and how she'd almost died when I was born because of that disgraceful procedure. My father was enraged that day, and said that the Quran mentioned circumcision as a way of protecting women from temptation. But when she refused to accept this and asked him to prove his claim, he went away in defeat, as usual. But the next day he came back with 'clear proof,' in the form of a fatwa by Sheikh al-Faki declaring that circumcision makes women more fertile and also protects them from intercourse with the jinn, for the jinn preferred to sleep with uncircumcised women.

"Poor Karima had to suffer through that terrible procedure: they cut away the most sensitive areas and then stitched her closed, leaving just a small opening for her to urinate through. My father wanted to have Halima circumcised on the same day and be done with it, but my mother managed to save her from this by postponing the procedure. Karima suffered for at least a year because of that mutilation. She was hemorrhaging blood, and nearly died from it. They tried everything to stanch the flow—coffee beans, olive oil, castor oil, date liquor—but none of it worked. Then my mother treated her with an infusion of wormwood, cactus, and some plants that grew in our region, and she finally recovered. But during that time she suffered from a horrible fever, and couldn't sleep at all. She raved incomprehensibly in her delirium, and my mother could only make out a single sentence that Karima repeated over and over again, 'I don't ever want to get married!' My mother gave her a compress of water, warm vinegar, and cactus oil to ease her pain and keep down the fever that was racking her body. And she swore that she'd never allow Halima to be circumcised, even if the jinn themselves showed up."

"But where's the sense in that kind of procedure?" Sandra asked.

"There is no sense in it, Sandra. The people believe that circumcision increases a man's sexual pleasure and decreases a woman's. They say it's God's reward for women, and that it purifies and sanctifies them—as if women were impure. Our society is dominated by men, and looks for every way to enhance the sexuality of the men while taking it away from the women. A man is happy when his wife's pleasure is stifled and repressed, for it means she's become 'virtuous' in his eyes, yet he quickly gets angry at her for not wanting sex, and starts looking for a substitute."

Sandra's extremely interested in this subject, and asks me dozens of intelligent questions, almost as if she's testing me. Uncharacteristically for her, she gets upset about things I have no control over. I can understand where she's coming from, however, for in spite of everything I'm still a man from that militant male society, and the humiliation that I myself experienced there doesn't change that fact.

Hakima jumps onto the bed to join us, and we cast aside that heavy topic of conversation. I enthusiastically try to translate a few Arabic jokes for Sandra, and get a bit carried away with my performance. At first, I think that she understands everything, because she can't stop laughing. But when I'm done telling jokes, she says, "I didn't understand a single word!"

"Then what are you laughing at?"

"I'm laughing at your incredible delivery! And because Hakima's tickling my feet!" This time, we both laugh together.

On Sunday morning, neither of us can remember when we went to sleep that night; or rather, when sleep came to us.

14

Vienna International Airport–Monday, May 10, 1999

"This is the last call for Egypt Air flight 802 to Cairo. All passengers should proceed to Departure Gate A immediately."

The weather outside the airport is cloudy and rainy. The announcement of the last call fades away. Completely drenched, the cat shivers pitifully.

Vienna, the seventh district—Saturday, January 9, 1999

I open the door of the apartment and walk inside; I am surprised that Hakima doesn't rush at me like she usually does. I take off my shoes and hear a faint movement behind the closed living room door—I thought I had left it open in the morning. It's three in the afternoon, and Sandra won't be back from her brother's place for another two hours. I open the door to the living room, and am amazed when a large group of people with Sandra at their head all cry out, "Surprise!"

It's a party for my thirty-second birthday, which is two days from now, but Sandra decided to celebrate it on Saturday so that more of my friends could be there. Now I understand why she kept asking me in the morning what time I'd be home from work. And so we have another wonderful party, less than two weeks after celebrating New Year's Eve. I wasn't expecting to receive so many wonderful gifts. My favorite is Sandra's, of course: an annual pass to the Palm House. The party goes deep into the night, with no break in the laughter and conversation. But Sandra seems exhausted and has dark rings around her eyes. I watch her from a distance as she slowly eats a little bit of cake, leaving the rest on her plate. But she still joins in the conversations.

Starting at three in the morning, our friends gradually file out, the last of them leaving at five, whereupon Hakima comes out and joins us. Sandra and I sit down for a bit to recount some of the stories we'd heard that night. Then we start quickly cleaning up the place, for I know that Sandra won't be able to fall asleep until the apartment is in order again. I ask her to sit down and rest from her long day, but she refuses, and together we gather up the last traces of the party. I wash the dishes while she dries them, and all the while we laugh about the stories and jokes our friends had told that night. We finally head to bed together, exhausted, as dawn appears in the window. Before we fall asleep, Sandra says, "Don't forget! We're going to the Palm House in the afternoon to celebrate your birthday on our own!"

At the Palm House, we recall our first visit here two years ago. We sit down on the very same bench. Everything seems the same as it was back then: the weather outside, and the calm and warmth inside the Palm House. The memories come back as if no more than a moment had passed, or as if we'd never once left this place of ours the past two years. Hakima only gets up twice the whole time we're there, and eventually falls asleep on Sandra's lap. I remember the dream I had two years earlier: I was walking in a strange dark place, and could see nothing. I didn't know where I was going, or where I had come from. But I could hear a cat and followed it; it saved me from being lost.

The past few weeks, that dream has been in dialogue with another long dream that I keep having, and that keeps being interrupted. I try hard to remember some of it so I can tell Sandra about it now, but to no avail. Suddenly, like a magician, Sandra pulls out a large photo album. I'm touched by this gesture, for I've been pestering her to show me pictures from her childhood. I had seen some of the photos once at her grandmother's place in Krems, but it seems that Sandra brought a lot more pictures back from our visit with her family at Christmas. I know that all these pictures will spur on questions from me, and help me learn more about Sandra's life.

We laugh at the first pictures, where Sandra is just an infant. Her beauty is still captivating, and she reminds me of the two dolls I bought for Karima and Halima many long years ago now. The pictures follow in quick succession: soon she's crawling, and then taking her first steps. Then she's at school and on class trips, and trips with friends and family, and trips of her own as well. We fall silent when we get to her pictures from the ballet academy, and she flips through them in evident pain as I stop my flow of questions. Finally, we come to pictures of our friends, and pictures of the two of us in many different places: by the Danube; inside the Prater amusement park; in the Schönbrunn Palace and the Belvedere Palace; in Vienna's parks; at home; and in some of the cities we visited together. I can't help but laugh at how ridiculous I look in those winter clothes. And in most of our pictures, Hakima is either with me or with her, or right between the two of us. Sandra can tell how happy looking through the album makes me. I flip through it several times, lingering over the pictures in enjoyment. She finally closes the album and says, "This is a gift for you. I have enough pictures at my family's place. I wish I could see photos from your childhood as well."

The Palm House has become our second home. It feels so close to me. I've lived in it, and dreamed it in, and laughed, remembered, and gone through happy times and sad. I even loved in it. All of this in just two years.

I remind Sandra that she needs to take care of her medical tests, and tell her that I'll come to the hospital with her, "I'll work half-days starting tomorrow so I can be with you. My boss is a kind man, and he's comfortable with me now. I'm sure he won't say no."

The weather is sunny and clear today, for the first time this week. That rare blue sky is inviting us outside, and the large number of people filling the Palm House also drives us out—they seem to have a habit of loudly screaming at each other during perfectly normal conversations. As we head out, Sandra says, "I haven't seen the Schönbrunn Zoo for a long time. I read that they've made some changes there and given the poor animals more space. Why don't we go take a look?"

"Sure. At the very least, Hakima can see a few of her relatives."

Hakima is still fast asleep inside my coat as we make our way to the zoo. The animals bring back old memories. I remember my dog Samih and the cats we had when we were young back in Wad al-Nar. And I recall Sumit, Sheikh Sharif's home in Sudan, and the goat from the Eid al-Adha festival. I remember the soldier who saved me from captivity, and also the Zahra Stables in Ain Shams. I think about what the weather must be like in Sudan and Egypt at this time in January, in contrast to this country where we only rarely see the sun. The heaters are still on in our apartment, and we're still wearing our winter coats. "I wish I had the chance to work at this zoo again," I say to Sandra.

We sit down on a quiet bench in the warmth of the sun. There's a newspaper on it, and Sandra quickly flips through it, and shakes her head in what seems to be either disgust or wonder. Before I can get a question out, she asks, "Have you ever been mistreated for no good reason here?"

I laugh and reply, "For no good reason? I don't think there can be ill treatment without a reason. But one thing does come to mind. It was winter, about five or six years ago, and I was going to drop in on a friend of mine, but he wasn't home. It was extremely cold that day, so I went into a café hoping to drink something to warm up my frozen limbs. The owner of the café was busy with people who seemed to be his regular customers—they were all playing some kind of game. He had clearly seen me come in, and I was sitting in full view of everyone, but he didn't come over to me, and he ignored me every time I waved at him. I thought he must have bad eyesight, so I got up and went over to him and ordered a drink. He looked at me scornfully, as if I had just made some strange request. 'I don't serve foreigners!' he said sharply. I laughed, thinking he was joking, but he was adamant about it, 'We don't serve foreigners in this café!' While the customers looked at me in disbelief and said things I couldn't understand in their dialect. 'But this is a public café!' I told the owner. 'So what?' he replied, shrugging his shoulders and turning back to chat with his friends as if I wasn't there. I thought the situation would become even more ridiculous if I insisted on being served, so I put on my coat and left."

"Didn't you go to the police?" Sandra asked.

"Why?"

"To report the incident. It's against the law for the owner of any business to refuse service to someone without a valid reason."

"The man was very clear, and he certainly would have denied what had happened to a judge. Or perhaps, at best, he'd serve me a drink under pressure, and I'd sit there and drink it like poison. Do you really think that this man's behavior and prejudice can be changed by appealing to the law?"

"But the law . . . "

"Sandra, it's not a problem. People like him can be found everywhere. Most of them don't show how biased they are in public. You can't stop prejudice with law."

"But you could have gone after your rights!"

"Prejudice isn't a sickness that can simply be cured. Most prejudices are made of steel, and can't be melted."

Our long conversation is serious at times, and playful at other times. We're oblivious of the way we take back home, and suddenly we find ourselves standing in front of the gate to the building—Sandra looks for the key. Hakima hasn't moved around much all day, which is strange for her, and even the smells of the zoo failed to arouse her curiosity. I'm worried she may be sick. I can't seem to keep thoughts of illness out of my mind. In the past few days, I've been worried about both Sandra and Hakima.

Inside the apartment, Sandra asks me another one of her surprising questions. "You haven't told me about any of the women you met in Vienna," she says. "Didn't you have any adventures?"

"In the five years I spent here in Vienna before meeting the love of my life, I was with two women. I met the first one through Abu Darsh, of course. He had been pestering me and insisting that I start to meet some more women. I was still shy because of my weak German, but his presence put me at ease—he's such a joker, and he always lightens the mood of any situation. He introduced me to a woman named Eva from a well-off family. She was a young student, and was quite skinny. She chose the food she ate very carefully, and I noticed that she'd disappear to the bathroom after every meal. I wasn't concerned at first, but then twice I heard her vomiting in her apartment right after we'd eaten. I was worried about her and suggested we go see a doctor, but she assured me that she was fine. I found out later that she was anorexic. I got tired of trying to help her. She always pushed me away whenever I talked about it: she said it was none of my business. I was patient with her, but soon all we ever talked about were diets and anorexia and healthy eating, until I couldn't even enjoy a simple meal with her. So we broke up."

"And the other woman?"

"Frau Erika's responsible for that one. She kept asking me why I didn't have a girlfriend like all the other young men my age—someone to make me happy and add some excitement to my life. She told me I was very handsome and said my spoken German was much better now, and that I should go out at night and see the city and its people, rather than sitting at home in front of that stupid box all the time. Her words actually did inspire me, and gave me some confidence too. A little while later, I met a cashier from the nearby supermarket. Her name was Dagmar. She was beautiful and kind, but a bit strange as well. About three weeks after we first met, we were alone in her apartment for the first time. I quickly took off all my clothes, only to find her very calmly taking off each piece of her own clothing and folding them as she did so, as if she were about to put them all back in the closet! It was winter, and she had a lot of clothes on. She did everything in slow motion. I thought it was a joke at first, or some type of foreplay that I didn't know about, but it happened the next time as well, and she also told me not to touch her hair because she'd just had it done. When she started up with this again the third time I was over, I got up butt naked, took out her ironing board, and started ironing the clothes she was taking off. This caught her by surprise, but when I said that there were still a few wrinkles on her dress, she thought I was being serious! As soon as I finished the ironing, I put on my clothes and left.

"She had obsessive-compulsive disorder. We never got together again after that, and because of her I started going to a supermarket that was farther away. I was afraid of a new relationship after that. I felt that every beautiful woman was hiding some strange demon. I kept my guard up for a long time, until I finally met a woman whose only demon was boundless love."

Sandra laughed enchantingly. "Do you love me, Hamza?" she asks.

"Of course I don't."

I place my hand on her cheek as I say this, then gently pull away her hair and kiss her smiling lips. She closes her eyes and lets out that lovely deep sigh of hers. I stroke her neck with the back of my hand as she leans in for an even longer kiss.

Sandra repeats a few expressions from my stories, laughing. Then she falls into a deep sleep, like a child, the traces of a smile etched on the edges of her mouth. But lines of anxiety—and of something else I can't make out—furrow her brow, and I find no rest from the troubling thoughts in my head.

Feelings of secret regret are mixed in with the joy of having met someone so special—regret at not having met this person sooner, even though it was a coincidence that neither of us could control. This is how I feel now about Sandra. I somehow feel responsible for not having met her earlier, during my first years in Vienna, rather than at the end of five long years. But there's no way to change it now. More than any time in the past, I feel inadequate toward her. I feel there are things I should be doing for her, but I don't know what they are.

Sandra's condition worsens. She's clearly losing her appetite. Her nausea returns, and she starts to complain about pain in her stomach and her back. Her weight drops considerably in just a couple days. I go to the hospital with her to have her tests done. The tests that had been routine and normal at first now become more serious. The doctors order more tests and decide to keep her in the hospital. I stay by her side until late in the evening. The doctors appear one after another, but their silence and the look on their faces is not at all reassuring. A single phrase keeps coming out of their mouths, "We're not sure yet."

I spend a wretched sleepless night by myself in the apartment. My misery is compounded when I see that Hakima vomited while I was away—she looks bad. I bend down to take a good look at her while she slowly moves about. I lift her into bed with me: she falls asleep, but I do not. I pull out Sandra's photo album and spend a long time flipping through it. I remember the days we so recently spent together, those days that seem like a distant memory now. At dawn, I realize Hakima's not moving. I shake her, and she meows faintly. I'm relieved to hear her voice, and think back to something I once told Sandra, "If this cat were a person, she'd be a jazz singer with that voice of hers!"

I finally get a bit of restless sleep, waking up at eight. I shake Hakima once more, and her voice seems even fainter now. I check for the nearest veterinarian in the phone book and take Hakima there. She says Hakima's condition is bad. She gives her an injection, and gives me some medicine for her. I take her back to the apartment: she seems to be in a stupor, and is extremely weak and submissive.

At noon, I hurry to the hospital. Sandra asks me to call her father, for things seem serious. A group of doctors enters and take Sandra somewhere. I call her father, who arrives about two hours later with her grandmother and her brother. Sandra's not back yet.

This night is worse than the first one. But at least Hakima is doing better, which comforts me a little. My whole heart and soul are by Sandra's side. The doctors have yet to pronounce their final judgment.

On the third day, the doctors confirm that Sandra has pancreatic cancer. Her condition is advanced, and it's too late to operate. The only option is radiation treatment and chemotherapy, since the silent disease has already spread beyond her pancreas. I stay by her side at the hospital the whole day. She's exhausted, and falls asleep. A procession of friends and relatives streams into the room throughout the day, while I move around like a caged animal. I exchange brief words with everyone, but in truth I have no idea what I'm saying, and am oblivious of what everyone says to me. Sandra wakes up for a bit in the afternoon and tells me she wants to see Hakima.

Another sleepless night: being alone in the apartment like this is torture to me. As I lie on the bed, the lights coming in from the outside look like ghosts on the ceiling. I can see the forms of beasts wrestling with one another: strange predators and wild birds, and animals with fangs and long tongues and sharp claws. I toss and turn for a long time, and at dawn I lose myself in the same dream that I've been having the past few days, the dream I'd been trying to tell Sandra about ever since that day in the Palm House, but that kept slipping away from me.

The hunchbacked man is still in front of us in the long underground vault: the man with the new coat and old cap. We're still following him. Suddenly, I hear voices ringing out and calling to one another. The people gather in a circle around something, and I can hear them say, "A chest! A chest!" One after the other, they try to open it: with their hands and their legs, and even with blows. When it finally opens, a thick cloud of dust rises up. They surprise me by clearly calling out the names of all the things they find in the chest, as if they were at an auction or in a souk. All of them rush toward the dim rays of the flashlight, carrying or dragging things that I cannot make out. I'm too tired to go over to them, but I crane my neck to see better, and I'm all ears as well. "Maybe they've found a treasure chest!" I say to myself. Yet I still don't know why I set out and walked this long way with them, carrying this bag of mine. I recall how heavy it is, and quickly open it up and toss the large cookbook aside. Different voices come to me: rough voices and gentle ones, the voices of women and men, of young and old.

"These are military insignias!"

"And those are medals!"

"And these are . . . " (I can't understand the word.)

"And here are uniforms!"

"Look! These are scimitars!"

"No they're not, they're . . . " (Another word I do not know.)

"These are holy chalices!"

"And these are ancient ledgers!"

"These are . . . " (Again, I cannot understand the word.)

"And this is a medical book!"

"And these are flags!"

"Here are old law books!"

"No. Wait, yes. Those are . . . "

I hear the names of many other things, and also many words I don't understand. I think about opening up the Duden German dictionary I have with me, but it's too dark to read, and in any case I'd rather listen and try to remember the meanings of the words myself. Each item pulled out of the chest sends a handful of putrid dust my way, and I'm forced to plug my nose with my hand. The old hunchbacked man points his flashlight at the chest so the group can see what they're doing. Their shadows on the wall look like beasts wrestling with one another: strange predators and wild birds, and animals with fangs and long tongues and sharp claws. For a moment, all I can see are those wild shadows.

They need everyone's strength to move the heavy chest from its place. They seem to have forgotten about me, but they ask the old hunchback for help. He sets the flashlight on the ground, pointing it in the direction of the chest. It slowly starts to turn in the opposite direction, so he points it toward the chest again. But again it spins in the opposite direction. He leaves it and goes over to them, and the beam of the flashlight settles on an oil painting on the wall. I can barely make out its colors. The painting is covered in dust and cobwebs, and is hanging from a long chain on a nail that's beginning to bend downward. It's a picture of a woman: I can't tell how old she is, but her incredible eyes look reproachful, and her mouth is caught between a smile and an expression of sorrow. A metal swastika has been hung carelessly above the painting, on the same long nail that the painting is hanging from. The swastika is about the size of a man's arm, and seems to have been put there more recently than the painting, for there's less dust on it.

Forgetting my weariness, I stand up and grab the flashlight. I keep its light fixed on the painting as I approach it, for I seem to know the woman in the painting. The people notice me and call out for me to help, and then curse me for pretending not to hear them.

The swastika begins swinging back and forth like a big pendulum, and seems to grow in size as I advance. The huge painting slowly slips down the long nail, which has started to bend even further because of the weight. The people's voices gradually die down in the distance, but I can still hear them calling me names that are not my own.

I wake up in the morning, so tired and confused that for a few moments I have no idea where I am or what I'm doing here. In vain I try to understand the import of that strange dream. I lay there and stare at the ceiling for a few moments until my eyes settle on Hakima, who is lying by Sandra's pillow. She lets out a loud purr, and I smile.

I enter the hospital cautiously, my coat bulging. Sandra's not in her bed, so I ask the nurse about her. She assures me that Sandra's fine and will be back shortly. I wait nervously until Sandra comes in, wearing a nightgown and pushing a metal pole on small wheels in front of her: there's a container of solution hanging on the pole with a tube that runs into her arm. I help her lay down on the bed. She hears a meow and perks up. I smile and sit down beside her, looking around me like a thief—fortunately there's no one else in the room—before I open up my coat to reveal Hakima. I set her down beside Sandra on the bed and hide her beneath the sheet, but Hakima comes out and climbs up to Sandra's face, who kisses her happily while I keep a lookout to make sure that no nurses or doctors are coming. Sandra says that Hakima looks thin. I tell her about her illness and how I had taken her to the veterinarian a few days ago, and I say that Hakima's getting better and that there's nothing to worry about. Then Abu Darsh comes in carrying a bunch of flowers. He makes Sandra laugh until she hurts. And after he realizes that Hakima's there, he diverts the attention of a nurse who's about to enter the room by asking some strange question—she's more than happy to help him out, and leaves the room with him. Sandra's father arrives, and then her grandmother, then some friends. I leave late in the evening, taking Hakima with me, who had slept for several hours at Sandra's side.

The days go by, and I continue my daily visits to the hospital. Sandra's condition deteriorates, yet she still seems forbearing and calm, despite her gauntness and all of her lovely hair falling out. She asks me to bring her a picture of me and Hakima, so that we can always be with her there. And she surprises me by giving me a long lock of her hair, which she had cut off and saved for me before her first chemotherapy session.

I feel nothing but desolation and loneliness every time I return to the apartment. Hakima no longer welcomes me with her usual meowing, which I so long for, and she stops eating and drinking. I've lost my appetite as well. I don't have the time to visit the Palm House now, and in any case: what would it be like there without Sandra and Hakima?

Sandra remains calm and composed every time I see her, and her mind is clear despite all the pain. As for me, I can't hide my worries very well. The nurses tell me that they've never seen a patient as serene and forbearing as Sandra.

She's been writing in a journal during her time alone, and one day she tells me, "I want you to have this journal, Hamza."

"I'd rather you read it to me yourself one day."

My days in Vienna are downcast, and the nights have no flavor. I ask to work half-days for a while, and my boss agrees. I call Amm Rikabi and tell him about everything. His heart goes out to me, and he consoles me. I need him now more than ever. He asks me for Sandra's phone number in the hospital, and gives her a call. The next day, Sandra's still excited about the call. But we avoid talking about traveling to Egypt anytime soon. Sandra reminds me of the twenty-eight months we've spent together moment by moment. Her memory seems stronger now: she can recall the smallest details, and seems to be truly happy, while I struggle to hide my sorrow and my fear.

I get through my days by clinging to hopes I know are false. I feel so alone, despite all the friends who visit both me and Sandra. The past few days, I've felt like someone sitting in a train that's stuck in the station, and looking at the train across the way. I'm relieved for a moment when my train finally starts moving, happy to be done with the tedium and the waiting, and glad to be starting off on my journey. But soon enough I realize that it's the other train that's departing and not my own. As I gaze at where the other train used to be, I let out a bitter sigh that does nothing to ease my despair.

I come home early one day, and find Hakima in the bed, a place she usually never sleeps in—she's been sleeping a lot the past few days. I go over to her: she's completely submissive, and looks at me with feeble eyes. She lets out a sharp meow of pain when I pick her up. She feels as light as cotton in my hands. When I set her back down on the bed, she meows in pain again and crumples in a heap like a stuffed animal.

"What's wrong, Hakima?" I ask her. "Do you want to leave me here on my own?"

She's clearly in a bad way, and I rush her to the veterinarian. The assistant lets me go in immediately, since it's an emergency. The vet tells me she's very sorry: the only thing she can do for Hakima is to put her to sleep and free her from the pain.

The vet asks me if I want to stay with her or leave the room. Thus, from one moment to the next, I'm confronted with the harsh reality of the situation, and forced to make a quick decision. I ask her if there's any way to put this off, but she calmly shakes her head and tells me that Hakima is in such great pain that she can hardly move. I look at Hakima, who looks back at me and very weakly lets out that old meow of hers one last time.

"I'll stay with her. But please be gentle when you give her the injection."

The vet prepares the injection while I kiss Hakima over and over again. I lift her up to look in her eyes. I feel great warmth in my chest and my heart, which I know will turn cold in the coming days without her. My breath rattles in my throat. The needle looks so cruel in the veterinarian's hand. Intense pain runs through me as Hakima lets out a single meow, like the cry of a baby, and loses consciousness. The vet injects her once more, mercifully, in the heart, and I feel Hakima's soul flow through my fingers.

I head back toward the apartment with her, but I pass our building by and keep walking, with Hakima at my chest. I walk through some of the nearby streets. I'm not sure how many times I pass by our building, and I'm not sure what's keeping me from going up to the apartment. Hakima's warmth slowly turns into a mournful cold.

I finally enter the building, and head up the steps slowly and heavily. Once inside the apartment, I call Sandra to check up on her, but I don't tell her about what has happened. When she asks me about Hakima, I change the subject by telling her that I have the photo she asked for, and that I'd come visit her that afternoon. She says that my voice sounds strange, so I tell her I just woke up from a deep sleep on the sofa.

I leave the apartment with Hakima pressed against my chest inside my coat. I can feel how cold and stiff she is. She seems much smaller than she's ever been the past seven years. I have a small spade in my coat pocket, and some incense sticks that the mute woman gave me years ago near the al-Hussein mosque in Cairo.

I don't know what tram I took, nor how I made it here to the Palm House. I go inside and take a seat on the same bench that the three of us always sit on. I don't really know what I'm doing. I sit there like a statue for a long time. The emptiness of the place at that hour puts me at ease, and I start to hum and sing out loud, my hands on Hakima at my chest. My voice doesn't come out clearly, but seems to pass through Hakima's body, which muffles it. I look at the palm and stand up. I grab the spade and start digging directly beneath the tree. The ground is hard, but I work quickly, sometimes with the spade and sometimes with my hands, until the hole is large enough. I take Hakima out of my coat and kiss her. Her eyes are still open, but their spark has gone out. I put her in a small canvas bag, along with a few sticks of incense, and bury her. Then I collapse back onto the bench, as exhausted as if I'd just dug a whole trench. I sit in front of the palm tree and look at that small mound of earth beneath it. I think back to the day I found her, seven years ago: small and homeless, and suffering like me from the cold of the street. I recall my long life with her. And I remember how Hakima brought me luck: she was the reason I met the greatest love of my life. The tape of my memories plays all the way through, stopping at this very moment, in front of this bulge of ground beneath the palm tree. I get up to level it out a bit so that it won't attract attention. Then I pick a stone from the adjacent fountain and set it on top of her grave.

The palm tree looks like it's trembling. The warm air inside the Palm House causes something like tears to well up in my eyes. I sit back down, weary and alone, and almost lose consciousness before I remember that I'd promised to visit Sandra.

The announcement is repeated, "This is the last call. Egypt Air announces . . . ."

I don't hear the rest of the announcement. Everything looks murky and unclear from behind the thick reinforced glass. It's like a scene from an absurdist play: people keep hurrying by as if they were trapped in some monotonous nightmare.

Sandra makes me swear not to cry in front of her, and also not to cry when she's gone. She makes me swear to try to imagine her face instead, and remember the beautiful time we spent together. And she makes me swear many other things as well.

It's the first of May, a national holiday. It falls on a Saturday this year, and public transportation won't start running until noon. I want to visit Sandra in the morning today, for tomorrow will be her twenty-seventh birthday, and I want to be the first to congratulate her, and give her my present a day early, before all her friends come. So, just like I did years ago in Cairo, I decide to make another pilgrimage with my gift: the lantern that I have wanted to give her for so long. I set off on foot from the seventh district to the ninth, through the alleyways and streets of Vienna. I take a new route this time, though I'm not sure why. The way is not nearly as long as the one in Cairo was years ago, but it's raining, and my eagerness to see the expression on Sandra's beautiful face when I give her this present makes the way seem much longer than it actually is.

I'm still very happy about having gotten the lantern back from the Turk yesterday. He repaired it even better than I'd hoped. I passed by his shop several times the past few weeks and did not find him; I thought he had disappeared forever. The people who worked in the store beside his said that he had gone to Istanbul. But he came back. He told me he had taken the lantern with him to Turkey, and that he had repaired it in his village in the Izmir province. He found the right glass and the right colors there. He said that a few people had offered to pay quite a bit of money for the lantern, but he had of course refused. I thanked him profusely, and paid him more than he asked for. The lantern truly looks brilliant now. And its story makes me happy: it has passed through three different continents, and will finally settle, in a few moments, in Sandra's hands. I hurry up, panting, and soaked by my own sweat and the rain.

This is the face I've wanted to see with that lantern. Sandra holds onto it joyfully while I tell her its long story, and the distances it has traveled: all the way to Izmir in Turkey, and on foot across both Cairo and Vienna. I get up and put a blue candle in the lantern, and sing her Happy Birthday.

Tears of joy fill her eyes, and I can tell she wants to get up. I embrace her a bit too forcefully and she lets out a groan: I can feel how weak she is. I lighten the pressure of my embrace, but I don't stop pressing her against my chest. Her calm breathing passes through me, and I can feel her rib bones protruding through her back with my hands.

We spend some lovely peaceful time together. We talk about this and that, as if one of us were about to leave on a trip. She asks me about Hakima, of course, and I hesitate. I'm not sure if I should lie to her or not. I'll blame myself as long as I live for any lie I tell her now. But the truth will hurt her, and she can't take any more pain.

I tell her the truth, and the tears stream from her eyes. But she quickly regains her composure. She tells me she could feel it the last time I was here, and that she had had a dream about Hakima. She says the dream was strange but comforting: she had seen Hakima in a beautiful place with many other animals. I tell her where I buried her. "What a lovely resting place she has," Sandra says with a smile. "I wish I were well enough to go visit her with you."

We manage to turn the conversation to happier topics, despite the sadness in the air. Sandra asks me if I'm still listening to Asmahan, and I tell her I am. She says that she couldn't sleep last night, and that Asmahan's song kept going through her head, and she realized that she actually had large parts of it memorized. Suddenly, she starts singing part of the song in that beautiful voice of hers—still delightfully mispronouncing the hard Arabic 'h'—while I sit there, amazed.

"Nights of joy in Vienna,
a breeze from Paradise.
Enjoy your youth in Vienna,
this garden of Paradise.
Why do you let the days
go by without delight?
Rejoice, enjoy the music!
Take joy, enjoy the music!
Let your heart swim and fly in this world,
and grant it a companion."

The next day, Sandra's twenty-seventh birthday, her room is filled with loved ones. Her father sits beside her and holds her hand. Her grandmother stands up, then sits down, then stands up again, softly saying prayers. Her mother finally arrives as well: she had been away on a trip with her husband, and had only just heard the news. She seems utterly exhausted. Sandra speaks to her lovingly. Then Sandra's brother arrives with his wife and Susanne. They've brought her a large bunch of roses. Susanne pounces on her just like she always does: this hurts Sandra, but she masks the pain with a smile. I watch her from the corner of the room, never once taking my eyes off her face. And every now and then she flashes her broad smile at me.

They permit us to have the celebration in the hospital's common room. I help the nurses push her bed into the middle of the room, and I hear her laugh for the first time in a long while. Abu Darsh is there spreading good cheer as usual, and he tells Sandra about his latest adventure. He was riding the subway yesterday without a ticket when a ticket inspector came up to him. He told the inspector that it was Labor Day, and that since he was a laborer in this country, it was his right to ride for free that day. He struck up a long conversation with the inspector, and the two of them kept on talking until they finally got off the subway and walked out of the station together. When they were safely outside, he said to the inspector, "How can you prove that I was ever in the subway now?"

After everyone has left, I take Sandra back to her room and sit down beside her. I beg the nurse to let me stay an extra hour that night, and she feels for us and leaves us alone. Sandra reads a few of the birthday cards and looks at some of her presents. Then she asks me to take all the gifts to the apartment, but says I should leave the cards, the roses, and the lantern there with her.

As promised, I don't cry once Sandra is gone. Even if I wanted to cry, I wouldn't be able to. Everything has happened so suddenly, without any warning: it's as if an earthquake has wrecked my life and all that we built together. Everything has ended sooner than expected. I feel as I'm waiting for this dream to be over, waiting to wake up from this nightmare and return to life. But the dream goes on this time, and now it has swallowed up Sandra as well. All I have left is a feeling of loss and longing, and also her journal. She's written down the lyrics of Asmahan's song in Latin letters on the first page. She also recorded her last wishes in that journal: that I should keep going back to the Palm House, without sorrow or grief; that, on each visit there, I should imagine her sitting beside me, and also imagine Hakima still moving around between us, as usual; that I should listen to Asmahan and to the CDs she gave me; that I should sing along with them again, like I used to do; that I should listen to Mozart and Bach to recall the sweetest moments of our love; that I should finish my long story for her, which I hadn't quite told to the end; that I should tell her about any new dreams I've had whenever I visit her grave; that I should read the journal she gave me in the one place I love above all else, the Palm House; and that, after she's gone, I should invite all our friends over to the apartment to listen to the music she loved and remember her as if she were there with us, for she will be there in spirit.

This last written testament shook me to the core. Each request was written on a separate page.

I tell Abu Darsh that I need someone who can carry out an urgent task for me. I quickly tell him what I have in mind, and he finds me someone for the job. At dawn the next day, I set out for the cemetery with the man, and bring the lantern with me. Once there, I stop for a bit at Valerie's grave, which I had visited several times with Sandra.

The miserly clouds allow only a little sunlight through. I stand there in silence. The man asks me if this is the grave, but I shake my head. Scenes of Amm Rikabi and Valerie pass through my mind, as if I had seen them together with my own two eyes. I say Valerie's name several times, trying to recall a distant voice: the voice of Amm Rikabi. The sun's rays disappear for a moment, and the man follows me to Sandra's grave, which is some distance away in the same row as Valerie's. The man fastens the lantern to the marble slab that covers the grave, and the sun's rays make it seem as if the lantern is lit up. I pay the man for his work and thank him. Then I put a lighted blue candle inside the lantern and stay there alone with her. I walk around the grave several times, then stop and stand in front of it for a long while. Another tape of recent memories plays in my mind. I remain frozen to the spot until the candle has melted away entirely, and replace it with another. My breathing is shaky. I feel quite worked up, so I calm myself by softly humming, which slowly turns into singing: I don't know what song the words were from, or how they came into my mind just then. I keep on singing while the colors of the lantern convulse in the candlelight—everything convulses, in fact, and a layer of twilight passes over my eyes, like steam on a pane of glass.

I read Sandra's newly etched name on the tombstone, and bend over to straighten the wreaths of flowers.

I return to the Palm House and sit down in front of the palm tree, which remains like a witness to the living and the dead. Sandra's lock of hair is pressed against the skin of my chest—it still smells like her. The bulge of ground beneath the palm is a bit smaller now. Bright sunlight escapes from the clouds, so I put on my sunglasses. I feel weak. I don't want to give in to my sorrows, or stir them up again. I want to control my thoughts, direct them toward anything other than what has been occupying my mind this whole time. But I can't. I remember one of Sandra's last wishes: I imagine her beside me, along with Hakima, and I'm granted a brief reprieve. I recall Sandra's face, her eyes, her mouth, and her hands. I remember how generous and lighthearted she was. When I manage to bring her fully back to mind, the image soothes me, and I fall into a deep sleep. Because of my sunglasses, no one there notices that I've left the world.

I see myself being born from my mother's womb at dawn, beneath a palm that is as short as a fig tree. I hear nothing. My mother's face looks relaxed, despite her weariness. She sleeps, but I stay awake, looking at her face. Everything around me seems strange.

On the evening of that same day, the day of my birth, I become a child about one year old. I hear voices I do not understand. My mother's smell is soothing, and I suckle her delicious milk. The sun comes out that night, and I grow to two or three years old. My father comes and joins us for the first time, his huge frame blocking the sun. It looks as if he's wearing a dark mask over his face. His rough voice terrifies me, and I cling to my mother. I'm a seven-year-old boy the next morning. I rush down a long path without knowing the reason for my haste. I stop running in front of what looks like a river or a sea. Several animals arrive there. I join them and we all head into a forest—there's a cat on my right and a dog on my left. We stop in front of a towering palm tree. The other animals take counsel and decide that the three of us should climb it, and that the first one to the top will be the winner. I scamper up the palm as lightly as a squirrel, but the dog quickly passes me, and then the cat passes both of us. I regain the lead by a large margin, however, and soon I find myself alone at the crown of the palm, laughing and waiting for the two of them to join me. But they don't come up. Suddenly, the palm begins to grow upward into the air. This new game delights me at first, but it soon becomes too much for me: everything beneath me starts to dwindle, and I feel afraid.

Then the palm bends and sets me down in some distant land beyond the river or sea where I had been. A bull as massive as a mountain is stuck in the ground there. A group of people has surrounded it, though they cannot tell what it is because of its enormous size. They rip off pieces of its flesh with their nails and teeth, and devour them voraciously. The bull looks pitiful, but it does not make a sound. A ceaseless stream of tears is pouring like warm rain from its eyes and onto the people, who are now lying there, completely relaxed. The sight of them is disconcerting: their faces look normal except for their teeth, which stick out like those of sharks or crocodiles. Blood is dripping from those long fangs of theirs.

A girl standing near the bull's head proclaims that she doesn't eat meat. I'm worried that she's like the others, and am relieved when her smile reveals a normal set of teeth. I walk over to her, and she gives me a fruit that looks like a pomegranate. The second I bite into it, I feel a great desire to kiss the girl. She lets me.

I sink into the kiss, and suddenly find myself in a colorful garden. There's a large square in the middle of it, and people are passing by dragging heavy chests and other objects, and muttering in strange voices. I catch sight of a man in the distance: he's standing on a raised platform and laughing in mockery as he orders the people to go this way and that. They carry out his orders submissively, without any grumbling. Some of his helpers are preparing new loads for the people, and others are standing with whips and lashing anyone who stops or slows down, or who even looks up toward the man on the platform. I try to scream and get the people's attention, but no sound comes out of me. The commander standing on the platform waves his stick at me like a conductor, and all his helpers converge on me in a threatening manner.

Sandra appears at that instant and takes my hand. I feel safe the moment her hand touches mine. We run together, fearlessly, and the people stop dragging their loads as our laughter echoes through the square. We can hear the sounds of other people's laughter in the distance now. We stop, relaxed, and throw ourselves onto the fresh turquoise-colored grass. Sandra kisses me and whispers in my ear, "You'll remain with me like this forever."

She pulls a candle out of somewhere and lights it. "Try to put it out," she says.

I blow as hard as I can, but it does not go out. "This candle is your soul, Hamza," she whispers in that lovely voice of hers. "No one can put it out, not even you."

I peacefully close my eyes while familiar-looking animals lie down near us and protect us. I can see people approaching in the distance as well, and I recognize them one after the other. I joyfully cry out each of their names, and the names of their mothers as well. As the warmth from Sandra's hand courses through my body, she speaks to me in a language I've never heard before but can still understand, "This is paradise. This is paradise, Hamza."

I leave the Palm House like someone returning from a long voyage. I wander through the city streets, stopping at places we used to go to together. I feel so much loss. The places all seem so much smaller now than they were before, when I visited them with Sandra, and sometimes Hakima. Yet at the same time they seem much vaster now, as vast as the void. I feel oppressed, and also utterly lost. At times the people's voices seem muffled to me, and at others they ring absurdly in my ears. Every place I enter is full of noise, yet I still feel so alone. I'm amazed that everyone can laugh like this—so easily. I try to remember the last time I laughed, to no avail.

I move from café to café throughout the evening and late into the night, unaware of what I'm ordering and drinking. I enter the apartment just before dawn with a headache and a nauseous feeling in my stomach: it's a miserable condition to be in, but it distracts me from a reckless thought that has crept into my mind. I call Abu Darsh and wake him up at that early hour. I tell him that I want to travel to Egypt as soon as possible. I'm not sure if this is the right decision, but I've reached a point of utter despair. I want to go back to the south: perhaps the change will do me good. "Being alone in this apartment is killing me," I tell him. "What am I supposed to do with all this silence?"

Abu Darsh tries to calm me down and convince me to put off the trip for a bit. He suggests that I move into his apartment for a few days, but I cut him off, saying, "This emptiness is greater than I can bear, Mustafa!"

By the following afternoon, Abu Darsh has a ticket for me to travel to Cairo in two days.

The announcement is repeated: "This is the last call for Egypt Air flight number 802 to Cairo . . . ."

Abu Darsh and I arrive late at the airport on a rainy day. He tells me to hurry up and check in while he parks the car. I had hastily stuffed some clothes into my suitcase. In my handbag, I packed Sheikh Sharif's stone and the three black stones from Wad al-Nar, and a few others things as well: the lock of Sandra's hair, her photo album, a picture of Hakima, the tape by Asmahan, the CDs that Sandra had given me, and also a few recordings of Mozart and Bach.

I wind my way through the terminal with my heavy bags, but the thoughts in my head weigh me down more than the luggage does. I'm not sure where I'm going. I simply follow the flow of people, paying no attention to the signs. I stop to rest and set my bags down for a bit, even though I haven't walked more than fifty meters. It feels as if I'm carrying the weight of the world. I've stopped near an emergency exit. Despite the thick glass, I can hear the thunder reverberating outside. When I hear the words "Egypt Air" in an announcement, I grab my suitcase, and the handle breaks. I stand there, not knowing what to do.

I can hear a cat meowing. At first I think my mind is playing tricks on me, and that I'm imagining Hakima. But then I hear it again. I look around me, but all I can see are people moving in that strange quickness they have. At that moment, the emergency door opens and two security men come in. The meows are coming from outside the door. I open the door a bit, and there's a terrible peal of thunder, as if it were the end of the world. The sky is grey, and the rain pours down mercilessly. I see a small drenched cat at the corner of the wall. I call out to it to come over to me, but it seems terrified of the thunder. Its meowing reminds me of Hakima. Without thinking, I head toward it, and the door silently closes behind me. I dry it off a bit, and then pick it up in my arms to go back into the terminal. But the door doesn't open from the outside.

It's extremely cold behind that thick reinforced glass. Everything looks murky and unclear through it. It's like a scene from an absurdist play: people keep hurrying by as if they were trapped in some monotonous nightmare. I knock on the door, but no one opens.

I can't hear anything from inside the airport above the noise of the thunder and the pouring rain. But I make out what looks like someone with a large backpack who's dragging a heavy suitcase and moving much more slowly than everyone else. I knock on the door again, and the person stops and opens it. It's a young woman. I thank her and tell her that I'd been trapped out there for over a quarter-hour, and that I've missed my flight. She laughs and says that she's just missed her flight as well because she hadn't set her watch properly. She sees the cat, which is still trembling in my arms. I wipe some more water off it, even though I'm more drenched than it is. It's meowing loudly now, and seems to be feeling better.

"Is that your cat?" the woman asks me.

I look at the animal, which lifts its head up and stretches its left paw out toward me, as if it had heard the question. "Yes," I answer without hesitation.

"What's its name?"

"Nur," I reply.

At that instant, I see Abu Darsh running and breathing heavily. He laughs when he sees me, and pounces on me in that wonderful way of his, embracing me with genuine happiness as if I'd just come back from a long trip. "You're too late, Hamza! The fates are smiling! Every cloud has a silver lining, and every missed flight as well!"

He looks at me in joy, and in his eyes I can see the tears he's trying to hold back. He starts speaking to the woman, and grabs a nearby cart and puts my broken suitcase and my handbag on it. I push the cart while he charmingly asks the woman if he can help her with her bag. "I'd like to invite both of you for a coffee at the airport café until the weather clears a bit," he says.

The four of us get going. Abu Darsh looks at the woman, while the woman looks at me, and I look at Nur, trying to make out her features. She meows and lightly scratches my face, and I smile for the first time in a long while. I kiss Nur and put her in my coat. She scratches me a bit at first, but then calms down and pokes her head out. We walk to the café together. I no longer hear the thunder.

Glossary

Abu Hurayra: this name literally means 'the one with the kitten' or 'the father of the kitten,' but Abu Hurayra is also the name of one of the most famous narrators of Hadith, or sayings ascribed to the Prophet Muhammad (this historical Abu Hurayra was one of the Prophet's companions)

Abu Kura'ayn: literally, 'the one with the legs'; the name could perhaps be translated as 'Daddy Longlegs'

Abu Libas: literally, 'the one with the underpants'; the name could perhaps be translated as 'Underpants Sami'

Abu al-Nar: literally, 'the one of the fire (nar)'; Hamza is called this because the name of his native village is Wad al-Nar

adhab: 'torment'

ahlan wa-sahlan: 'greetings' or 'welcome'

Allahu akbar: God is great

aqeeqa: a celebration that occurs seven days after the birth of a child, and where the child's hair is cut and an animal is slaughtered

argoun palm: a species of fan palm native to the Nubian desert

Bab al-Hadid: another name for Midan Ramsis, a square in the center of Cairo which is now also the site of Cairo's central train station (Ramsis Station); 'Bab al-Hadid' literally means 'Gate of Iron' and refers to the iron gate that Salah al-Din (Saladin) built in the twelfth century AD, and which was torn down in 1847 to make room for the train station

balila: a sweet drink consisting of stewed wheat and milk

Banat al-Kadayis: 'the cat's daughters'

beide: 'both' in German

bio: 'organic' in German (as in: organic fruits and vegetables)

al-Darib: 'the (mentally) afflicted' or 'the afflicted one'

dhal: the ninth letter of the Arabic alphabet

Eid al-Adha: the Feast of the Sacrifice, which commemorates Abraham's (Ibrahim in the Islamic tradition) readiness to sacrifice his own son at the command of God, before God intervened to save the boy by having him sacrifice a ram instead. The Eid generally involves the slaughter of an animal.

Eier kaput: a grammatically incorrect German phrase that translates to 'eggs broken'

Farid al-Atrash: a famous Syrian-Egyptian oud player, composer, singer, and actor

Fasching: the name for the Carnival celebration in Austria (as well as Germany and Switzerland)

Fatiha: the first chapter of the Quran. It is read when someone has died, in addition to many other occasions.

fuul: stewed fava beans, a staple of Egyptian cuisine

gondayl: a type of yellow date

guwannabana: fruit from the soursop tree

Hagg or Hajj: polite form of address for an older man, or for a Muslim man who has made the Hajj pilgrimage to Mecca

haggana: literally, 'camel riders'

halawa tahiniya: a sweet paste made of tahini, honey, and nuts

al-Hilal: the name of a Sudanese soccer team; it literally means 'the crescent moon'

hilba: an infusion of fenugreek

hilw-murr: the name of this spice literally means 'bittersweet'
al-Hut: this name literally means 'the whale'
Iblis: another name for the Devil in the Islamic tradition
Ibn Kadisa: 'son of the cat'
Ich arbeiten, du arbeiten. Woher kommen du? Du kommen Afrika?: ungrammatical German that translates to 'I work, you work. Where you from? You from Africa?'
Iftar: the meal breaking the fast after sunset during Ramadan
ismaha Ann: 'her name is Ann'
Jabal al-Tayr: 'Birds' Mount'
Jibril Shal al-Bahr: this name literally means 'Gabriel who bore the sea'
al-Kabbal: this name literally means 'the shackler'
karama: a special gathering to welcome back someone who has been away, and wherein an animal is usually slaughtered
karkaday: an infusion of hibiscus, served either hot or cold
al-Kayyal: this name literally means 'the weigher'
al-Khattaf: this name literally means 'the snatcher'
khawaga: a usually derogatory term in the Egyptian dialect used to denote a westerner
khayl al-zahra: 'the brilliant horses'
kisra: traditional Sudanese flatbread
al-kizan: this word, which literally means 'jugs' (for example, of water), is used in the Sudanese dialect as a derogatory term for overly pious men
kolkhoz: a collective farm in the former Soviet Union
Krone Zeitung, gnä Frau!: German (Austrian dialect) for 'the Krone newspaper, gracious lady!'
al-kunkan: an Egyptian card game similar to rummy
kushari: a dish of macaroni, rice, and lentils, served with garlic and tomato sauce
Lukanda al-Firdaws: 'Paradise Hotel'
madida: a pudding made from a type of clover
mahlab: a spice made from the extracted seed kernels of the St. Lucie cherry

Mama Mabsuta: literally, 'happy Mama'; the name could be translated as 'Momma's Boy Sulayman'
al-Marrikh: the name of a Sudanese soccer team; it literally means 'Mars'
Medinat al-Shams: 'the City of the Sun'
Mohamed Mounir: a famous Egyptian singer born to a Nubian family in Aswan
Muhammad Abduh: a key figure of the Egyptian Nahda, or Renaissance, of the late nineteenth and early twentieth centuries. He was a liberal Islamic reformer, and is considered by many to be the founder of Islamic modernism.
morgen: 'tomorrow' in German
al-Murada: the name of a Sudanese soccer team; it literally means 'the giants'
al-Na'am: 'the ostrichers'
nar: fire
National Salvation Revolution: the 1989 military coup in which Omar al-Bashir came to power in Sudan
Nur: 'light' in Arabic (as in: rays of light)
Nuwwar: 'blossoms'
Oyes klor: 'all right' in Viennese dialect
Pass: 'passport' in German
Pfui! Um Gottes Willen!: 'Ugh! Good God!' in German
al-qabawat: the vaults
Qasim Amin: one of the main figures of the Egyptian Nahda, or Renaissance, of the late nineteenth and early twentieth centuries. He is perhaps best known for his advocacy of women's rights.
Sabir: 'patient' or 'forbearing'
sahlab: a drink made from the salep plant
Salah ibn al-Badiya: a well-known Sudanese singer
Samih: 'gracious'
Scheisse: 'shit' in German
Semmel bread: a type of Austrian (and German) roll or bun
Shahryar: the king in *A Thousand and One Nights*. Betrayed by his wife, he takes a new wife each night and then kills her in the morning,

until he meets Scheherazade. She tells him story after story, always leaving them off at a point of suspense, so that he has no choice but to spare her life for one more night.

shakshuka: a North African dish of eggs cooked in a tomato and onion sauce

Sharif: 'honorable'

sharmut: strips of thinly sliced meat

Tafelspitz: a traditional Austrian dish of broiled tri-tip

tunboora: a stringed instrument similar to a large lyre

Umm Kulthum (1898–1975): probably the Arab world's most famous singer of the twentieth century

Uthman Darab Sidru: this name is best translated as 'Uthman Chest-Beater'

uzzab: 'bachelors'

al-'Uyun: 'the springs'

wayn: 'where' in several Arabic dialects

weeka: dried crushed-up okra

die Weise: 'the wise one' in German

die Weisse: 'the white one' in German

Wien: 'Vienna' in German

Willkommen: 'welcome' in German

Wirk: 'thigh'; the name could perhaps be translated as 'Muhammad the Thigh'

Woher kommen Sie: 'Where are you from?' in German

ya Satir: literally, 'O Protector'; this is said when someone enters another's home so that the occupants know to prepare themselves

zay: the eleventh letter of the Arabic alphabet

Zunbat: best translated as 'backstabber' here, the word is derived from 'zunba' or 'zumba' in the Egyptian dialect, which denotes the act of stabbing someone in the back or betraying them

Modern Arabic Literature
from the American University in Cairo Press

Bahaa Abdelmegid *Saint Theresa* and *Sleeping with Strangers*
Ibrahim Abdel Meguid *Birds of Amber* • *Distant Train*
No One Sleeps in Alexandria • *The Other Place*
Yahya Taher Abdullah *The Collar and the Bracelet* • *The Mountain of Green Tea*
Leila Abouzeid *The Last Chapter*
Hamdi Abu Golayyel *A Dog with No Tail* • *Thieves in Retirement*
Yusuf Abu Rayya *Wedding Night*
Ahmed Alaidy *Being Abbas el Abd*
Idris Ali *Dongola* • *Poor*
Rasha al Ameer *Judgment Day*
Radwa Ashour *Granada* • *Specters*
Ibrahim Aslan *The Heron* • *Nile Sparrows*
Alaa Al Aswany *Chicago* • *Friendly Fire* • *The Yacoubian Building*
Fadi Azzam *Sarmada*
Fadhil al-Azzawi *Cell Block Five* • *The Last of the Angels* • *The Traveler and the Innkeeper*
Ali Bader *Papa Sartre*
Liana Badr *The Eye of the Mirror*
Hala El Badry *A Certain Woman* • *Muntaha*
Salwa Bakr *The Golden Chariot* • *The Man from Bashmour* • *The Wiles of Men*
Halim Barakat *The Crane*
Hoda Barakat *Disciples of Passion* • *The Tiller of Waters*
Mourid Barghouti *I Saw Ramallah* • *I Was Born There, I Was Born Here*
Mohamed Berrada *Like a Summer Never to Be Repeated*
Mohamed El-Bisatie *Clamor of the Lake* • *Drumbeat* • *Hunger* • *Over the Bridge*
Mahmoud Darwish *The Butterfly's Burden*
Tarek Eltayeb *Cities without Palms* • *The Palm House*
Mansoura Ez Eldin *Maryam's Maze*
Ibrahim Farghali *The Smiles of the Saints*
Hamdy el-Gazzar *Black Magic*
Randa Ghazy *Dreaming of Palestine*
Gamal al-Ghitani *Pyramid Texts* • *The Zafarani Files* • *Zayni Barakat*
Tawfiq al-Hakim *The Essential Tawfiq al-Hakim*
Yahya Hakki *The Lamp of Umm Hashim*
Abdelilah Hamdouchi *The Final Bet*
Bensalem Himmich *The Polymath* • *The Theocrat*
Taha Hussein *The Days*
Sonallah Ibrahim *Cairo: From Edge to Edge* • *The Committee* • *Zaat*
Yusuf Idris *City of Love and Ashes* • *The Essential Yusuf Idris*
Denys Johnson-Davies *The AUC Press Book of Modern Arabic Literature* • *Homecoming*
In a Fertile Desert • *Under the Naked Sky*
Said al-Kafrawi *The Hill of Gypsies*
Mai Khaled *The Magic of Turquoise*
Sahar Khalifeh *The End of Spring*
The Image, the Icon and the Covenant • *The Inheritance*
Edwar al-Kharrat *Rama and the Dragon* • *Stones of Bobello*

Betool Khedairi *Absent*
Mohammed Khudayyir *Basrayatha*
Ibrahim al-Koni *Anubis • Gold Dust • The Puppet • The Seven Veils of Seth*
Naguib Mahfouz *Adrift on the Nile • Akhenaten: Dweller in Truth*
Arabian Nights and Days • Autumn Quail • Before the Throne • The Beggar
The Beginning and the End • Cairo Modern • The Cairo Trilogy: Palace Walk
Palace of Desire • Sugar Street • Children of the Alley • The Coffeehouse
The Day the Leader Was Killed • The Dreams • Dreams of Departure
Echoes of an Autobiography • The Essential Naguib Mahfouz • The Final Hour
The Harafish • Heart of the Night • In the Time of Love
The Journey of Ibn Fattouma • Karnak Cafe • Khan al-Khalili • Khufu's Wisdom
Life's Wisdom • Love in the Rain • Midaq Alley • The Mirage • Miramar • Mirrors
Morning and Evening Talk • Naguib Mahfouz at Sidi Gaber • Respected Sir
Rhadopis of Nubia • The Search • The Seventh Heaven • Thebes at War
The Thief and the Dogs • The Time and the Place • Voices from the Other World
Wedding Song • The Wisdom of Naguib Mahfouz
Mohamed Makhzangi *Memories of a Meltdown*
Alia Mamdouh *The Loved Ones • Naphtalene*
Selim Matar *The Woman of the Flask*
Ibrahim al-Mazini *Ten Again*
Yousef Al-Mohaimeed *Munira's Bottle • Wolves of the Crescent Moon*
Hassouna Mosbahi *A Tunisian Tale*
Ahlam Mosteghanemi *Chaos of the Senses • Memory in the Flesh*
Shakir Mustafa *Contemporary Iraqi Fiction: An Anthology*
Mohamed Mustagab *Tales from Dayrut*
Buthaina Al Nasiri *Final Night*
Ibrahim Nasrallah *Inside the Night • Time of White Horses*
Haggag Hassan Oddoul *Nights of Musk*
Mona Prince *So You May See*
Mohamed Mansi Qandil *Moon over Samarqand*
Abd al-Hakim Qasim *Rites of Assent*
Somaya Ramadan *Leaves of Narcissus*
Mekkawi Said *Cairo Swan Song*
Ghada Samman *The Night of the First Billion*
Mahdi Issa al-Saqr *East Winds, West Winds*
Rafik Schami *The Calligrapher's Secret • Damascus Nights*
The Dark Side of Love
Habib Selmi *The Scents of Marie-Claire*
Khairy Shalaby *The Hashish Waiter • The Lodging House*
The Time-Travels of the Man Who Sold Pickles and Sweets
Miral al-Tahawy *Blue Aubergine • Brooklyn Heights • Gazelle Tracks • The Tent*
Bahaa Taher *As Doha Said • Love in Exile*
Fuad al-Takarli *The Long Way Back*
Zakaria Tamer *The Hedgehog*
M. M. Tawfik *Murder in the Tower of Happiness*
Mahmoud Al-Wardani *Heads Ripe for Plucking*
Amina Zaydan *Red Wine*
Latifa al-Zayyat *The Open Door*